HE WAS ALREADY WATCHING ALTHEA.

He seemed oblivious to the rowdy antics of his friends and the addition of three scantily-clad women to their party, one of whom was openly vying for his attention. He was interested only in Althea, gazing at her as if he could see through the stretchy fabric of her form-fitting dress, through her silk thigh-high stockings and lace underwear, right down to the shivering flesh beneath.

As Althea returned his hot, bold gaze, she, too, lost track of her surroundings—the loud music, the flashing strobe lights, the sea of writhing bodies on the dance floor, the buzz of laughter and conversation. Everything faded into a distant blur as her world narrowed to focus solely on *him*.

Dark, handsome, virile. Utterly mesmerizing . . .

AFRICAN AMERICAN

No One But You

MAUREEN SMITH

Dafina Books

Kensington Publishing Corp.

http://www.kensingtonbooks.com

DAFINA BOOKS are published by

Kensington Publishing Corp.
850 Third Avenue
New York, NY 10022

All Kensington Titles, Imprints, and Distributed Lines are available at special quantity discounts for bulk purchases for sales promotions, premiums, fund-raising, and educational or institutional use. Special book excerpts or customized printings can also be created to fit specific needs. For details, write or phone the office of the Kensington special sales manager: Kensington Publishing Corp., 850 Third Avenue, New York, NY 10022, attn: Special Sales Department, Phone: 1-800-221-2647.

Dafina and the Dafina logo Reg. U.S. Pat. & TM Off.

ISBN-13: 978-0-7582-2740-9
ISBN-10: 0-7582-2740-X

First mass market printing: December 2008

10 9 8 7 6 5 4 3 2 1

Printed in the United States of America

To every reader who ever asked for Damien's story.

Acknowledgments

My thanks and heartfelt gratitude to Special Agent Victor McCollum, for patiently answering my many questions and for not calling me a liar every time I promise him that I'm taking a break from writing about FBI agents!

My wonderful editor, Kate Duffy, whose guidance and unwavering confidence in me give me wings to soar.

And, of course, much love to my supportive family and friends who endure months of neglect without a word of complaint. Well, maybe just a *little* grumbling, but you're entitled!

Chapter 1

Baltimore, Maryland
Friday, October 3
Day 1

Claire Thorndike smoothed on a coat of red lipstick, pressed her lips together to evenly distribute the color, then leaned back to inspect her image in the vanity mirror. The wide green eyes that stared back at her were dramatically accentuated by the smoky eye shadow and mascara she'd applied minutes before. Her long auburn hair—the envy of those jealous bitches at her high school—cascaded to her pale bare shoulders in lustrous, rippling waves. But as gorgeous as her hair and makeup were, the pièce de résistance was the sheer white negligee that clung to her lithe, curvaceous body. She looked like a virgin bride on her wedding night. Wholesome and demure, yet irresistibly seductive— which was the effect she'd been going for.

James was going to love it.

As she placed a dab of Clive Christian's No 1 perfume behind her ears, on her wrists, and between her perfectly perky breasts—courtesy of a $15,000 boob job last year—

Claire could feel her pulse racing in anticipation of the night to come.

After four weeks of corresponding via MyDomain and secretly e-mailing each other, Claire was finally going to meet her cyberlover, the smart, funny, gorgeous man who'd swept her off her feet in a way no lamebrain jock at school had ever come close to accomplishing.

But Claire was no idiot.

She'd watched enough *Dateline* specials to know the dangers involved in hooking up with strange men over the Internet. She'd heard horror stories of naive young girls who wound up getting raped or killed by the sadistic pervs they'd met in some chat room, and Claire had always shaken her head in disbelief at the appalling stupidity demonstrated by the victims.

Youth is never an excuse for stupidity, as her AP English teacher was fond of saying.

Amen, sister!

Before agreeing to meet James that evening, Claire had taken the necessary precautions by enlisting the services of a discreet private investigator, who'd run a complete background check on James—without his knowledge, of course. The P.I. hadn't come cheap, but the peace of mind he'd given Claire was worth every red cent she'd paid him out of her allowance.

What was money to her anyway? Her father was a multimillionaire.

At the thought of Spencer Thorndike, Claire's lips curved in a slow, satisfied smile. Her father would never approve of her online romance. Although James was intelligent, handsome, and successful, he was also older than Claire. Much older.

And he was black.

Which made him even more perfect.

Claire could think of no better way to get back at her

mean, domineering father than by falling in love with a man who was nothing like him. Spencer Thorndike would have a stroke if he knew that while he and his bimbo of a trophy wife were enjoying their annual ski trip to Vail, his seventeen-year-old daughter was rolling between *his* imported silk sheets with a tall, dark, and handsome stranger.

Oh yeah. Her father would really have a—

Whump!

Claire started at the sudden loud noise. Her gaze flew across her large bedroom to the window, where a strong gust of wind had slammed against the windowpane, rattling it. The bony, brittle branches of a giant oak tree, gnarled like an old woman's fingers, scraped against the glass. Night had fallen, leaving the forested hills and grounds shrouded in darkness.

With a slight frown, Claire rose from the vanity chair and crossed to the window. As she started to draw the heavy curtains closed, she stopped short. And stared into the night.

She'd caught a glimpse of something in the darkness. Movement?

Or her own pale reflection?

Claire stepped away from the window, the fine hairs lifting on the back of her neck.

Get a grip, she silently commanded herself. *There's no one out there. You're just paranoid because you know you'll be in deep shit if Dad ever finds out you had a strange man in the house.*

But he won't find out, she reminded herself. *He and your wicked stepmother are thousands of miles away at a private ski resort. They're probably not even thinking about you. So chill out!*

Taking a slow, deep breath, Claire stepped to the window again and peered through the darkness. The night was suddenly still, the rush of wind having died down. There was no one out there. No boogeyman lurking in the shadows. No Peeping Tom spying on her from behind a pair of binoculars.

But as Claire quickly closed the curtains, she found herself regretting, not for the first time, the remote location of her home, a Tudor mansion built of stone and glass and perched high on a hill that overlooked the manicured suburbs of Mount Washington in northwestern Baltimore City. It wasn't that she minded living on sixty acres of land that boasted a natural lake, beautifully tended gardens, an equestrian complex, and plenty of scenic riding trails. The sprawling estate, which had been featured in many magazines and had hosted a number of visiting dignitaries and Hollywood A-listers, offered far better accommodations than the cramped two-bedroom apartment in northeast D.C. she'd briefly shared with her mother, who'd not only lost custody of Claire after her bitter divorce from Spencer Thorndike but had been gullible enough to sign a prenup when they'd first gotten married twenty years ago.

No, Claire wouldn't have given up the mansion for anything. But she sometimes wished she lived closer to her friends from school. Hell, on lonely nights like these, she wished she lived closer to *anyone.*

Stop it, she told herself. *You're being ridiculous.*

Not having any neighbors actually worked to her advantage. She'd never have gotten away with inviting James over if she'd had to worry about nosy neighbors telling her father about her late-night visitor. That was why she'd given the housekeeper, the butler, the cook, *and* the chauffeur the night off. Insurance. That was also why she'd disabled her father's high-tech security system, which often made her feel like she was living in some damn futuristic prison. Between the surveillance camera at the front gate, the motion sensors on the property, and the security alarm inside the house, Claire felt like she couldn't take two steps without being tracked. If she ever found out that her father had installed hidden video cameras in the house, she'd kill him, so help her God.

Claire glanced at the clock on her antique nightstand. 8:30 P.M. James was supposed to arrive at nine, which gave her a little more time to finish getting ready. Downstairs in the living room, she had a bottle of Bordeaux on ice next to a cozy fire. In the CD player, the hauntingly seductive wail of John Coltrane's sax—James's favorite—was waiting to be enjoyed.

It was going to be a perfect night, Claire thought dreamily. One she would never forget.

As she moved from the window, she heard it. The soft creak of a floorboard.

Claire froze. Fear pulsed through her blood.

Was someone else in the house?

Calm down. It's just your imagination. You live in a house that was built in 1929. Old houses make noise. You know that.

But she suddenly felt a draft across her skin, as if there were someone in the room with her.

Claire remained perfectly still, scarcely breathing as she strained to listen for approaching footsteps. But all she heard was the gentle whisper of the wind outside, the soft scrape of tree limbs against her window. Nothing sinister or out of place.

Maybe she should call James to see if he was on his way. She'd feel a lot safer once he arrived.

But as she started toward the dresser, where she'd left her cell phone earlier, a dark, hulking figure suddenly appeared in the open doorway.

Claire screamed.

Dressed entirely in black, his head covered by a ski

mask, the intruder slowly advanced on her. Deadly silent and menacing.

Terror gripped Claire. "Who are you?" she cried. "What do you want?"

But he remained silent, deliberately stalking her as she backed toward the window. *Oh God, oh God, I don't want to die. Please help me!*

Her frantic gaze swept around the room, searching for something she could use as a weapon. Spying a wooden baseball bat mounted on one wall—autographed by her longtime crush Derek Jeter—she lunged for it.

But it was too late.

In no time at all the intruder was upon her, a strong, heavy male whose weight forced her to the hardwood floor. She landed with a painful thud, the long hem of her negligee tangling with her bare legs. She screamed and flailed against him as he straddled her.

Oh God, she thought in horror. *He's going to rape me before he kills me!*

Something hard and cold was pressed against her neck, and then a jolt ripped through her body. Thousands of volts of electricity burned through her veins.

Claire let out a whimper before surrendering to unconsciousness.

Chapter 2

"Hey, beautiful, can I holler at you for a minute?"

With a cursory glance, Althea Pritchard sized up the stranger who'd approached her as she emerged from the restroom. Five foot six. Late twenties. Wearing a shiny silk shirt opened to the middle of his hairy chest. Reeking of cheap cologne.

Not her type. Definitely.

"Tell you what," Althea said over the bass-heavy hip-hop music blaring through the crowded Baltimore night-club. "Let me have a few drinks first, then maybe we can talk."

He opened and closed his mouth, looking as if he were trying to determine whether he'd been rejected.

Before he could decide, Althea made her escape, weaving her way through a throng of sweaty, gyrating bodies to reach a small table in the corner occupied by two attractive black women. They were laughing at her as she approached.

"You poor baby," said Keren Childers as Althea slid into the empty chair beside her.

"He's been watching you ever since we arrived," Kimberly Rhodes added, her dark, expressive eyes twinkling with mirth. "We watched him get up and follow you when you went to the restroom."

Althea scowled at her two longtime friends. "You could have warned me I was being stalked."

Keren laughed. "We tried to, but you left your cell phone in your purse at the table, remember?" Pointedly she passed Althea the Louis Vuitton handbag she'd been guarding in her absence.

Kimberly said, "Besides, we knew you could take care of yourself if that fool tried something crazy, like actually following you *into* the bathroom." She shook her head, grinning. "I'd have given anything to see the terrified look in his eyes when you shoved your Glock in his face."

Althea chuckled, lifting her untouched strawberry margarita to her mouth. "It wouldn't have come to that."

Kimberly looked disappointed. "Too bad. What good is being an FBI agent if you can't arrest every loser who hits on you?"

Althea sputtered on her drink, laughing. "What kind of question is that? I didn't become an FBI agent so I could go around threatening and arresting harmless people!"

A speculative gleam filled Kimberly's dark eyes. "Now that you mention it, why *did* you become an FBI agent? I mean, you could have been a—Ouch!" She shot an accusing glare across the table at Keren. "Why'd you kick me?"

Keren gave her a smile etched in steel. "This is Althea's first night back in town, remember? We're here to celebrate and have a good time, not rehash the past."

The past.

Those two words descended upon the small table like an ominous gray cloud, thick and heavy with the promise of rain. Althea knew all too well about *the past*. She'd spent the last eight years, and thousands of dollars in therapy, trying like hell to bury the past. But every so often it resurfaced, the way an empty conch shell washed ashore after a storm.

She had returned home, to the place where her life had changed forever, hoping to put the painful memories behind her once and for all. Joining her friends for a carefree night on the town was just what the doctor ordered—literally. A month before leaving Seattle, Althea had kept her final appointment with her therapist, Zachary Parminter, who she'd been seeing for three years. During that last session, she'd promised Dr. Parminter that she would learn to find a healthy balance between her personal life and her demanding career. And she intended to keep that promise.

On Monday morning, she would report to her new assignment at the FBI field office in Baltimore and immerse herself in the business of hunting criminals.

But tonight she wouldn't think about work. Tonight she would let her hair down and cast aside all her inhibitions. She'd drink margaritas, laugh like she had not a care in the world, and dance the night away.

"Speaking of arresting people," said Kimberly, her gaze riveted on the entrance to the club, "would you happen to have an extra pair of handcuffs on you, Althea?"

Althea frowned over the salted rim of her cocktail glass. "Why?"

"'Cause I want to make an arrest. That brotha who just walked through the door is so damn fine it should be against the law!"

Laughing, Althea and Keren followed the direction of their friend's gaze. For once, Kimberly had not exaggerated. The man who stood in the entryway scanning the crowded nightclub was tall, well over six feet. He was darkly handsome in a well-cut blazer, pleated charcoal trousers, and a white shirt open to the strong column of his throat. He had broad shoulders and a wide chest that tapered down to a trim, athletic waist and long legs. Midnight black hair was cropped close to his scalp. His skin was rich mahogany, stretched taut over broad cheekbones, a strong masculine nose, and a rugged jaw. His eyebrows were thick, black slashes, and his mouth was firm and sensual.

For some reason he struck Althea as vaguely familiar, though she knew she'd never met him before. *No way* would she have forgotten someone like him.

As his dark, piercing eyes roamed around the room, Althea was surprised to find herself willing him to glance her way.

And then, suddenly, he did.

The moment their eyes met, Althea felt like the air had been knocked from her lungs. An unexpected heat curled through her blood. Despite the people who passed between them, intermittently blocking their line of sight, their gazes remained locked for several charged seconds.

A burst of rowdy male voices, rising above the music from a table across the room, drew the man's attention. With one last lingering look at Althea, he moved off to join his party.

"Lord have mercy," Kimberly breathed, making an exaggerated show of fanning herself as she craned her neck to stare after him. "Lord have *mercy*."

Keren laughed. "You can say that again."

Althea was silent, watching as the sexy stranger threaded his way through the crowd, oblivious to the admiring looks of women he passed. He stopped at a table occupied by a large group of men, half of whom, judging by their flushed faces and raucous laughter, were already drunk or well on their way there. At the newcomer's arrival, the entire group erupted into a loud chorus of "Happy Birthday."

The stranger laughed, a pair of deep dimples flashing

in his lean cheeks. There was *nothing* cherubic or adorable about those dimples. They were masculine and irresistibly wicked, the kind that made a woman want to cross her legs.

Which Althea did. *Tightly*.

As his friends ended their off-key birthday tribute, the man, still grinning, claimed an empty chair at the head of the table. The waitress quickly materialized with another round of drinks. An attractive young brunette with ample breasts spilling over the neckline of her too-small halter, she made a point of serving the birthday boy first, pouring his beer into a tall glass, then leaning over him with an arm draped across his chair for the sole purpose of treating him to an eyeful of cleavage—much to the delight of his comrades, who whooped and roared with approval.

With a pang of irritation, Althea watched as the sexy stranger whispered something into the waitress's ear that made her throw back her head and laugh with genuine pleasure. She gave him a sultry smile and a wink before leaving the table, the seductive sway of her hips drawing the lustful eye of every male within a hundred feet.

"Men," Keren pronounced in disgust, shaking her head. She glared after the departing waitress. "I bet those aren't even real!"

Kimberly laughed. "Now, now. Don't be jealous," she teased, gently patting her friend's hand. "You're a successful CPA. I'm sure you can afford your own breast implants. Hell, it might even help you get that promotion you've been slaving for."

Keren scowled at her. "Kiss my ass."

This time both Althea and Kimberly laughed.

The three women lapsed into companionable silence for a few minutes, content to nurse their margaritas and people-watch before venturing onto the dance floor.

They had been friends ever since their days at Elizabeth

Seton, an all-girl Catholic high school near their hometown of Upper Marlboro. Whether outsmarting their irascible headmistress or supporting one another in student-council election campaigns, they had always been inseparable. Over the years they'd kept in touch, even when Althea broke with Seton tradition and decided to attend a coed university instead of joining her two friends at Spelman. After years of attending all-girl schools, she'd been ready for a change, welcoming the opportunity to match wits with her male counterparts in the world of academia. As a premed major at the University of Maryland, Althea had spent countless hours studying and memorizing the unabridged version of *Gray's Anatomy* and had endured the rigors of biology and organic chemistry courses alongside egomaniacs who believed that women had no place in college, let alone medical school. She'd had to work twice as hard as her male peers to prove herself, never imagining that these early experiences would prepare her to someday compete—and survive—in the testosterone-dominated FBI.

When Althea learned two months ago that she'd been transferred to the Baltimore field office, Keren and Kimberly were among the first few people she'd called. It was Keren who'd suggested that they celebrate her return home by having dinner at their favorite restaurant at the Inner Harbor, followed by a night of dancing at one of the most popular nightclubs downtown.

As Althea reached for her margarita, she felt a light, prickling awareness ripple across the surface of her skin. As if guided by an invisible force, she turned her head and homed in on the sexy stranger she and her friends had been ogling earlier.

He was already watching Althea, a silent, focused observation that made her pulse go haywire. He seemed oblivious to the rowdy antics of his friends and the addition of three scantily-clad women to their party, one of whom was openly vying for his attention. He was interested only in Althea, gazing at her as if he could see through the stretchy fabric of her form-fitting dress, through her silk thigh-high stockings and lace underwear, right down to the shivering flesh beneath.

As Althea returned his hot, bold gaze, she, too, lost track of her surroundings—the loud music, the flashing strobe lights, the sea of writhing bodies on the dance floor, the buzz of laughter and conversation. Everything faded into a distant blur as her world narrowed to focus solely on *him.*

Dark, handsome, virile. Utterly mesmerizing . . .

At that moment he glanced away, bending his head toward the beautiful woman at his side as she murmured something in his ear. He listened briefly, then nodded. With a smile full of seductive promise, the woman rose from the table and sashayed toward the restrooms near the back of the club.

Without a second thought Althea downed the rest of her margarita and stood, drawing curious looks from her friends.

"Where are you going?" they asked in unison.

Althea smoothed her silver jersey dress over her thighs. "To dance with the birthday boy."

She moved swiftly and purposefully through the crowd, like a woman on a mission. Which she was. She'd seen something she wanted, and now she was going after it.

You only live once.

When Althea reached the noisy table across the room, several pairs of eyes swung in her direction. But she only had eyes for the birthday boy, who stared at her with an expression of surprise mingled with unmistakable pleasure.

Althea gave him her most beguiling smile. "Would you like to dance?"

"Absolutely," he said, his voice a deep, husky growl that made her belly quiver. He unfolded his lean body from the chair and stood with a fluid grace that reminded Althea of the leashed power of a panther prowling through the jungle.

Just as she'd suspected, he towered over her five feet six inches. She'd thought he was good-looking the moment she laid eyes on him, but seeing him from across the crowded room was nothing compared to the up close and personal view. But even as gorgeous as he was, it was his eyes that ensnared Althea. They were black as midnight, heavy lidded and penetrating. They stared down at her with a searing intensity that scorched her nerve endings and left her feeling a little weak.

Swallowing hard, Althea slipped her palm into the warmth of his big hand and steered him away from the table, not missing the knowing looks and grins his friends gave him. Normally she would mind the lewd innuendo reflected in their gazes, but tonight was different. Tonight she didn't care about anything but having a good time, and she'd found just the right man to help her achieve that all-important goal.

The dance floor was packed with couples swaying to a slow, sensual number beneath a mirrored disco ball. Althea led her partner through the crowd, finding an available spot somewhere in the middle.

As he drew her into his arms, she slid her hands up the hard, muscled wall of his chest and curved them around his neck. The moment their bodies came together, heat sizzled through her veins, igniting her blood. He stared down at her, their faces a scant few inches away. Her heart thundered. The look in his eyes pulled at something deep within her, something that made her ache with an indescribable longing.

She managed a soft, demure smile and lowered her

head to his shoulder as they began swaying to the music. He smelled incredible. Like soap mingled with just a hint of an expensive, woodsy fragrance. Probably Armani.

"What's your name?" he asked. His voice was an intoxicating baritone—deep, potent, and incredibly sexy. It made the back of her neck tingle, as if he were caressing it with his hands, his lips, his warm breath.

She almost forgot he'd asked her a question until he chuckled softly. "Ah, a woman of mystery."

Althea lifted her head from his shoulder and smiled into his dark eyes. "Althea."

He nodded, his mouth curving in a smile that revealed strong white teeth. "Damien."

So that was his name. *Damien.* A strong, masculine name. It definitely suited him, Althea decided.

"Happy birthday, Damien. Hope it's been a good one."

"It is now," he said huskily.

She felt a thrill of pleasure at his words. *Don't get carried away,* an inner voice warned. *After tonight you'll never see this man again. Remember that.*

"How many years?" she asked.

"Thirty-four."

Althea nodded, mentally processing the fact that he was eight years older than her.

Glancing over his shoulder, she spied the beautiful woman who'd been seated at his table earlier, vying for his attention. She stood just beyond the edge of the dance floor, nursing a drink and openly glowering at them.

Althea felt only the slightest twinge of guilt. After all, it wasn't *her* fault that the other woman had left Damien unattended long enough for Althea to make her move. And if it hadn't been Althea, it would have been someone else. God knows there had been no shortage of women ogling him that evening.

"I know this might sound like a bad pickup line," Damien said, gazing at her, "but you look familiar to me."

Althea gave him a wry look. "You're not going to tell me that I look like Kerry Washington, are you?"

He chuckled. "No, I wasn't. But now that you mention it, you *do* bear a striking resemblance to her. Why? Is that a problem?"

"Not at all. I think she's gorgeous, and I love her movies. But if I had a dime for every time someone told me I look like her . . . Well, you get the point. Anyway, I was thinking the same thing about you. You look familiar to me, but I know we've never met before."

Damien shook his head. "There's no way I would have forgotten meeting you," he said huskily.

Althea's insides melted. She gave him a sultry smile. "I thought the same thing."

He smiled, soft and intimate, and pulled her closer.

As the slow, seductive ballad segued into another, she resettled her head upon his shoulder and closed her eyes, emptying her mind of everything but this moment. She reveled in the strength of his arms around her. The hardness of his chest and abdomen rubbed against her breasts, the friction enough to make her nipples pucker against her lace bra. His firm, muscled thighs slid along hers as he turned her slowly in a circle, one hand at the small of her back, the other at her waist. The heat of his touch seared her, penetrating the soft fabric of her dress. When his hip brushed against hers, she felt the thick, rigid length of his erection. A soft gasp escaped her throat. Desire pooled between her legs, dampening the crotch of her panties.

She fought to control her ragged breathing as his arms tightened around her, holding her closer. As they danced in slow circles, their bodies moving as one, it was as if nothing and no one else existed outside their embrace. The heat emanating from every point of contact seemed to forge them together.

With her head resting on his shoulder, Althea's gaze riveted on the full, sensuous curve of his bottom lip. She wondered what it would be like to kiss him, to feel those soft, sexy lips gliding against hers before they trailed lower, to the aching swell of her breasts, and lower still, to the hot, pulsing flesh between her legs.

When she lifted her eyes to his, she found his dark, smoldering gaze already fixed on her face, as if he'd intercepted her thoughts.

Her lips parted, but before she could draw her next breath, Damien slanted his head over hers and seized her mouth with such searing possession she felt as if she might drown. She arched into him, moving higher in his arms to match herself more equally to his height. It didn't matter that they were in public or that he was a complete stranger to her. All that mattered were the explosive sensations he aroused in her, almost terrifying in their intensity.

She pressed her aching breasts to his chest and felt the deep timbre of his voice vibrating through her body when he groaned. Her hips ground mindlessly against his, seeking the enticing bulge she'd encountered just minutes before.

With another husky groan, Damien deepened the kiss, sliding his silky tongue past her lips and devouring her mouth until she was breathless and clinging to him. Soon they were both panting hard.

Althea pulled back and stared up at him. Her face was hot, her lips parted and swollen as her breath sawed in and out of her lungs.

Flashing strobe lights revealed the raw hunger in Damien's dark, glittering eyes as he gazed back at her. "Althea—"

She pressed a finger against the seam of his warm, soft lips. "Shhh." Reaching on tiptoe, she drew his head down to hers, leaned close, and let her lips brush his earlobe, making him shiver in response.

"Take me home," she whispered in his ear.

He lifted his head and stared down at her, searching her face as if he couldn't quite believe what he'd heard.

Althea cupped his face in her hands and kissed him so boldly and provocatively there could be no doubt in his mind what she wanted.

When she drew away, Damien grabbed her hand and started purposefully from the dance floor, plowing through the crowd as effortlessly as Moses parted the Red Sea.

Althea gave a breathless little laugh as he tugged her along. "Where should we—"

"Whoever lives closest," he growled over his shoulder. "I'll drive."

Chapter 3

It was the most impulsive thing Althea had ever done in her life.

And *that* was saying a lot, considering her track record.

Three years ago, she'd unexpectedly dropped out of medical school and joined the FBI, shocking her family, friends, and everyone else who knew her.

Now, as she left the nightclub with a perfect stranger, her life-altering decision not to practice medicine suddenly seemed like child's play in comparison.

During the short drive from the club to the downtown apartment building Althea had recently moved into, she and Damien let their fingers twine sensually and shared heated looks in the shadowy interior of his Tahoe. By the time he parked in front of her building, Althea was so aroused, so impatient to be with him, that she had to force herself to sit still and wait for him to open the passenger door for her.

As she fumbled to unlock the door to her sixth-floor unit, she could feel the heat radiating from his body as he stood close behind her, his warm breath caressing the nape of her neck. She crossed the threshold of her apartment, flipped a light switch, then stepped aside to let him enter.

She dropped her purse and keys on the cherry sideboard in the foyer. Trying to be a good hostess, she asked, "Would you like something to drink? I have—"

Strong arms grabbed her and turned her around. Althea had only a fleeting glimpse of Damien's expression—his heavy-lidded eyes blazing with fierce arousal, his nostrils slightly flared—before his dark head slanted over hers.

The moment their mouths locked, Althea had no more coherent thoughts.

Damien's hands held her head as he ravaged her lips. His need was unmistakable, intense. Althea found herself crushed against his hard chest, enfolded in his body. His tongue plunged inside her mouth, sensual and demanding. Her tight, achy nipples knotted against his blazer, and she clung to him, desperate for more. Their teeth scraped. Althea thought she tasted blood, but she was beyond the point of caring.

One of his impossibly hard thighs slid between hers, hiking up the hem of her dress. Friction swelled her clitoris. Desire, the kind she had never before experienced, the kind she had believed existed only in erotic fiction and in her secret fantasies, overwhelmed her. She rode Damien's thigh. *Hard.*

He uttered something unintelligible, his voice low and guttural. He lifted her easily in his arms, walked a few steps, and deposited her on a hard surface. It took Althea a dazed moment to realize it was the antique sofa table in the living room.

He moved between her legs, kissing her savagely as he shoved up her dress and palmed her wet, throbbing sex through her lace panties. Althea moaned, her hips arching off the table to press against his big hand. His long, skilled fingers teased and stroked her labia until a shaking moan rose in her throat. When he slipped one finger inside her, Althea felt the first tiny explosion, a preview of what was to come, and she cried out.

Damien grasped her buttocks and held her tightly against his thick erection, which promised unparalleled heights of ecstasy. She wrapped her arms around his neck, her breathing rapid and shallow. He crushed his mouth to hers, and their tongues mated frantically while their bodies surged against each other.

Althea reached for and unzipped his trousers, gasping when he sprang hot, thick, and long into her hands. Her mouth watered. Greed filled her. A greed that was pure, raw hunger.

Their gazes locked as she slid off the table and knelt before him. She wrapped her lips around his engorged shaft and tried to swallow him whole.

Damien let out a harsh groan, a sound of both pleasure and torment. He thrust hard and deep into her mouth, and she laved and sucked him like it was a matter of survival. She held his buttocks as he thrust faster, again and again.

When he swore loudly and bucked against her as he came, she sucked harder, swallowing every last drop he emptied into her.

Afterward he didn't collapse on the floor. Instead he cradled her face between his hands and leaned down to kiss her. Althea kissed him back, still tasting his salty-sweet cum, their mouths soon tearing insatiably at each other.

With a savage oath, he bent and lifted her back onto the table. She raised her hips, and he grasped the waistband of her panties and quickly dragged them down her legs and over her stiletto boots. She quivered with anticipation as he stood there for a prolonged moment, his hungry, possessive gaze devouring the sight of her. She imagined how she must look to him, her thick black hair disheveled, her dress hiked up to her bare waist, her long legs spread open to reveal the slick, glistening folds of her sex.

"Beautiful," he whispered huskily.

Althea felt a shiver of warmth puddle in her loins. She wanted him inside her, hard and deep.

She almost wept with relief when he retrieved a condom from his pocket and sheathed himself with practiced ease. She reached up and slid his blazer from his broad shoulders, impatiently casting it aside. That was as far as she got before Damien pushed her back onto her elbows and settled between her legs. He nudged her thighs wide and knifed into her, filling her with every swollen, aroused inch of him. She cried out wildly and clutched him, her nails raking down his back, her legs locking around his waist.

As he pounded in and out of her, she shouted hoarsely in pleasure and encouragement. She wanted more, faster, harder, and he was only too willing to oblige her. Soon the entire apartment was filled with the orchestra of their fierce lovemaking, their desperate cries and moans punctuated by the wet suck-and-slap sounds of their bodies.

The sensations thundering through Althea's body were almost too intense to call pleasure. She couldn't bear the building pressure, and when she finally erupted, it was in an endless series of spasms that wrenched a loud, broken sob from her.

The spasms had barely abated when Damien pulled out of her. "Turn around," came his rough command.

Althea obeyed without hesitation, and when he took her from behind she screamed, pain mingling with the erotic pleasure. He thrust hard, his body slapping against her backside, his strong fingers digging into her buttocks. She moaned uncontrollably, her hands splayed on the table, her breasts bouncing up and down with his deep, powerful strokes.

Their coupling was so good it was almost unbearable. She couldn't take it. She tried to push him away, only to pull him closer. When he reached between her legs and traced his thumb around her clitoris, she arched backward like a bow. And fell apart.

They came violently at the same time.

When it was over, when Damien shuddered and collapsed on top of her, their lungs heaving for air, Althea could not find the strength to move. Neither, apparently, could he. They remained like that for several minutes, slumped weakly over the table, his throbbing penis buried deep inside her.

When Althea could frame a coherent thought again, she realized that her throat felt raw from all the screaming she'd done. She wondered if any of her new neighbors had heard, and promptly decided she didn't give a damn.

There was a wet suctioning sound as Damien eased out of the slick clasp of her body and raised himself off her. He turned her over and lifted her back onto the table, gently brushing away the damp tendrils of hair that clung to her face.

Althea curved her arms around his neck and gazed into the molten darkness of his eyes. His lids were at half mast, and the soft glow of lamplight washed across the hard angles and planes of his face. He was sexier than any man had a right to be, and tonight, he was all hers.

One night only, she reminded herself, lest she become too greedy. A man like Damien made it easy for a woman to beg for more.

"Happy birthday," she whispered.

"Mmm," came the deliciously husky rumble. "You have no idea."

Althea couldn't help but smile. She brushed her lips across his forehead and the strong bridge of his nose, then kissed his closed eyelids, telling herself she was crazy for indulging such a tender impulse.

"I took you away from your own birthday party," she murmured.

He laughed softly. "You don't hear me complaining."

"True." Unable to resist, she dipped the tip of her tongue into the wickedly sexy dimple carved into his right cheek. She delighted in the small tremor that shook him.

"Spend the night with me." The words were out before she could stop them.

Not that she would have.

His thick black lashes slowly lifted. The eyes that bored into hers were smoldering pools of onyx.

Without a word, he swept her into his arms and started purposefully toward the bedroom.

Saturday, October 4
Day 2

Althea awoke to the brilliant warmth of sunshine bathing her face. Without opening her eyes, she yawned and stretched languorously in the four-poster bed, like a cat rousing from an afternoon nap. She couldn't have slept more than a few hours last night, but she had never felt more refreshed in her life.

As she slowly opened her eyes, a soft, satiated smile curved the corners of her mouth. What a night. What an absolutely incredible night. One she would definitely remember for a long time, if not for the rest of her life.

Rolling over, she found herself alone in the rumpled bed. She didn't know whether to feel relieved or disappointed. Which was ridiculous. Of course she should be relieved that Damien had snuck out of her apartment sometime in the middle of the night without saying good-bye. By doing so, he had spared himself the awkwardness of having to make promises he didn't intend to keep, such as *I'll call you* or *Let's do this again sometime.*

Actually, he'd done them *both* a favor by disappearing before she woke up. Althea would have been mortified if he'd felt compelled to lie to her or, worse, if he had genuinely wanted to see her again.

What they'd shared had been a one-time thing, a night of no-holds-barred sex between two mature, consenting adults. No mess, no fuss. No strings attached. Those were the rules.

So why did she find herself wondering what time he'd left and how long he'd been gone?

Althea frowned at the ceiling.

Last night she'd told herself that having a one-night stand with a sexy, gorgeous man like Damien was all she needed, but now, in the sobering light of day, she wasn't so sure. The truth was that she'd never been the type of woman who took strangers home for casual sex and engaged in meaningless flings. No, *she* was the type of woman who'd once saved herself for someone special, someone who genuinely cared about her and was interested in more than just claiming the prize of her virginity. That someone had been her college sweetheart, and although, ultimately, he'd betrayed her in the worst possible way, Althea had never regretted giving herself to him.

Just as she had no regrets about sleeping with Damien.

The memory of their savage lovemaking long into the night made her belly quiver on a wave of sexual arousal. She remembered the erotic invasion of his tongue in her mouth and the searing intensity of his gaze as he carried her into the bedroom. She remembered the way he'd wrapped her fingers around the bedpost and held them there while he thrust into her. One hard, long stroke after another until she was screaming in ecstasy and begging for mercy.

The sex with Damien had been so spectacular, so unlike anything she had ever experienced before, that she half wondered if she'd dreamed the whole encounter. But, no, the throbbing ache between her thighs, the musky scent clinging to the rumpled linens, and the indentation on the pillow beside hers were all too real.

When the phone rang she groaned softly, resenting the intrusion. She reached across the nightstand and picked up on the final ring. "Hello?"

"Althea Lynette Pritchard, you got some splainin' to do!"

Althea chuckled dryly. "Good morning to you, too, Keren. I was wondering who would call first—you or Kimberly."

"We've *both* been trying to reach you on your cell phone all morning! I finally remembered that you gave me your new home number before you left Seattle. Girl, I can't believe you went home with a complete stranger last night!"

Althea grinned at her friend's scandalized tone. "Okay, um, did you happen to *see* that particular stranger?"

"Of course I did! Every woman at the club did. He was fine as hell. But that's not the point. You left with a perfect stranger after just one dance! Did you two even have a chance to exchange names before you hightailed it out of there?"

Althea bristled. "Of course we did." *First names anyway.* "Look, did you call to lecture me or get the salacious details of my, ah, evening?"

Keren grumbled, "I called to make sure you were all right." She paused a beat. "*And* to get the salacious details!"

Althea laughed. "I thought so."

When she offered no more, Keren prompted impatiently, "Well?"

Smiling, Althea toyed with the edges of her satin duvet. "Well, since we all took a cab to the club last night," she began, "I brought him to my apartment so I wouldn't have to worry about catching a ride home afterward."

"But you've got unopened boxes all over the place." Keren had always been the practical one. Kimberly wouldn't have given a rat's ass about the state of Althea's apartment while Damien was there.

"All the boxes are gone," Althea said. "Didn't I tell you? My aunt came over earlier this week when my stuff arrived from Seattle and unpacked everything for me. It was such a wonderful surprise."

"That was very thoughtful of her," Keren agreed. "Now get back to—"

But Althea suddenly bolted upright. "Oh my God! I forgot to plug in my alarm clock yesterday. What time is it?"

"Ten-thirty. Why?"

"I'm supposed to be meeting my aunt and uncle for lunch in an hour!"

Keren groaned in protest. "But I wanted to hear—"

"I have to go." Althea flung back the covers and swung her legs over the side of the bed.

"Do you have to go *now*?"

"Yes! Look, they didn't complain when I told them I'd be spending my first night back in town with friends. The least I can do is show up on time to eat with them."

"Oh, all right. I need to get out and run some errands anyway." Keren heaved a deep, resigned sigh. "Will you call me later?"

"Of course. And tell Kimberly I'm okay." Althea paused with a wicked grin. "*Better* than okay."

She hung up on Keren's groan of frustration and hurried into the adjoining bathroom to take a shower.

As she stood beneath the hot spray, her thoughts strayed once again to Damien and the events of last night. She'd thrown caution to the wind by approaching him at the club and asking him to dance, setting the stage for what would become the most incredible night of her life. An unforgettable night. That was all it had been, and that was all it could ever be. Damien's disappearing act was proof that he felt the same way. He hadn't stuck around to have a cup of coffee with her, or even to indulge in one last tumble between the sheets. Before the first pink rays of dawn lightened the sky, he had gotten dressed and snuck out of her apartment with the stealth of a cat burglar.

Judging by the amount of female attention he'd been receiving at the club, it wouldn't have surprised Althea to learn that he did this sort of thing all the time. By this time next week, she would be nothing but a distant memory to him. He would remember her only as the bold, freaky woman with whom he had spent an amazing few hours on the night of his thirty-fourth birthday. He and his friends would laugh about it the next time they visited the club, which would probably be the following weekend.

Not that it mattered one way or the other, Althea reminded herself as she rinsed soap off her body. It made no difference whether Damien remembered her, or in what manner. They would never see each other again.

Which was as it should be.

She'd had her one night of carefree fun, and now it was time to move on. With any luck, by tomorrow afternoon she'd be buried to her nose in tough new cases that would keep her too preoccupied to dwell on thoughts of Damien No-Last-Name and the mind-blowing night of passion they had shared.

Besides, Althea mused, in a city the size of Baltimore, what were the odds of running into him again anyway?

Chapter 4

Damien Wade stood under a pounding shower spray, his head bowed and his eyes closed as he let the hot water pour over his body. His muscles ached, and he was operating on less than four hours of sleep. But he wasn't complaining.

Not after the incredible night he'd just had.

He smiled as vividly erotic images stole through his mind. When he'd agreed to celebrate his birthday with friends at the downtown nightclub, never could he have imagined that the celebration would end with him making love to the most beautiful, exciting woman he'd ever met—a woman he hadn't known existed before that evening.

And to think he'd almost missed her.

After a long, trying day at the office, Damien had been looking forward to spending a relaxing evening with his eleven-year-old daughter India. It was a long-standing tradition for the two of them to celebrate his birthday together, which usually meant dinner at his favorite restaurant followed by a trip to the skating rink, which was *her* favorite pastime. It didn't really matter where they went or what they did, as long as they could spend quality time together. Six years ago when Damien lost custody of India, he'd promised her that he would always be part of her life, and despite her mother's efforts to the contrary, he'd kept his promise.

When Angelique called him at the office yesterday to let him know that India wouldn't be joining him that evening, he'd thought his ex-wife was up to her old tricks again, until India herself got on the phone and in a small, tremulous voice asked him if he'd be mad if she attended her first middle-school dance instead of spending his birthday with him. Damien hadn't known whether to laugh or cry over the startling realization that his little girl was growing up right before his very eyes. He gave her his blessing and told her to have a good time at the dance.

When he hung up the phone, Marshall Blake, who'd been shamelessly eavesdropping on the conversation, stood and peered over the cubicle at Damien. "Tough break about the kid standing you up. But now you have no excuse not to hang out with the fellas tonight." Before Damien could refuse, he said, "Come on, Wade. It's your birthday—live a little!"

It turned out to be the best piece of advice Marshall Blake had ever given him.

The moment Damien stepped into the noisy club last night he'd noticed Althea. In a crowd of other women dressed in skimpy skirts and diaphanous tops that left little to the imagination, *she* alone had caught his eye. Beautiful brown skin, sultry eyes, and a lush, tempting mouth that promised untold pleasures. Just remembering the things she'd done to him with that mouth sent a hard shudder through him.

When their eyes met, the connection between them had been visceral, electric. He'd almost forgotten about his friends waiting for him somewhere inside the nightclub, and even after he was settled at his table, he couldn't stop looking across the room, looking for *her*. When she came over and asked him to dance, he felt like he'd just won the lottery. By the time he kissed her halfway through the second song, he was so aroused he actually ached. They couldn't make it out of the building fast enough.

But as incredible as last night had been, Damien knew it had to be a one-time thing. Between his demanding career and sharing the responsibility of raising an eleven-year-old daughter, he had no room in his life for a relationship. And he preferred it that way. Relationships could be tricky, and although he'd dated frequently in the six years since his divorce, he had yet to meet a woman who made him want to take another trip down the aisle.

Until last night, a voice whispered.

Damien frowned, giving himself a hard mental shake. Nothing had changed for him overnight. After all, he reasoned, if great sex with a beautiful woman was all he needed, he would still be married.

Never mind that he'd felt a powerful connection to Althea that transcended the physical act of sex. And never mind that their lovemaking had been out of this world, like nothing he'd ever experienced before. None of that mattered. He and Althea were two mature, consenting adults who'd enjoyed a mind-blowing night of passion, and although Damien cringed at the term *one-night stand*, that's exactly what it had been. A one-night stand. An isolated encounter. When he crept out of her apartment at the crack of dawn that morning, he knew he was doing what they both wanted, what they both expected. No empty promises, no strings, no drama. Hey, he didn't make the rules of the game; he just followed them.

And if he found himself unable to stop thinking

about her, well, he'd just have to deal with it. After all, he told himself, he couldn't think about her *forever*.

Comforted by the thought—if not entirely convinced—Damien stepped out of the shower stall and reached for his towel, wrapping it loosely around his waist. As he brushed his teeth, he wiped at the misted mirror, surveyed his reflection, and decided he could go another day without shaving. It was Saturday, and the only people who would see him today were his family and some close friends, who had planned a surprise birthday party for him that he'd accidentally learned about when he overheard his mother whispering on the phone with Imani, his sister-in-law. Damien knew he would have to put on an Oscar-worthy performance when he arrived at his mother's house that afternoon and all those people jumped out at him yelling "Surprise!"

Chuckling at the thought, he rinsed out his mouth and left the bathroom.

He pulled up short at the sight of his ex-wife, Angelique Navarro, perched on a corner of his bed, her glossy dark hair swept over one shoulder, her long legs crossed as she leaned back on her elbows, looking as if she had every right to be there.

He frowned at her. "What the hell are you doing here?"

Angelique arched a perfectly sculpted brow. "In your house or in your bedroom?"

"Both."

Instead of answering, she ran an appreciative eye over his bare chest, where droplets of water still clung to his dark skin. "You always *were* too damn sexy for your own good, Damien Wade," she purred.

There was a time that hearing those words from her would have driven Damien wild with lust. If this had been six years ago when they were still married, before things turned sour, he would have dropped his towel where he stood, walked over to her, and stretched her out on the bed, where he would have made love to her long into the afternoon.

But this *wasn't* six years ago. Too much had happened since then, too much bad blood now flowed between them. They could never return to the way things used to be, could never reclaim the innocence and blind optimism they'd possessed as infatuated college sweethearts who suddenly found themselves facing parenthood. In the eleven years since India's birth, they'd gone from being two crazy kids in love to two people who barely tolerated each other.

Which was what made Angelique's presence in his bedroom so unnerving.

Months before their brief, disastrous marriage had ended they'd stopped sleeping together. Angelique started hanging out at nightclubs with her single friends, leaving Damien and India to fend for themselves at home. Although she'd been smart enough not to get caught, he'd always suspected she was cheating on him. She was a beautiful, desirable woman who turned male heads wherever she went. Her sudden lack of interest in their marriage bed told Damien she was getting what she needed elsewhere. On the few occasions when she *did* try to sneak into bed with him, he was so angry and disgusted with her behavior he couldn't even bring himself to touch her. He'd learned the hard way that whenever his selfish, manipulative wife tried to seduce him, she usually wanted something in return.

Part black, part Cherokee and part trouble, his mother used to say about Angelique. If only he'd remembered that *before* he married her.

"What do you want?" he demanded.

Hurt flared in Angelique's light brown eyes at his

harsh tone. "Why do I have to want anything? Why can't I just drop by to say hello to you?"

His lips curved cynically. "Because you've never just 'dropped by to say hello.' And haven't you ever heard of waiting downstairs in the living room like a normal visitor?"

"I *was* waiting downstairs, but you were taking too long, so I came up here to make sure you were all right." Her eyes narrowed speculatively on his face. "You never used to take such long showers before. What were you in there thinking about?"

"Where's India?" Damien asked, ignoring her question. "I've told you before she's too young to be left home by herself."

"I didn't leave her at home," Angelique snapped, sitting up on the bed. "Your mother and Imani came to the apartment to pick her up, claiming they were taking her shopping and out to lunch. But I know good and damn well they're all running around getting last-minute stuff for your surprise party." She paused, a malicious gleam filling her eyes as she looked at Damien. "I'm so sorry. You weren't supposed to know about that. It just, well, slipped out."

Damien believed *that* about as much as he believed she'd been on the pill the first time they had unprotected sex. "Do you mind?" he said pointedly, nodding toward the door.

She didn't take the hint. Deliberately. "You know, I think it's pretty trifling that your family hasn't bothered inviting me to your party," she said bitterly.

He scowled, crossing over to his dresser. "What do you want me to do, Angelique?" He'd stopped calling her Angel a long time ago. There was nothing remotely angelic about her. "I'm not even supposed to know about it."

"It's not just your birthday party I'm talking about!

It's Reggie's parties, Garrison's parties, Imani's parties, your mother's parties! It's christenings, graduation ceremonies, award banquets, holiday dinners, summer vacations. I've been excluded from just about every Wade family gathering for the last six years!"

Damien's face hardened as he turned and stared at her. "You had your opportunity to be a member of my family," he said coldly, "and as I clearly recall, you told each and every one of us to go to hell."

Her face reddened. "I was angry! Your family was trying to take India away from me by testifying in court that I was a bad mother!"

"No one said you were a bad mother," Damien corrected her, his voice clipped. "They answered truthfully when asked about your lack of parental involvement before, and during, our two-year marriage. Even the judge agreed that you'd been irresponsible and downright negligent on numerous occasions."

"And yet he gave *me* custody of our daughter," Angelique shot back spitefully.

Damien didn't so much as flinch, even though her words had struck a raw nerve. "That's right," he said in a cool, carefully measured voice. "The judge awarded you custody because he wanted to give you a second chance to redeem yourself, to prove you could be a good mother to India."

Angelique sneered. "If memory serves me correctly, he also had some concerns about *your* job as an FBI agent. The long hours, the traveling, the amount of casework you bring home. Let's not sit here and pretend you deserved custody of India any more than I did."

"Why are we having this conversation?" Damien growled, his patience wearing thin. "Is it because you weren't invited to my damn birthday party? Or do you have a better reason for breaking into my house and camping out in my bedroom while I took a shower?"

"I didn't break in," Angelique said tightly. "I used India's key."

"Operative word being *India's*—not yours."

"I don't have a key to your house."

"My point exactly." He reached for the towel draped around his waist. "Now if you'll excuse me, I'd like to get dressed. *Without* an audience."

Angelique gave him a slow, deliberate once-over, lingering on his crotch in a manner designed to either embarrass him or elicit a surge of lust. He felt neither.

And she knew it, too. "I don't understand what the big deal is, Damien," she said testily. "I've seen you naked a million times. Hell, we've seen *each other* naked a million times. No matter what else was going on in our relationship, we never had a problem appreciating each other's bodies. If it makes you feel more comfortable, I'll even take off my—"

"Angelique."

She paused, her hands stilling on the hem of her shirt as she stared at him.

"Get out."

Recognizing the steely glint in his eyes, she huffed out a sigh that was part resignation, part frustration, and reluctantly rose from the bed. Halfway to the door she turned back, holding up a white slip of paper between her fingers.

"I almost forgot," she said. "I found this on the staircase. It must have fallen out of your pocket when you came home last night."

Damien recognized the business card he'd received from a woman at the nightclub. On the back she had written, *Call me tomorrow. You won't be disappointed.* He'd forgotten about the card—and the woman—as soon as Althea had appeared at his table. And he doubted very seriously that Angelique had found the card on the staircase, as she claimed. The blazer and trousers he'd worn last night were still slung across the bench at the foot of his bed. More than likely she had gone through his pockets while he was in the shower.

"Looks like you had a good time last night," she said coolly.

"You could say that."

She shook her head. "And to think India was feeling guilty about ditching you on your birthday. She felt so bad she hardly even enjoyed the school dance. She wanted to rush over here first thing in the morning to make sure you hadn't cried yourself to sleep." Her lips twisted mockingly. "Little did she know that Daddy celebrated his birthday just fine without her."

Damien said nothing. He refused to rise to the bait.

A nasty, possessive gleam filled Angelique's eyes. "Are you going to call her?" she asked, tapping the card with a manicured fingertip.

"None of your damn business. Now get out."

She hesitated for a moment, then walked over to the nightstand and slapped the card down, right beside the phone. "There. I'll make it easy for you."

Damien clenched and unclenched his jaw, watching as she retraced her steps to the door. Before he could reach for his towel, however, she paused once again and turned to look at him. Her expression was thoughtful, brooding.

"We were good together once," she said softly. "I remember how terrified and excited we were when we found out we were having a baby. We didn't care that we were only juniors in college, or that our families thought we were throwing our lives away. We were determined to prove them wrong. It was us against the world. Do you remember?"

Damien frowned. "Where is all this coming from, Angelique?"

She held his gaze, and for the first time in years, he thought he saw genuine vulnerability in her eyes. "Maybe I wish things had turned out differently for us. Maybe I regret the way I took you for granted. Maybe I'm starting to realize what a good thing I had, what a good man I had. Maybe I'm hoping that you, me, and India can be a family again someday."

Damien stared at her, unmoved by her words, unthawed by the plaintive note in her voice. "That train left the station a long time ago, Angelique," he said flatly.

She flinched, her chin lifting a proud notch. "It's not like I came over here to beg you to take me back or anything."

"Good. I'd hate to see you waste your time." Turning away dismissively, Damien pulled open his dresser drawer and reached for a pair of dark briefs, making it clear to Angelique that the discussion, and her visit, were over.

He thought he heard her mutter, "Never say never," but when he glanced over his shoulder, the doorway was empty.

Althea stood in the entryway of an upscale Baltimore restaurant that overlooked the Inner Harbor. She scanned the crowded dining room until her gaze landed on a handsome black couple in their early sixties seated at a table that offered a sweeping view of the water below.

Her face broke into a wide smile.

Without waiting for the maître d' to escort her, she hurried across the room toward her aunt and uncle.

Louis Pritchard looked up first, and when he saw Althea approaching, a huge, delighted grin swept across his face.

"There she is!" he said, rising quickly to his feet. "There's our baby girl!"

Althea had barely reached the table before she was swallowed in the solid warmth of her uncle's embrace, and then her aunt's, who showered her face with kisses before standing back to give her an approving once-over.

"You look wonderful," Barbara Pritchard exclaimed.

Althea smiled. "I could definitely say the same about you."

The years had been good to her aunt, who looked effortlessly elegant in a fitted herringbone jacket worn over dark silk trousers. Several years ago she'd decided to let nature take its course, and now she sported a head full of silver hair cropped in sleek, stylish layers. Her cream-colored skin remained smooth and firm, and her figure was as svelte as ever.

Louis Pritchard was tall and broad-shouldered, a powerfully built man accustomed to taking control, whether he was delivering a speech on the Senate floor or leading his family through a crisis. His salt-and-pepper hair was neatly trimmed, and whether he was wearing a William Fioravanti wool suit or jeans and a Redskins jersey, he always managed to look handsome and debonair.

Once they were all seated, and the waiter had departed after taking their orders, Barbara reached over and squeezed Althea's hand on the linen-covered table.

"We're so glad you could meet us for lunch, sweetheart," she said warmly.

Althea grinned. "I wouldn't have missed it for the world. Especially since Uncle Louie is treating," she added, winking playfully at him.

He laughed good-naturedly and tweaked her nose, the way he'd done when she was a child.

Louis and Barbara Pritchard were the only parents Althea had ever known. When her young, crack-addicted mother died a few hours after giving birth to her, her aunt and uncle had stepped in to raise her. After years of struggling with infertility, they'd regarded Althea as a precious gift from God, their miracle baby. They gave her the best of everything, showering her with all the love and affection she could ever want or need. They had always been a tremendous source of strength for her, a safe haven. And although they were shocked, even disappointed, by her decision not to become a doctor, they put aside their own feelings and gave her their unconditional support. When she graduated from the FBI Academy three years ago, no one cheered or clapped louder than Louis and Barbara Pritchard. The bond Althea shared with her aunt and uncle had made it difficult for her to stay away from home for so long, and now that she was back, she realized just how much she'd missed them.

She smiled at her aunt. "I can't thank you enough for unpacking my things and putting my apartment in order before I arrived, Aunt Bobbi. The place looks absolutely wonderful."

"Oh, you don't have to keep thanking me," Barbara said, patting her hand affectionately. "I knew you wouldn't have time to worry about unpacking once you started working, and I didn't want you living out of boxes for months on end. Besides, like I told you, I didn't do all the hard work by myself. I had plenty of help from the ladies at church, who have always considered you one of their own anyway."

Althea's smile softened. "I'll have to thank each of them personally when I see them at church tomorrow."

Barbara beamed with pleasure. "They'd like that very much. Everyone was so excited when they heard you were coming back home."

"Not as excited as *we* were," Louis said, buttering a roll and passing it to Althea. "We were afraid the Bureau would send you to Alaska before letting you return home."

Althea grinned, nibbling on the hot, crusty roll. "I've only been in the Bureau for three years. It takes most agents several years to be assigned to their office of preference—*if* it ever happens. I'm fortunate to be back in the area this soon."

Although there was a time she'd never wanted to step foot in Maryland again. When she left home nearly eight years ago, she knew it would be a very long time before she found the courage to return. Everywhere she looked, everywhere she went, she'd been reminded of the harrowing ordeal she'd suffered at the hands of a violent psychopath. Moving halfway across the country had been a desperate attempt on her part to outrun the memories, the horrifying nightmares that plagued her sleep every night. But after all these years of running and hiding, she was ready to face her demons and put the past behind her. It was time to reclaim her life once and for all.

"How are Keren and Kimberly doing?" Barbara asked as the waiter materialized with their starter salads and drinks. "We haven't seen or spoken to them since your graduation ceremony three years ago."

Althea reached for her white wine. "They're both doing well. Keren is knocking on the door of a promotion at her accounting firm, and Kimberly thoroughly enjoys working at Calloway by Design," she said, citing a large graphic design company headquartered in Washington, D.C.

"From what Nick Hunter tells me," Louis said, "his wife Rachel is thrilled to have Kimberly on board. She says Kimberly is one of her best designers, and the clients really love her work."

Althea smiled proudly. "That doesn't surprise me. Kim is very talented. Always has been. Remember the program and invitations she designed for your thirtieth wedding anniversary celebration?"

"Of course," Barbara chimed in. "We still receive compliments on them. And let's not forget the interactive Web site she designed for your uncle when he ran for Congress."

Louis chuckled. "I truly believe that Web site did more for my candidacy than any campaign speech or promise I could have ever made."

Althea grinned at him over the rim of her wineglass. "So that means you'll have to utilize Kimberly's services again when you run for president in four years."

Barbara groaned softly. "Oh, please. Let's not talk about that yet. I'm *still* getting used to being the wife of a senator, even though I've had several years to adjust. I don't even want to *think* about becoming First Lady."

Her husband and niece laughed. They knew, as did Barbara, that Louis Pritchard's bid for the White House was a foregone conclusion among his supporters and many Beltway insiders. He had enjoyed a successful political career that spanned three decades, starting out as a tough, no-nonsense prosecutor before working his way up to state's attorney, a position he held for fifteen years. When he became county executive, the highest elected office in Prince George's County, everyone knew it was only a matter of time before he would set his sights on Washington. And they were right. Within five years he was elected to the U.S. Senate, where he continued working tirelessly for his constituents, earn-

ing the respect and admiration of his colleagues and
solidifying his reputation as a man of character and
integrity.

As a child Althea had worshipped her uncle and
thought he could do no wrong. Although she was older
and wiser now, she still believed he was the smartest,
most caring, and most honorable man she had ever
known. He was the standard by which she judged all
other men, including the few she'd dated. So far, none
had measured up.

Damien certainly had potential, a tiny inner voice whispered.

"Did you and the girls have a good time last night?"
Barbara asked, stirring sugar into her hot tea.

"We had a great time," Althea answered, as intensely
erotic images from the night before flashed through her
mind, bringing a hot flush to her cheeks. She cleared
her throat. "It was good catching up with Keren and
Kimberly again. I missed them."

A silent look passed between Louis and Barbara.
"We've been debating whether or not to tell you about
a recent phone call we received," Barbara said slowly.

Althea felt the muscles tightening in the back of her
neck. She divided a wary glance between her aunt and
uncle. "A call from who?"

Louis looked like he had a bad taste in his mouth.
"Malik Toomer."

Althea blinked, surprised. "*Malik* called you?"

Barbara nodded, watching her carefully. "He heard
through the grapevine that you were moving back to
Maryland. He wanted us to give him your phone number
so he could call you, maybe invite you to one of his
games. You know, of course, that he got traded to the
Washington Wizards two years ago."

Althea nodded, fully aware of Malik Toomer's failures—
and more recent successes—as a professional basketball

player. "So what did you tell him when he asked for my number?"

"I told him to go to hell," Louis growled.

Barbara grimaced. "You had some other choice words for him as well. Things that would make my sainted mother roll over in her grave if I repeated them."

Althea laughed, even as she gave Louis a censorious look. "Uncle Louie, how many times have I told you that a man in your position has to watch what he says to people, because you never know when your words might come back to haunt you?"

"I don't care," Louis grumbled, shoving aside his empty salad plate. "That boy has a lot of damn nerve calling us to ask for your number. He's lucky your aunt took the phone from me when she did, or he *really* would have gotten his feelings hurt!"

Barbara gave him a look. "You called the boy a lying, cheating, overrated basketball player who doesn't deserve to breathe the same air as your niece. Believe me, I think his feelings were *plenty* hurt."

"Uncle Louie," Althea groaned, shaking her head in disbelief. "I know you meant well, but you shouldn't have said those things to Malik."

"Why not?" Louis demanded, his dark eyes sizzling with temper. "Listen, baby girl, I held my tongue when you first told us why you and Malik were breaking up. Even though I could see how hurt you were, I stayed out of it because you asked me to. But I've never forgotten what that boy did to you, the way he betrayed your trust and deserted you at a time when you needed him the most. The fact that he had the unmitigated audacity to call my house, after all these years and after the disgraceful way he treated you, tells me that he still doesn't get it. So I took the opportunity to set him straight, and I make no apologies for that."

Silence descended over the table as the waiter appeared with their meals. Three plates of crab cakes, which was the house specialty, served with a heaping of garlic mashed potatoes and seasoned greens.

The conversation resumed as soon as the waiter moved on to the next table. "Despite what your uncle thinks about Malik," Barbara said gently to Althea, "I do believe he genuinely cared about you. I don't believe he ever meant to hurt you."

"But he did," Althea said quietly. "He slept with my best friend, then lied to me about it for months. I had to learn the truth from someone else, someone who thought I already knew. And Uncle Louie is right. Malik did abandon me at a time when I needed him the most. In the weeks and months after I was returned home, Malik was missing in action. I couldn't even count on his friendship, which was supposed to be the foundation of our relationship. I knew it was difficult for him, having to deal with an emotional wreck of a girlfriend who'd just survived a kidnapping. We were young, and neither of us was prepared to handle the aftermath of such a traumatic ordeal. I didn't expect Malik to have all the answers or know the right words to say, nor did I expect him to make my pain, my fears, my nightmares, go away. But I did expect him to be there for me, as someone who claimed to love and care about me. But he wasn't. He pulled a disappearing act. And although I've worked through my feelings of anger and betrayal and disillusionment, that doesn't mean I'm ready to welcome him back into my life. Truth be told, I may never be. And I'm okay with that."

By the time she'd finished speaking, Louis and Barbara had tears glistening in their eyes. They reached over, each taking one of Althea's hands on the table.

"I've always believed you deserved much better than

the Malik Toomers of the world," Louis said with quiet solemnity. "When God sends you the right man, you will know. He'll be someone worthy of you, someone deserving of your love, loyalty, and trust. But I know I also speak for your aunt when I tell you that marrying you off is the *last* thing on our minds right now. Ever since you called to tell us about your transfer to Baltimore, we've been dancing on air and counting our blessings. We're so grateful to have you back home, with us, where you belong."

Barbara said tenderly, "Welcome home, Althea."

Althea smiled at her aunt and uncle, her throat constricted with emotion. "It's good to be home," she said, and meant every word.

Chapter 5

"Good morning, Claire. Rise and shine."

Balancing a breakfast tray in his hands, he stood in the doorway and stared across a shadowy expanse to the bed where seventeen-year-old Claire Thorndike lay bound, gagged, and blindfolded. As he opened the door wider a sliver of light from the corridor spilled into the cold, windowless room and slanted across her silent, unmoving form.

"Claire?"

Once again, she did not stir at the sound of his voice.

He stepped into the room, his footfalls silent on the concrete floor as he slowly walked over to the bed. He set the tray down on a small table beside the bed, then turned to examine his prisoner with the clinical detachment of a coroner. She lay on her side, curled in a fetal position with her arms pinned behind her, her wrists tightly bound. The tangled, wavy mass of her long auburn hair spilled across her head, concealing her lovely face. He had changed her into a pair of jeans and a sweatshirt from her closet, because the sheer white negligee she'd been wearing was all wrong. She was supposed to be dressed like a college student, not a harlot.

She was supposed to be dressed the way *she* had been.

He sat on the edge of the bed and gently smoothed her disheveled hair off her face. "Claire," he called again softly, his voice a lover's caress. "Time to wake up."

She stirred then, struggling against the pull of the drugs he had given her earlier. He'd needed to sedate her, to stop her violent thrashing on the bed and to silence her hysterical, horrified screams.

She moaned fitfully, the sound muffled behind the strip of duct tape plastered across her mouth. He would have preferred a cloth gag, but everything had to be perfect, right down to the minutest detail.

He smiled inwardly, anticipation heating his blood at the thought of what lay ahead. But, no, he couldn't allow himself to look too far into the future. He had to be patient and bide his time. The successful outcome of his plan depended on his patience, his diligence. His cunning.

He would not fail.

"You must eat now," he said softly to his captive. "I brought you breakfast."

Claire made a small whimpering noise and tried to back away from him on the bed.

His mouth curved in a slow, predatory smile she couldn't see. "I'm going to remove the tape so you can eat, Claire. Don't bother screaming. No one can hear you. No one *will* hear you."

He felt her body trembling even before he touched her. Slowly he peeled the duct tape away from her mouth, which was incredibly soft and lush. She'd been wearing lipstick when he took her—a bright, garish red that made her look like a whore. That, too, had been all wrong. So he'd wiped her lips with a damp washcloth until not a trace of the offensive red color remained.

"There, now," he murmured, slowly wadding up the tape. "Isn't that better?"

"W-Who are you?" she whispered fearfully. "W-What are y-you going to do to me?"

He laughed, the soft, eerie sound echoing around the cold, cavernous room. "Ah, Claire. Sweet, young, beautiful Claire. Don't trouble yourself with such matters. All you need to know is that you are in good hands."

"M-My dad is rich," she said pleadingly. "If y-you want m-money—"

Again he laughed, more harshly this time. "I don't need or want your father's money."

How typical of the wealthy to assume that their problems could be solved with money. Typical and arrogant. All the riches in the world could not save Claire Thorndike from the fate that awaited her. The fate he would deliver.

"Are you . . . going to kill me?"

"No more questions, Claire," he said mildly. "It's time to eat."

Her lips began to tremble. "I-I'm not hungry. I w-want to go home."

"You're not going home, Claire."

"Please," she sobbed, her voice rising shrilly. "Please let me go! *Please!*"

He carefully removed a needle and syringe from the tray on the table and grasped her left arm. Her terrified screams ripped through the room, bouncing off the walls and ricocheting through his brain.

He emptied the contents of the syringe into her veins, and a moment later she fell silent, her body going limp.

He rose from the bed and pulled the single white sheet over her body, tucking her in as calmly and lovingly as if she were his own child. He even took a moment to brush the hair off her face.

"Sweet dreams, Claire," he whispered in the utter stillness of the room. "You won't be alone much longer. *She* will come for you soon enough."

And when she did, he would be ready for her.

Welcome home, Althea.

Chapter 6

By seven-thirty on Monday morning, Althea was on her way to the Baltimore field division, which served as headquarters for Maryland and Delaware. Not unlike a kid on the first day of school, she was excited and nervous about her new assignment. She was eager to tackle tough new cases and, yes, make a good impression on her colleagues. She had worked hard to get where she was, but she knew she still had a long way to go to prove that she belonged in the Bureau instead of medical school. There were many who still considered her the new kid on the block, although the very nature of an agent's work meant she'd had to learn more in three years than the average worker learned after several years on the job.

As she skillfully maneuvered through downtown traffic, Althea flipped through radio stations in search of some smooth jazz. She'd had her fill of campaign coverage and the political commentary that had increasingly dominated the airwaves as the November election drew near. Now all she wanted to hear was something soft and mellow, something to soothe her jittery nerves before she reached the office.

She settled on WSMJ 104.3 just as the host was announcing the songs he had played in the previous segment. ". . . And now in late-breaking news, Baltimore police are reporting the disappearance of seventeen-year-old Claire Thorndike, who is the daughter of real estate developer Spencer Thorndike."

Althea tensed, her hands tightening on the steering wheel.

"According to police sources," the radio host continued, "the teenager was apparently taken from the family's home near Mount Washington while Thorndike and his wife were out of town for the weekend. An AMBER Alert has been issued by the Baltimore Police Department, and Spencer Thorndike is expected to make a statement during a press conference scheduled this afternoon. We'll keep our listeners posted as more details become available in this developing story."

Frowning deeply, Althea began flipping through radio stations, seeking more news about the kidnapping even as a fist of instinctive tension curled in her stomach. While this certainly wasn't the first abduction she'd heard or read about since her own harrowing ordeal, something about *this* one put her on edge.

And she knew why.

It had been nearly eight years to the day that she was kidnapped.

A chill ran through her, twisting and coiling in the pit of her stomach. Memories rushed to the surface of her mind, a deluge of painfully vivid flashbacks. She saw herself standing on the dark, deserted street corner, waiting for the shuttle bus to take her across campus to Malik Toomer's apartment. She saw the flickering street lamp, heard the faint rustling of tree leaves. She saw the dark, nondescript sedan creeping down the street toward her, thinking nothing of it until it was too late.

Sunday, October eighth—the day her life changed forever.

Today was Monday, October sixth.

Eight years later.

Calm down, Althea told herself. *Don't jump to conclusions. There's no connection between what happened to you and Claire Thorndike's abduction. And for all you know, there may be another explanation for her disappearance. She might have run away from home to get back at her father for some perceived transgression. Teenagers do that sort of thing all the time. The police may have acted prematurely in issuing an AMBER Alert. You've been in law enforcement long enough to know the first response is not always the right response.*

But, Althea thought grimly, she'd also been in law enforcement long enough to know there was no such thing as coincidence.

The Baltimore field office was located in an industrial area of the city surrounded by brick commercial buildings. As soon as Althea arrived at the office, she went straight to see her new boss—Special Agent in Charge Edward Balducci.

When she rounded the corner and saw that his office door was closed, she hesitated, deliberating whether to knock or come back when he was available. But she didn't want to wait. What she needed to discuss with Balducci was too important to put off until later.

Just as she raised her fist to knock, the door suddenly opened.

Althea gasped in shock.

There, standing in the doorway of her boss's office, was the man who had given her more orgasms in one night than she'd ever had in her entire life, the man who'd had her screaming his name and clawing his back in the middle of hot, mind-blowing sex.

The man she'd never expected to see again.

He was staring down at her with a dumbstruck expression that mirrored her own. He was as darkly handsome and virile as she remembered, wearing a dark suit with a crisp white shirt and a blue-and-gray-striped silk tie.

After several long moments, Althea regained the power of speech. *"Damien?"*

"Althea." That deep, potent voice washed over her, through her. "What are you doing here?"

"I, uh, work here."

"You do? Since when?"

"Today is my first day. I just got transferred to this field office. Wait a minute." She swallowed. "Do you . . . Are you an *agent?"*

Damien nodded, and Althea inwardly groaned. Oh great. Just great. Of all the men at the nightclub she could have gone home with, she had to choose a fellow FBI agent. What were the odds?

"Wade," an amused male voice spoke from inside the office, "why are you guarding my door like a bouncer?"

Wade. The name reverberated in Althea's mind. *Damien Wade.*

Why did that name sound so familiar?

"You here to see Balducci?" Damien murmured, his dark, penetrating gaze roaming across her face.

Althea nodded. "Yes. If you're finished with him. . . ." She trailed off, glancing pointedly at the doorway, which he was still blocking.

He stepped aside, but only a little. As Althea brushed past him to enter the office, her shoulder grazed his broad chest. To her mortification, her nipples hardened and a melting warmth rushed to her loins. Their eyes met and held before she dragged her gaze away.

Her first day was not turning out at all the way she'd planned.

Special Agent in Charge Edward Balducci was already rounding the corner of his large desk to greet her. "Althea Pritchard," he said with a warm, dimpled smile that flashed white against his deep olive skin, courtesy of his Italian blood. "Welcome to your new digs."

Althea smiled a bit unsteadily. "Thank you, sir. I'm glad to be here."

Ignoring her outstretched hand, Eddie grabbed her in a quick bear hug, then drew back to chuck her lightly on the chin, the way a big brother would. "How you been, kiddo?"

"Good. Really good."

Piercing hazel eyes softened on her face. Eddie Balducci understood, better than most, the tremendous import of her response. The first time he'd met Althea, she was an emaciated, shell-shocked figure huddled in the backseat of his partner's truck just minutes after she'd fled from her abductor. Speaking to her in soothingly gentle tones, Eddie had taken her statement before helping her into a waiting police cruiser that rushed her to the nearest hospital. In the years that followed, she'd never forgotten him or his partner, Garrison Wade, who had saved her life that fateful night.

Wade . . . Wade . . .

Suddenly Althea spun toward the doorway, where Damien Wade was already staring at her in stunned recognition. "Oh my God," she whispered. "You're Garrison Wade's brother!"

He nodded, his eyes never leaving hers as he stepped farther into the office. "And you're Althea Pritchard. *The* Althea Pritchard."

She nodded.

"No wonder you looked so familiar!" they chorused in unison.

With his arms folded across his chest, Eddie divided a curious look between them. "Wait a minute. Don't tell me this is the first time you two have ever met?"

"Not quite," Damien murmured. "We met for the first time on Friday night."

"Really?" Eddie's surprised gaze returned to Althea, whose expression betrayed nothing. "Didn't you guys meet at Garrison and Imani's wedding seven years ago?"

Althea shook her head. "I wasn't there, remember? I had joined the Peace Corps that summer, and I couldn't make it back from Africa in time to attend the wedding."

"That's right," Eddie said, nodding slowly. "And after that you transferred to Stanford to finish your degree and attend med school. So I guess you and Damien wouldn't have had too many other opportunities to meet."

Althea nodded, staring at Damien. "But I should have known who you were the minute I saw you. You look so much like your big brother."

Damien's mouth curved in a slow, crooked grin that made her pulse leap. "I'm better looking," he drawled.

Althea laughed. "I'm going to call Garrison and tell him you said that!"

"Go ahead." Damien winked. "He already knows it's true."

"Hmm. Well, I think Imani might have something to say about that. How *are* they doing anyway? I'm ashamed to admit I haven't spoken to them in over a year."

"They're doing well, and so are the kids. Little G and Soraya are five and three. Imani still loves teaching at the University of Maryland, and you probably already heard that Garrison is the assistant director in charge at the Washington field office."

"I did hear. I called to congratulate him when it was

announced. That was a wonderful promotion, and well deserved. *Both* of your promotions," Althea said, beaming proudly at Eddie. He smiled in return.

"Now that Imani knows you're back," Damien said, "I'm sure she'll be calling to invite you over for dinner."

"I'd like that very much." Althea smiled ruefully. "After everything they did for me, I should be inviting *them* over for dinner."

"There will be plenty of opportunities for that," Eddie said. "If I have anything to say about it, you, *signorina*, will be in Baltimore for a very long time. Now, was there something you wanted to talk to me about? You looked like you had a lot on your mind when you walked into the office earlier."

Besides wanting to jump Damien Wade's bones? "Actually, there *is* something I wanted to discuss with you."

"Sure," Eddie agreed, gesturing her into one of the visitor chairs across from his desk.

As Althea sat down, Damien started from the room, saying, "I have phone calls to return."

Althea watched him go, admiring his lithe, powerful strides. At the door he paused and looked back, his dark eyes capturing hers. "I'll be seeing you around."

Althea swallowed. "Looks that way."

Moments after he left the office, her body still tingled with awareness. Her overwhelming attraction to Damien Wade was the absolute last thing she needed or wanted, especially now, when she was trying to reclaim her life and establish herself at a new field office. She cursed the stroke of fate that had allowed her to single *him* out and take *him* home for the first and only one-night stand she'd ever had.

"Althea?"

Too late, Althea realized she'd been staring at the door in the wake of Damien's departure. Turning around quickly, she found Eddie watching her with an amused, speculative gleam in his eyes. A slow flush crawled up her neck.

"Sorry." She hesitated, biting her bottom lip. "Has he . . . How long has Damien been with the Bureau?"

"Almost seven years. He joined against Garrison's wishes, and has since proven to be one hell of an agent, one of the best I've ever worked with." His lips curved. "It's in their blood. Their father was a cop, and from what I hear, a damn good one."

Althea nodded. She seemed to remember Garrison once mentioning that his father had been a police officer. Funny how she remembered *that*, yet somehow she'd forgotten him telling her that his younger brother was an FBI agent.

Giving herself a mental shake, Althea turned her attention to the matter that had brought her to her boss's office in the first place. "I heard about the Thorndike kidnapping on the radio this morning," she began.

Eddie nodded, his expression grim. "Hell of a thing."

"Yes, it is." Althea hesitated, then sat forward in her chair. "I'd like to work with Baltimore PD on this case."

"No." His refusal was swift, unequivocal. As if he'd already anticipated the request.

Althea frowned. "Why not?"

"Because I've already assigned an agent to work with the BPD."

Her heart sank. She'd gotten there too late. "Who did you assign?"

"It doesn't matter," Eddie said firmly. "The point is, it won't be you. Look, Althea, you just arrived here. I know your squad supervisor has plenty of other cases you can sink your teeth into."

"I want to sink my teeth into *this* one."

Eddie shook his head, his thick black hair gleaming

under the recessed lighting. "No can do. I've already got someone on it, and you know how territorial the local boys get when we send too many of our own. They think we're trying to take over."

Althea couldn't argue with that, so she tried a different tack. "Just let me tag along. I've never worked one of these cases before. I know I could learn a lot from—"

"Sorry, kiddo. It's not gonna happen."

And suddenly she understood why.

Her eyes narrowed on his face. "You're trying to protect me. You think that my involvement in the kidnapping case will bring back too many bad memories."

He just looked at her, neither confirming nor denying her accusation.

Althea took a long, deep breath and said in a carefully measured voice, "With all due respect, sir, I didn't join the FBI to be coddled or handled with kid gloves. I joined the FBI to catch criminals, to make a difference."

"I know that," Eddie said just as evenly, leaning back in his chair. On the bookcase behind him were photos of his gorgeous wife Annabella and their two small children. "I've always supported your decision to join the Bureau, Althea, and I have no intention of preventing you from doing your job—especially since I've heard nothing but great things about you and your work ethic. But the Thorndike case is being handled by another agent, and you're just gonna have to accept that."

Althea stared at him, struck by a new realization. "Oh my God. You're worried that this might be a copycat. You're worried that this case might have something to do with what happened to me eight years ago."

A muscle clenched in his jaw. "I didn't say that."

"You didn't have to. You're thinking it."

Eddie hesitated. "The thought crossed my mind, yes," he reluctantly admitted. "But that doesn't mean anything.

The reality is that hundreds of kids are abducted every year. We have no concrete reason to assume that Claire Thorndike's abduction has anything to do with what happened to you."

"Even though the timing is suspicious," Althea said quietly. "Yesterday—Sunday—would have been exactly eight years to the day I was kidnapped."

When Eddie said nothing, she asked, "Do the police know when Claire was taken from her house?"

"They believe it was sometime on Friday evening. When Spencer Thorndike and his wife returned home from their trip yesterday, Claire's alarm clock was going off. She'd set it for six A.M. on Saturday because she had to attend a program at Johns Hopkins at eight o'clock."

"What kind of program?"

A long pause. "It was an informational session. For high-school seniors interested in a premed summer internship."

Althea felt the air escape from her lungs, soft and shaky. A whisper of foreboding snaked down her spine.

She had been a premed major in college.

Watching her carefully, Eddie said, "It could be purely coincidental."

"If you really believed that," Althea said softly, "you wouldn't be trying your damnedest to keep me off the case."

He held her gaze for a moment, then glanced away with a muffled curse. "There was a small piece in one of the local newspapers about a week ago. I don't know how it got leaked that you were being reassigned to Baltimore, but it did. That means any crackpot out there who read the article could be behind this thing. If I let anything happen to you, your uncle will nail my ass to the wall. I've never been one to back down from a fight, but a powerful U.S. senator who may be president one of these days isn't someone I care to have as an enemy."

"So you're going to let my *uncle* dictate the type of investigations I handle?" Althea demanded in outraged disbelief.

Eddie scowled. "That's not what I said."

"But that's what you're implying!" she shot back. "If my uncle thinks a case might be too dangerous for me, then it's off-limits. Is that how it's going to work around here?"

"Damn it, Pritchard! If there's some psycho out there reenacting your abduction, I don't want to play right into his hands by putting you on this case. I don't want to use you as bait for whatever sick game he might be playing!"

Althea met his gaze unflinchingly. "If Claire Thorndike's disappearance has anything to do with my abduction," she said levelly, "we both know the perp is going to involve me whether I'm investigating the case or not. Rather than sitting around on my hands waiting for him to make a move, I'd rather be doing whatever I can to help catch the son of a bitch."

Eddie's mouth thinned to a grim line. Averting his gaze, he reached for a pen and began tapping it furiously against a stack of files on his desk, torn between his desire to protect her and his sworn obligation to treat her the same as any other agent.

Althea waited, her breath shallow in her lungs.

The noise of ringing phones, the buzz of conversation interspersed with occasional laughter, and clicking keyboards could be heard from the maze of cubicles and desks outside the office.

After what seemed an eternity, Eddie looked at Althea. "Just as your uncle did when you were kidnapped, Spencer Thorndike has already gone straight to the top of the food chain to request the Bureau's assistance in locating his daughter. Director Grayson himself called me first thing this morning. He wanted to emphasize the importance of working cooperatively with the local police department, but he also wanted us to put in some extra face time with Thorndike. Let him know that we're as committed to finding Claire as we were to finding you eight years ago."

Althea nodded her understanding. Spencer Thorndike was a wealthy, powerful man who would think nothing of crying foul if his daughter's abduction did not warrant the same level of urgency that Althea's had. He'd have no qualms about going to the media with claims that Senator Louis Pritchard had a pattern of using his political connections to obtain special favors from the FBI. While the Bureau—and her uncle, for that matter—had survived worse accusations, the director liked to avoid the appearance of impropriety whenever possible.

"I'm sending Damien to interview the Thorndikes after the press conference this afternoon," Eddie said decisively. "You can accompany him."

Althea was so relieved by his decision that it took a delayed moment for the rest of his words to register. "Damien? You've assigned Damien Wade to be the case agent?"

"Yes. Do you have a problem with that?"

"N-No. Not at all." *Liar.*

"Good. Damien can bring you up to speed on everything you need to know." Eddie pinned her with a stern look. "I expect you to *support* Damien in this investigation, not try to take over. I expect you to give him your full cooperation and defer to his judgment as the senior agent on this case. If I hear that you're being a troublemaker or taking unnecessary risks, I'm yanking you. Are we clear on that?"

"Absolutely, sir. Thank you for giving me this opportunity."

When the phone on his desk rang, Althea got up and broke for the door before he could change his mind.

"Althea?"

She turned in the doorway. "Yes, sir?"

Eddie's expression was somber. "Don't make me regret my decision."

The unspoken words hung in the air between them, a silent plea from one friend to another: *Don't get yourself killed.*

"I won't," Althea said quietly.

Eddie held her gaze for another moment, then reached for the phone, dismissing her.

Althea left the office, her mind already on finding Claire Thorndike and bringing her home safely.

No matter what it takes, she silently vowed.

Chapter 7

When Althea Pritchard was kidnapped eight years ago, the story captured national headlines and fueled a media feeding frenzy. Damien, who was a senior in college at the time, had been too wrapped up in his own life and his own problems to follow the abduction case as religiously as others had. After taking an unplanned three-year hiatus from college to work full-time and take care of Angelique and India, he'd gone back to school. He knew that getting a degree was the best way for him to maximize his earning potential, which was absolutely critical if he wanted to continue supporting his family. The challenge of juggling a full course load, a part-time job, an internship, and the demands of raising an active toddler whose mother could seldom be found proved to be more difficult than anything Damien had ever experienced in his life. On most days he hadn't known whether he was coming or going.

So when a girl named Althea Pritchard went missing, he could do little more than pray for her safe return and hold his own daughter close to his heart before tucking her into bed every night.

Never in a million years could he have imagined the

twist of fate that would not only bring Althea Pritchard into his life but pair them together on a kidnapping case that bore many similarities to her own abduction.

One too many similarities, as far as he was concerned.

That morning as he drove to Spencer Thorndike's northwestern Baltimore home, Damien couldn't decide what bothered him more: Althea's involvement in a case that might prove to be too much for her to handle or the fact that he'd been forced to work alongside her, a woman who was only supposed to be a one-night stand.

Judging by the tension radiating from Althea, who sat ramrod straight and silent beside him in the black SUV, she wasn't terribly thrilled about the situation either.

As he weaved in and out of downtown traffic with practiced ease, he stole surreptitious glances at her. In a navy blue designer pantsuit with her black hair swept back into an elegant bun, she looked cool, composed, and professional. Too cool. Too composed. Too professional. Looking at her, Damien found it hard to reconcile the aloof, buttoned-down stranger she'd morphed into with the seductive femme fatale who'd approached him at the nightclub, then invited him back to her apartment for a night of intense, no-holds-barred sex. Try as he might, he couldn't stop thinking about *that* woman. Couldn't stop fantasizing about her, dreaming about her. Wanting her. He was half tempted to turn to Althea and demand to know what she'd done with the woman he met on Friday night.

"The light is green."

Damien didn't realize he had been staring at her until she spoke, breaking into his thoughts. He tore his gaze from her and pulled off just as the car behind him honked. Damien scowled into the rearview mirror as if the other driver could see him.

Althea made a small coughing noise behind her

hand, and when Damien glanced at her, he realized she was trying very hard not to laugh.

He felt his own lips twitching. "What's so funny?"

She shook her head, those sultry dark eyes glittering with mirth. "Has anyone ever told you that you drive like you're the only one on the road?" Even as the question left her mouth, Damien suddenly swerved around a vehicle that was testing his patience by moving too slow.

He threw Althea a sheepish grin. "Sorry."

She gave her head another shake. "I hope the Bureau took out extra auto insurance on you," she said dryly.

Damien chuckled. "What can I say? I grew up in the city—I learned how to drive on these crazy streets." He shot her a teasing sideways glance. "Not that I would expect a suburban princess to know anything about that."

Althea choked out a laugh. "Hey! Who're you calling a suburban princess?"

Damien grinned. "There are only two of us in this vehicle, and I sure as hell wasn't talking about myself. Besides," he drawled, "I don't recall hearing any complaints about my driving skills when we were rushing to get to your apartment on Friday night."

To his delight, Althea actually blushed. "That was a low blow," she grumbled, averting her gaze to the window.

"Sorry. I saw an opportunity and I took it."

"And what opportunity would that be?"

"The opportunity to bring up the elephant in the room we've both been avoiding."

He felt, rather than saw, Althea stiffen. She did not turn from the window.

Undeterred, he continued, "I think it goes without saying that neither of us expected to see each other again after Friday night. I know you were as shocked as I was when we ran into each other this morning."

"That's putting it mildly," Althea muttered darkly. "I thought I was hallucinating."

Damien suppressed a smile. When he'd opened his boss's door that morning and saw Althea standing there, he'd known by his body's primal reaction to her that *he* wasn't hallucinating.

"We never actually got around to talking about our jobs that night," he said.

"Or our last names," she added.

"Yeah. Right." He cleared his throat. "Anyway, the point is that I understand how awkward this must be for you, being new to the Baltimore field office. I want you to know that what happened between us will stay between us. I have no intention of telling Balducci, or anyone else, that you and I slept together. You have my word."

After a prolonged moment, Althea turned her head and looked at him. "Thank you," she said quietly. "I appreciate that."

He nodded.

Suddenly she frowned. "Oh no. I just thought about something. What about your friends—the ones who were at the club that night? I don't suppose there's any chance they don't work for the Bureau?"

Damien grimaced. "There were only two who didn't," he admitted.

Althea groaned, covering her face with her hands. "I'm ruined."

"No, you're not."

"Yes, I am. Sooner or later I'm going to run into those guys, and they're going to take one look at me and recognize me as the ho you went home with that night."

Damien scowled. "First of all, if anyone calls you a 'ho,' I'm kicking their ass up and down the damn street. Second of all, the fellas aren't gonna gossip about you, 'cause they'd be putting my business out there as well, and they know I don't play that. The only one who's on our squad is Marshall Blake, and he's on vacation this week. As soon as he gets back I'll give him a call, make sure he knows what's what." His tone gentled. "Don't worry. What happened between us is nobody's business but ours, and I'm going to make sure it stays that way."

Althea gave him a small, grateful smile. "Thank you." She hesitated, biting her lush bottom lip, looking like she wanted to say more. Finally she did. "I don't make a habit of, ah, picking up strangers at nightclubs, or anywhere else for that matter. You were the first man I've ever been so, ah, reckless with."

Damien sent her a long look. "I had an incredible time with you."

She held his gaze. "It was absolutely amazing."

His body stirred. The blood heated in his veins.

"That said," Althea murmured, "it can never happen again."

"I know." His mind knew, but his body was an entirely different matter. "I have a rule against mixing business with pleasure."

She looked relieved. "So do I."

Damien inclined his head. "Then we're going to get along just fine, Special Agent Pritchard."

Spencer Thorndike's residence was a sprawling sixty-acre estate just on the outskirts of Mount Washington, an exclusive white enclave known for its quaint New England setting, stately mansions, manicured parks, and top-performing schools. The Thorndike mansion was a stone and glass Tudor perched high on a hill and guarded by a tall iron fence. The property boasted a natural lake, well-tended gardens, equestrian facilities, and miles of scenic riding trails.

It was only fitting that the man who'd made his fortune in real estate development would live in such grandeur, Althea thought.

As they approached the estate, she noted several news vans parked on either side of the private road. The occupants of the vans eyeballed her and Damien as they passed by in their federal-issue SUV.

"The feeding frenzy has begun," Althea murmured, realizing it must have been the same way when she was abducted eight years ago.

When Damien glanced at her, she knew he was thinking the same thing.

They continued up the long road before he braked to a hard stop beside the intercom panel outside the gate. Ignoring the aggrieved look Althea gave him, he buzzed down the window just as a voice crackled from the intercom speaker. "Yes?"

"Special Agent Damien Wade, FBI."

The gate rolled silently open, then closed behind them. The reporters made no attempt to rush in after them, perhaps realizing that they wouldn't get very far now that the feds had arrived. Or perhaps because their desire to respect the family's privacy actually outweighed their desire to make deadline. Althea suspected the former.

A pair of gleaming luxury vehicles—a Rolls Royce and a Lamborghini—sat in the circular driveway in front of the house, along with three police cruisers. Claire Thorndike's car had been confiscated by the crime scene unit to be vacuumed and analyzed for possible trace evidence left by her abductor.

Damien pulled up behind the last of the squad cars and killed the engine.

Althea looked at him. "Is this the part where you tell me to let you do all the talking?"

Damien met the subtle challenge in her gaze. "Is that how they treated you in Seattle?"

"Well, no, but Balducci said—"

"If you get out of line, believe me, I know how to reel you back in. I don't play power games, Althea, unless it's absolutely necessary."

Althea flashed him a grateful smile.

Damien climbed out of the SUV and came around to open the passenger door for her, and together they started up the walk toward the imposing house. While they waited to be let in, they studied the front door in silence. No sign of forced entry. What about the back door? The windows?

A butler dressed in black finally answered the door and ushered them inside a cavernous entry hall, where a massive wrought-iron chandelier hung from the second-story ceiling. A uniformed police officer sat beside a glossy mahogany table reading *The Baltimore Sun* and drinking a cup of coffee. He acknowledged Althea and Damien with a brief nod. They responded in kind.

"Mr. and Mrs. Thorndike are still with the police," the gaunt, unsmiling butler informed them in hushed tones. "They requested that you wait in the parlor until they conclude their meeting, which should be shortly. This way, please."

Althea and Damien followed, their footsteps clicking against inlaid marble floors. They were led into a luxurious parlor filled with English antiques and silk-upholstered furnishings. A sedate fire crackled in the granite fireplace, although it was an unseasonably warm seventy degrees outside. A silver serving set had been placed on a Hepplewhite sideboard that had been polished to a hard shine. On nearly every surface throughout the room, Althea could see black fingerprint powder left by the crime scene unit. She knew it must have taken several hours, and three times the number of crime scene technicians, to comb through the sprawling mansion in search of physical evidence. Talk about trying to find a needle in a haystack.

She and Damien were seated on a chintz sofa near the hearth. "Would either of you care for tea or coffee?" the butler offered.

"No, thanks," Damien declined.

Althea accepted a cup of tea with two sugars.

As soon as the butler departed from the room, Damien rose from the sofa and wandered over to a built-in bookcase that held an assortment of framed family photographs. He reached for an eight-by-ten portrait of a smiling Claire Thorndike astride one of her father's prize horses, her green eyes sparkling with laughter, her long auburn hair cascading to her shoulders. The beautiful young socialite at her leisure. Beside that was another photo of her in a pink off-the-shoulder dress at her junior prom last spring. She looked like an all-American teenager, which was why this photo had been chosen over the other to be distributed to all media outlets. The rationale was that the viewing public could sympathize more with the missing girl's plight if they didn't have to be reminded of her enormous wealth.

As Damien studied more photographs, Althea sipped her tea and glanced around the room at oil portraits framed in gold leaf that depicted scenes of vintage American life: a sleek greyhound taking first prize at a dog show, dapper-dressed gentlemen cheering at the Kentucky Derby, Southern belles enjoying a leisurely afternoon of tea and beignets.

Damien turned at that moment, holding up a photo of Spencer Thorndike and a woman less than half his age. Suzette Thorndike, his second wife.

"Oh my God," Althea whispered, so as not to be overheard. "She could be Claire's big sister!"

Damien nodded, his mouth quirking at the corners. He returned the photo to the shelf and rejoined her on the sofa just as they heard approaching footsteps.

A moment later Spencer and Suzette Thorndike entered the room, linked arm in arm. In his late fifties, the real estate mogul was of medium height with a trim physique and a neat, expensive haircut and dye job that made him look years younger. Even in dark jeans and a sweater, he exuded an air of wealth and importance.

His wife was a tall, strikingly beautiful redhead in a silk blouse, cashmere slacks, and Prada pumps—the epitome of style and sophistication. The resemblance between her and Claire Thorndike was so strong they could pass as sisters. Althea wondered how Claire felt about her father marrying a woman who not only looked like her but wasn't even old enough to be her mother. And then Althea wondered how Suzette Thorndike felt about her teenage stepdaughter.

Althea and Damien rose from the sofa to introduce themselves to their hosts. Althea didn't miss the way Spencer Thorndike's eyes widened slightly when he heard her name. She also noted that Suzette's green eyes were red rimmed and puffy, as if she'd been crying for several hours.

"Thank you for coming," Spencer greeted Althea and Damien, shaking their hands in turn. "I spoke to Director Grayson this morning, and he assured me that finding my daughter would be the Bureau's top priority."

Althea doubted that the FBI director would have made such an unrealistic promise, but she refrained from saying so.

Once they were all seated, Damien removed a mini-cassette recorder from his breast pocket and placed it on the center table. He clicked it on after the Thorndikes agreed to be taped.

"Agent Pritchard and I are here to help any way we can to bring back your daughter," Damien began, "but we're going to need your full cooperation and patience. I know you've both already given your statements to the police, so I apologize in advance if any of our questions seem redundant. We're going to cover a lot of the same ground, but I always believe in erring on the side of thoroughness."

Spencer and Suzette nodded somberly. "We understand," Spencer said. "We just want Claire back home, safe and sound. We want this nightmare to be over."

Suzette gave his hand a comforting squeeze, and they shared a brief, tremulous smile.

"Before I begin the interview," Damien said, "I have to ask both of you what may be an unusual question since Claire's car was here, but considering that her purse, cell phone, and bookbag are gone, do you have any reason to believe she might have run away from home?"

The couple exchanged startled glances. "Absolutely not," Spencer answered unequivocally. "Claire would never do anything that reckless and irresponsible. That's not even a remote possibility."

Suzette nodded vigorously in agreement.

"Even if she was angry?" Damien pressed. "Even if she felt she'd been unjustly punished for something, she wouldn't run off to a friend's house to give herself time to cool down?"

"No," Spencer clipped. "Claire may be headstrong and a little spoiled, but she's not impulsive. And she's certainly not mean-spirited enough to hide out at a friend's house when she knows we're over here worried sick about her!"

Damien nodded. "I had to ask. It's my job to ask the tough questions."

Suzette glanced hesitantly at her husband. "If Claire ever did want to get away from home," she said slowly, "she wouldn't go to a friend's house. She would go to her mother's apartment in Washington, D.C." She paused for a moment. "Like she did before."

"You mean Claire has run away to her mother's apartment before?" Althea asked, speaking for the first time.

Spencer scowled. "That was two years ago. And she wasn't running away from home. She was going through a difficult phase where she only wanted to be with her mother, whose job as an environmental lobbyist seemed very 'exciting' and 'purposeful' to Claire. Her enchantment didn't last very long, however. After spending a week at her mother's tiny, cluttered apartment and having no servants to wait on her hand and foot, Claire was more than ready to come back home."

Althea nodded. "I understand that your wife, Madison—"

"*Ex*-wife," Suzette corrected tightly.

"My apologies," Althea smoothly amended, noting the cold, territorial gleam that had filled the other woman's eyes. "I understand that your ex-wife, Madison, is out of the country on business, Mr. Thorndike. Attending an environmental summit in Edinburgh, Scotland."

"That's right. She's been contacted and is supposed to be flying home tomorrow. The police have already been to her apartment—Claire isn't there. Not that I expected her to be," he added, giving his wife a look that conveyed his displeasure with her for raising the possibility in the first place.

Interesting, Althea thought. When Damien glanced briefly at her, she knew he'd caught the look as well.

"When was the last time the two of you saw Claire?" he asked the couple.

"Thursday morning," Spencer replied. "She dropped us off at the airport before going to school. As you know, we spent the weekend at a ski resort in Colorado."

Damien nodded. "I understand this was an annual trip for you. So it wasn't the first time you've left Claire home by herself."

"No, it wasn't. But she's hardly home by herself," Spencer said almost defensively. "There are four members of my household staff who are always here—the housekeeper, the butler, the cook, and the chauffeur."

"But they weren't here on Friday night," Damien noted.

"No." Spencer clenched his jaw, his expression murderous. "Claire gave them the weekend off."

"Do you know why? Did she tell you she was planning to do that?"

Spencer shook his head. "According to what the staff told me, Claire was thinking about spending the weekend at a friend's house—her best friend Heather Warner—so she told the staff their services wouldn't be needed. Needless to say, I gave every last one of them a piece of my mind."

Althea could only imagine. "We'd like to talk to the staff, as well as to Miss Warner."

"That's fine. They've all been interviewed and cleared by the police already, but if you think you might learn new information, be my guest." He hesitated, then added almost reluctantly, "Heather claims she had no plans with Claire. She told us she didn't know that Claire was planning to spend the weekend at her house. The last time she saw or spoke to her was after school on Friday, and Claire didn't mention anything about wanting to hang out."

"Then why would Claire make up that story?" Althea asked, although she had already guessed the answer.

Spencer's dark eyes hardened with anger. He averted his gaze, his jaw locking tightly.

Suzette answered, "We think she was planning to invite someone over here. A boy from school, perhaps."

"Why do you think that?" Damien asked evenly.

Suzette glanced at her husband, who remained sullen and silent. "Whenever we go out of town," she explained, "Spencer makes a point of taking inventory of his wine collection. He can account for every last bottle in the wine cellar. When we arrived home on Sunday afternoon, a bottle of Bordeaux was missing."

"Not just any bottle," Spencer growled. "It was the year 1985—*the* standout vintage of the decade."

Seeing the silent look that passed between Althea and Damien, Suzette gave a little laugh that sounded forced. "Listen to yourself," she gently chided her husband. "You're going to have Agents Wade and Pritchard thinking you're more concerned about your missing Bordeaux than your missing daughter."

Spencer looked shamefaced. "That's ridiculous. Nothing could be further from the truth. I didn't even think about the damn wine until the police arrived and asked me if anything was out of place. Once we spoke to Heather and realized what Claire must have been planning that evening, *that's* when it occurred to me to check the wine cellar. After I discovered the missing bottle of wine, it was easier to put two and two together."

Damien nodded. "Neither of you spoke to Claire at all over the weekend?"

"No." Spencer looked guilt-ridden. "Claire doesn't like to hear from us when we go on trips. If we call, she thinks we're trying to check up on her, like we don't trust her. So we reached an agreement. Unless there's an emergency, or unless we're going to be out of town for a week or more, we don't call her, and she doesn't have to call to check in with us."

Althea couldn't remember a time her aunt and uncle had ever been so permissive with her. Even now that she was an adult and led a busy life, they worried if they didn't hear from her after two days.

If Claire Thorndike survived this ordeal, it would be a very long time before her father let her out of his sight again.

"So when you arrived home on Sunday afternoon," Damien probed, "you didn't notice anything else out of place or missing? Nothing else had been taken—jewelry, heirlooms, clothing, electronics? Nothing had been disturbed?"

"No. Nothing."

"There were no signs of a struggle? Nothing to indicate exactly what Claire may have had planned for the night?"

Spencer said bitterly, "If you're asking whether there was a romantic table set for two, soft music playing on the stereo, or wilted rose petals floating on water in her bathtub, the answer is no, Agent Wade. We did not return home to a scene of seduction. We returned home to a *crime scene.* Claire's alarm clock was blaring, and her bed had not been slept in. Someone waltzed into this house and snatched my little girl, and no one is doing a damn thing—" He broke off, his voice cracking with emotion.

Blinking back tears, Suzette reached over and took his hand. He turned to her, and they leaned their foreheads against each other's, silent and mournful.

Damien waited an appropriate length of time before speaking again, his voice quiet and compassionate. "I can't pretend to know how difficult this must be for you, Mr. and Mrs. Thorndike. I have an eleven-year-old daughter, and I couldn't even imagine what I would do if anything happened to her. Believe me when I tell you that Agent Pritchard and I, along with the police, will do everything in our power to help bring your daughter home safely."

They turned to him, eyes bright with unshed tears, soft, quivery smiles on their faces. "Thank you," Spencer whispered.

Suzette said wonderingly, "You don't look old enough to have an eleven-year-old daughter, Agent Wade."

Damien's mouth curved in a lazy grin. "Funny, that's what *she* always tells me. Mostly when she's trying to sweet-talk her way out of trouble."

Spencer and Suzette laughed.

Althea watched the exchange, admiring the ease with which Damien had comforted the suffering couple, enabling them to forget, even for a moment, that their daughter was missing.

She waited a full minute before returning to the matter at hand. "Mr. Thorndike, we understand from the police report that your security system was disabled on Friday. Which means everything was turned off—the surveillance camera on the electronic gate, the motion sensors on the property, the security alarm inside the house. Everything."

Spencer nodded grimly.

"According to the security company," Althea continued, "whoever disabled the security system used a passcode known only to you, Mrs. Thorndike, Claire, and the household staff, all of whom said everything was on when they left the house at five P.M. The company rep who spoke to the police said the system was shut off at 5:18 on Friday afternoon." Althea paused. "Do you think Claire might have turned off the security system to make it easier for her guest to gain access to the property without your knowledge? I imagine she wouldn't have wanted him—whoever he was—showing up on the surveillance camera when he arrived."

Spencer hesitated, then nodded grudgingly. "That sounds plausible. Claire hated our security system. She complained about it all the time, said it made her feel like she was a prisoner. She used to claim that living out in the middle of nowhere made her feel isolated enough; she didn't see the need for all the extra layers of security." His mouth twisted bitterly. "The very thing she hated could have saved her life and kept a monster out of our home."

No one said anything for a moment, reflecting on the tragic irony of his words.

"The perpetrator would have had to know that the security system was off," Damien pointed out quietly. "He wouldn't have taken a chance on coming all the way out here, to a well-guarded property, unless he knew the coast was clear."

"Which is why the police believe she was abducted by whomever she was meeting that night," Suzette said shakily.

"It's highly possible," Damien agreed. "Or it could have been someone else who was familiar with the family's routine, someone who may have known that Claire would be home alone for the weekend and that she would open the door without question if she recognized them. I'd like to get a list of the people who have had access to your property in the last sixty days. Repairmen, delivery people, the cable guy, door-to-door solicitors. I'd also like a complete list of your employees and contractors."

Spencer paled. "You think whoever took Claire may have worked for me?"

"We have to consider the possibility, Mr. Thorndike. The majority of children who are abducted either know the perpetrator or are familiar with the individual in some way. Given how wealthy you are, you know we have to consider ransom as a possible motive."

Spencer nodded unhappily. "The police have already put a tap and tracer on the house line, and they've assigned a team to monitor the phone in case the kidnapper calls to make a ransom demand. The damn thing has been ringing off the hook all morning. Family, friends, reporters, but no one with any leads or information about Claire." His wistful gaze drifted toward the phone on the sideboard table. Its silence seemed to mock him.

"Can you think of anyone who might have wanted to get back at you by harming your daughter?" Damien asked. "A disgruntled former employee? A contractor who didn't get one of your construction jobs? An angry competitor?"

Spencer blew out a harsh, frustrated breath, scrubbing a hand over his face. "Hell, that could be just about anyone. I've fired lazy workers, awarded jobs that disappointed the losing bidders, pissed off people in the county zoning and planning offices, butted heads with politicians and community activists over my selection of a construction site. I've been in business for over twenty years, Agent Wade. My guess is you don't have to look very far to find enemies I've made on my way to the top."

"I don't doubt that," Damien murmured.

"That said, I honestly can't think of anyone who would be vindictive enough, *deranged* enough, to kidnap my daughter to get even with me."

"It happens, unfortunately. It's an angle we have to explore."

Althea nodded in agreement. "But getting back to the individual Claire may have invited over to the house that night. Do either of you have any idea who that might have been?"

Spencer and Suzette glanced at each other before

shaking their heads. "She had a boyfriend at school," Spencer said, frowning, "but she broke up with him three months ago."

"Did she tell you why?" Althea asked.

His face darkened, his lips compressing. "Claire doesn't tell me anything anymore. But one day I overheard her on her cell phone talking to Heather about it. Apparently Claire found out that Josh—her boyfriend—was cheating on her with another girl at school. She was very upset about it. Moped around here for weeks. I hated seeing her like that. I almost went up to the school to have it out with that dumb jock, but Suzette begged me not to. She said Claire would be humiliated and would never forgive me for interfering. She was right, so I stayed the hell out of it."

Fragments of her recent conversation with her uncle floated through Althea's mind. *Even though I could see how hurt you were, I stayed out of it because you asked me to. But I've never forgotten what that boy did to you, the way he betrayed your trust and deserted you. . . .*

She shoved the thoughts aside. "Is it possible that Claire and Josh got back together? And maybe she didn't want you to find out because she knew you would be mad?"

Spencer frowned, shaking his head. "Not a chance. Claire isn't a very forgiving person. Once you cross her, she never forgives, and she never forgets."

"And she's such a beautiful girl," Suzette added. "She could have her pick of any boy she wants. Taking Josh back, after the way he'd humiliated and betrayed her, would have made her look desperate to her friends and classmates."

"And desperation has never been a Thorndike trait," Spencer avowed. "Anyway, the police already questioned Josh. He says he and Claire haven't spoken to each other in three months, ever since they broke up. And he has an alibi for Friday night. He was on a date—with the same girl he and Claire broke up over. They went to the movies, then to her house afterward. He still had the ticket stub and his credit card receipt, and the girl verified his story. She said they were together all night. Apparently her mother sees nothing wrong with allowing her teenage daughter's boyfriends to sleep over," Spencer added derisively.

Damien nodded slowly. "What was Claire like on Thursday morning when she dropped you off at the airport?" he asked. "How did she seem?"

"She was in a great mood that morning. Which was a bit unusual."

"What do you mean?"

"Whenever Suzette and I go on a trip, Claire sulks for a few days before we leave. Not because she wants us to take her or anything. I just think she feels left out sometimes. She was only twelve years old when her mother and I split up. The divorce was"—he pursed his lips, searching for an appropriate word—"acrimonious. Very bitter. Claire felt caught in the middle, like she had to choose sides. I regret that her mother and I handled things the way we did, but at the time it seemed unavoidable. Anyway, it took Claire some time to adjust after I remarried." Spencer smiled ruefully at his wife. "I think it's fair to say you and Claire had a bit of a rocky start."

Suzette laughed dryly. "Just a bit."

"Their relationship is much better now," Spencer assured Althea and Damien. "The point I was making is that Claire still gets a little moody from time to time as a result of the divorce. But she was very upbeat on Thursday morning."

Suzette said, "We were both a little surprised when she offered to drive us to the airport. Our chauffeur always drops us off and picks us up from the airport whenever we travel. But Claire insisted on doing the honors that morning. We joked that she was in a hurry to get rid of us."

Spencer frowned darkly. "In light of what we now know, it looks like we weren't too far off the mark."

Althea asked, "She didn't mention spending the weekend at Heather Warner's house?"

Spencer shook his head. "All she talked about was attending the information session at Johns Hopkins on Saturday morning. She was really looking forward to it."

"For the premed summer internship, right?"

He nodded. "Claire has always wanted to study medicine. She loves horses, and when she was a little girl, she talked about becoming a veterinarian and healing sick animals. But as she grew older, she decided it was more important to her to heal people." A soft, poignant smile touched his mouth. "People who don't know Claire often make the mistake of assuming she's nothing but a spoiled rich girl who cares only about shopping and spending her father's money. They're always surprised to learn that she's a straight-A student enrolled in honors classes, she's president of the student government as well as the French Club, and she made school history this year by becoming the first female captain of the debate team."

Althea smiled gently. "She sounds like an extraordinary young woman. You must be very proud of her."

"We are. We *both* are," Spencer said, taking his wife's hand. They smiled sadly into each other's eyes.

"Does Claire have a MyDomain page?" Althea asked.

"Yes, she does. The profile is set to private so that it can be viewed only by her friends and people who know her. That was my stipulation." He supplied the information that would enable them to access the Web page.

"The police have already taken her computer to check her e-mail messages, Internet activity, files on her hard drive."

Damien nodded briskly. "Good. That might provide some promising leads."

"They're checking her cell phone records and are working with the phone company to monitor any activity on that number. I pay an additional monthly fee for Claire's text messages to be stored on their server, should I ever need to access them. So the police will be able to go through those transcripts and share them with you. They brought their K-9 dogs and spent most of yesterday searching the grounds of the estate. They even went over the driveway carefully, checking for freshly leaked oil or an unfamiliar tire tread. Nothing." Spencer sighed. "They also went through the entire house and dusted every room for fingerprints, although they warned me that the chances of getting a positive hit were a million to one."

"I'm afraid that's true," Damien concurred. "Assuming Claire was taken from inside the house, I can almost guarantee the perpetrator wore gloves, possibly even shoe covers so he wouldn't leave behind trace evidence. And again, since there were no signs of a struggle anywhere in the house, it makes it that much more difficult to know for certain what actually happened that night." He paused. "Her purse, cell phone, and bookbag are gone. Do you know if any articles of clothing are missing?"

Spencer looked askance at his wife, who shook her head helplessly. "I've checked the closet three times," she said, "but nothing seems out of place. Honestly, Claire has so much clothes that trying to figure out what may or may not be missing is like searching for a needle in a haystack."

Spencer nodded in agreement. Turning back to Althea and Damien, he said, "The police have a theory that

Claire was taken from her bedroom as she was getting ready for her date on Friday night. Her makeup was still spread out on the vanity table, and one of her dresser drawers was partially open, as if she was in the middle of getting dressed when she was interrupted."

"Which drawer?" Althea asked.

Spencer looked uncomfortable.

"Her lingerie drawer," Suzette supplied. "Where she kept her nightgowns."

Althea nodded, mentally filing away the detail.

"The two of you are more than welcome to check out her room if you want," Spencer offered. "The police have it roped off to keep the household staff from going in there, but I know they wouldn't object to you guys taking a walk-through."

Before Althea could open her mouth to say yes, Damien said smoothly, "Thanks, but that won't be necessary. We'll wait for the lab results from the crime scene unit and go from there. In the meantime, if you could get me those lists I asked for, we can coordinate our efforts with the police and start doing some interviews."

Spencer nodded, rising with his guests. "I've heard the statistics. I know that the odds of finding a missing person alive diminish with each hour, each day they're gone. But I'm not giving up on Claire." He looked at Althea. "Do you know what gives me hope, Agent Pritchard? *You.* You were missing for over a month, and I know there were many who believed you would never make it back home. But you did. You were found, and you were returned safe and sound to your family." He swallowed hard, tears misting his eyes as he stared at her. "I've never been a religious man, Ms. Pritchard, but I believe that your very presence in our home this afternoon is a sign from God, a sign that Claire *will* be found alive and returned to us. Because if there's anything we all learned from your abduction and recovery, it's that miracles do happen."

"Why did that make you uncomfortable?" Damien asked Althea as they drove away from the Thorndike estate a few minutes later.

She didn't have to ask what he meant. "Why would you think it made me uncomfortable?" she countered.

"I'm good at reading people." His mouth curved wryly. "Occupational hazard."

Althea smiled a little. "All right. Maybe I *was* a bit uncomfortable by what Thorndike said. Someone kidnapped that man's daughter, and the hard, cold reality is that she may never be found. I don't want to be the reason he won't be able to face that reality."

Damien looked at her. "It sounds like you already believe Claire is dead."

"I don't," Althea said with quiet conviction. She turned her head to stare out the window and added softly under her breath, "In fact, I can almost guarantee that she isn't."

Because you know he's waiting, her conscience whispered. *Waiting for you.*

Chapter 8

Before returning to the office, Althea and Damien
stopped at a sports bar and grill near the Inner Harbor
to grab a quick lunch and compare notes.

Mulligan's, once a popular hangout for cops, was
neat but impossibly tiny inside. It was after three, so
thankfully the lunch crowd had long since dispersed.

Damien led Althea to a booth in a private corner of
the restaurant, and after they had ordered their meals,
he looked across the table at her. "What did you think
of Suzette Thorndike?"

Althea chuckled dryly. "You mean the trophy wife?"

Damien grinned. "How'd I know you were going to
say that?"

Althea arched a brow. "So you didn't think the same
thing?"

"Of course I did. But I knew you'd say it first. Women
are always harder on their own."

Althea frowned. "I wouldn't be hard on anyone who's
going through such a difficult time." She paused. "That
said, I'm not sure Suzette Thorndike is as distraught
over Claire's disappearance as she wanted us to believe."

"What makes you say that?" Damien murmured.

"A gut feeling. Thorndike even admitted that his wife and Claire had a rocky relationship."

"*Had.* As in past tense. He said things are better between them now."

"I don't buy it. In fact, I'd bet my next paycheck that Claire and Suzette still can't stand each other. Claire probably resents having a stepmother, especially one who's not that much older than she is. And Suzette probably resents having to share her husband with his bright, beautiful teenage daughter. I mean, think about it. They're both competing for the same thing."

"Spencer Thorndike's affection."

"Exactly. I watched Suzette's face when her husband was bragging about Claire's accomplishments. Her smile looked forced. It was like she was annoyed but trying very hard not to show it."

"So she and Claire are jealous of each other. What are you getting at?"

Althea shrugged, watching as the waiter approached with their food. "I don't know."

"Of course you do." Damien looked vaguely amused. "Why don't you just come right out and say it?"

Althea waited until their meals and drinks had been placed on the table and the server had moved on before she spoke again. "I'm just floating some theories here. What if Suzette had something to do with Claire's abduction? What if she hired someone to do it while she was away?"

Damien poured ketchup on his burger and shook salt onto his thick-cut French fries. "Go on. I'm listening."

"What if she decided she was tired of sharing her husband with Claire? Or what if she found out that Claire will eventually inherit Spencer's fortune? We both know that money is always a motive for murder."

Damien nodded. "That's true. But it's not as if Spencer

is on his deathbed or anything. He's only fifty-eight years old, and he appears to be in excellent shape. Barring an accident or some terminal illness, Suzette may have a long wait before she'd get her hands on his money. Unless you're suggesting that she plans to off *him* next," he added wryly.

"Crazier things have happened," Althea pointed out, picking up her grilled chicken sandwich.

"Can't argue with that."

Damien bit into his burger, and they ate for a few minutes in contemplative silence.

Despite the theory Althea had just proposed, she couldn't shake the sense of foreboding that had gripped her the moment she'd heard about the kidnapping. She couldn't dismiss the feeling that Claire Thorndike's disappearance was somehow connected to her own abduction. And she wasn't alone. Eddie Balducci had the same fears.

Which meant she wasn't crazy or paranoid.

The deep timbre of Damien's voice interrupted her thoughts. "What about Spencer Thorndike?"

Althea glanced up from her plate. "What about him?"

"Did his grief seem genuine to you?"

Althea nodded. "You?"

"It seemed genuine enough." Damien's expression turned sardonic. "But that doesn't mean anything. I've known of cold-blooded killers who wept uncontrollably when recounting the gruesome details of the crimes they'd committed."

Althea made a face. "Even if Spencer didn't have an alibi—being in Colorado at the time of his daughter's abduction—I wouldn't suspect him. The only thing I find somewhat unsettling about him is his taste in women. Do you think he consciously set out to marry a woman who's almost an exact replica of his teenage daughter?"

Damien's mouth twisted into a grim smile. "Are you suggesting that Spencer Thorndike secretly has incestuous feelings toward his daughter? What a warped little mind you have, Ms. Pritchard."

She gave him an ironic smile. "Occupational hazard. We're trained to think the worst of people."

He chuckled, taking a sip of his Coke. "Maybe he has a thing for redheads," he suggested. "Maybe Suzette looks like his ex-wife."

"Maybe. I guess we'll find out when we meet the former Mrs. Thorndike." Althea ate a forkful of potato salad, which she'd chosen over fries, and chewed thoughtfully. "I would have liked to check out Claire's room. Why did you turn down Thorndike's offer?"

"Because I wanted to demonstrate to our friends in the police department that we're not trying to take over their case. If we had stepped foot in Claire's bedroom, after the crime scene team already went through it, that's the message we would've been sending to BPD—that we don't think they're competent enough to handle the investigation." He paused. "I happen to think they are."

"So do I," Althea said, impatience edging her voice. "But I also believe we have more resources at our disposal, more experience to bring to the table."

"Maybe," Damien agreed, his tone mild. "But we both know how this works. Unless we have reason to believe there's been a violation of federal law, this is a routine kidnapping case, which means it stays under local jurisdiction. We're here to assist, not take over."

Althea said nothing. She knew he was right, but damn it, she hated the idea of taking a backseat role in this investigation. Too much was at stake, and now that Claire had been missing for three days, time was their enemy.

Sensing her frustration, Damien said, "When I first joined the Bureau, I promised myself I would never get into turf wars with the local police. My father was a cop, one of the best. Whenever I find myself thinking I'm smarter, more hardworking or better than someone else just because I'm a fed, I think of my father. And that always brings me back down to earth."

Althea scowled at him. "Point taken," she grumbled, suitably chastened.

"Believe me," Damien said, wiping the corner of his mouth with a napkin, "I'm as eager to dive into this case as you are. As soon as I drop you off at the office, I'm heading over to the police station to meet with Detective Mayhew, who's the primary on the investigation. He's got a twenty-four-hour head start on us, so I hope he's in a sharing mood so we don't have to waste precious time duplicating efforts."

Althea nodded. "I'm sure they've already checked out Claire's MyDomain page to see who she's been talking to and what she's been talking about. With any luck, they might already know the identity of the mystery guest she invited over to her house on Friday night."

"I'll find out. Whoever took Claire had a reason for sterilizing the scene, de-staging it like that."

Again Althea nodded. "I've been thinking about that, too. I've been picturing Claire getting all gussied up for her blind date, primping in front of the mirror, giddy with excitement. Her lingerie drawer was found open, so maybe she had put on a sexy negligee for her date. I can imagine her putting on some soft music, lighting some candles, building a cozy fire. Maybe he was bringing dinner, so she told him she would take care of the wine. She wanted to impress him, so she chose the Bordeaux. Maybe they ate first, and afterward when he tried to make a move on her, she got cold feet and refused him. Things got out of hand, and he became aggressive, violent. He killed her, then panicked when he realized his prints were all over the place. So he had to sterilize the scene. He clears the dinner table, takes the wine bottle with his prints on it, blows out the candles, removes the CD in the stereo, basically puts everything back the way it was before he arrived."

Damien nodded slowly, thoughtfully. "I can see it going down like that."

Althea tried not to be pleased by his words. "Talk to Mayhew. Sounds like he may have a different theory based on the appearance of her bedroom."

"I'll get his impressions. In the meantime, why don't you pull up some information on Suzette Thorndike, see if you come across anything interesting."

"Will do." Unable to resist any longer, Althea reached across the table, pilfered one of his fries, and stuffed it into her mouth.

Damien grinned at her. "Little thief."

Althea laughed. "Sorry. I've been wanting to do that since our meals arrived. Don't get me wrong. My potato salad is delicious, but those fries looked too yummy to resist."

"I told you they're good. You should have ordered them."

She shook her head. "I'm really trying to cut back on fried food. When I had lunch with my aunt and uncle over the weekend, I ordered crab cakes as a little home-coming treat to myself. Oh, man, they were *so* good—definitely worth every gram of saturated fat they contained. I figured that should do me for a while." Even as she spoke, she found herself eyeing Damien's plate, sorely tempted to snag another French fry.

He nudged the plate toward her, his dark eyes glinting with mischief. "Go on," he murmured coaxingly. "Indulge yourself a little more. You know you want to."

Althea laughed, even as she wondered how many

unsuspecting women Damien had tempted into sin with that deep, sexy voice of his. "You are so wrong, Damien Wade! See, I thought you had my back."

He grinned, flashing those dangerous dimples. "I do."

"No, you don't. If you *really* had my back, you would keep that plate away from me, or smack my hand if I tried to take another fry. But I see how you are. You . . . you *enabler*!" she said accusingly, making it sound like the dirtiest word in the English language.

Damien threw back his head and roared with laughter. The deep, rumbling sound was so appealing, so downright infectious, that Althea started laughing, too. A couple seated a few tables away glanced over at them curiously.

When the moment had passed, Althea smiled at Damien. "Maybe this won't be so bad after all."

"What?"

"Working with you. We seem to be getting along okay."

Damien shook his head slowly, holding her gaze. "Believe me, that was never my concern. I think we already demonstrated that we get along just fine, Althea."

She averted her eyes, heat stinging her cheeks at the reminder of just how well they'd "gotten along" on Friday night, and into the wee hours of the next morning.

Shoving the thought aside, she racked her brain, casting about for safe conversational territory. "I didn't know you had a daughter. An eleven-year-old, at that."

Damien gave her a small, knowing smile. "Yet another one of those topics we never actually got around to discussing that night."

Althea didn't think her cheeks could get any hotter.

He chuckled, taking pity on her. "But, yes, I do have a daughter. Her name is India."

Althea smiled. "Pretty name."

"Her mother named her after India.Arie, her favorite singer at the time."

Althea stole a glance at his big, masculine hands, which were covered with a fine dusting of black hair. No wedding band. Thank God. She hadn't even asked him if he was married, she realized, slightly mortified. She'd just assumed he was free to go home with her and screw her brains out all night long.

"I'm divorced," Damien said with an amused glint in his eyes, as if he'd caught her covertly checking his ring finger.

"That's good," Althea blurted without thinking. Then, realizing her gaffe, she hastened to clarify herself. "I mean, it's not good that you're divorced. I meant—"

He chuckled softly. "I know what you meant, Althea. As incredibly beautiful and tempting as you are, I wouldn't have spent the night with you if I was still married. I'm not that kind of guy."

Relieved, Althea reached for her Coke. "Does your daughter live with you?"

"No. She lives with her mother in East Baltimore. But I see her nearly every weekend, and she spends the summers with me."

Althea smiled at him. "The two of you must be very close."

"We are," Damien said with a tender little smile. "She's my heart."

Althea was touched. All too often the media perpetuated stereotypes of young black men who were deadbeat fathers, incapable of supporting their families and being role models to their children. Althea was always pleased to meet strong, responsible black men who shattered the negative stereotypes. Damien Wade was no exception.

She smiled teasingly at him. "Well?" she said expectantly.

He gave her a puzzled look. "Well what?"

Althea rolled her eyes in mock exasperation. "I'm waiting for you to whip out your wallet and show me every single photo you have of your daughter."

He laughed. "Oh, is that right?"

She grinned. "If you were a woman, I wouldn't have to prompt you."

"I'm sorry," Damien said smilingly, reaching inside his breast pocket. "I didn't realize there were rules about this sort of thing."

"Of course, silly. Any good parent knows that discussions about their children *must* be accompanied by a slide show."

Damien opened his wallet and passed it across the table, grinning. "I don't know about any slide show, but here's the most recent photo of India. The rest are at home."

Althea took his wallet, studying the photo of a smiling young girl with a smooth bronze complexion and thick, curly black hair that hinted at her mixed ancestry. While she may have inherited her mother's coloring and hair type, India Wade, with her glittering dark eyes, full lips, and wide, dimpled grin, looked just like her father. She was at that awkward preadolescent stage where her ears were still a little too big and her small, bony shoulders had not rounded out enough to fill her pink T-shirt. Nonetheless, Althea could already tell that the girl would one day blossom into a stunningly beautiful woman.

"You're in trouble," she said to Damien as she passed the wallet back to him. "In a few years the boys are going to be fighting all over themselves, knocking down your door to get to India."

"And I'll be waiting for them," Damien promised with a cool, narrow smile, patting the 9mm concealed beneath his suit jacket.

Althea laughed, shaking her head. "Poor India. She'll

be lucky if she goes on her first date before the age of thirty-five."

"I'm not *that* unreasonable." He paused. "I was leaning more toward thirty."

"Thirty!" Althea threw a packet of artificial sweetener at him, and he laughed.

They were still chuckling quietly as they left the restaurant and headed back to the office.

Althea's cell phone rang as she climbed out of the SUV ten minutes later and thanked Damien, who had rounded the fender to open the door for her. She waved good-bye to him and answered the phone without glancing at the number displayed on the caller ID screen.

"Special Agent Pritchard," she said briskly.

"Why, hello there," a warm, familiar voice greeted her. "This is Imani."

A delighted smile swept across Althea's face. "Hey, Imani! It's so good to hear from you."

"I hope you don't mind. I called Eddie, and he gave me your new cell phone number."

"Of course I don't mind. I've been meaning to call you and Garrison to let you guys know I'm back in town."

"And *I've* been meaning to call you ever since Eddie told us you'd been transferred to Baltimore, but time just got away from me, between the kids and work and my needy husband." She laughed, a sound of contentment that bordered on sheer bliss.

Althea smiled softly. If anyone deserved to be happy, it was her former college professor, who'd been through more than most people Althea knew. "It sounds like marriage and motherhood agree with you," she said warmly.

Imani chuckled. "You could say that. Hey, listen, is Damien with you?"

"No, he just dropped me off at the office."

"Oh, good! I wanted to invite you to a surprise birthday party we're throwing for him next Saturday."

"*Next* Saturday? But wasn't his birthday this past Friday?"

"It was. We just got together for cake and a small family dinner. But the real celebration will be held next Saturday. Damien doesn't have a clue. He thought the party would be *last* Saturday, the day after his birthday, but we fooled him. To his credit, he didn't look surprised or disappointed when only family members showed up at his mother's house for dinner."

Althea was confused. "Wait a minute," she said, pausing outside the entrance to the office building. "How did Damien find out about his own surprise party in the first place?"

"His mother and I set him up. We let him think he'd overheard us planning the party. We figured we wouldn't be able to keep it from him entirely, so we decided to trick him with the dates. It seems to have worked." Imani laughed, inordinately pleased with herself. "So can you make it next Saturday, Althea?"

Althea had already decided that the less interaction she had with Damien outside of work, the less likely she'd be to sleep with him again. But she couldn't very well refuse an invitation from the woman who, along with her husband, had saved her life eight years ago.

Besides, Althea reasoned, there would be dozens of people at the party. She had a better chance of being seduced by Damien at the office than at a party attended by all his family and friends.

"Althea?"

"I'd love to come," she said easily. "Thank you for inviting me."

"It's gonna be so much fun! We rented out his favorite

sports bar and hired a deejay, so make sure you bring your dancing shoes."

Althea chuckled. "Will do," she said, but her response was drowned out by a passing delivery truck, blaring its horn at another motorist on the congested street. She lifted her head, absently scanning her surroundings before turning away and pressing the phone closer to her ear.

Imani said, "I know you're busy, so I won't hold you up much longer. How was your first day at the new field office?"

"Great. Everyone has been very warm and welcoming. I don't know if they're *always* this friendly to newcomers or if they're only being nice to me because Eddie threatened to fire them."

Imani laughed. "Probably a combination of both." She sobered after a moment. "I heard about the high school student who was kidnapped over the weekend. I don't suppose there's any chance you're *not* involved in the investigation?"

Althea said nothing. She'd already had the same conversation with her aunt and uncle, who'd called her twice that morning to express their concerns. Even her therapist, Dr. Parminter, had called from Seattle to make sure she was okay, probably worried that this kidnapping would send her into some sort of emotional relapse.

Now you know I'm available any time if you need to talk, Althea, he'd assured her in his kind, tranquil voice. *I mean it. You can call me whenever you want.*

On the other end of the phone, Imani expelled a long, deep breath. "We figured as much."

"We?"

"Garrison and I. As soon as we heard about the kidnapping this morning, we knew you'd want to be involved in the case. You want to help find Claire Thorndike."

"Of course. It's my job to help find missing people." Never mind that this case had the potential to undo all the progress she'd made in eight years of therapy. Never mind that this case had the potential to take a very personal—and deadly—turn at any moment.

"You just got back home," Imani said quietly. "Don't you think it's a little too soon to tackle something like this?"

Althea closed her eyes, pinching the bridge of her nose at the onset of a mild headache. She knew Imani meant well, and she had every right to be concerned about Althea, considering that she, too, had been terrorized by the same psychopath who abducted Althea and held her captive for a month before he went after Imani. The two women had survived the most horrifying ordeal of their lives, becoming pawns in a madman's twisted game of revenge and murder. Imani knew, better than anyone, the horrors Althea had endured at the hands of their sadistic captor. Imani understood the fears and nightmares that had kept Althea awake every night for weeks after their rescue. The experience had bonded the two women like nothing they could have imagined. Their relationship had evolved from that of professor and student, mentor and protégé, to co-survivors. Sisters whose bond transcended blood. Althea owed Imani her life. If she hadn't devised a scheme to distract their kidnapper while Althea escaped and ran for help, they both might have been killed on that harrowing night. Which was why Imani should understand, better than anyone, why Althea felt compelled to help find Claire Thorndike and bring her home safely.

It was her turn to be the rescuer.

"I'm not going to lecture you," Imani said solemnly. "I didn't do that even when you were one of my students. I respect the fact that you're a mature, responsible adult, a trained professional whose job is to catch dangerous criminals and help put them behind bars. But if I can't convince you to change your mind about working this abduction case, will you at least promise me one thing?"

Althea smiled into the phone. "What's that?"

"Don't try to be the hero. If at any point you sense you're in danger, or if you find that the case is bringing back too many painful memories and you're starting to feel overwhelmed, please let someone know. Whether it's me, Garrison, Damien, your aunt and uncle, Eddie, hell, your therapist back in Seattle. You have an entire network of people who care about you and want you to be safe. Please, *please* confide in one of us if this case starts getting to you in any way. Will you promise me that?"

"Yes," Althea said, meaning it. "You have my word."

There was an audible sigh of relief on the other end. "Thank you," Imani whispered. She hesitated, then added after another moment, "It's good to have you back home, Althea, although I wish your homecoming didn't have to be tainted by a kidnapping—the very thing that caused you to leave in the first place. I just pray that Claire Thorndike is still alive. And I hope to God that there's absolutely no connection to what happened eight years ago. I hope the timing is nothing more than a tragic, terrible coincidence."

"Me, too," Althea murmured.

But even as she ended the call and ducked inside the federal building to begin her search for an unknown predator, she knew her hope was in vain.

He watched her.

Climbing out of the black sport utility vehicle, lifting her hand in a brief wave to her partner—the brother of the man who had killed her abductor that fateful night. Damien Wade, a rising star in the Bureau who had erupted from his big brother's shadow to establish a place for himself through sheer force of will. Brash, tenacious, an expert marksman with killer instincts and a sharp, methodical mind. He would prove to be a formidable opponent when the time came.

Formidable, but not invincible.

From a dark, nondescript sedan parked across the street, he had watched her. Talking on the cell phone. Laughing one minute. Looking grim and resolute the very next. He'd watched her, wondering if she was thinking about him, wondering if she could sense his presence less than one hundred yards away.

She was so beautiful. Oh, she'd been pretty enough before, he realized, but in the nearly eight years she'd been away from home, she had really come into her own. Voluptuous curves had replaced the slender, almost boyish angles of her body. He imagined what was hidden beneath the sensible pantsuit she wore. Dark nipples; skin like smooth, melted chocolate; and a soft nest of curls at the juncture of her thighs. A mild afternoon breeze worked to loosen the bun at the back of her head, stirring tendrils of black hair that brushed across her sensual face.

As he stared at her, every molecule, every fiber of his being homed in on her, the sounds of traffic around him receding to a low-frequency hum. When she suddenly glanced in his direction, her dark gaze skimming over the line of parked cars, his heart jolted. His pulse drummed with anticipation, pounding in his brain.

She was so close. So temptingly close.

After all this time, after years of poring through old newspaper clippings, police reports, interviews, tran scripts. After committing every minute detail to memory, she was finally within his sights again.

Althea Pritchard.

The FBI's very own success story.

She was a poster child for the law enforcement community, a missing girl who had been safely recovered through the hard work and collaborative efforts of a task force headed by one of the Bureau's top guns. Althea served as a glowing reminder that the good guys had prevailed, triumphing over evil. And three years ago, she had gone from being a victim of violent crime to a crime-fighting crusader. It had all the makings of a Hollywood blockbuster.

The script he had in mind would not appeal to an audience looking for a typical happy ending.

But it would be brilliant. Unforgettable. A masterpiece.

Of that he was certain.

As Althea disappeared inside the office building, a smile crept across his face.

The stage had been set. The cast had been chosen.

Rehearsals were over.

Lights . . . Camera . . . Action!

Chapter 9

It was after seven when Damien returned to the office that evening.

The building was mostly deserted, the majority of personnel having already left for the day. He rode the elevator to the floor designated for the Violent Crimes and Major Offenders program, otherwise known as the VCMO squad. The "bull pen," as it was called, was a large area with a series of connected desks, with groups of desks separated by cubicles.

He found Althea alone inside her cubicle. She had draped her suit jacket across the back of her chair and loosened her black, shoulder-length hair. One hand maneuvered the computer mouse while the other absently massaged her scalp. With her arm raised to her head, the pale silk of her blouse pulled taut across her firm, round breasts.

Damien's mouth went dry.

He wished he could walk over to her, lean down, and brush his mouth against the warm, silky skin at the nape of her neck. He could almost hear a soft murmur of pleasure escaping her lips before she turned her head, offering her mouth for his hot, hungry kiss. He imagined lifting her slightly and settling her sweet, lush bottom on the edge of the desk, then stepping between her long legs. He imagined their tongues tangling erotically, their hands tearing impatiently at each other's clothing—

"Oh good. You're back."

The sound of Althea's voice broke into his fevered musings. He blinked, and realized that she was staring at him with a slightly quizzical expression.

Damien swore softly under his breath, scrubbing a hand over his face as if to erase the tormenting images from his mind. It was no use. The impressions, along with vivid memories of their lovemaking, were burned into his brain. He'd need a damn lobotomy to remove them.

"How did it go with Detective Mayhew?" Althea asked. "Was he in a sharing mood or what?"

Damien tugged his tie loose as he strode toward her cubicle. "We spent most of the afternoon out in the field, coordinating the ground search efforts and organizing uniforms to canvass the surrounding area and talk to potential witnesses." He grimaced. "But given how isolated the Thorndike property is, it's not very likely that anyone saw anything that night. It's not as if they have neighbors."

"A fact that definitely worked to the perp's advantage," Althea murmured.

Damien propped a shoulder against the cubicle wall. "We can always hope for a jogger to come forward, someone who may have wandered off the beaten path that night and wound up in the vicinity of the estate while the abduction was in progress."

Althea snorted dubiously. "We should be so lucky. So what are they doing about the surveillance camera footage?"

"They've assigned a team of investigators to review sixty days' worth of video footage. But they've already

established that the hours between 5:18 P.M. on Friday
and 2:30 P.M. on Sunday, when the Thorndikes returned
home, can't be retrieved."

Althea nodded.

Damien could tell by her grim expression that she was
thinking the same thing he was, that Claire Thorndike
couldn't have known that her decision to disable the
security system in order to conceal the identity of her
mystery date may have doomed her. Not only had she
made it easier for a predator to enter her home and
kidnap her, but not having any surveillance footage
during that critical time frame would make it that much
harder for them to track down a suspect.

"The police have set up a hotline to take tips from the
public," he continued. "As you might imagine, they've
already received a ton of calls, reported sightings around
the city of a teenage girl matching Claire's description.
Mayhew dispatched K-9 search teams to investigate
some of these areas, but so far nothing has panned out.
Before I left the station, dozens of volunteers from the
community had shown up offering to organize a group
search. They're scheduled to meet at the old fire hall on
Reisterstown Road at eight-thirty A.M. on Wednesday
morning. This gives them more time to get the word out
to the community and solicit more volunteers. Not only
that, but the school principal has agreed to cancel school
for the day to allow students to participate in the search
efforts."

"Mmm. Very generous of him."

"*Her*," Damien corrected. He sent her a chiding grin.
"You disappoint me, Pritchard. I thought a feminist
like you would be above making those types of gender
assumptions."

She grinned at him. "And I thought a progressive
male like *you* would be above assuming a female agent

is a feminist just because she wears a badge and carries a big gun."

He arched a teasing brow. "So you're not a feminist?"

"I don't categorize myself as one."

"Good. 'Cause I'm not a progressive male. I've never been too crazy about the idea of women fighting in wars, I think a female presidential candidate *should* wear a skirt every once in a while, and I happen to like pulling out chairs and opening doors for women."

"Yeah, I noticed that," Althea said, her dark eyes glittering with mirth. "I was going to tell you that while I certainly appreciate the gesture, it's really not necessary. We're going to be spending a lot of time on the road together. I don't want you to feel obligated to open the car door for me every time we go somewhere."

Damien's mouth twitched. "I never do anything out of a sense of obligation. I do things because I want to. I like opening doors for you. What's the problem?"

She laughed, shaking her head in helpless defeat. "I don't know. Nothing, I guess. I'm being silly. It's just that I don't know what to do with myself—with my hands—while I'm waiting for you to come around and open the door for me. I feel . . . I don't know. Like I'm not in control."

He grinned at her. "God forbid you should surrender control for five whole seconds." His eyes narrowed suspiciously. "Are you sure you aren't a feminist?" Althea shot him a baleful look, and he laughed. "Tell you what. Why don't you just fold your hands neatly in your lap, and I'll make every effort to get to your side as quickly as possible. How does that sound?"

She regarded him in mild amusement. "This whole chivalry thing is really important to you, isn't it?"

He chuckled. "My mama raised three gentlemen. What can I say?"

Althea smiled softly. "You're really something else, Damien Wade."

He inclined his head. "I'll take that as a compliment."

"You should."

Their gazes held. The moment stretched into two.

Althea was the first to glance away, looking unsettled. "I take it that Detective Mayhew hasn't had a chance to check out Claire's computer yet."

"He's got someone working on it. He says he should know more by tomorrow morning. What've you got for me?"

"Pull up a seat," she offered.

Damien grabbed the empty visitor chair in a corner of the cubicle and nimbly straddled it. Glancing at Althea's computer screen, he saw that she'd been reading through Claire Thorndike's MyDomain page.

Following the direction of his gaze, Althea said, "Claire had a lot of friends, and not just the kids she went to school with. She made new friends online and met different people from around the world. It took me more than two hours just to read through all the comments and messages that had been left for her."

"Find anything interesting?"

"Potentially." Althea turned back to the computer, and Damien slid his chair across the floor, pulling up beside her. Her tantalizing scent teased his nostrils— soap mingled with a hint of the maddeningly seductive fragrance she wore.

With a supreme effort, he forced himself to ignore his raging libido and concentrate on what she was telling him.

"Joshua Reed, handsome captain of the swim team and Claire's philandering ex boyfriend, told the police he hadn't spoken to Claire in three months, right?"

Damien nodded. "Right."

Althea pointed to the screen with a manicured fingertip. "As recently as a week ago, the two of them were sending messages to each other. Josh initiated the contact, leaving a comment on her page about some cool photos of herself she'd recently uploaded. When Claire didn't immediately respond, he sent her a private message a day later asking her how long she planned to ignore him. He apologized for the way he had hurt her and said he'd made a huge mistake."

Damien skimmed the message in question, frowning when he reached the last line. "What does MUSM stand for?"

"Miss you so much." Althea grinned at him. "Don't do much text messaging, do you?"

He chuckled. "Nah," he drawled. "My daughter, India, does enough of that for both of us."

"Well, you'd better get with the times, Pops," Althea said teasingly. "Chat-speak is the way of the future. Pretty soon everyone will be communicating in this language. All of our briefings and reports will be written in chat-speak, complete with smiley faces and the full range of emoticons."

Damien gave a mock shudder, feeling very much like a relic. "God, I sure as hell hope not."

Althea laughed, patting his hand consolingly. "Don't worry. If it ever comes to that, I can be your translator."

Damien smiled. "I'm gonna hold you to that," he said, resisting the urge to capture her hand and lace their fingers together. "How did Claire respond to Josh's apology?"

A rueful grin curved Althea's lips. "She basically told him to go to hell. She said he blew his chance to be with a real woman, and as far as she was concerned, he and his new girlfriend—aka 'the skank'—could kiss her lily-white ass."

Damien grimaced. "Ouch."

Althea snickered. "Tell me about it. Gee, you think Spencer was exaggerating when he said his daughter isn't a very forgiving person?"

"Obviously not. Please tell me Josh had the good sense to walk away with his manhood still intact."

"Nope." With two clicks of the mouse, Althea pulled up another message. "He fired back at her, blaming *her* for their breakup, saying she was self-absorbed and always put her own needs above his. He predicted that by the time their senior prom rolled around, she would regret letting him go. To which Claire responded. YGTBKM. SWL."

"Translation?"

"'You've got to be kidding me. Screaming with laughter.'"

Damien shook his head, smiling grimly. "Double ouch. Damn."

Althea looked unsettled. "Here's what Josh wrote back."

Damien peered at the screen. *WSAT.*

He frowned. This time he took an educated guess on the translation: *We'll see about that.*

He met Althea's gaze. "You think he was threatening her?"

"Sure as hell sounds like it. Although it's hard to say whether he was threatening her with the prospect of having to attend the prom without him—"

"Or threatening to get back at her for breaking up with him." Damien's frown deepened. "He has an alibi for Friday night," he murmured, thinking aloud.

"Right. He was at the movies with Brandi, the new girl-friend, then he allegedly spent the night at her house. But what if the alibi is bogus? What if Josh asked Brandi to lie for him? What if he really went to the movies with her but dropped her off afterward and headed to Claire's house?"

Damien said nothing for a moment, turning over the

theory in his mind. He knew it was entirely plausible that Josh Reed was responsible for Claire Thorndike's disappearance. It was standard protocol for investigators to look closely at the husband or boyfriend whenever a female victim was involved. Josh might have driven to Claire's house that night intending to reason with her, perhaps hoping that she would give him a second chance if he appealed to her in person. But if Claire still refused him—or "screamed with laughter" in his face—he may have become desperate, even enraged. Enraged enough to lash out at her. To kill her. Damien had seen enough crime of passion cases in his seven-year career with the Bureau to know that nothing was beyond the realm of possibility when it came to scorned lovers. But his gut instinct told him that while Josh Reed may have been a lousy boyfriend to Claire and an insensitive jerk after the fact, he hadn't harmed her.

Damien glanced at the computer screen, at Claire's brightly decorated MyDomain page. The date of Josh's last message to her was October 1. Just two days before she disappeared.

"If he has nothing to hide," Althea speculated, "then why did he lie to the police about the last time he'd spoken to Claire? Why did he tell them it was three months ago when he just e-mailed her last week?"

"Maybe he thinks online communication isn't the same thing as actually *speaking* to a person," Damien suggested.

Althea gave him a look. "Semantics. And even if that were the case, he could have at least *mentioned* his recent e-mail exchange with Claire."

"Maybe he was embarrassed. She was pretty hard on him. Or maybe he didn't want the police to know he and Claire had traded insults just a few days before she went missing, because he didn't want to give them any reason to suspect him—as we're doing now."

Althea frowned, shaking her head. "The bottom line is that he lied to the police. And we've both been trained to suspect anyone who lies when questioned by the police."

Damien inclined his head, conceding the point. "You're forgetting one thing, though."

"What's that?"

Damien clasped his hands together over the back of his chair. "We've been operating under the assumption that Claire invited someone over to her house on Friday night. If Josh went over there and saw another guy with her, I'm pretty damn sure he would have told the police—if for no other reason than to take the focus off himself."

Althea pursed her lips thoughtfully. "That's very true. But what if the mystery date hadn't arrived yet? What if Josh got there first and took Claire? Then we're looking at the possibility that someone out there may have arrived at the house afterward, realized that something was amiss, panicked, and left without calling the police."

Damien nodded. "Or he may have thought Claire simply got cold feet and decided not to let him into the house. He saw her car in the driveway, saw lights on inside, and figured she was home. Unless he actually entered the house to search for her, he had no way of knowing anything was wrong, therefore he wouldn't have had a reason to call the police." He paused. "Especially if he wasn't supposed to be there in the first place."

Althea stared at him, comprehension dawning. "Because he's an older man. Or he's married. Or both."

"Exactly."

Althea swiveled away from the desk to face him. "What if Claire were having an affair with one of her father's business associates? What if she fell in love with him and asked him to leave his wife, but he refused? So what if she retaliated by threatening to tell her father about the affair, which caused the guy to panic and kill her?"

"It's possible. Hell, anything's possible. That said, I don't think Josh had anything to do with Claire's disappearance."

Althea frowned. "He's got motive and opportunity. This might be a classic case of 'If I can't have you, no one will.' I'm sure he knew that Mr. and Mrs. Thorndike would be out of town this weekend on their annual ski trip. I don't think it's a coincidence that he reached out to Claire a week before she disappeared. And I'm not ready to let him off the hook for lying to the police. What is he hiding?"

Damien hummed a thoughtful note. "Tell you what. How about we pay him a visit tomorrow afternoon, see if we can get some straight answers out of him?"

Althea nodded. "I think that's a great idea. I also think we should talk to Heather Warner. She's Claire's best friend—she *has* to know more than she's telling anyone."

"I agree. Which is why I think you should speak to her alone. If she feels more comfortable being interviewed by a woman, she might open up to you."

"You've got a point."

"I say we divvy it up. I'll talk to Josh. You talk to Heather."

"Works for me."

"Good." Damien hitched his chin toward the computer screen. "Did you come across any other red flags?"

"Possibly. As I said earlier, it took me some time to read through all the comments and messages on Claire's page." Althea paused. "How familiar are you with My-Domain?"

Damien scowled. "Familiar enough," he said darkly.

"India keeps begging me to let her have a page. Her mother agreed to it, but I've adamantly refused. I don't trust these social networking sites, and I sure as hell don't like the idea of some pervert viewing online photos of my daughter and sending messages to her. I told India she's too damn young to have a MyDomain page, and the only 'social networking' she needs to be doing is at school."

Althea grinned, making an exaggerated show of edging away from him. "Have I told you how positively terrifying you are when you go into protective papa-bear mode?"

Damien chuckled grimly. "At the risk of sounding like a dinosaur—which you've managed to make me feel twice today, thank you very much—the world we live in today is a pedophile's paradise. The Internet has given these predators access to kids like never before. I don't have to give you the statistics. We both know that every year an alarming number of children are coerced into pornography and lured away from their homes by predators they met online. I'm not saying that social network sites like MyDomain are entirely to blame; that would be too easy. Adults have to do a better job of educating kids and monitoring their Internet activity. If we as parents don't protect our children, who the hell will?"

When Althea smiled softly at him, he cleared his throat, looking sheepish. "Sorry. I didn't mean to go off on a tangent. You asked a simple question, and I jumped on my soapbox."

"It's all right," Althea said. "India is very lucky to have such a vigilant father looking out for her. And, hey, it doesn't hurt that you're also an FBI agent."

Damien grinned ruefully. "Tell that to India. She can't decide whether my job is a blessing or a curse."

Althea let out a short laugh. "Give her a few more years.

By the time she's sixteen and ready to start dating, she'll think it's a curse."

Damien smiled briefly. "Back to what you were saying. You found another red flag on Claire's MyDomain page?"

"Maybe. Maybe not. As I was reading the comments and messages left for her, I came across one dated almost three weeks ago. What I was going to explain earlier is that on MyDomain, comments are posted for public viewing, while messages are sent privately to the owner of the page. On September 19, Claire received a message from another user by the name of COLTRANEFAN."

"As in, a fan of John Coltrane, the jazz musician?"

Althea nodded. "The message was brief and cryptic, almost deliberately so. 'I hope you liked it.'"

"That's all it said? 'I hope you liked it?'"

"Yes, that was it. Just one line, no signature. That was the only message Claire had received from this user. I looked through her sent mail to see if she had responded, but I couldn't find anything, and unfortunately, all sent mail is automatically deleted after fourteen days. When I tried to access COLTRANEFAN's page, I got a message saying the profile was no longer available."

Damien frowned. "You think the user closed the account?"

"Looks that way. So now I've got all these questions racing through my mind. Is he the mystery date Claire was expecting on Friday night? Did he remove his My-Domain page before, or after, she was abducted? And *why* did he remove it? To keep his identity a secret? To make sure there was nothing connecting him to a missing girl?"

Damien's nerve endings tightened. This could be it, he realized. This could be the break in the case they were looking for. The break they desperately needed.

But he knew from experience that it was never that easy.

Althea continued, "I called the company headquarters in California to obtain the account information for COLTRANEFAN. The rep I spoke to balked at first. He started feeding me the company line about their privacy policies, their sworn commitment to protecting the legal rights of their customers, told me I needed to get a subpoena, et cetera, et cetera. I told him that COLTRANEFAN was a person of interest in a federal kidnapping investigation and if he didn't get me what I needed in twenty-four hours, I would dispatch the meanest, ugliest agents from our San Francisco field office to come and arrest his sorry ass for obstruction of justice." She flashed a sweet, beguiling smile that belied the aggressiveness of her threat. "Guess what? He promised to have those answers for me first thing in the morning. He even said he'd provide a detailed report of the user's account activity over the last thirty days." Her smile turned sharp, triumphant. "It pays to be a bitch with a badge."

Damien let out a bark of laughter, and Althea grinned.

Shaking his head at her, he said, "Damn, Miss Pritchard. Remind me never to get on your bad side."

She chuckled, exiting the MyDomain Web site.

Damien glanced at his watch and saw that it was already eight-thirty. It had been a long day, and this was only the beginning. "It's getting late," he said. "Why don't we call it a night and regroup tomorrow morning?"

Althea nodded, tilting back her head and closing her eyes as she massaged the muscles between her neck and shoulder blade. Damien ran his gaze over the sleek curve of her throat, his mind filled with an erotic image of her, head flung back, lips parted on a soundless cry as she rode him through a mind-shattering orgasm that left them both gasping and clutching each other long afterward.

"I didn't get a chance to run the background check

on Suzette Thorndike," Althea murmured, her eyes still closed, oblivious to the way Damien was staring at her. "I had to put in a little face time with our squad supervisor. He gave me a tour of the building and briefed me on some cases he wants me to assist with, in addition to the kidnapping investigation."

"Don't worry about it," Damien said huskily. He cleared his throat. "Doherty's a pretty reasonable guy, but if he gives you a hard time about working the Thorndike case, just let Balducci know. He can take care of it for you."

"Mmm. I don't doubt that. But I just got here. I don't want to make any enemies if it can be avoided."

Damien smiled to himself, silently congratulating her. Although Althea had been with the Bureau for only three years, she'd already learned that the key to surviving the ranks was knowing how to play the game, and knowing when to play your hand. The nature of her relationship with Eddie Balducci was public knowledge. The special agent in charge was her biggest advocate, and everyone knew it. But Althea would not exploit their friendship, using it as leverage over her peers and supervisors. She wouldn't make the mistake of expecting or demanding preferential treatment. She would earn her stripes the right way—through hard work, talent, and tenacity.

Damien's appreciation for her went up a notch.

Rising from the chair, he said with deliberate casualness, "Wanna grab a bite to eat?"

Althea glanced up from stuffing files into her leather briefcase and met his gaze. "You mean dinner?"

"Yeah," he said, pushing his chair back into the corner. "You know, the meal most people eat in the evening?"

She gave him a look. "I know what dinner is."

He chuckled softly. "Just making sure. You made it

sound like a foreign concept. So yes or no? I know a great little Italian restaurant not far from here, in Little Italy. Best risotto and lasagna in the city—just ask Balducci. We don't even have to talk about the case. We're going to eat, sleep, and breathe it for however long it takes to find Claire. Tonight is about nothing more than good food and good company."

Althea hesitated, pulling her lush bottom lip between her teeth, indecision reflected in her dark eyes. He could see that she was tempted by the offer, tempted to say yes.

He waited, surprised to realize just how much he *wanted* her to say yes. They'd spent most of the day together, and it still hadn't been enough for him.

That's when he should have known he was in trouble.

At length Althea shook her head. "Two meals in one day? I don't think that's such a good idea."

Disappointment washed over him. Trying to play it off, he drawled humorously, "Are you objecting to eating two meals in one day, or eating both of those meals with me?"

She grinned, rising from her chair. "Don't be obtuse. You know very well what I meant. As tempting as your offer sounds, I'm going to pass on dinner, and you know why. Besides, I need to get home and finish organizing my office. My aunt unpacked everything for me, but she didn't know how I wanted things arranged."

Damien angled his gaze toward the ceiling, affecting a wounded look. "My pride is in tatters. She'd rather organize files than have dinner with me."

Althea snorted out a laugh. "Oh *puh-leeze*! Don't you dare give me that wounded-male-ego act, Damien Wade. We both know you aren't exactly hurting for female companionship. I was at the club that night, remember? I saw those women throwing themselves at you, while the rest of them—myself included—couldn't keep their eyes off you. You could walk out this door right now, snap your fingers, and have as many women as you want lined up to have dinner with you." She bumped him playfully with her shoulder on her way out of the cubicle. "Now be the gentleman you are and walk me down to the garage."

"With pleasure," Damien murmured, wondering how she would react if he looked her straight in the eye and told her that the only woman he wanted to have dinner with was her.

Chapter 10

One of the things Althea knew she would miss about Seattle was her downtown loft with its scenic views of the city and proximity to her favorite shops and restaurants. When she learned she was being transferred to Baltimore, she'd enlisted the help of her aunt and uncle to find an apartment that shared many of the same amenities as her place in Seattle. On their first outing, they struck gold. They'd called her from the rental office, excited about the treasure they'd found on the city's bustling West Side. Trusting their judgment, Althea signed a lease and paid the nonrefundable security deposit. The first time she stepped foot in her new bachelorette pad was the day she arrived from Seattle, and she wasn't disappointed. The spacious two-bedroom apartment was within easy walking distance of the Inner Harbor, the Central Business District, and Lexington Market, the world's largest openstall food market, where she could buy fresh fruit and produce every day. Her unit featured modern appliances, hardwood floors, a fireplace, and floor-to-ceiling living room windows that offered a spectacular view of the downtown skyline. And because her uncle couldn't persuade her to move back home, he'd insisted on a controlled-access building complete with a twenty-four-hour front desk attendant and an intercom system. It was either that, he warned, or he would hire a bodyguard for her.

When Althea calmly pointed out to him that no respectable FBI agent would have a bodyguard, Louis Pritchard said, "We almost lost you once, baby girl. When it comes to your safety, I'm not taking any chances."

As Althea stepped off the elevator that evening and started down the narrow corridor to her apartment, she passed one of her neighbors, an attractive white man in his early thirties who lived two doors down. In response to her polite nod of greeting, he grinned at her, an odd, suggestive gleam in his blue eyes.

"How's it going?" he said cheerfully.

"Can't complain," Althea replied.

He snickered. "I'll bet," he muttered under his breath as he continued down the hall.

Pausing at her door, Althea stared after him, puzzled. When he glanced over his shoulder at her, still grinning, a slow flush crawled up her neck. Inwardly she groaned, mortified to realize he must have overheard her and Damien going at it on Friday night. They hadn't exactly been quiet, especially *her*. She'd moaned and screamed so many times her throat felt sore afterward. At the time she'd been too far gone to care if anyone else heard her, but now, in the face of her neighbor's unabashed amusement, she was horrified. Now, instead of being known as the quiet, considerate neighbor who kept to herself—a reputation she'd enjoyed in Seattle—she would be known as the noisy, not-so-considerate neighbor who screamed like a banshee during wild, all-night sex marathons.

How utterly embarrassing.

Althea let herself into her apartment, thinking that she should have added *thick walls* to her list of requirements when she started hunting for a new place to live. Of course, she couldn't have known at the time that thick walls would become a necessity for her. She'd certainly never needed them in Seattle, where her love life had been practically nonexistent. She'd dated so sporadically that sex became a rare indulgence, something she engaged in just to remember what it felt like. And none of those sexual encounters came close to what she'd experienced with Damien Wade.

Too bad you won't be enjoying any encore performances, she lamented, dropping her purse and keys on the foyer table and setting down her briefcase. She'd been so damn tempted to accept Damien's dinner invitation back at the office. *Tonight is about nothing more than good food and good company*, he'd told her. And although she knew better, she'd actually found herself considering his offer. *It's just dinner*, the voice of temptation whispered. *It's just two colleagues sharing a harmless meal.*

And then it would be just a touch, just an embrace, just a kiss, and before she knew what was happening, they would end up back at her apartment. And this time it would be more than just sex.

It would be the beginning of a dangerous addiction.

She could not—*would not*—let that happen.

It was one thing to have a torrid one-night stand with a complete stranger. But sleeping with that same stranger, after discovering that he was actually a colleague, was just asking for trouble. She'd spent the last three years working hard to be taken seriously by her colleagues and superiors in the Bureau, many who believed her decision to quit medical school and join the FBI had been the rash, emotional reaction of a fragile young woman still suffering from posttraumatic stress. These were the same people who believed that Althea wouldn't last more than six months at the Bureau. But she'd proven them wrong and, in the process, had gained their respect. She wasn't about to compromise her reputation or principles by getting involved in an office relationship that could go sour at any time.

Not that your reputation or principles can give you multiple orgasms or keep your bed warm at night.

Sighing deeply, Althea peeled off her cashmere jacket, hung it up in the hall closet, and crossed the living room to build a fire. The temperature had plummeted, bringing a chill to the air.

And somewhere out there, a seventeen-year-old girl was being held captive by an unknown predator.

Althea shuddered, rubbing her arms against a chill that came from deep within.

She wandered over to the windows and gazed out at the bright, twinkling lights of downtown Baltimore, cloaked in night.

All day long she'd held herself together, maintaining a detached, professional facade as she went about the business of investigating Claire Thorndike's abduction. She knew that the slightest chink in her armor, any hint of weakness or instability, would signal to Damien, and their boss, that she wasn't ready for a case like this. So she'd remained outwardly cool and composed, showing little sign of emotion, conducting herself as if this was just another case to her. But now that she was alone, in the privacy of her own home, the mask slid away, apprehension pressed down on her like an anvil, and her mind surrendered to her deepest, darkest fears and suspicions.

She knew what it was like to be alone, confused, terrified. To wonder if you had seen your family and friends for the very last time. She knew what it was like to sob hysterically and plead for your life, desperately hoping to get through to the madman who held your fate in his hands. And she knew what it was like to cling to a shred of hope that help was on the way, even as the long, dark days turned into weeks.

The more Althea delved into the investigation, the more convinced she became that her abduction and Claire Thorndike's disappearance were somehow connected. The similarities between the two cases were too uncanny to be ignored. For starters, she and Claire shared similar backgrounds. Although Louis Pritchard was no real estate tycoon, over the years he'd reached a level of success in his political career that enabled him to afford the best of everything for his family. When he became county executive while Althea was in middle school, they'd moved into a large stone house in an exclusive gated community. The house, Althea mused, sat alone at the top of a hill.

Just like the Thorndike estate.

She, like Claire, was an only child. And she, too, had been an overachiever, excelling academically and serving as president of various student organizations. She'd wanted to become a doctor and had entered college as a premed major, just as Claire would have done next year.

And last but certainly not least, they'd both been cheated on by their boyfriends.

Althea frowned. She knew that the details of her personal life had been splashed across the pages of countless newspapers during the course of her kidnapping investigation. Hungry reporters had camped out at the university she attended to interview her friends, classmates, professors, anyone remotely acquainted with her. When her boyfriend Malik Toomer became a suspect, the media speculated that he may have killed Althea when she confronted him about his infidelity.

Whoever abducted Claire must have followed Althea's

kidnapping case very closely. But the only way the perpetrator could have known that Josh Reed cheated on Claire was if he knew one or both of them personally.

Althea turned from the window and crossed the living room, mentally rifling through the list of people connected to the missing teenager. She grabbed a notepad and a pen from the table in the foyer and began making a list, her mind working faster than she could write. *Friends, classmates, teachers, school administrators, doctor, dentist, household staff, parents' friends and business associates.*

She paused, tapping the pen against the notepad as she pondered another theory. The psychopath who kidnapped Althea eight years ago had singled her out solely because of her relationship with her professor and mentor, Imani Wade. Imani had been his primary target; Althea was the unwitting pawn he'd used to punish Imani and lure her into his sinister web of revenge and murder. If Claire's abductor was following the same pattern, then it was highly possible that his next target was someone close to Claire, someone she considered a mentor. One of her teachers, maybe. Or an old riding instructor, or a former supervisor. On her MyDomain page, she'd mentioned a summer job at a nonprofit animal-rescue shelter in Baltimore. She'd described it as "a lot of hard work, but fun and incredibly meaningful."

Althea strode to her office, sat down at the desk, and turned on her computer. She pulled up Claire's My-Domain page and scrolled down the screen until she reached the Hobbies and Interests section where Claire mentioned the summer job from last year. Althea jotted down the name and address of the animal-rescue shelter, then quickly read through the new comments that had been posted by Claire's friends and classmates who were hoping and praying for her safe return. Conspicuously, no comments had been left by Josh Reed.

"What are you hiding, kiddo?" Althea muttered in the silence of the room. "Whatever it is, I'm going to get to the bottom of it."

But assuming she was on the right track with the copy-cat theory, even she had to admit that Josh seemed an unlikely suspect. He'd been only nine when Althea was abducted. She couldn't see him dredging up an eight-year-old case in order to kidnap and possibly murder his ex-girlfriend.

Stranger things have happened.

Althea frowned, staring at Claire's smiling image on the computer screen. Somewhere out there, someone knew what had happened to the missing teenager. That someone had waited until the day Althea returned home, nearly eight years later, to emerge from the shadows.

Taking Claire had been his first move.

Only time would reveal his ultimate endgame.

Outside in the darkened parking lot, Damien hankered for a cup of strong black coffee as he pored through a report he'd printed out before leaving the office. Every so often his gaze strayed to Althea's fourth-story apartment, where the lights glowed invitingly from the living room. Through the closed curtains, he saw her shadow passing back and forth in front of the windows as she moved around inside the apartment. He frowned, his gut tightening at the thought of an unknown predator spying on her from the shadows of the parking lot, patiently biding his time, waiting for the perfect opportunity to strike.

It was that suspicion, that unnamed fear, that had brought Damien there that night.

After seeing Althea off two and a half hours earlier,

he'd returned to the office and run a background check on Suzette Thorndike. While he waited for the report, he'd reflected on his earlier conversation with Eddie Balducci, who'd summoned Damien back to his office after his meeting with Althea that morning. When a grim-faced Eddie informed him that Althea would be assisting him with the Thorndike investigation, Damien was surprised.

"Don't you think it's a little too soon for her to be handling a case like this?" he demanded.

"Of course," Eddie bit off tersely. "Not only that, but her life may be in danger."

Damien had listened, with a mounting sense of dread, as Eddie explained the similarities between Althea's kidnapping and Claire Thorndike's disappearance, disturbing similarities that could not be easily dismissed.

Eddie finished by saying, "Make no mistake about it. I don't want Althea anywhere near this case when I know there's a very real chance she could get hurt. But she insists on helping, and damn it, if her involvement can somehow lead us to Claire Thorndike, that's a chance I'm willing to take."

Damien let his boss know, in no uncertain terms, what he thought of his willingness to use Althea as bait to draw a dangerous psychopath out of hiding. Then, realizing he may have revealed too much about the nature of his relationship with Althea, he'd left the office without another word. He spent the rest of the morning berating himself for losing his cool, something he rarely ever did. He told himself he had no right to feel so protective over a woman he hardly knew, a woman who probably wouldn't welcome his interference. So he'd vowed to treat Althea the same way he treated every other agent he worked with, which meant he wouldn't ask her to step down from the case—no matter how much he wanted to.

But as the day wore on and he learned more about Claire Thorndike, the harder it became to suppress his misgivings.

Seated at his cluttered desk that evening, he'd grabbed a notepad, flipped to a blank page, and created two columns under the headings *Similarities* and *Differences*. In the first column, he jotted down the similarities between Althea and Claire. *Young female, only daughter, honor student, aspiring doctor, prominent father, affluent upbringing, cheating boyfriend.*

In the second column, he recorded the differences. *Race, one year apart in age at the time of abduction.*

When he'd finished writing, he stared down at the list, chilled by what he saw. The similarities between the two victims outnumbered the differences. There was no disputing that. Add to that the timing of the abductions— less than a week apart—and a cold knot of dread tightened in Damien's stomach.

When he left the office that night, he wasn't surprised to find himself driving to Althea's apartment. He parked in an empty visitor spot near the front of the building, slid his seat as far back as it would go, and prepared to settle in for the long haul. He didn't know what he expected to accomplish by staking out her apartment. All he knew was that he felt compelled to be there, and he'd never been one to ignore his instincts.

At eleven-fifteen, when the lights went out in Althea's apartment, Damien gave his undivided attention to the printout he'd brought from the office.

Twenty-eight-year-old Suzette Cahill Thorndike was born and raised in a small fishing town on Maryland's Eastern Shore, the eldest of five siblings. An aspiring actress, she left home at the age of seventeen and moved to Baltimore, where she held a number of waitressing jobs before landing a position as a production

assistant at Center Stage Theater. It was there that she
met her first husband, Patrick Farris, a prominent in-
ternist who ran his own private practice in Baltimore.
After they were married, Farris, who served on the
boards of various arts councils, used his connections to
help his wife land some community theater roles. Two
years into their marriage, the wealthy physician was
sued for malpractice by five former patients who accused him of sexual misconduct. Not only did the lawsuit cost him his practice, his medical license, and his
reputation, but shortly afterward his young wife filed
for divorce, citing emotional distress caused by his infidelity. Suzette Cahill walked away with more than half
of Farris's remaining assets—a cool two million dollars.

Within a year, the wealthy divorcee was remarried to
real estate mogul Spencer Thorndike, whose vast fortune made Patrick Farris look like a pauper.

The girl from a backwater fishing town had done
very well for herself, Damien thought sardonically. But
that didn't mean she'd gotten rid of her stepdaughter
to get her hands on all of Thorndike's money, as Althea
had conjectured.

If anything, Suzette's ex-husband seemed a more likely
suspect in Claire's disappearance. Patrick Farris lost just
about everything in the aftermath of the malpractice
lawsuit; he must have viewed Suzette's desertion as the
ultimate betrayal. At a time when he'd needed her the
most, she'd not only left him but took more than half of
his money with her. He definitely had motive for wanting
to get back at her. There was a strong possibility that the
unknown subject, or Unsub, they were looking for was a
sexual predator. If Farris was capable of molesting his
patients, he was certainly capable of molesting his
ex-wife's beautiful stepdaughter.

Damien frowned, questions and hypotheses churning in his brain like mathematical computations. What if Farris kidnapped and murdered Claire for the sole purpose of framing his ex-wife for the crime? Surely he realized that investigators never ruled out the parents whenever a child went missing. Was he setting up Suzette Thorndike to take the fall? Would the police suddenly "stumble upon" evidence that implicated her in her stepdaughter's disappearance?

Damien frowned a second time, chilled by another possibility. What if Farris intended to abduct and murder Suzette to complete his revenge? Could she be the next victim?

Pulling out his laptop, Damien quickly entered Patrick Farris's name and identifying data into the Bureau's National Crime Information Center, a computerized database accessible to law enforcement agencies nationwide. If Farris had a criminal history, Damien would know by tomorrow morning.

As he was closing his laptop, his cell phone jangled. When he dug it out of his breast pocket and saw that his daughter was calling, he felt an instinctive twinge of alarm.

He answered quickly. "Hey, sweetheart. Is everything all right?"

"Hi, Daddy," India greeted him cheerfully. "Everything's fine. I just wanted to call and see how you're doing."

Damien smiled, the tension ebbing from his body. "I'm good, baby girl. But why are you still up? It's almost eleven-thirty."

"I know. I couldn't sleep. You're not at home, are you?"

"No, sweetheart. I'm out."

"Are you on a stakeout?"

Again he smiled. "Something like that."

India hesitated, and Damien could see her sitting crosslegged on her canopy bed, frowning up at the ceiling and twirling a thick lock of hair around her finger because she never remembered to wrap it at night.

"What's on your mind, kiddo?"

India issued a long, deep sigh. "I'm worried about you, Daddy."

"And why is that?" he murmured, although he already had an inkling. Over the years, he and India had had many heart-to-heart conversations about the dangerous nature of his job. Although she was proud of him for "protecting innocent people and putting away the bad guys," she made no secret of the fact that she'd much rather have him working as a doctor, a teacher, or a garbage man than a federal agent. *You're always chasing bad men, but what if they turn around one day and start chasing you?* she'd once demanded of him, tiny fists planted on her narrow hips, unshed tears shimmering in her eyes. Although Damien gently recited the statistics to her, telling her that only forty-nine FBI agents had been killed in the line of duty since the Bureau was founded in 1908, India remained convinced that he was in mortal danger as long as he was an FBI agent.

So when she announced that evening that she was worried about him, he automatically braced himself for another spirited lecture about the hazards of his occupation.

But India surprised him by saying, "I think you need another wife."

Damien let out a choked laugh. *"Excuse me?"*

"I think you should get married again. Before you tell me I'm too young to know what I'm talking about," she hastened to add, "let me just tell you why I said what I did. Are you listening?"

"I'm listening," he drawled, distinctly amused.

India blew out a heavy breath, as if she were about to impart some unpleasant news. "You're lonely, Daddy."

"I am?"

"Of course." As if the answer should be obvious. "Don't *you* think so?"

"I, uh, hadn't really thought about it. What makes you think I'm lonely?"

"You live all by yourself."

Damien grinned. "So do a lot of people."

"And *they're* probably lonely, too. The other thing is, you spend your birthday with me every year."

"What's wrong with that?"

"Nothing! I think it's great that you like celebrating your birthday with me, and we always have the best time." Her voice gentled. "But, Daddy, I want to know that you'd *still* have fun if I couldn't spend the day with you. If you were married, I wouldn't have to worry about that. I know your wife would make your birthdays special, the way Aunt Imani always does for Uncle Garrison. You know what I mean?"

"I think I understand," Damien said, his tone somber. "You're dumping me for some beady-headed boy at school."

"Daddy!" India protested.

Damien chuckled softly. "I'm just giving you a hard time, baby girl. You know how much I enjoy spending my birthdays with you, and I appreciate your concern for me. But don't you worry your pretty little head about me. I meant it when I told you I wasn't mad that you couldn't make it on Friday. You're growing up, sweetheart, and that means a whole new world is opening up to you. Believe me, I understand that. You don't have to feel guilty if you want to go to a school dance or a friend's party that happens to fall on my birthday. I'm cool with that. I really am."

India mumbled dispiritedly, "Mom says you had a good time on Friday night, but I didn't believe her. I thought she was just telling me that to make me feel better."

Damien swallowed. An image of his and Althea's naked, writhing bodies flashed through his mind. He gave himself a hard mental shake. "I had a good time," he assured his daughter. "Take my word for it."

"Okay," India said, sounding relieved. But a moment later she was sighing deeply again.

Damien smiled. "No wonder you can't sleep. Got a lot on your mind tonight, don't you?"

"Yeah. I guess so." She hesitated another moment, then blurted, "I think Mom misses you."

His smile faded. "Baby girl—"

"Last week I walked in on her looking through your wedding album. She closed it really fast when she saw me, but it was too late. And, Daddy," she added, lowering her voice to a hushed whisper so as not to be overheard, "I could be wrong, but I think Mom had tears in her eyes."

Damien flexed his jaw, turning his head to stare out the window. India was only five years old when he and Angelique split up. In the aftermath of their bitter divorce and protracted custody battle, Damien swore he would never again put his daughter in the impossible position of having to choose between her parents when it came to her love and loyalty. He refused to allow her to become a tool, a possession to be bickered over. To that end, he never bad-mouthed Angelique; in fact, he rarely discussed her at all. It was an unspoken agreement between him and India, one she'd always seemed perfectly content with.

Until now, apparently.

"I didn't tell you that to make you feel sorry for Mom or anything," she said in a low monotone. "I just . . . thought you should know that she misses you."

"Is that what this is about, India?" Damien asked quietly. "You want your mother and me to get back together?"

"No! I mean, not really. Well . . . maybe. It's just that you both seem so lonely. Mom still goes out with her friends all the time, but she doesn't seem very happy. Maybe if you guys were married again, things would be better this time."

Damien wondered fleetingly if Angelique had put India up to this phone call, but no, he knew his daughter well enough to realize that the concerns she'd just expressed were very much her own.

In a gentle but firm voice, he said, "You know I'd do just about anything to make you happy, India. Unfortunately, getting back with your mother isn't one of them."

"Do you hate her?" his daughter whispered, as if fearing the answer.

Damien pushed out a deep, weary breath. "No, baby girl, I don't hate your mother. I did, once. But I don't anymore. That said, I don't want to give you any false hopes about our relationship. Your mother and I have done a lot of things to hurt each other, things we can never take back. I know you think we're both lonely—and maybe you're right—but believe me when I tell you we're better off apart than we are together. Anyway, sweetheart, the most important thing is that we both love you very much, and nothing will ever change that. Do you believe me?"

"Yes," India said in a small voice.

Damien frowned slightly. "You don't sound too convinced."

"I am." India sighed heavily. "You've always told me the truth, Daddy. No matter what, you've never lied to me or treated me like a dumb little kid."

He smiled softly. "That's because I've never thought you were a dumb little kid. Far from it."

"Thanks, Daddy." India held the phone away from her mouth and yawned, but Damien heard it anyway.

"It's almost midnight, kiddo. Time for you to get some shut-eye."

"Okay," she mumbled drowsily. Then, "Today in school everyone was talking about that girl who got kidnapped. Are you trying to find her, Daddy?"

"I am, sweetheart. A lot of people are."

"That's good. Her parents must be really worried about her. I hope you find her soon."

"Me, too," Damien murmured, scanning the darkened parking lot, as if the key to Claire Thorndike's whereabouts lurked in the shadows. As he said good night to India and disconnected the call, he sent up a silent prayer of thanksgiving that his daughter was safe and sound in her own home, in her own bed.

Just as he'd done when Althea Pritchard was kidnapped.

As he glanced at the list he'd made earlier, a chill swept over him that had nothing to do with the cold. On its heels was a foreboding sense of déjà vu.

From the shadowy interior of an old Honda Accord parked five rows away, near the back of the parking lot, he watched Damien Wade. The agent had arrived an hour ago and appeared to be in no hurry to leave.

He didn't know whether to feel amused or annoyed that Wade had intruded upon his nightly ritual of spying on Althea Pritchard inside her apartment.

That evening he'd watched through his military-issue binoculars as she stood at the living room window, staring out into the dark, wintry night with an apprehensive expression that told him she was thinking about the missing teenager. Thinking about *him*. Wondering who and where he was. The thought excited him, made his blood pulse through his veins and his cock throb with lust. He had just reached down to stroke himself when she suddenly disappeared from view.

He swore viciously, lowering the binoculars. He held his breath, waiting for her to reappear. As the minutes ticked past, he grew impatient, frustrated. His erection subsided.

After what seemed an eternity, a light clicked on in another room. And there she was, seated at the small wooden desk, the glow from the computer lighting her beautiful face. The back of the monitor faced the window, making it impossible for him to see what she was viewing on the screen. But he didn't have to guess. He knew she was on Claire Thorndike's MyDomain page, chasing down potential leads like the good little investigator she was. So smart, so tenacious. She would work at the puzzle until every piece fell neatly into place.

And then he would come for her.

After fifteen minutes at the computer she stood. As she raised her arms above her head to stretch, he was distracted by the sight of the Glock clipped to her belt holster. He had a vision of her standing with her long legs braced apart, her disheveled hair falling into her eyes as she trained the gun on him. He imagined her pulling the trigger, only to realize that the clip was empty. He imagined catching her easily as she turned to flee. Her desperate screams echoed in his mind, as real as the sight of her in his binoculars.

Suddenly she turned her head to stare out the window. For an arrested moment she seemed to catch his eye, to look right at him.

As if she knew he was there.

As if she understood that her fate awaited her in the dark, chilly night.

His heart thudded against his rib cage. He stared into her luminous dark eyes, rimmed with a thick fringe of black lashes. Anticipation heated his blood.

She came toward the window, a frown marring the smooth line of her brow. Was that fear reflected in her dark eyes? Or a sense of premonition?

Before he could decide, she snapped the blinds closed, and a moment later the room went dark. He had only a fleeting glimpse of her as she returned to the living room and quickly drew the curtains, shutting him out.

He'd remained hidden in the shadows, silently praying for one last sight of her before he departed for the night. He was just about to give up when a familiar black SUV pulled into the large parking lot and claimed an empty visitor spot near the front of the building. He frowned, wondering what sort of business had brought Damien Wade to Althea's apartment at such a late hour. He waited, an awful kernel of suspicion forming in his mind. He could think of only two reasons a man visited a woman in the middle of the night. To deliver bad news or to seduce his way into her bed.

But that couldn't be, he thought, his frown deepening. She'd only arrived in town on Friday, and to his knowledge, she and Wade met for the first time this morning. Surely Wade wouldn't have the audacity to make a move on her so soon.

She's a beautiful, sexy woman. Of course he wouldn't waste time trying to seduce her!

The stranger tensed, struck by the possibility that Althea and Damien Wade had met before this morning. He'd been occupied with Claire for several hours on Friday night, getting her settled into her new dwelling. By the time he made it to Althea's apartment, it was after midnight. He'd stayed for only two hours, long enough to satisfy himself that she wasn't out partying on her first night back in town.

But perhaps he'd missed something. Wade's presence there that night was suspicious . . . unsettling

He waited, but the agent made no move to get out of the SUV. After ten minutes, he realized that Wade was not there to seduce Althea but rather to watch over her. To protect her.

How sweet, he thought with a cold, mocking smile.

It amused him to realize how quickly Althea had cast her spell over her new partner. Wade barely knew her, and already he was willing to risk his life for her. Just as his brother had done for Althea's mentor eight years ago.

It was perfect. He couldn't have planned it better himself.

Because he knew that when the time came, Wade would not be able to save her from the destiny that awaited her.

No one would.

The thought brought another smile to his face. "Just you wait," he said, his voice the barest of whispers in the stillness of the night.

He trained his binoculars on the black SUV and saw that the agent was on the phone. While Wade was preoccupied, the stranger eased the car door open and slid out of the Honda, which belonged to a tenant who was out of town for a week.

Crouching in the darkness, adrenaline humming through his veins, he closed the car door with a soft click. Knowing that Wade would be checking his rearview mirror, he crept toward the back of the parking lot, keeping low to the ground. When he reached the line of trees that bordered the lot, he straightened to his full height, a figure cloaked in black, and disappeared into the shadows.

Chapter 11

She was huddled on a bed in a corner of the cold, dark room.

Her wrists were tied tightly behind her back, cutting off her circulation. A coarse band of cloth knotted around her head blindfolded her, heightening her sense of helplessness, fueling her terror. She was alone in the room, but she thought she could feel him nearby, breathing silently, watching her. A malevolent presence that taunted her.

She didn't know where she was, didn't know how long she had been there. Days, maybe weeks. She wanted to go home, but she knew he wouldn't let her. He was going to kill her. She knew that, too. Knew it with chilling certainty.

Somehow she had to find a way to escape. But how? She was a prisoner, at his complete mercy. She ate when he told her to, used the bathroom when he told her to, slept when he drugged her. She was as powerless as a child.

Suddenly she heard a match striking. She tensed, hot

fear lancing down her spine. She squinted against the tight blindfold, straining to make out the silhouette of her captor. But she saw nothing but darkness.

And then came the footsteps. Slow, deliberate, approaching her from across the room. Her heart pounded violently against her ribs. Her insides twisted with panic and dread.

She heard the soft hiss of a flame as he drew near, felt a whisper of smoke across her skin.

He stopped in front of her. She began trembling, her teeth chattering so hard they rattled in her skull.

"You've been a naughty little girl, Althea," the voice whispered, soft and menacing. Eerily familiar.

She felt the cold tip of a blade pressed to her throat. And then, without warning, the blindfold was unceremoniously ripped from her head.

She looked up and found herself staring into the face of evil incarnate.

"No!"

Althea's eyes flew open, the sound of her own scream echoing in the silence of her darkened bedroom.

She bolted upright in bed. Her heart drummed wildly in her chest, her body was drenched in sweat, and the vivid nightmare lingered in her mind as clearly as if she'd just lived through the horrifying experience.

"It was just a dream," she whispered shakily, feeling weak and disoriented.

Just a dream, her mind echoed. But the thought brought her little consolation.

A pounding headache had started at the base of her skull and moved upward. Her hands shook as she pushed her damp hair out of her face and glanced at the digital clock on her nightstand. The red numbers glowed eerily in the darkness. 4:20.

Dropping her head into her hands, she massaged her

temples. It had been two years since she'd had one of her nightmares. Two years.

She'd been home four days, and the dreams had already started again.

And this is just the beginning, an inner voice warned ominously. *You know this is the beginning*.

Althea shivered, closing her eyes.

She'd spent the last several years in therapy, talking through her darkest fears and baring her soul on a monthly basis. But that had been from the safe confines of Dr. Parminter's plush downtown office, thousands of miles from here. Time and distance, along with a controlled dose of antianxiety meds, had taken the edge off her memories, perhaps giving her a false sense of peace. A false sense of security. Now that she was back home and surrounded by everyday reminders of her ordeal, it was clear that it would take more than therapy to help her bury the past once and for all.

Before she could fully commit herself to finding Claire Thorndike, she had to confront her own demons.

And she knew just where to start.

Althea threw back the covers and slid from the bed, padding barefoot to the bathroom to turn on the shower.

Twenty minutes later she was dressed in dark jeans, an angora sweater, and a pair of thick-soled boots. She stuffed her 9mm into her belt holster and strapped her backup service revolver to her ankle.

Before walking out the door, she swallowed two aspirins, hoping they would take the edge off her headache before she reached her destination. She needed to think clearly, needed her wits about her should there be any surprises.

As she left the apartment, she wore a grim, resolute expression.

It was time to face the ghosts of the past.

* * *

The cabin was waiting for her as the first blush of dawn lightened the sky.

Even framed against the vivid backdrop of the sunrise, the abandoned property had a sinister look. No amount of sunlight could chase away the shadows that fell down from the surrounding trees, shrouding the old cabin in perpetual gloom. It squatted amid rotting, overgrown grass; the windows were boarded up, and the wood showed signs of decay.

Althea parked right in front and climbed out of her dark sedan. As she stared at the deserted building, she wondered if it was possible for evil to linger in a place long after the source of evil had been destroyed.

She swallowed, feeling a strange sense of disquiet. As if she were being watched from inside the house.

Don't be paranoid, she told herself. *There's no one here. No one but you and your memories. Now hurry up and get it over with.*

Althea ducked inside the car, leaned across the driver's seat, and removed a flashlight from the glove compartment. She closed and locked the door, then did a slow scan of the yard before approaching the cabin.

A stiff morning breeze rustled the tree leaves, amplifying the sense of isolation and gloom that surrounded the property.

A fine chill threaded through her.

Telling herself she had no reason to be spooked, she stepped onto the porch and clicked on the flashlight. She stepped over a fallen board that had been pried loose from the door, probably by the same vandals that had spray painted profanities across the PRIVATE PROPERTY— KEEP OUT sign posted at the main entrance. She fully expected to find the place trashed, littered with empty beer cans, fast-food wrappers, discarded condoms, and other debris left by the vandals.

But the moment she crossed the threshold, she saw nothing but the memories that rushed to the surface of her brain.

She saw the mounted animal heads on the timber walls, alongside macabre African masks with sinister black eyes and twisted, gaping mouths. She saw candles lit throughout the room, their flickering flames casting long, writhing shadows against the walls.

Althea shuddered, blinking several times to banish the haunting images. As her vision cleared, she noticed the shafts of daylight seeping through the cracks in the wooden boards that covered the windows.

She shone her flashlight around what had once been the living room. It was empty, and unless her eyes were deceiving her, the hardwood floors appeared to have been swept clean.

By whom?

After glancing around the room, Althea knelt and ran her finger across the floor. It was covered in a thin layer of dust. Not as much as one would expect in a house that hadn't been occupied in eight years.

She swept her flashlight across the floor, searching for footprints, but it was still too dark and gloomy to accurately make out anything.

Ignoring a whisper of unease, she stood and continued through the darkened room, creeping deeper inside the silent cabin, moving stealthily through the shadows. When she reached the open doorway that led down to the cellar, she paused.

Outside she could hear the wind moaning softly through the trees. Her heart thudded against her sternum. Her fingers tightened around her Glock.

You're gonna get your black card revoked. No black woman in her right mind would go down there alone.

Stop it! There's no one down there. It's just your over-wrought imagination. You can do this. You have to do this!

Leading with the flashlight, Althea started down the narrow stairwell, descending into the dark bowel of the cabin. Her heart rate accelerated after each step. In her mind's eye, she saw herself racing up those same stairs in a mad, desperate flight for survival. *Get help, get help, get help*, she'd chanted to herself that night as she fled from her captor. Leaving Imani Wade behind with the madman was the hardest thing she'd ever had to do, but she knew her escape was their only chance for survival.

On the last step Althea came to a stop. Her heart was hammering painfully now. Her legs suddenly felt unsteady.

And she knew why.

There, at the end of the dark corridor, was a closed door that led into the room where her life had changed forever. The room where she'd been held against her will for thirty days. The room she'd come to think of as her prison. Her final resting place.

The saliva dried in her mouth. Not for the first time since her arrival she questioned the wisdom of her decision to come there. Maybe it was too soon. Maybe she wasn't ready for this.

You've come this far, a voice whispered. *You can't turn back now.*

Shoring up her resolve, she stepped off the stairwell and continued down the corridor, the beam of the flashlight cutting a path through the darkness. The air was dank, stale, filling her constricted lungs.

As she neared the closed door at the end of the hall-way, that's when she heard it.

A faint noise from above.

Her blood froze.

She whirled around, her pulse drumming in her ears as she strained to listen. She thought she heard the soft scrape of a boot on hardwood. The fine hairs on the nape of her neck lifted. Her skin prickled with awareness.

She tightened her grip on the Glock and held her breath, listening. But there was nothing but silence.

An unearthly silence.

And yet she knew she hadn't imagined the noise. She wasn't alone. She could sense another presence somewhere inside the cabin. Whoever it was had seen her car parked outside. He knew she was there.

Nervous sweat broke out on Althea's skin. A chilling fear seized her by the throat.

Training and instincts kicked in, and she turned off the flashlight so as not to give her position away. Flattening herself against the cold cellar wall, she edged back toward the staircase, leading with her weapon. Her nerves were stretched so taut they were about to shatter.

She heard the creak of a floorboard on the landing above her.

She swallowed, her finger tightening on the trigger. She heard the soft tread of approaching male footsteps. The intruder came to a stop at the top of the stairwell.

Her breathing grew shallow, uneven.

"Althea?"

Relief flooded her bloodstream at the sound of the deep, familiar voice. Her knees turned to water.

"Damien?" *Thank God!*

Hurriedly shoving her Glock and flashlight into the waistband of her jeans, Althea raced up the stairs and ran right into Damien's arms, which closed around her with stunning force. Trembling with relief she clung to him, wanting to burrow deeply against him, to lose herself, even for just a moment, in the strength and protection he offered.

He drew back after several moments and gazed down at her, brushing his hands over her hair and her face. "Are you all right?" he demanded.

She nodded quickly. As the adrenaline rush ebbed from her body and the fear receded, she suddenly felt like an idiot. She'd let her nerves get the best of her. She was a well-trained federal agent—an *armed* federal agent—and she'd just behaved like some hapless little blonde trapped in a haunted house on the set of a horror movie.

"I'm fine," she said when Damien continued gazing worriedly at her.

His expression darkened. "What the hell are you doing here?"

"I—" She glanced back, staring down the dark stairwell. How could she explain what she was doing there without sounding like a nutcase—which, judging by the look on his face, he already thought she was?

"I had to come," she said simply.

Damien frowned darkly. Without another word, he grabbed her hand and led her purposefully from the cabin. Under normal circumstances Althea would have protested being manhandled like that, but at the moment she was so eager to escape the gloomy cabin it didn't matter to her *how* she left.

Once outside they started toward her car, where Damien's black SUV was also parked. He did not let go of her hand as they walked, their bodies close, their breaths mingling in the frosty morning air.

When they reached her dark sedan, he turned to her, his thick black brows still furrowed together. "You shouldn't have come here alone," he growled. "Someone could have followed you here—someone other than me."

"I know. I wasn't thinking. I just . . . Wait a minute." Althea stared at him, her eyes narrowed suspiciously. "How did you know I would be here?"

A muscle clenched in his jaw. "When I showed up at your apartment this morning and saw that your car was gone, I got a little worried. So I tracked you down."

It took Althea a moment to remember that the vehicles issued to agents were equipped with GPS tracking devices. She didn't know whether to be annoyed or grateful that Damien had used the technology to hunt her down like some rogue agent. Or, worse, a damsel in distress.

"You mean you followed me all the way out here, an hour away from Baltimore, because you were worried about me?"

Damien looked slightly uncomfortable. "Yes," he muttered, adding irately, "damn it."

Althea felt a twinge of pleasure and told herself she was a crazy fool for caring that this man—whom she barely knew—was so concerned for her safety that he'd gone out of his way to make sure she was okay.

A sheepish grin tugged at the corners of her lips. "Thanks for caring. And for following me out here." She hitched her chin toward the abandoned cabin. "I was a little, ah, creeped out in there."

"I noticed. You were shaking like a leaf." Damien followed the direction of her gaze, studying the building in silence for a few moments before returning his attention to her. "That must have been very difficult for you," he said quietly. "To come back here, after all this time."

Althea said nothing, surprised to find tears suddenly clogging the back of her throat. It occurred to her, then, that she'd left the cabin without seeing the room where she'd been held captive, which was the main reason she'd driven out there that morning. But it didn't matter.

At that moment, all she wanted was to put as much distance as possible between herself and this place.

She glanced at her watch. It was barely six-thirty. "What were you doing at my apartment so early anyway?"

"I wanted to let you know what I learned about Suzette Thorndike, bounce some theories off you."

Althea nodded, unlocking the car. "Sounds good. We can discuss it over breakfast—I'm buying."

Damien smiled, slow and sexy. "Works for me."

He held the door open for her. Grinning and shaking her head in resignation, Althea ducked inside the sedan and started the ignition, welcoming the blast of heat that poured into the car, warming her face and hands.

Through the rearview mirror she watched as Damien folded his tall, powerful frame into the driver's side of his SUV. She'd been so preoccupied with escaping from the spooky cabin that she hadn't noticed just how good he looked. He was dressed in a gray turtleneck sweater that clung to his broad chest and dark jeans that hugged his firm, muscled butt. *Yummy.*

As she waited for him to get settled in the SUV, her gaze strayed back to the old cabin. It didn't seem as desolate and menacing now that she was no longer alone. Maybe she'd—

Suddenly Althea tensed, a whisper of unease crawling down her spine as she stared out the window. She could have sworn she saw movement inside the cabin, a shadow that passed in front of the living room window.

She stared intently, not moving or blinking, until her eyes began to sting, forcing her to close them for a few seconds. When she opened them again, there was no boogeyman leering at her from the doorway or wielding a bloody knife. Whatever she thought she'd seen a moment ago was gone.

It's just your overactive imagination, she told herself. *Being inside the cabin, after all these years, was even more unsettling than you thought it would be. Your memories and fears, combined with your overwrought nerves, got the best of you. Besides, girl, you couldn't have seen anything. The windows are all boarded up.*

Althea frowned, fighting a tremor that had nothing to do with the cold.

She knew her mind was probably playing tricks on her. And yet as she pulled off a moment later with Damien following close behind, she couldn't dismiss the prickling sensation that someone else had been inside the cabin with her before Damien arrived.

Someone with sinister intentions.

Someone innately evil.

He watched her leave.

Hidden in the shadows of the old cabin, he watched Althea drive away from the property followed by Damien Wade, who was riding her bumper so hard he ought to be pulled over for tailgating.

The stranger frowned.

Wade was becoming something of a nuisance. First he'd shown up at Althea's apartment last night, and now he'd appeared here, at the remote rural cabin everyone had long since forgotten about. The authorities, the media. Everyone.

Everyone but her.

He had always known she would eventually find her way back to the cabin, back to the place where it had all started. Still, he hadn't expected to see her there so soon, on that particular morning. He'd gone there himself to meditate, guided by the spirit of his predecessor, Anthony Yusef, the visionary who had given him the inspiration for his masterpiece. He was in the middle of praying when he heard a car coming down the road. If he'd been down in the cellar—inside the Sacred Room, where Althea's essence remained—he wouldn't have heard the approaching vehicle. And if he hadn't had the foresight to park in his secret hiding place on the other side of the property, she would have discovered him. And then their reunion would have had an entirely different outcome.

A regrettable outcome.

But by the time she had entered the cabin, he was hidden in an old crawl space that enabled him to observe her, undetected. He'd intended to remain out of sight until she finished what she came there to do and left. But when she had crept downstairs to the cellar, he couldn't resist the overwhelming temptation to follow her. The thought of seeing her in the Sacred Room, a scenario he'd imagined so many times he'd lost count, gave him a rush like nothing he had ever experienced before.

But just as he had reached the doorway to the cellar, he heard the approach of another vehicle outside.

A surge of rage swept through him at the sight of Damien Wade. *Interfering bastard!*

Still, despite the agent's unexpected arrival, he knew he could have taken Althea if he'd really wanted to. He could have taken her the moment she stepped through the door. He could have knocked the gun out of her hand and subdued her with a blow to the back of her head, using her own flashlight. He could have carried her unconscious body out the back door and taken her to his hideout in the woods.

But it was too soon. It wasn't her time yet.

The successful outcome of your plan depends on your patience, he repeated the familiar mantra to himself like a prayer. *It depends on your diligence. Your cunning.*

After all the hard work and meticulous planning that

had gone into bringing his masterpiece to fruition, he would not make the mistake of ruining everything because he was too eager. Because he could not resist temptation.

Because Althea had unwittingly walked right into his path.

He knew it would not be the last time.

And when her time came, there would be no Damien Wade, no cavalry to rescue her.

He smiled inwardly, feeling a deep sense of satisfaction.

Soon enough, Princess.

Soon there will be no one but you.

And then you will have to reckon with me.

Chapter 12

An hour and a half later, Althea was seated beside Damien in a private corner booth in the café where they had stopped for breakfast. The restaurant, located on the outskirts of Baltimore, was abuzz with ringing cash registers and the noisy chatter of morning commuters who'd stopped in to fill up on coffee and fresh-baked goods before braving the traffic.

She and Damien had waited only ten minutes for the corner booth to become available. And then, to further ensure their privacy, they'd sat next to each other with their backs facing the room so that no one could read their lips.

"So you're telling me that Suzette Thorndike's *ex-husband* could be our perp?" Althea asked after Damien brought her up to speed on everything he had learned about Patrick Farris.

Damien nodded, raising his cup of coffee to his mouth. "That's exactly what I'm telling you. Farris has the motive and, according to the NCIC report that was e-mailed to me this morning, he already has a criminal history. In addition to the allegations of sexual abuse cited in the lawsuit by his former patients, he was also charged with three counts of aggravated sexual assault last year—charges that were later dropped by the victim."

Althea frowned. "I hope whatever he paid her was worth it," she muttered grimly. "Not only for herself, but for his next poor, unsuspecting victim."

"Which may be Claire Thorndike." Damien took a long sip of his coffee.

"Do we have a current address for the good doctor?"

"Yeah. He sold the house he once shared with Suzette—too many bad memories, I guess—and now lives all the way out in Solomon's Island. I was thinking about paying him a little visit today. Care to join me?"

"Hell, yeah. Just try to stop me." Althea forked up the last of her ham and cheese omelet and chewed thoughtfully for a moment.

Out of the corner of her eye, she saw Damien studying her profile with a soft, lazy smile. "I can see the wheels turning," he murmured. "What's going through that beautiful head of yours?"

Althea ignored the way her traitorous heart fluttered at his words, just as she'd been forcing herself to ignore his clean male scent and the heat and energy that radiated from his body. The moment he slid into the booth beside her and his knee accidentally brushed hers, making her belly quiver, she'd started having serious doubts about the wisdom of their decision to sit on the same side of the booth. She needed to concentrate on the investigation, but Damien's nearness was threatening her ability to breathe, let alone concentrate.

Belatedly remembering that he'd asked her a question, she said, "I was just wondering about Suzette and Spencer Thorndike. Neither of them mentioned the ex-husband when we asked them if they could think of anyone who would want to hurt Claire. Given the way

Suzette's marriage ended, I would think Farris's name would have made the short list of potential enemies."

Damien nodded, conceding the point. "Maybe they didn't think about him because I asked only about Spencer's enemies," he suggested.

"Still. His name should have come up at least once."

A shadow of cynicism curved Damien's mouth. "Maybe Suzette thinks she's caused him enough pain and suffering. It wasn't bad enough that she bled him dry in the divorce settlement. Maybe she thought implicating him in her stepdaughter's abduction would have added insult to injury."

Althea made a face. "I think you give her more credit than she may deserve. This is a woman who benefited a great deal from her husband's downfall, and within a year of leaving *him,* she was married to a multimillionaire. I don't think she does anything that isn't advantageous to her."

"All right. I'll play along. How does she benefit from not mentioning her ex-husband as a possible suspect in her stepdaughter's abduction?"

"I don't know." Althea pursed her lips, deep in thought for a moment. "What if Suzette and Patrick Farris are in on it together? What if he came to her and threatened to expose some dirty little secret from her past if she didn't agree to help him recoup some of his fortune?"

"Are you suggesting that Farris kidnapped Claire in order to demand a ransom from Spencer Thorndike?"

"I think it's highly possible. I mean, just think about it. It's the perfect revenge. He blackmails his opportunistic ex-wife, causes *her* some pain and suffering, then walks away with a huge chunk of her new husband's money."

Damien frowned. "Whatever dirt he has on Suzette would have to be major enough to convince her to go along with a scheme like that. She has too much to lose. If Spencer finds out that she was involved in his daughter's abduction, she goes to prison *and* he divorces her—assuming he doesn't kill her first. It's a lot for her to risk."

"True, but maybe she can't afford *not* to take the risk. Maybe the alternative—her secret being exposed—is simply not an option for her. We've both learned in our line of work that people will go to extreme lengths to protect their deep, dark secrets and avoid scandal. If Suzette agreed to the kidnapping scheme, she obviously felt she had no other choice. Desperate times call for desperate measures."

Damien said nothing, absently stroking his stubbled chin between his thumb and forefinger as he mulled over her theory. He hadn't shaved that morning, and the shadowed growth on his jaw only added to his raw sex appeal.

Stop it! Althea ordered herself.

Oblivious to her predicament, Damien murmured thoughtfully, "So the question would be, what did Farris recently learn about Suzette? He obviously didn't have any dirt on her during the divorce proceedings, or the outcome would have been a hell of a lot different."

Althea snorted. "Yeah. He would've been able to keep her hands off his money."

Damien slanted her an amused look. "You're pretty hard on Suzette. You don't think she was entitled to *some* compensation after the pain and suffering Farris put *her* through during their marriage? I mean, it couldn't have been easy for her to find out that her husband was sexually abusing his patients. I'm sure she felt betrayed and humiliated, not unlike the wives of these politicians who are brought down by sex scandals. Would you begrudge any of *those* women for leaving their husbands and taking them to the cleaners?"

Althea grinned ruefully. "All right. Point taken. I guess my problem with Suzette is that there seems to be a pattern with her. A pattern of seeking out wealthy men."

Damien chuckled dryly. "Why are you dancing around the word? Just come right out and say it. You think she's a gold digger."

"Fine. I think she's a gold digger. And when it comes to those types I don't put anything past them. Hell, for all we know, Suzette might have *paid* her ex-husband to take Claire off her hands—permanently."

"Anything's possible," Damien said. But Althea could tell by his expression that he still wasn't sold on the idea of Suzette Thorndike being their prime suspect. He added, "I'll dig even deeper into her background, see if I trip over any skeletons."

Althea nodded and took a sip of her lukewarm coffee. "I should be hearing back from the MyDomain folks in a few hours—it's still early on the West Coast. I'm eager to learn the identity of COLTRANEFAN. With any luck, *he's* the mystery date we've been looking for."

"We should be so lucky." Damien glanced at his watch. "Detective Mayhew's supposed to call me this morning to let me know what they found on Claire's computer. That might give us some clues to work with as well."

"I hope so," Althea murmured. "We need all the help we can get."

Damien said nothing, the grim expression on his face mirroring what she was thinking. Claire had been gone for nearly five days now, and so far they had no viable leads and no suspects. The countdown had begun, and time was their enemy. Twenty-four was the magic number. If the missing person wasn't found in the first twenty-four hours, the odds against finding the victim went up with every passing minute.

But you were found, Althea reminded herself. *You were*

missing for thirty days, and just when you had given up hope of making it out of that cabin alive, you were rescued.

She only prayed that Claire would be as lucky.

"You haven't touched your cinnamon roll."

Althea glanced at the saucer to her right, where a large cinnamon bun slathered with creamy icing beckoned enticingly to her. She groaned. "Oh God. What was I thinking, ordering *that* on top of an omelet?"

Damien grinned. "Don't feel bad. Very few people who walk in here can resist getting one of those cinnamon rolls."

"I couldn't possibly eat the whole thing by myself. Want half?"

Damien shrugged. "Sure, why not? I could use a good sugar rush to get the juices flowing."

"Long night?" Althea asked, using a knife to cut the large cinnamon bun in half.

"You could say that."

Althea took her half, then passed the saucer to him. *"Bon appétit."* She bit into the soft pastry and let out a deep, languorous moan. "Oh my God. That is *sooo* good."

"Most definitely," Damien agreed around a smiling mouthful.

Althea shook her head in amazement. "I think this is the best cinnamon roll I've ever had in my life. Damn, there goes my diet," she complained.

Damien chuckled, polishing off his half and reaching for a napkin to wipe his sticky fingers. "You don't need to be on a diet, anyway."

She laughed. "How would you—" She broke off mid-sentence, heat suffusing her cheeks at the memory of Friday night. "Never mind."

Damien gave her a soft, knowing smile before murmuring, "You've got a little icing on the corner of your mouth."

Althea ran her tongue back and forth across her lips. "Did I get it?"

He shook his head, his eyes darkening. "Here, let me help you."

Her pulse quickened as he reached over, using the pad of his thumb to gently wipe the corner of her mouth. Then, holding her gaze, he licked the dab of icing off his thumb. Her nipples tingled, and her insides quivered.

"There," he said huskily. "All gone."

Althea swallowed hard. "Thanks."

They gazed at each other for a long, charged moment that was interrupted by a coolly amused feminine voice. "Well, isn't *this* cozy?"

Althea felt Damien tense as they turned in unison to stare at the gorgeous woman who had materialized at their table. She appeared to be African American, with a strong trace of Indian ancestry. Five foot seven, early thirties, glossy dark hair that hung past her shoulders, and an hourglass body poured into a Baby Phat knit jumper dress.

The moment Althea saw her, she knew who she was.

"Hello, Damien," the woman said, but she was staring at Althea, her light brown eyes narrowed in shrewd speculation. "Aren't you going to introduce me to your friend?"

Damien said evenly, "Angelique, I'd like you to meet one of my colleagues, Althea Pritchard. Althea, this is Angelique Navarro, India's mother."

The ex-wife.

Althea smiled politely. "Nice to meet you."

"Likewise," Angelique murmured, her mouth curving in a smile that was more predatory than friendly. "How long have you and my ex worked together?"

"Not very long. Today's our second day together."

"Really? Well, you seem to be getting along quite

well," Angelique observed, looking meaningfully at the empty space across from them. She seemed to be waiting for one or both of them to explain why they were sharing the same side of the booth. When no explanation was forthcoming, her lips thinned with displeasure.

Damien glanced pointedly at his watch. "Aren't you going to be late for work?" he said. "It's almost eight-thirty."

Angelique didn't take the hint. "Oh, I'll get there when I get there," she said with a dismissive wave of her manicured hand. "Now that I've been promoted to communications manager, I can pretty much come and go as I please."

Damien looked vaguely annoyed by her obvious reluctance to leave him and Althea alone. "Angelique works at a professional membership association downtown," he informed Althea, who nodded without comment.

"Damien and I met in college," Angelique volunteered. "We were both journalism majors, so we took a lot of the same classes. He was a little shy back then, so I had to make the first move, even though I'd caught him checking me out several times. He claimed he would've eventually worked up the nerve to ask me out, but I wasn't taking any chances. There were too many other vultures circling." She smiled sweetly at Althea. "Know what I mean?"

Althea didn't miss the implication or the veiled warning behind the words. "I do know what you mean," she said, cool and composed. She flashed the other woman a smile etched in steel. "Gotta watch out for those vultures."

"Exactly."

Damien's expression darkened. "We should be heading back to the office," he said to Althea.

She nodded, reaching for her purse. "I'm ready whenever you are."

He rose from the table, removed a ten-dollar bill from

his wallet, and dropped it on the table to cover the tip. For a moment, as he stood beside Angelique, Althea could see what an attractive couple they made, with his dark good looks and her exotic beauty. Her stomach twisted at the thought, for reasons she didn't care to examine.

As she slid to the end of the seat, Damien reached down and helped her gently to her feet. The proprietary gesture did not go unnoticed by Angelique. Her eyes narrowed as a cold, territorial gleam filled them.

She turned suddenly to Damien. "I don't know whether or not India told you about the homecoming dinner for parents that's coming up in a couple of weeks. It's something the school came up with this year, as a way to get more parents and families involved in the homecoming festivities. India would really like for both of us to attend the dinner with her."

Damien nodded briefly. "She didn't mention it, but I'll talk to her this evening and get more details."

"But you *will* come, right?"

"I have to check my schedule and get back to you."

"All right. I know it would mean a lot to our daughter to have us there together, like old times." Angelique gave him a soft, winsome smile and stopped just short of batting her eyelashes.

Damien looked down at her, deadpan, a solitary muscle bunching in his jaw. "I have to go, Angelique."

"Of course," she purred in a voice like oiled silk. "I don't want to hold you up. I know you have important cases to get to." She turned to Althea with another one of those saccharine smiles. "It was a pleasure meeting you, Aretha."

Althea didn't bother correcting her. She knew the mistake had been deliberate, and she wouldn't give the other woman the satisfaction of knowing she'd gotten under her skin. In more ways than one.

But as she and Damien walked out of the crowded café a few minutes later, she muttered under her breath, "From now on, just call me the queen of soul."

Damien gave a low, mirthless chuckle. "Sorry about that."

"You don't have to apologize. I'm a big girl—I can handle it. Besides, you're not responsible for her actions."

But as Damien helped Althea into her car—while a fuming Angelique looked on from the doorway of the restaurant—Althea realized that the other woman had just given her yet another reason not to become romantically involved with Damien. Between the kidnapping investigation and her ongoing battle to reclaim control of her life, the last thing she needed was the drama of dealing with a jealous, vindictive ex-wife.

Damien couldn't pinpoint the exact moment he'd decided he had to have Althea again.

As of yesterday morning, he'd been in full agreement with her that their one-night stand had to remain just that—a one-night stand. When he told her about his policy against dating colleagues, he hadn't been lying. He'd never dated anyone who worked for the Bureau, although not for lack of opportunities. Over the last seven years he'd received his fair share of propositions, but he'd never been tempted enough to break his own rule about keeping his professional life separate from his personal life.

Until now.

Until Althea.

He wanted her like no other woman he'd ever wanted

before. And the more he told himself he couldn't have her, the more he wanted her. Craved her.

Damn it all to hell.

Just what he needed at this time in his life. A craving.

In the aftermath of his disastrous marriage and the devastating custody battle that resulted in India being taken away from him, Damien had had to work overtime to put the shattered pieces of his life back together. Literally. He'd thrown himself into his job with a ferocity, a single-minded focus that earned him a reputation for being "intense" and "brooding." His family worried constantly about him, convinced that his obsession with his cases rendered him incapable of coping with the reality of his own dysfunctional life. And they were right. Hunting criminals gave him the perfect excuse to escape into the minds of others—others who had far more problems than *he* did.

For giving his all to the Bureau, he was rewarded with the respect of his peers and supervisors, who doled out letters of commendation and put him in charge of various task forces. But the price he nearly paid for being a workaholic was the loss of his daughter—again. After missing three court-appointed visits with India due to work, Damien realized he was in serious danger of causing irreparable damage to the relationship he'd spent years cultivating with his daughter. He had to step back and reassess his priorities, and in the process, he'd learned to stop using his job to anesthetize the pain and anger that had consumed him during the course of his disastrous marriage and in the ensuing custody battle.

Over the last two years he'd finally gotten his life under some semblance of control. His relationship with India was stronger than ever, and although his family still accused him of being a workaholic, he'd at least developed an internal mechanism that warned him when he'd reached his limit, when he was dangerously close to crossing the line between duty and obsession.

Which was why Althea Pritchard posed such a problem.

A woman like Althea had the power to drive a man to the point of obsession. Look at him. He'd spent most of the night camped outside her apartment, lurking in the dark like some stalker. He'd gone home only to grab a few hours of sleep and take a shower. When he returned to her apartment and found her car gone, he'd panicked, fearing that something terrible had happened to her. Once he picked up her vehicle on the radar and he realized where she was headed, his fear doubled. He went after her, trying not to imagine the worst, that she'd been kidnapped by the same sadistic predator who took Claire Thorndike, a psycho who planned to reenact Althea's abduction by returning her to the place where she'd been held captive.

The relief Damien felt when Althea burst from the cellar, shaken but unharmed, was unlike anything he'd ever felt before. He never wanted to let her out of his sight again.

Which was crazy.

He had no proof to substantiate his belief that her life was in danger. He had a list that drew some uncanny, disturbing parallels between two abduction cases. And he had a gut instinct that warned him something was not right. Neither would be enough to convince Althea to remove herself from the case.

But he sure as hell intended to try.

What do you expect her to do? his conscience mocked. *Go into hiding until Claire is found—dead or alive?*

Damien frowned, switching lanes. Actually, that wasn't such a bad idea. He wished he could somehow talk Althea into taking a leave of absence and laying low for a while, but he knew she'd never agree to such a suggestion, and, quite frankly, he didn't have a right to expect her to just because they'd slept together.

But his reasons for wanting her off the case were perfectly legit. Not only was she risking her life by remaining involved in the case, but her presence was a distraction to him. The time and energy he spent worrying about her safety were time and energy that should be spent on the investigation. With a young girl's life at stake, he couldn't afford any distractions. He had a job to do, and if Althea was the intended victim of an unknown predator—as he suspected—he had to keep his perspective.

He was so absorbed in his thoughts that he didn't realize he'd cut off another driver until he heard the testy blast of a horn behind him.

"My bad," he muttered, even as Althea's amused voice echoed in his head. *Has anyone ever told you that you drive like you're the only one on the road?*

Glancing in his rearview mirror, Damien saw that she had fallen several car lengths behind him, which meant she'd probably missed his near collision. Good. He didn't need another lecture from her about his reckless driving skills.

As he hung a right at the next intersection, his cell phone trilled. He picked it up and answered brusquely, "Wade."

"Agent Wade, this is Detective Mayhew. I promised to let you know what we found on Claire's computer."

"Go for it."

"Nothing unusual on her hard drive. Miscellaneous stuff like school reports and projects, photos, downloaded music, favorite videos, movies, YouTube clips. As for her Internet activity, she visited many of the same sites the average teenager would—MyDomain, Facebook, popular music download sites, online fashion magazines, the American Idol Fan Site, the Web sites of various colleges and universities. No porn, Daddy Dearest will be happy to know."

"That's reassuring," Damien said. One of the telltale warning signs that a minor may have had contact with an online sex predator was the discovery of pornography on the child's computer.

"She bookmarked a ton of sites," the detective continued, "but there was only one that raised a red flag. It was a local private detective agency. Charm City Investigations. Seems that Claire visited the Web site two weeks before she disappeared."

Damien frowned. "Why would Claire need the services of a private investigator?" he wondered aloud.

"That's what I intend to find out. I'm heading over there now to speak to the owner. Why don't you meet me there? I might need you to throw your weight around in case this guy tries to play hardball about client confidentiality, yada yada. He might not talk to a cop, but he'll sing to a fed."

Damien chuckled dryly. "I'll meet you there. We can play good cop/bad cop. What's the address?"

Mayhew rattled off the information, then said, "Before I forget, in case you were thinking about talking to Josh Reed anytime soon, forget about it."

"Why?"

"The kid's lawyered up," Mayhew grumbled in disgust. "The attorney went over my head and called the commissioner first thing this morning. It seems that someone leaked to the press that we'd questioned Reed as a possible suspect, and now he's receiving threatening phone calls and being harassed by reporters. The lawyer said the next time we go anywhere near his client, we'd better be serving an arrest warrant, 'cause the kid won't be granting any more interviews. Period."

"Shit," Damien muttered under his breath. He was afraid something like that would happen. The media's involvement in kidnapping cases always provided a mixed bag of blessings and curses. On one hand their nonstop coverage helped the authorities disseminate important information to the public, which occasionally led to crucial breaks in cases. On the other hand, in their eagerness to get the scoop and trump their competitors, media outlets had a penchant for releasing sensitive details to the public that compromised investigations. Damien had experienced the utter frustration of watching a trail go cold because the perpetrator went deep underground after being tipped off by a news report.

Still, he couldn't help thinking that Josh Reed's haste to secure legal representation didn't exactly bolster his claims of innocence. Maybe Althea was right. Maybe the kid *was* hiding something.

"What about the girlfriend?" Damien asked. "Brandi Duplantis. Is she lawyered up, too?"

Mayhew snorted. "Not yet, but give her time. The day's still young. Besides, there's no point in talking to her again. She and her mother already vouched for Reed's whereabouts on Friday night. Push them too hard and they *will* get a lawyer."

Damien frowned. He knew the detective was right. "Any red flags come up on the cell phone records?"

"Nope. The last call Claire made was to her best friend Heather Warner on Friday morning. Heather says they often spoke to each other before school to find out what the other was wearing, a practice that started a few years ago when they both showed up to school one day wearing the exact same outfit. *Like, oh my God!*" Mayhew exclaimed in a perfect mimicry of a scandalized teenage girl.

Damien laughed. "Hey, that's not bad."

The detective chuckled dryly. "I've got two teenage daughters. I hear them yakking in my damn sleep. Anyway, the last call Claire received on her cell phone was on Friday afternoon. It was her gynecologist's office, calling to confirm her appointment on Monday morning. We're still going through the phone records, but so far everything's checking out." He let out a deep, ragged sigh of frustration. "I gotta tell you. If Claire *was* meeting someone that night, she sure as hell did a good job of covering her tracks."

"Maybe. Maybe not," Damien murmured, thinking about COLTRANEFAN. After Althea went home last night, he'd called Mayhew to let him know about the cryptic message left on Claire's MyDomain page. The detective, an eighteen-year veteran on the force who'd seen and heard just about everything, wasn't terribly optimistic about this particular clue leading to a break in the investigation.

As Damien hung up the phone and made an illegal U-turn to head back in the direction he'd just come from, Althea's earlier words about COLTRANEFAN echoed through his mind. *With any luck, he's the mystery date we've been looking for.*

Amen to that, Damien thought grimly. *We need all the luck we can get.*

Chapter 13

At ten-thirty A.M., Althea received the phone call she'd been waiting for.

"The user's name is James Odem," the MyDomain representative began without preamble. There was no trace of hostility in his voice over the way he'd been bullied into violating a client's privacy; he now sounded eager to cooperate and be a good citizen. "He's a forty-seven-year-old neurosurgeon from Baltimore. He created the account on September 5 and closed it a month later, on October 4."

"What time?" Althea interrupted, taking notes. "What time did he close the account on Saturday?"

"Ten-twenty A.M. Eastern standard time."

The morning after Claire was taken from her home. "What's the process for closing an account? Does it take long?"

"Not at all. Less than five minutes. All you have to do is log in to your page, click on the link that says Home, go to Account Settings, and select Cancel Account. You're directed to another page where you have to confirm your choice to cancel the account. Once that's done, the profile is deleted."

"Are users asked to complete a survey whenever they close an account?"

"Yes. It's a quick questionnaire that helps us identify areas of improvement and keep track of the number of users who may be switching over to our competitors."

"Did Dr. Odem fill out the survey?"

"According to our records, no, he did not. But he doesn't have to. It's on a voluntary basis."

"What can you tell me about his account activity? Did he update the page very often? Did he have a lot of friends?"

"He logged in to the account every day, usually in the evenings between the hours of nine and eleven P.M. He updated the page once a week."

"With photos?" Althea asked hopefully. "A new blog entry?"

"No. There was no blog, and there were no photos of Dr. Odem on the page. He had a very clean, basic layout that included a slideshow of John Coltrane's album covers. His page was more or less devoted to the works of Coltrane. He added a new song every week. As for friends, he only had ten, and most of these were pages devoted to other jazz musicians. He did have one friend that he corresponded with on a regular basis." There was a brief pause. "It was Claire Thorndike, the missing girl from the news."

Althea found herself moving to the edge of her chair. "How often did he and Claire correspond?"

On the other end, she heard papers rustling before the rep answered, "Pretty often. At least three times a week. It looks like Dr. Odem deleted all comments and messages on the page before closing his account."

The son of a bitch was trying to cover his tracks. "Is there any way you can retrieve all of the messages to and from Claire?"

There was a slight hesitation. "I have to check with Legal. I could be wrong, but you might need a court order to obtain message transcripts. You know—privacy issues, FOIA, and all that."

"I don't have time to get a court order," Althea said quietly. "A teenage girl is missing, and the key to her disappearance may lie in the contents of those messages. Your competitors have always worked cooperatively with law enforcement. I hope we can expect the same from you."

There was a long, nerve-stretching pause. "It may take a few more hours. We're having some technical issues with our server. But, yeah, I should be able to get those messages for you. Hopefully by close of business."

"Good. That would be very helpful. Could you also send me a screenshot of Odem's page?"

"Sure. No problem."

"Let me give you my fax number." After rattling off the number, Althea asked, "When was the last time Dr. Odem sent a message to Claire?"

"Umm . . . Thursday, October 2. At 10:35 P.M."

The day before she disappeared. "Did she respond?"

"Doesn't look like it."

"All right. Thanks for your time and cooperation."

"I hope it helps."

"You and me both," Althea muttered, her nerve endings humming with excitement.

As she hung up the phone, she glanced over her cubicle wall and saw Damien striding purposefully toward her. He nodded briefly to the greetings that were called out to him by other agents in the bull pen, but his gaze never wavered from Althea. The determined set of his jaw and the glittering triumph in his dark eyes told her he was on to something.

Something big.

Her pulse quickened with anticipation. "I just got off the phone with the rep from MyDomain," she said, swiveling around just as Damien reached her cubicle. "He gave me the 411 on COLTRANEFAN. His name is James Odem, and he's a neurosurgeon from Baltimore. But something tells me you already know that."

Damien nodded, grabbing the visitor chair and nimbly straddling it. "Two weeks ago, Claire paid a visit to the owner of Charm City Investigations. She hired him to run a background check on a man she'd recently met online. She wanted to make sure he was who he said he was before she agreed to meet him in person. Everything checked out. His job, his credit, his home address, and, most important, he had no criminal record."

"So Claire and Odem set up a date," Althea concluded. "On Friday night. While her parents were out of town."

"Looks that way."

"At least she had the sense to get him checked out."

Damien grimaced. "For all the good it might have done her. The P.I. said Claire seemed a little uneasy about the whole thing, kept saying she'd never done anything this risky before, hooking up with strangers online. Before she left the detective agency, she joked that if anything happened to her, the P.I. would know who was responsible. As soon as Mayhew and I walked through the door and showed him her photo, he turned white as a damn sheet. I think that's the only reason he cooperated with us—he felt guilty."

Althea scowled. "Apparently not guilty enough to come forward when he first heard about the kidnapping," she groused. "Damn it. Aren't there laws prohibiting private investigators from taking on clients younger than eighteen?"

Damien gave her a wry look. "Not in the state of Maryland. And I don't know of any P.I.s who would turn down a paying customer, especially one wearing designer clothes and pulling out a wad of dough from a $10,000 Hermès purse. Anyway, the police are bringing Odem in for questioning. I thought you'd want to ride with me to the station. On the way there, you can fill me in on your conversation with the MyDomain folks."

Althea was already reaching for her jacket. "Let's go."

Dr. James Odem was a reasonably attractive black man in his late forties with close-cropped hair sprinkled with gray, a neat goatee that framed thin unsmiling lips, and fathomless dark eyes that betrayed no emotion as he sat at a table in the main interrogation room, his long, lean hands folded calmly in his lap. He wore a well-cut blazer, pleated gabardine trousers, and Gucci loafers that gleamed under the room's bright fluorescent lighting. He was medium height with a trim, athletic build he'd probably honed at some exclusive fitness club.

He seemed more annoyed than nervous at the prospect of being questioned by the police about his possible involvement in a high-profile kidnapping. While he waited to be joined by Detective Mayhew and Damien— who'd deliberately kept him waiting while they, along with Althea, observed him from the other side of the one-way mirror—Odem consulted his Rolex watch, heaving an impatient sigh every three minutes.

Damien disliked the man on sight.

And he could tell, by the way Odem watched him enter the room, that the feeling was mutual.

Damien stood with his shoulder propped against the wall and his arms folded across his chest in a decidedly negligent pose, while Mayhew sat down at the table opposite their suspect. The detective was a stocky man of medium height with craggy features, shrewd blue eyes that crinkled at the corners when he smiled—which was rarely—and graying brown hair that seemed perpetually mussed. He wore dark slacks, a cheap pinstriped tie, and a rumpled sport coat that fit him a little too snugly across the shoulders.

"How long is this going to take?" Odem demanded, addressing Mayhew. "I'm due in surgery in three hours."

"It's up to you how long this interview lasts," the detective answered blandly. "If you're forthcoming with us, then we don't have to spend all day in here. And if it's all the same to you, Doc, I'd just as soon not do that. It doesn't take long for this room to start heating up like a fucking sauna—pardon my French—and I don't know about you, but I've never cared for those damn things. Of course," he added with a self-deprecating grin, "on my salary, this room in the middle of summer is the closest thing to a sauna that I can afford."

Odem offered a thin, condescending smile. "Please spare me the inane small talk, Detective. I don't need to be lulled into a false sense of security with your overworked-underpaid-public-servant-just-doing-my-job routine. Just get to your questions so that I can be on my way."

"Touché," Mayhew muttered, pretending to be affronted as he withdrew a mini-cassette recorder from the breast pocket of his rumpled sport coat and set it down on the table. "Just trying to be hospitable. Oops. No pun intended."

Damien chuckled softly, drawing Odem's gaze back to him. There was something in the other man's dark eyes that put him on edge—a glimmer of malice tinged with something else, something indefinable.

Had they met before? Damien wondered. He'd never stepped foot inside Mercy Harbor, the local hospital where Odem worked as an attending physician, and they sure as hell didn't travel in the same social circles. So why did he get the uncanny feeling that Odem recognized him?

As Damien returned the surgeon's silent gaze, a ghost of a smile played at the corners of Odem's mouth. As if he were privy to a joke Damien wasn't.

What the hell?

"All right, gentlemen. Let's begin, shall we?" With a dramatic flourish Mayhew leaned across the table; clicked on the recorder; then stated the names of everyone in the room, the date, and the time.

"Dr. Odem, the reason we brought you in for questioning this morning was so that we could learn more about the nature of your online relationship with Claire Thorndike, who, as you know, has been missing since Friday. We understand that over the last month, the two of you have corresponded regularly via MyDomain."

"That's correct," Odem said evenly. "Miss Thorndike and I met online about a month ago. She was learning about John Coltrane at school, for her music appreciation class. She happened to stumble across my page one day while surfing the Internet, and she left a comment telling me how informative the page was, and how much she enjoyed it. Naturally I responded, thanking her for the feedback. She wrote back immediately, and as we began communicating, we realized we had a lot in common."

"You did realize, of course, that you were 'communicating' with a seventeen-year-old girl," Damien drawled sardonically.

"Of course I knew," Odem said coolly. "But the last time I checked, Agent Wade, there are no laws against socializing online. That's why they're called social networking sites."

"Is that all you and Claire were doing?" Damien asked softly. "Socializing?"

"Of course. Claire was interested in learning more about John Coltrane. I happen to consider myself a Coltrane aficionado. Claire also told me she planned to become a doctor. Again, this was an area I felt I could be of some assistance to her."

"It sounds like you had quite a lot to teach Little Miss Thorndike," Mayhew observed. "You were developing something of a mentor–mentee relationship."

"You could say that. Claire is an extremely bright, ambitious young lady. It was refreshing to encounter such intelligence and poise in one so young. I told her she would make an excellent doctor one day."

"Assuming she gets that chance," Mayhew murmured. Odem said nothing. His face was expressionless.

"Did Claire ever suggest that the two of you should meet in person?" the detective asked.

"As a matter of fact, she did. After we'd been corresponding for two weeks, she hinted that maybe I could give her a tour of the newly remodeled surgery wing at Mercy Harbor. She said that might help her decide on a specialty to pursue."

"And how did you respond to her suggestion?"

"I told her that since her father's generous endowments over the years had made the new wing possible, she could probably ask him to arrange a private tour of the entire hospital, if she wanted."

"You knew that Spencer Thorndike had donated money to the hospital?" Damien interjected.

Odem looked over at him. "Of course. He's one of our biggest donors." He paused. "There's not an employee at Mercy Harbor who doesn't know that."

Damien held his gaze for a moment, then shrugged dispassionately. "Maybe. Maybe not."

There was a barely perceptible tightening of Odem's lips, but he didn't respond.

"Why didn't you want to give Claire a tour of the surgery wing?" Mayhew asked.

Odem pulled his gaze from Damien to look at the detective. "I didn't think Claire was really interested in a tour," he said.

Mayhew arched a brow. "You thought she was only using that as an excuse to hook up with you?"

"That's correct. My suspicion was confirmed a day later when she came right out and asked me if we could meet sometime. She said she'd really enjoyed getting to know me online, and she thought it would be nice if we could get together in person."

"And what did you say?"

Odem looked Mayhew in the eye. "I told her I wasn't comfortable with that."

"Why not?" the detective pressed, sounding vaguely amused. "Because you didn't *want* to meet her, or because you were afraid you'd wind up the victim of some *Dateline* sting operation?"

Odem smiled grimly. "You must think I'm stupid, Detective. I'm well aware that the legal age of consent in Maryland is sixteen. You and I both know that if I had wanted to meet Claire, I wouldn't have been breaking any laws."

"Then why were you uncomfortable about meeting her?"

"I had my reasons."

"That's not an answer."

Silence fell over the table as the two men stared at each other. After a moment, Odem let out a measured sigh between his teeth. "If you must know," he said, seeming to choose his words with care, "I was concerned that Claire was developing feelings for me."

Mayhew exchanged meaningful looks with Damien. "What kind of feelings?" the detective asked.

Odem frowned in exasperation. "Do I have to spell out everything for you, Detective?"

Mayhew chuckled dryly. "Afraid so. *You're* the brain surgeon in the room, not me."

"Fine. I believed Claire was falling in love with me."

"Did she tell you that?"

"Not in so many words, but I knew what was happening. She told me constantly how much she admired me, how special I was becoming to her. She said the highlight of her day was coming home and reading messages from me." He pursed his lips for a moment. "Claire is a very sensitive, misunderstood young woman. Despite how wealthy her father is, and no matter how many expensive gifts he showers upon her, what she craves more than anything is attention. I don't think Spencer Thorndike realizes just how lonely his daughter is, how starved for affection and approval."

Mayhew grinned, leaning back in his chair. "Hey, that's pretty good, Doc. For a second there you really had me thinking I was talking to my old shrink."

Odem's lips compressed in an expression of disgust. "You asked me to explain myself," he said tersely, "and then you ridicule my response?"

"I'm not ridiculing you, Doc," Mayhew said, holding up his hands in mock surrender. "No, sir. I wouldn't dream of it. I can definitely understand how Claire might have become infatuated with you. A smart, successful, good-looking doctor who took such an interest in her life, her dreams, her goals. If what you say about her is true—that she craved attention—then it's no wonder she wanted to meet you in person. It sounds like you were giving her all the attention, affection, and approval her father wasn't. You're, what, thirty years older than her? Maybe she saw you as a father figure."

"Perhaps," Odem murmured, but something in his expression conveyed his displeasure with the notion.

"So what you're telling us," Damien drawled, "is that you never agreed to meet Claire in person? The two of you weren't planning to get together on the night she disappeared?"

Odem met his gaze unflinchingly. "No. We weren't."

"Then why did she tell her best friend otherwise?" Damien lied with a straight face.

The surgeon didn't so much as blink. "I can't imagine why Claire would have told her best friend something like that, because it wasn't true. We never made any plans to meet."

"So you had no problem chatting with her online, but you drew the line at meeting her in person?"

"That's right."

"And how did Claire feel about that? Did she get angry? Did she think you were rejecting her by refusing to meet her?"

Odem hesitated. "She may have felt that way. The tone of her next two messages to me was noticeably cooler, briefer. She didn't say she was upset, but I could sense it."

"Did that give you second thoughts about seeing her?" Mayhew asked.

"No. But it did make me wonder whether or not I should continue our online correspondence."

"Is that why you closed your MyDomain account?"

"That was a big part of the reason, yes," Odem admitted, with a look of mild discomfiture. "The other reason was that I didn't have as much time to update the page, and I was beginning to receive a lot of unwanted friend requests. I just decided it wasn't for me anymore."

"So you intended to stop corresponding with Claire altogether. Just like that. Cold turkey."

"Yes. MyDomain was the only means by which we communicated. We didn't exchange e-mail addresses or phone numbers, if that's what you're asking."

"We know. We already checked her computer, and there are no e-mails to or from you on any of her personal accounts." Damien paused. "Did you tell Claire you were deleting your MyDomain page?"

"I told her I was thinking about it, but I didn't feel it was necessary to go into all the reasons."

"You wanted to spare her feelings."

"You could say that."

"When was the last time you sent a message to her?"

"Wednesday, I believe. In the evening."

Damien waited a beat. "Are you sure?"

Odem held his gaze for a prolonged moment, then shrugged dismissively. "It could have been Thursday. I'm not sure. I've been on a grueling surgical rotation at the hospital, so the days tend to run together for me." He paused. "Now that I think about it, yes, it was Thursday. Around ten-thirty."

"Did Claire respond to your message?"

"No, she didn't."

"How did you think she would react on Saturday morning when she went to your page and saw that it was gone?" Damien probed.

"I didn't give it too much thought, to be honest with you. I assumed she would understand since I'd already told her I was thinking about deleting the profile." Odem glanced at his watch and frowned. "Is this going to take much longer?"

"Just a few more questions, Doc," Mayhew chimed in, clasping his hands on the table as he leaned forward in his chair. "Where were you on the night of October 3 between the hours of five-thirty P.M. and two A.M.?"

"At home. I left the hospital at seven-thirty, stopped at the store to pick up a few things, then went home, where I remained for the rest of the night."

"Can anyone vouch for that?"

"I don't know, Detective," Odem said levelly. "I'm single and I live alone, and my neighbors know I work long, crazy hours. It was Friday night. Most of them had probably gone out for the evening. If I had known I would need an alibi, believe me, I would have made plans with someone or volunteered for another shift at the hospital. As it was, all I wanted to do when I got home was take a long, hot shower and crawl into bed. And that's exactly what I did."

"You didn't make or receive any phone calls? Get on the Internet?"

"No."

How convenient, Damien thought. "There's something else I've been wondering about, Dr. Odem. Maybe you can clear it up for me. I noticed that on Claire's My-Domain page, all comments and messages from you had been deleted from her file. It was almost as if she was going out of her way to make sure no one found out about your correspondence. What do you have to say about that?"

"Nothing. I can't speak for Claire. I won't presume to know her reasons for deleting my messages. She told me her father had the password to her account. Maybe she thought he'd get the wrong idea if he read the messages."

Mayhew snorted out a laugh. "*I* sure as hell would. No offense, Doc, but there are a lot of perverts prowling around on the Internet. If I found out one of my teenage daughters was getting real friendly with some guy she met online—a guy who's thirty years older than her—you'd better believe I'd get the wrong fucking idea. And then I'd get my twelve-gauge shotgun and go hunting for the son of a bitch. But, hey, that's just me."

Odem smiled narrowly. "I suppose I should consider myself lucky that Spencer Thorndike hasn't come hunting for me."

"Not yet, anyway." Damien regarded the surgeon in silence for a moment, his head tipped thoughtfully to one side. "Aren't you wondering how we found you if Claire dutifully deleted all her messages to and from you?"

Odem said nothing.

Damien smiled. "She left one message, dated September 19. She must have forgotten to delete it, or maybe she left it there on purpose, as a clue for the police should anything happen to her. It was a brief message. Cryptic. Almost deliberately so, my partner noted. You said, 'I hope you liked it.' That was it. Do you remember what that was about?"

"Of course," Odem said smoothly. "I had recommended a Coltrane song for Claire to listen to. 'Equinox,' one of my personal favorites. I told her to download the song and listen to it. I sent her a message later that evening telling her I hoped she liked it." A slow smile reeking of arrogance spread across his face. "I'm afraid it was nothing more sinister than that, Agent Wade. Sorry to disappoint you."

Damien lifted one shoulder in a nonchalant shrug. "I had to ask. It seemed odd that it was the only message we could find from you." He pushed off the wall and slowly wandered over to the table. "I'm sure you've figured out by now that we're still waiting to receive the message transcripts from MyDomain. And I'm sure you also know that although your account is closed and Claire deleted her messages from you, the company's technicians are able to pull them off their server. I assume the transcripts will corroborate everything you've told us today about your online relationship with Claire."

Odem met his gaze evenly. "I don't expect any surprises."

Because you've made sure there won't be any, you smug son of a bitch.

Damien decided it was time to play their ace in the hole. "One more thing before you leave, Dr. Odem."

Very calmly and deliberately, Odem tipped his head back slightly to look up at Damien. He wore a bland, superior expression, as if he were bored with the entire interview. Mr. Cool. Mr. Untouchable.

We'll see about that.

Damien said silkily, "Are you aware that two weeks before she disappeared, Claire hired a private investigator to run a background check on you?"

Odem stiffened. For one brief, unguarded moment Damien saw shock, fear, and the anger of betrayal darken the other man's gaze before the impenetrable mask slid back into place. But by then it was too late.

Damien knew he had him.

"I take it you didn't know about the private investigator," he murmured.

"Obviously not." Odem pursed his lips in disapproval. "I have no idea why Claire would have hired someone to run a background check on me."

"Don't you?"

"No, I don't."

"That's odd. Because she told the P.I. she was supposed to be meeting you in person, but first she wanted to make sure you didn't have a criminal record or a wife stashed away somewhere." Like a predator stalking its prey, Damien slowly rounded the table, perched a hip against the edge, and crossed his arms. "Come now, Dr. Odem. Do you really expect us to believe Claire would have paid a grand to run a background check on you if she wasn't going to be meeting you?"

Odem held his gaze without blinking. "Clearly I underestimated the level of Claire's infatuation with me. I didn't realize she had become so obsessed with meeting me that she would go to such extreme lengths. Maybe she was hoping she would find something in the background check that she could use to blackmail me into having a relationship with her."

Damien stared at him, incredulous. "Let me get this straight. You're suggesting that Claire Thorndike, the beautiful daughter of a multimillionaire, was so desperate to date you, a doctor she'd met online, that she hired a private investigator to dig up dirt on you. Not for the purpose of protecting herself in case you turned out to be a psycho, but for the purpose of *coercing* you into a relationship with her?"

Across the table, Mayhew shook his head at the ceiling and muttered in disgust, "I've heard some really crazy shit in my time, but this takes the cake."

Odem clenched his jaw. "I've been the victim of a stalker before, a woman who wanted to be with a doctor so bad she wouldn't take no for an answer. She hung around my house late at night and left disturbing messages on my phone."

"Did you report this stalker to the police?" Damien challenged. "Is it on record anywhere?"

"No. When I threatened to press charges, she finally realized I wasn't interested in her and gave up. I never heard from her again. Obviously Claire was more delusional than I thought. That's the only explanation I can provide for her hiring a private detective to run a background check on me."

Damien just stared at him, and Odem stared back, stone-faced and defiant.

In the ensuing silence, a cell phone trilled. With a muffled curse, Detective Mayhew reached inside his breast pocket and dug out his phone. He checked the caller ID, swore a second time, then got up and left the room muttering a gruff apology.

Alone with Odem, Damien straightened from the table and walked around to claim the chair vacated by the detective. Odem eyed him warily as he reached into his back pocket and retrieved a pack of Marlboros.

He held it out to his guest. "Care for a smoke?"

"No, thank you."

"Of course. You probably aren't a smoker. Being a doctor, you know better. Good for you." Damien removed a lighter from his pocket, shook out a cigarette, and lit up. He drew a deep lungful of nicotine and slowly exhaled, watching Odem through twin streams of smoke released through his nostrils. "I quit several years ago, but this case is really starting to do a number on me, know what I mean? I don't think I slept more than an hour last night. I keep going over theories in my head and wondering if I'm missing something that's staring right in my face. It's frustrating as hell."

Odem calmly removed a speck of lint from his trousers. "I wish there was more I could do to help you, Agent Wade, but I'm afraid I've told you everything I know."

"Nah, see, I don't believe that. I think you've been holding out on me, man."

Odem arched a brow but said nothing.

Damien took a long pull on the cigarette and sent a curl of smoke into the air, watching it rise toward the water-stained ceiling before speaking again. "I think you haven't been completely honest about your feelings for Claire Thorndike."

Odem looked vaguely amused. "What makes you think that, Agent Wade?"

"Instincts." He sat forward, leaning across the table to suggest intimacy. "Can we speak off the record for a moment?"

Odem hesitated, darting a glance toward the mirror on the opposite wall. He'd probably watched enough *Law & Order* episodes to know they were being observed.

Damien reached over and clicked off the mini-cassette recorder. "Off the record," he promised.

Odem settled back in his chair, casually crossed his legs, and offered the barest hint of an indulgent smile, prompting Damien to continue.

"I didn't want to say what I'm about to say in front of Detective Mayhew. He's cool and all, and he'd probably swear up and down he doesn't have a racist bone in his body, but you and I both know how it is."

Odem looked bemused. "I'm afraid you've got me at a loss, Agent Wade. We both know how *what* is?"

"You know, how society works. Here you are—an intelligent, sophisticated, highly educated black man, a neurosurgeon at the top of his profession. And yet you know that for all the success you've achieved, there are still those who would look at you and see nothing but the color of your skin. Those are the same people who might work alongside you every day, might even invite you to tee time at their posh country clubs, but they would never, ever welcome you into their families." He leaned back in his chair, propped one big, booted foot on the table and took a slow drag on his cigarette. "I bet you thought about that when you started chatting with Claire. I bet you thought long and hard about how Spencer Thorndike would react if you were introduced to him as Claire's boyfriend. I bet you found yourself wondering what would bother him more—the fact that you're old enough to be her father, or the fact that you're dark enough to be her chauffeur."

Odem said nothing, a solitary muscle leaping in his jaw.

And just like that, Damien knew he'd struck a nerve.

He continued in the same confiding tone, man to man, one brother to another. "I don't have to give you a history lesson, but sometimes it seems that the more things change, the more they stay the same. We both know that the moment the media releases your name and photograph in connection to Claire's disappearance, folks are gonna be whipped into a damn frenzy. 'Black Man Kidnaps Wealthy White Heiress.' Oh, the headlines won't be that blatant, but we both know that's what will be uppermost in people's minds. The fact that you're a brilliant, well-respected surgeon with no priors will be an afterthought. Your race, and Claire's, will become the most important issue in this case. And *that's* why I think you concocted that whole story about Claire becoming obsessed with you. You knew that if you told the truth—that you *did* agree to meet her and you *were* actually at her house on the night she disappeared— you'd become the prime suspect. And given your age *and* your race, you knew you'd be tried and convicted in the court of public opinion before you ever stepped foot in a courtroom. So you're damned if you do, damned if you don't."

Odem skewered Damien with a look. "You're way off base, Agent Wade," he said, coldly and succinctly. "I didn't concoct any story. Everything I told you and Detective Mayhew was the truth. I never met Claire, nor did I have any intention of doing so."

"Do you like women?"

"*Excuse* me? What kind of question is that?"

"I think it's a legitimate one. You're forty-seven years old. No girlfriend. No kids. Never been married." Damien shrugged. "Maybe I *am* barking up the wrong tree. Maybe you're not into women."

Odem cut him a narrow look. "I assure you, Mr. Wade, that I'm very much into women."

"So you're telling me you were never even *tempted* to meet Claire? Not even a little bit?"

"No."

"Come on now," Damien cajoled, settling into his best you-can-trust-me guise. "I've seen the photos on her MyDomain page. Claire's a little hottie. I can definitely see how you might have wanted a piece of that, especially if she was practically throwing it in your face. I don't think anyone would have blamed you for setting up a date with her. I mean, personally, I prefer my women a little older, a little thicker. A little browner. But, hey, to each his own."

Odem stared across the table at him. "Don't presume to know what type of women I like, Agent Wade, just because we travel in different social circles." He flashed a cold, sharp smile. "In fact, it wouldn't surprise me at all to discover that you and I have the *exact* same taste in women."

Damien felt a distinct chill at his words. His eyes narrowed as he regarded the other man in silence. Tension hung thick and heavy between them for several moments.

Abruptly Damien scraped back his chair and rounded the table. Odem eyed him warily as he approached. Bracing one hand on the table, with the cigarette bristling between his fingers, Damien leaned down and brought his mouth close to the doctor's ear. "You've insulted my intelligence by coming in here and feeding me that bullshit about Claire becoming obsessed with you," he said in a low, controlled voice. "I've been patient so far, giving you opportunity after opportunity to come clean. But you've refused, because you think you're smarter than everyone else. But guess what? You're not so smart, Doc. If you were, you would have realized that lying about your relationship with Claire only makes you look guilty of something more, something worse. You may have done a good job of covering your tracks, but that won't be enough to keep me from digging and digging, until I get to the truth about you and Claire. And when I do, motherfucker, your ass is mine. Make no mistake about it."

He drew back and looked into the other man's dark eyes, which were simmering with leashed fury and something else. The veiled promise of retribution.

"Are you finished?" Odem said tightly.

Damien took a long drag on his cigarette and slowly, deliberately, blew a cloud of smoke into Odem's face. "I've only just begun," he murmured.

He watched as Odem surged to his feet and started angrily from the interrogation room.

"Be sure to see Detective Mayhew before you leave," Damien called after him.

Odem left without a backward glance.

Damien chuckled softly, then stubbed out his cigarette on the sole of his boot and dropped the butt in an empty coffee cup before strolling out of the room, whistling cheerfully.

Chapter 14

When James Odem had arrived at the police station for questioning that morning, Althea had taken one look at him and felt a whisper of recognition.

As she watched the interrogation from the other side of the one-way mirror, she'd racked her brain, trying to shake loose a memory of where she may have seen the neurosurgeon before.

She hadn't been home in nearly eight years, which meant she'd missed all the political fundraisers and formal dinners hosted by her aunt and uncle during his election bid for the Senate—events that James Odem might have attended. Years ago she'd gone to Mercy Harbor Hospital to visit a sick relative, but she didn't recall meeting anyone who resembled Dr. Odem. Had he been a guest lecturer for one of her undergraduate premed classes at the University of Maryland? No, she would have remembered something like that.

Yet she knew she'd seen the man *somewhere* before.

But as the interview got underway, she had forgotten about trying to place his face and concentrated on what he was saying. Or, rather, what he *wasn't* saying.

Almost from the moment he had opened his mouth,

it was clear that James Odem was lying. But no matter
how many questions Damien and Detective Mayhew
had thrown at him, or how much pressure they had put
on him, he never broke a sweat. He was as cold as the
steel instruments that were the tools of his trade.

It was only when he and Damien were left alone that
Althea had seen the first crack in his icy facade. She had
watched, both amused and fascinated, as Damien me-
thodically went to work on their suspect, crawling beneath his skin and poking around until he found his
weakness. When Damien had threatened James Odem,
the rage that filled the doctor's eyes was the first real show
of emotion he'd betrayed since the interview began.

Shortly afterward, he'd marched out of the interrogation room without glancing over his shoulder at
Althea, standing at the mirror. As she watched him go,
she felt that same inkling of recognition.

When Damien joined her a minute later, she passed
him a fresh cup of coffee she'd pilfered from a machine
nearby.

"Good work," she told him. "He needed to be knocked
off his pedestal, smug bastard. Blowing the smoke in
his face was a nice touch."

Damien flashed a crooked grin. "You liked that, huh?"

"Yeah. How long ago did you quit smoking?"

"Never started. Little interrogation tactic I picked up
my first year in the Bureau. Works best on arrogant
pricks with superiority complexes." He took a sip of his
coffee and grimaced. "God, that's awful. And I thought
our brew back at the office was bad."

Althea grinned. "I wouldn't know. Haven't had the
pleasure of tasting it yet." She sobered after a moment.
"I think you were dead-on about Odem's reasons for
lying about his relationship with Claire. I think he did
realize he'd become the prime suspect if he admitted

he was supposed to meet her that night. But does that mean he kidnapped her?"

"Not necessarily. But as I told him, if he lies about one thing, you gotta wonder what else he's lying about."

Althea agreed. "I'm hoping to have the message transcripts from MyDomain before the close of business. We can go through them together, see if there are any inconsistencies in Odem's story. But something tells me there won't be. For all he knew, we already had the message transcripts and were just trying to catch him in a lie. He would have been taking a pretty big chance on waltzing in here and outright lying to us about the contents of those messages."

"I know," Damien said, looking grim as he leaned back against the wall. "Which is why I think he and Claire had another means of communicating. I think at some point, Odem decided it was too risky for them to continue sending messages to each other through MyDomain, an account her father had access to. So they found another way to talk to each other about private matters, and they saved the safe, generic stuff for MyDomain."

"That's highly possible." Althea frowned. "But why go to so much trouble? Why keep up the ruse on MyDomain at all?"

"Because Odem is a smart man. As soon as Claire contacted him that very first time, it became a matter of public record. By the time he realized their friendship was evolving into something more, they had already exchanged a number of flirtatious messages. Assuming he was planning at that point to kidnap or murder her, he knew their correspondence up until that point was already documented, which meant he would be a person of interest if she came up missing. He also knew it might look suspicious if they suddenly stopped sending messages to each other. He wanted to be able to walk in here and tell us, like he just did, that their online correspondence was perfectly innocent, at least on his part. So he told Claire to open a secret e-mail account where they could openly talk, and they agreed to keep up the charade on MyDomain."

"Poor Claire," Althea murmured sadly. "She must have been caught up in the excitement, the rush of sneaking around behind her father's back and getting away with it. *She's* thinking she's having a secret rendezvous with her smart, sophisticated cyberboyfriend; all *he's* thinking about is covering his tracks."

Damien nodded grimly. "So now the question is, which computer did she use to open the secret e-mail account? She knew she couldn't do it from home, or else the IP address could be traced."

"That's true. She could have gone anywhere to use a computer—school, the public library, an Internet café. And she'd probably go to the same place to check her messages and write him back. We have to talk to her friends, find out where she hung out a lot." She frowned, questions swirling in her mind at warp speed. "How did Odem go about suggesting the idea to her in the first place? Did he risk sending a letter or a package to her house? Or somewhere else? Damn it. We've *got* to get our hands on those message transcripts ASAP."

"I agree," Damien said, straightening from the wall. "In the meantime, I'm gonna talk to Mayhew to see about putting a tail on Odem."

"Already taken care of," the detective said, walking up to them.

His expression was grim. "I assigned a uniform to follow Odem as soon as he left the building. But I've got even bigger fish to fry at the moment. I just got a call from Thorndike. Seems the media just released a story that we were questioning another suspect today. Thorndike was upset, wanted to know why he had to learn about it on the news like everyone else. I'm heading over to the house now to smooth his ruffled feathers and bring him up to date on the investigation. When he hears about Odem, the good doctor might be coming to *us* begging for police protection."

Damien shook his head, frowning. "You gotta do something about that leak in your department, Detective."

Mayhew scowled. "I know, I know. *Hell.* Just what I need. A damn leaky faucet. I'm gonna have to talk to the captain when I get back."

Althea said, "Have you had a chance to visit Claire's high school and talk to some of her teachers?"

"My partner and I made the rounds yesterday. They all had pretty much the same things to say about Claire—smart girl, outstanding student, true leader, an ambitious go-getter with a bright future ahead of her. They acknowledged that there had been some rifts between Claire's friends and a few other cliques, but nothing you wouldn't find in any other high school. Girls fight, they compete for boys and attention, they're catty to one another. And although some of her classmates might have been jealous of her, none of her teachers could think of a single person who would want to hurt her. Which, of course, is what they all say in these situations. No teacher wants to believe one of their own students could be a school shooter in the making or a violent psychopath capable of kidnapping and brutalizing a classmate."

"What about an employee—a janitor or cafeteria worker—who may have taken an unusual amount of interest in Claire?" Althea probed. "Someone who might have gone out of their way to talk to her, offer her assistance, things like that?"

Mayhew made a face. "We spoke to most of Claire's

friends, and none of them remembered her mentioning anything like that. They swear she would have told them if she'd ever felt weirded out by someone at school, whether it was a teacher or a janitor. Just to cover our bases, though, we asked the school secretary to provide a list of all custodial staff and employees that were terminated within the last six months. She's supposed to be faxing it over this afternoon. We'll run the names through the system and see if we get any hits. We also asked Claire's friends if they had noticed anyone suspicious hanging around the school, loitering around the parking lot, looking like they didn't belong. All of them said no. But that doesn't surprise me."

"Why not?" Althea asked.

"Have you ever been to the high school?"

Althea shook her head.

"Well, they've got a pretty good setup over there. It's a small private school, so part of the hefty tuition goes toward hiring a private security company to keep the little rich kids safe. There are two security guards posted on campus every day until six P.M. One circulates inside the building—especially during class change times and lunch—and the other patrols the grounds. The parents asked that the guards be in plainclothes, so the kids won't feel like they're in prison or attending some inner-city school plagued by crime and violence."

Damien chuckled dryly. "Can't have that."

Mayhew snorted. "Of course not. Anyway, the guards also have the authority to enforce school discipline policies. The principal told me that this helps keep the number of school fights down and discourages students from bragging about their wild keg parties out in the open." He shrugged. "If you ask me, I'd rather know up-front what they're up to so I can catch 'em in the act as opposed to them pretending to be perfect little angels in my face while they sneak around behind my back." He paused, grimacing. "Like Claire."

"Like Claire," Althea murmured in agreement, reflecting once again on the tragic irony that the teenager's secrecy may have enabled her abductor to get away with the perfect crime.

Damien said, "What about the computer lab at the school? We've been thinking that Claire must have used another computer to open a secret e-mail account and correspond more freely with Odem."

"If she did, she didn't do it at school," Mayhew said. "We spoke to the computer science faculty, and they said the computers are firewalled to prevent students from viewing inappropriate material and accessing the computers for personal use. They told us Claire wouldn't have been able to open an e-mail account or check any personal messages."

"So *that's* a dead end," Althea muttered in frustration.

Mayhew said, "We're still going through her PC and checking her instant message activity, which is stored on the hard drive."

"If Odem was smart enough to instruct her to open a separate e-mail account," Damien said grimly, "he was smart enough not to IM her at home. If he was *really* smart, he would have told her not to use any of her wireless devices to contact him. That means no laptop, PDA, cell phone, or we could trace her activity through her MAC address."

Mayhew frowned in confusion. "What the hell is a MAC address?"

"The Media Access Control address is a unique value associated with a network adapter," Damien explained. "In other words, it's a number that acts like a name for a particular network. Any wireless capabilities with a MAC address can be traced, so if Claire sent or received a message from Odem using her laptop, PDA, or cell phone, we could simply trace it through her MAC address, which, in the world of computer networking, is just as important as an IP address."

Mayhew scowled, passing a hand over his thinning cap of hair, mussing it even more. "The double-edged sword of modern technology," he muttered darkly. "There are so many damn methods of communication nowadays— e-mail, cell phones, text messaging, instant messaging, BlackBerrys. It's done nothing but create more fucking work for cops."

Althea and Damien chuckled quietly. The detective was right. Modern technology had been both a blessing and a curse to those in law enforcement. On one hand it enabled underresourced police departments to streamline cumbersome processes and procedures, which helped cops do their jobs better. But on the other hand, technology had spawned a new breed of cybercriminals, and keeping one step ahead of them could be a daunting task for many law enforcement agencies, which was why the FBI had launched the Cyber Investigations division for the sole purpose of combating Internet crime.

"If your cybertechs need any help pulling the data off Claire's computer, let me know and I'll send one of our forensic examiners over to lend a helping hand," Damien offered. "These guys can break passwords and decrypt files in their sleep."

Mayhew nodded. "I might have to take you up on that. We don't have the luxury of being territorial or letting our egos get in the way. We need all the manpower we can get. My partner's been out in the field since the crack of dawn this morning leading the ground search efforts, along with deputies from the sheriff's office, state police, and representatives from the National Center for Missing and Exploited Children. We've also got our mounted police unit involved to help with that rural area around the Thorndike property, and our divers are going to be dragging parts of the Chesapeake later today." He blew out a long, weary breath, exhaustion stamped into his features and adding to his haggard appearance. "We've covered a lot of ground in the last two days, yet it seems like we've barely scratched the damn surface."

Althea wanted to offer some words of reassurance, wanted to tell him they would find Claire and bring her back home. But she couldn't make that kind of guarantee. The harsh reality was that no matter how hard they worked or how much they willed Claire's safe return, they were all at the mercy of an unknown predator. She knew it, and so did the two men standing with her.

"You're doing a helluva job," she said to Mayhew instead, meaning it.

He gave her a brief, grateful smile. "I'm sure you've both already heard that we're convening a task force to compare notes on the investigation and make sure everyone is on the same page. We're having our first meeting tomorrow morning at eight-thirty at the old fire hall on Reisterstown, which we're using as our base of operations."

"I know where it is," Damien said. "We'll be there."

Mayhew nodded briskly, then glanced at his watch, a cheap, serviceable watch that was the complete opposite of the platinum Rolex worn by James Odem. "I'd better get over to Casa Thorndike and do some damage control before he sics the commissioner on me. God, I just love my job," he grumbled as he started away.

As Althea and Damien were leaving the station a few minutes later, Damien's cell phone rang. He picked it up and listened for a prolonged moment, then said in a clipped voice, "We're on our way."

When he ended the call and looked at Althea, she felt a knot of instinctive tension tighten in her stomach.

"Who was that?" she asked warily.

"Balducci. He said a package arrived at the office today." He paused. "It seems that the kidnapper has made contact."

Chapter 15

When they reached the office, they headed straight to the conference room where the special agent in charge was waiting for them, seated at the head of the long conference table with a grim expression on his face.

In the center of the table, in a clear plastic bag, was a yellow nine-by-twelve envelope with a metal closure and a torn flap. It was addressed to SAC EDWARD BALDUCCI. There was no return address. Right beside the envelope, also encased in plastic to preserve trace evidence, was a single sheet of white letter-size paper. Centered on the page was a printed message:

When the music changes, so does the dance.

The blood drained from Althea's head.

Without a word, she and Damien sat down across from each other at the table.

"It came this morning," Eddie said flatly. "When I returned from a meeting downtown, it was sitting there with the rest of my mail."

"Which your secretary puts on your desk every day," Damien said.

"Right. It was postmarked on Saturday. Sent first-class." Eddie paused. "It was mailed from Richmond, Virginia."

A silent look of comprehension passed between the three agents. But it was Damien who voiced what they were thinking. "He wants to make sure we're involved in the case. So he took her across state lines."

"Or he wants us to believe he did," Althea murmured.

No one posed the obvious question. It hung in the air like a specter, silent and ominous. *Why?*

Why did the kidnapper want the FBI to become involved in the case?

Why had he taken Claire Thorndike across state lines, which was a federal crime?

Because he wants you to play his twisted little game, Althea.

A chill of foreboding swept across her flesh.

She could feel the heat of Damien's gaze trained on her. He was worried about her.

Pretending not to notice, she stood and leaned across the table to read the cryptic note encased in plastic. *When the music changes, so does the dance.*

"I've seen this before," she said suddenly. "It's a West African proverb. It's often been used as a theme for Black History Month celebrations. The proverb is basically about re-creating yourself to meet every circumstance, without ever losing the essence of who you are."

Eddie frowned. "That doesn't sound very threatening."

"No, but there's definitely a message in there," Damien said. "The question is, who's the message about? And who is it really for?"

The room fell silent. Althea knew they were all thinking the same thing, that *she* was the intended recipient of the proverb, but no one wanted to say it.

"There's a reference to music," Althea said. "James

Odem was teaching Claire about Coltrane for her music class."

Damien and Eddie nodded thoughtfully.

Damien posed, "Maybe the perp is telling us that he's a chameleon, able to adapt himself to any situation. Able to escape detection."

Althea stared at him alertly. "I think you're right. I think that's *exactly* what he's telling us."

Eddie scowled. "Then it's a taunt. A catch-me-if-you-can arrogance."

"Which fits the profile of the type of predator we're looking for," Damien muttered. "Someone who thinks he's smarter than us. Someone like James Odem."

Again they fell silent.

"Looks like the note was generated on a laser printer on standard copy paper," Eddie observed, shifting focus. "Which means it could have been sent by anyone."

Althea nodded. "And the envelope was addressed to you, which doesn't give us any clues into the sender's identity. Any crackpot with Internet access could look up your name and the address of the Baltimore field office."

"Right," Damien agreed. "And he knew that by sending it directly to the SAC, it wouldn't get lost in the shuffle. It would be taken seriously, given priority status."

Eddie nodded. "I was waiting for the two of you to arrive and have a look at it before I handed it off to the lab guys." He heaved a deep sigh. "I think we can all safely assume the chances of lifting a usable print are a gazillion to one."

Althea and Damien nodded in reluctant agreement. Whoever had sent the note was smart, cunning, meticulous. He—or she—would not have been careless enough to leave fingerprints, or any other trace evidence, that could lead the authorities right to his doorstep. This was a game to him.

A deadly game he intended to win.

Althea suppressed another shudder and asked, "Is it possible he's a Virginia resident?"

"Not likely," Eddie answered. "I think he traveled there specifically to mail the note. But just to be on the safe side, I already contacted our field office in Richmond and gave the SAC the postal code from the envelope. They're going to check out any abandoned buildings and warehouses in the area and talk to locals. Maybe someone saw a girl matching Claire's description around the time the letter was mailed. It's a long shot, but worth a try."

Damien nodded. "They should also take a photo of James Odem up to the post office, see if any employees recognize him. The note was mailed on Saturday, which was only three days ago. We might be lucky enough to get a positive ID."

"If he's our guy," Althea qualified, sitting back down.

"How did it go at the police station?" Eddie asked.

Damien gave him a quick rundown of that morning's interview with James Odem. When he'd finished, Eddie shook his head, frowning deeply. "Sounds like he's definitely lying about something. But he's got a lot to lose. By tomorrow morning his name and photograph will be splashed all over the news in connection to Claire's disappearance."

"Guess he should have thought about that before he decided to hook up with a teenage girl," Damien drawled, unsympathetic.

"Assuming he's not responsible for her disappearance," Eddie said, "he's got to be the unluckiest son of a bitch ever. Of the thousands of men every year who meet underage girls online, this poor bastard had to meet the girl who goes missing."

Damien grimaced. "I'm not ready to give this guy a pass. He walked in there and lied to our damn faces."

"What if he didn't lie?" Althea countered philosophically. "What if he was telling the truth about Claire becoming obsessed with him? Would that be so impossible? He's an attractive, intelligent, successful doctor who gave her the time of day. Never underestimate the power of male attention on an impressionable, lonely young woman." She hesitated, pursing her lips in thought for a moment. "You know, when I was in college, I met an older man in a chat room. He seemed very smart and sophisticated, and he was easy to talk to. I had a boyfriend at the time, but I found myself confiding in this man, this complete stranger. I shared personal things with him, things I hadn't even told my best friend. It felt good to talk to someone who didn't know me, who wouldn't judge me. I don't know. Maybe if I wasn't dating the star basketball player, I might have developed feelings for my chat buddy. Of course," she added sardonically, "I didn't know at the time that he was a professor at my university and a bona fide scumbag."

"I remember," Eddie said darkly.

"You've just proven my point," Damien growled. "Grown men who spend hours online chatting with young girls don't automatically deserve the benefit of the doubt when it comes to criminal behavior."

"But my chat buddy isn't the one who kidnapped me," Althea pointed out quietly.

Damien frowned, but said nothing. Neither did Eddie.

"And now that I've brought up the elephant in the room," she said in a calm, measured voice, "I think it's time we start exploring the very real possibility that we're looking at a copycat here. We've all been thinking about it. The arrival of this note forces us to confront it head-on. So who wants to go first?"

Damien and Eddie traded glances, but neither spoke.

A wry smile curved Althea's mouth. "All right. *I'll* go first. I've come up with a victim profile by compiling a list of the similarities between myself and Claire Thorndike at the time of our abductions, and there are too many of them to be ignored. As soon as I walked in here and saw this note, the first thing that went through my mind is, this is how it started before. With a note. A message from the kidnapper."

Damien nodded, his expression grim. "After that, your bookbag was found at a convenience store. Deliberately left there by the kidnapper."

Althea nodded. "Once we learned that Claire's purse, cell phone, and backpack were missing, I knew why. The perp took them as souvenirs. My hunch is that he's going to contact us at some point to let us know where we can locate those items. And he's not going to leave them just anywhere. It's going to be strategic. Anthony Yusef"—there was a time she couldn't utter her abductor's name without shuddering—"left my bookbag at the convenience store because it was symbolic for Garrison. And he knew that, because he'd already taken the time to learn everything he could about Garrison. So now we have to think like the Unsub. What does he know about us? We can already assume he knows plenty about me, but what has he learned about you, Damien? Or about Eddie?"

The two men exchanged tense, wary glances.

"Asking these questions allows us to get into his psyche," Althea continued. "What makes him tick? What's his motive for kidnapping Claire? Does he want fifteen minutes of fame, or does he have an ax to grind?

Is he just some nutcase out there who became obsessed with the news of my abduction all those years ago, or could he somehow be connected to Anthony Yusef—or one of us? If we can focus on answering these questions, maybe we can begin to narrow the scope of our investigation, narrow the range of suspects. And that could bring us closer to finding this son of a bitch before it's too late."

Eddie nodded slowly. "You're right, Althea," he said gravely. "About everything. Truth be told, I've been in denial about this whole thing, because I didn't want to accept the possibility that you could be in serious danger. I *still* don't want to think about it, but that's me reacting like a friend instead of an agent. That's not only a disservice to you, but to Claire and her family. I've got a job to do. We *all* have a job to do. So let's get to it."

Meeting adjourned, they rose from the conference table with the practiced efficiency of an elite team preparing for action. Reaching for the envelope and the note occupying the center of the table, Damien said, "I'm heading down to the lab to talk to the forensic guys about lending their resources to BPD. I'll hand these off while I'm there."

"Thanks," Eddie said. "And tell them to put a rush on it."

"Naturally."

"I assume we have to let Detective Mayhew know about the note," Althea said.

Damien grimaced. "We can't keep him out of the loop on such an important development, especially now that a task force has been convened. But that leak in his department is going to be a problem. If we don't keep this note out of the media, we all know it could set off a floodgate of copycats. We don't have the time or manpower to pore through a bunch of notes sent by every nutcase out there who wants a piece of the action. Nor do we want to give the perp the satisfaction of having his poetry read on the airwaves. I say we let him sit and stew, wondering if we've received the note and wondering what we're gonna do about it."

Eddie nodded. "You're one hundred percent right about everything. But we can't risk alienating the local boys by withholding evidence. So tell Mayhew about the note before the task force meets tomorrow, but make it clear to him that if it gets leaked to the press, we're holding him personally responsible." He smoothed down his silk tie as he started toward the door. "I'm going to call the folks in Richmond to let them know about Odem. Maybe they can make it to the post office before it closes. Think you'll have those message transcripts by the end of the day?" he asked, glancing over his shoulder at Althea.

"I sure as hell hope so." As she made to follow him from the room, Damien grasped her upper arm, gently but firmly detaining her. Althea turned and stared up at him questioningly as Eddie departed, leaving them alone.

"What—"

"Just for the record," Damien said in a low, dangerously soft voice, "I don't like this setup."

Althea frowned. "What setup?"

"Your involvement in this case. I think it's a bad idea. You said it yourself—there are too many similarities between you and Claire Thorndike to be ignored. That tells me this psycho, whoever he is, may be coming for you next."

Althea swallowed. "I'm aware of that," she said evenly.

"I don't think you are."

She bristled. "What the hell is that supposed to mean?"

Damien moved a fraction closer and Althea stepped back almost reflexively. His dark, intense gaze drilled into her, pinning her to the door she suddenly found herself against. Her pulse spiked, although she couldn't tell whether it was from a burst of anger or Damien's sudden nearness.

"You're a good agent, Althea. A damn good one. But I don't think you're being very smart about this situation. What part of 'Your life may be in danger' don't you understand?"

Her temper flared. "With all due respect, Damien, I graduated from the Academy just like you did. I took an oath to serve and protect just like you did. We put our lives on the line every day because that's what we signed up for. I'm not going to stop doing my job just because some head case out there wants to frighten and intimidate me."

Damien scowled. "Maybe you *should* be frightened and intimidated. We don't know what kind of lunatic we're dealing with, Althea. We don't know what he's capable of. Your involvement in this case just plays right into his hands, and you're a damn fool if you can't see that!"

Althea narrowed her eyes and tipped her head back. "As I already told Balducci when he shared his concerns with me, if this case is in any way related to what happened to me eight years ago, the Unsub is going to involve me whether I'm helping with the case or not. Rather than hiding in a corner like some coward, I'd rather be on the front lines of battle trying to catch this bastard. And *that's* what I intend to do, whether you like it or not."

Damien clenched his jaw, his expression hardening. "I don't have time to hold your hand or look after you. Just so we're clear."

Her chin lifted in defiance. "I never asked you to do those things. And just so we're clear," she said, coldly mocking him, "just because we spent one meaningless night together doesn't mean you have a say in anything

I do. You don't know me, and I don't know you. I've moved on since Friday night. If you can't do the same, maybe *you* should ask to be reassigned."

His nostrils flared. Something dark and dangerous flashed in his eyes.

Without another word he brushed past her, yanked the door open, and stormed out of the room, leaving her more shaken than she cared to admit.

Chapter 16

Damien spent the rest of the day out of the office. After dropping off the kidnapper's note and speaking with one of the Bureau's forensic examiners, he struck off for Solomon's Island, using the thirty-minute drive to clear his head and get his mind back on the investigation— where it belonged.

He arrived at Patrick Farris's small clapboard house along the river, hoping to catch the retired physician off guard. But Farris wasn't home.

He found one of his neighbors mending a net inside a tiny fishing boat docked at the pier. As Damien approached, the man stared at him with a mixture of curiosity and suspicion. Damien identified himself, flashing his credentials and watching as the man's eyes widened with surprise and a touch of alarm.

"Is he in some kind of trouble?"

"Not at all," Damien said smoothly. "I just wanted to ask him some questions about a case I'm working on. Nothing urgent."

The neighbor informed him that Farris was out of town visiting his son and daughter-in-law, who'd just welcomed their second child into the family.

"Does Dr. Farris live here alone?" Damien asked casually.

"Yep. Well, his son stays with him from time to time."

"The one from—"

"No, not the one who lives in Virginia. That's Kyle. I'm talking about his other son. The younger one—Corbin."

Corbin Farris. Damien made a mental note to run the name through the system as soon as he returned to the office. He also filed away the fact that Farris's oldest son lived in Virginia, where the note had been mailed from. He'd check him out as well. Couldn't hurt.

"Are Dr. Farris and Corbin pretty close?" he asked, keeping his tone casual.

"You could say that. They spend a lot of time together when Corbin is here, go fishing and sailing a lot. My sense is that Corbin likes to keep to himself. Even when he goes into town, he doesn't interact much with the locals. Just goes about his business. His father says the boy never really recovered from his mother's death. Breast cancer, poor thing." The man shook his head mournfully, and Damien offered his condolences.

He made small talk for a few minutes, then handed the friendly neighbor his card and asked him to call when Patrick Farris returned from his visit. The man agreed, albeit warily, and Damien thanked him for his time and headed back to Baltimore, deciding that his trip to the remote waterfront fishing village hadn't been a total bust after all.

He made use of his time on the road, checking voice mail messages and returning phone calls pertaining to other active cases. When he got back to the office, he ran the names of Kyle and Corbin Farris through the database to see if they, like their father, had criminal histories. Within an hour he had his answer. Both men were clean. But that didn't mean they should be eliminated

as possible suspects. On the contrary. What Damien
had learned from the neighbor about Corbin Farris
had piqued his curiosity; it was a thread he intended to
follow. To that end, he accessed Motor Vehicle Administration records, pulling up photographs of Patrick Farris
and his two sons. He printed out the photos, then faxed
them over to the SAC in Richmond with a brief, self-
explanatory note: *Persons of interest pursuant to Thorndike
case. Linked to Virginia area.*

Shortly afterward Damien left the office, deciding to
help with the ground search efforts although he knew,
instinctively, that Claire Thorndike would not be found
anywhere near her northwestern Baltimore home.

If she's found at all, he thought, a dark thought that
matched his even darker mood.

Already dressed in the jeans and boots he'd put on
that morning, he spent the next several hours tramping
through grassy terrain alongside hundreds of other law
enforcement personnel, the air fogged with their breath,
electric with their tension and the noise of helicopter
blades pounding above. When a cold drizzle began to
fall around eight-thirty, they called the ground search for
the night and told everyone to regroup at the old fire
hall at eight-thirty A.M. tomorrow. Chilled to the bone,
wet and exhausted, the officers and deputies and patrol-
men had trudged back to their waiting vehicles, eager to
return to the warmth of their homes and families, yet
disheartened that their efforts had yielded no clues into
the missing girl's whereabouts.

During those adrenaline-charged hours, Damien had
been too focused on his task, on the investigation, to
dwell on thoughts of his heated argument with Althea.
But as he drove home that night, bone-weary and frustrated from the lack of progress they'd made that day,
his thoughts strayed inexorably to Althea.

Her caustic parting words hammered at his brain, taunting him with the singular refrain: *Just because we spent one meaningless night together doesn't mean you have a say in anything I do.*

He didn't know what ate at him more. The fact that she'd stubbornly refused to remove herself from the case or the fact that she'd referred to the most incredible night of his life as *meaningless.*

Meaningless?

Damien scowled blackly, charging through a yellow light just as it clicked to red.

It shouldn't have bothered him so damn much. After all, Althea was right. They didn't really know each other. They were two strangers who had been drawn to each other by mutual desire, a fierce, irresistible attraction. Now that they had been paired together on what could be the biggest case of their lives, they needed to be focused on the task at hand. Obviously Althea understood that better than he did. *I've moved on since Friday night,* she'd told him. The fact that he couldn't seem to do the same left him feeling surly and frustrated, filled with self-loathing for his own weakness.

He'd never been this hung up on a woman before. Not even in college when he first started going out with Angelique, the beautiful, popular journalism major practically every guy on campus wanted to date—or screw, depending on who you asked. She'd been attracted to Damien because he hadn't given her the time of day—literally. When she'd strolled up to him after class one morning and asked him for the time, he'd raised a brow at the slim gold watch peeking beneath the cuff of her tight sweater and asked, "Something wrong with your watch?"

Angelique had laughed, claiming she'd forgotten she was wearing one, even though they both knew better.

Years later, when Damien reflected on that encounter, he realized that Angelique had started off their relationship with a lie, albeit a small white one. She'd pursued him aggressively that semester, inviting him to lunch and dinner, to the movies and concerts, even to her dorm room for an all-night study session, which would include cramming for midterms followed by a series of "pleasurable stress-relieving activities." Although Damien found her sexy and beautiful—he wasn't blind—he knew she wasn't his type. As an introvert—some called him shy—he'd never been attracted to self-absorbed, high-maintenance women, and his instincts told him Angelique Navarro fit this bill to a tee. But the more he turned her down, the more relentless she became. He was a challenge for her, one she'd set her sights on winning.

And after a while, she began to grow on him. He found himself noticing just how smart she was, how charming she could be, and the bond she shared with her large family reminded him of his own close-knit relationship with his mother and his two older brothers. So when he found Angelique sobbing quietly in a corner one morning after class, and she told him her grandmother had just died—a woman who'd helped raise her—Damien's heart had melted with compassion. He'd skipped classes for the rest of the day to keep her company, to console her through the first wave of grief. They made love that night, and by the time he accompanied her to her grandmother's funeral three days later, they were officially an item.

At the height of his relationship with Angelique, when he still viewed her flaws through rose-colored glasses and her come-hither smile could still induce butterflies in his stomach, he'd never felt as dangerously unbalanced as he did now.

Over a woman who'd pretty much just told him to go to hell.

Damien swore under his breath, disgusted with himself for giving a damn.

When his phone rang, he dug it out of his back pocket, pressed Talk, and growled, "Wade."

There was a brief pause, followed by a low, rumbling chuckle on the other end. "Bad day at the office?"

It was his older brother Garrison.

"You could say that," Damien muttered, but with a little less rancor than before. "When'd you get back from the conference in San Antonio?"

"This afternoon. Imani dropped the kids off at Ma's house, picked me up from the airport, and took me out to dinner. We just got back, so I thought I'd call and check up on you, Little Man."

Although only six years older than Damien, Garrison was the only father figure he'd ever known. Damien was only four years old when their father, a retired cop, left home after a long, torturous battle with depression. It was Garrison, not their eldest brother Reggie, who'd stepped up to the plate to fill their father's shoes, forced into manhood by circumstances beyond his control or comprehension. When their schoolteacher mother was too tired after a long, stressful day or was busy grading a mountain of papers in the evenings, it was Garrison who'd looked after Damien, checking his homework, rationing his snacks before dinner, and supervising his bath time. It was Garrison who'd taught him how to throw a mean left hook, then had kicked his ass when he got suspended from school for fighting. It was Garrison who'd taught him about the birds and the bees, then bought him a pack of condoms when he turned fifteen and decided he'd met *the one*, a pretty mall rat with a mouthful of braces who had eagerly facilitated his passage into manhood. And it was Garrison who'd been his sounding board and kept him sane—and nonhomicidal—during the lowest periods of his rocky, ill-fated marriage.

For as long as Damien could remember, his brother had always been there for him, a source of strength, guidance, and support. In many ways, Damien owed him his life. Which was why Garrison was the only one who could get away with calling him "Little Man."

Damien said now, "Before you ask about the abduction case—which I know is part of the reason you called—I have to ask about our girl. Did you get a chance to see Korrine while you were in San Antonio?"

Garrison laughed. "How'd I know that would be the first thing out of your mouth? Of course I saw Korrine while I was there. You know she's still on maternity leave."

"Yeah, I heard. How's she doing?"

"She's doing great, and her daughter Kaia is beautiful. She looks just like Korrine. They had me over to their ranch for dinner. Man, they've got an incredible piece of land out there. Rafe and I got to talking after dinner, and let me tell you, he had me seriously thinking about taking some of those acres off his hands and building a nice big home out there."

"Seriously?"

"Seriously."

Damien snorted out a laugh. "Yeah, right. Like you and Imani would ever relocate to Texas. Even if she agreed to leave her family—which is highly unlikely—you know Ma would be heartbroken if you left her."

"I know, I know. She's always talking about how good it is to have all her boys together again now that Reggie moved back home."

Damien grinned. "That's right, man, so you can't break up the family. Sorry."

Garrison chuckled softly. "Maybe when Imani and I retire. I'm not lying when I tell you how beautiful and peaceful it is down there. God's country. You'll see what I'm talking about. Rafe and Korrine invited all of us down to the ranch next summer. Korrine said we have to introduce Little G and Kaia to each other—I think she's already planning their wedding."

Damien laughed, thinking fondly of the woman who'd taken him under her wing when he joined the FBI seven years ago. Although Korrine Friday had only been with the Bureau a year longer, she'd willingly shown Damien the ropes, sharing a wealth of knowledge that, combined with his brother's mentoring, had helped Damien become the agent he was today. Back then, he'd sometimes wondered if a relationship could have developed between them if he wasn't married, and if Korrine wasn't married to the job. A consummate professional, she'd always kept things strictly platonic between them, respecting his marriage and sharing his conviction that business and pleasure should never mix—qualities that made him admire and appreciate her even more. Although he'd teased her about deserting him when she was transferred to San Antonio three years ago, no one was happier than Damien when he found out that she'd met and fallen in love with Rafe Santiago, her new squad supervisor. *Sometimes it's okay to bend our own rules a little,* she'd smilingly confided to Damien at her wedding.

He found himself reflecting on those words now, which, of course, only made him think about Althea.

He swore under his breath, forgetting he had an audience this time.

"What's on your mind, Little Man?" Garrison asked quietly.

"What *isn't* on my mind?" Damien grumbled darkly as he slowed for a traffic light. Although the streets were mostly deserted, he figured he wouldn't push his luck this time.

"I heard about the kidnapping while I was in San Antonio." Garrison blew out a long, weary breath. "The first thing I thought was: Damn, not again."

"I know," Damien murmured.

"The timing, man. Almost eight years to the day. I don't like it."

"Join the club."

"Imani called me, then Eddie. Please tell me someone's been able to talk some sense into Althea about not working on this case."

Damien said nothing. His jaw was clenched too tight.

"Damn it," Garrison growled. "She's even worse than Imani. We argued for over an hour when I told her I planned to hire a bodyguard to look after her and the kids until this nutcase is found and locked up. She didn't mind hiring someone for Little G and Soraya while they're at daycare, but she objected to her routine being altered and having to worry about a bodyguard following her around campus and into her classrooms. I told her I'd rather inconvenience her a little now than plan her damn funeral later."

"You did the right thing," Damien said grimly. "The hard, cold truth is that she was targeted by a deranged psychopath eight years ago, and for all we know, she could be in danger again. Until we've got the perpetrator behind bars, we can't afford to take any chances."

"I killed that bastard," Garrison muttered, the old fury edging his deep voice. "I put a bullet between his eyes. This isn't some horror movie, where the killer keeps coming back to life after being shot, burned, drowned and electrocuted. I watched Anthony Yusef die, then personally attended his funeral just to make damn sure he was buried six feet under. As far as I know, he had no living relatives, no mentally unstable children who could have crawled out of the woodwork after all these years to avenge his death."

"We're exploring all possibilities, running the gamut of theories," Damien said.

As he drove home, he brought his brother up to speed on the investigation, telling him about the interview with James Odom, Althea's blackmail theory involving Suzette Thorndike and her ex-husband, and the cryptic note from the kidnapper, the latter of which induced a string of harsh expletives from Garrison.

Damien smiled wryly at his brother's language. "I hope Imani and the kids are already in bed," he drawled.

"They are. Damn it, that note sounds like something Yusef would have left behind."

"I guess that's the point. But my suspicion is that whoever took Claire wants us to know he's smarter than Yusef, more cunning and elusive. I think it would be a mistake to label him a copycat and assume we've got him all figured out. Althea thinks he's going to follow a pattern, and that's a good starting point for us to work from. But my gut tells me this guy has something entirely different up his sleeve, something we may not see coming until it's too damn late."

Garrison heaved a long, ragged breath, resigned to the truth of his brother's words. "Is there any way you can convince Althea to lay low for however long it takes to find this lunatic?"

Damien scowled. "I already tried. She flat out refused. Unless Balducci reassigns her, she isn't going anywhere, and he has no intention of removing her from the case.

Why don't you talk to him? He's your best friend and
your son's godfather. Maybe you can talk some sense
into him."

"I can definitely try. But I know where he's coming
from. He's stuck between a rock and a hard place. Althea's
a good agent, one who happens to bring a unique perspective to this investigation that could be invaluable. If
Eddie removes her from the case because he's worried
about her, people will accuse him of treating her differently because they're friends. But if this goes bad and
Althea winds up getting hurt or killed, Eddie will be cru-
cified for not doing more to protect one of his agents
when he knew she was in danger. He's damned if he
does, damned if he doesn't."

"Cry me a river," Damien said mockingly, unsympathetic.

Garrison let out a short, grim laugh. "Don't be like
that. You know Eddie and I made a lot of enemies when
we got promoted to head the Baltimore and Washington field offices. We're only forty years old. Most agents
don't climb through the ranks as fast as we did, and
there are many who believe we only got this far because
Louis Pritchard is good friends with Director Grayson,
and to repay us for finding his niece, Pritchard put in a
good word for us. I mean, let's face it. Althea's abduction was a high-profile case, and the Bureau received a
ton of positive publicity after everything went down.
Eddie and I were awarded merits of honor and treated
like heroes for months afterward, which still makes me
cringe just thinking about it. The point is, we're both
under a lot of pressure to prove we legitimately earned
our positions. There's not a lot of room for missteps. So
cut Eddie some slack."

"Sellout," Damien groused.

Garrison laughed good-naturedly. "Be kind to your
boss. He always has nothing but good things to say about

you." He paused, a note of sly insinuation creeping into his voice as he added, "Wanna know something interesting he told me yesterday when he called?"

"Not particularly," Damien muttered, although he already had a pretty good idea.

Garrison said, "He told me how strange you and Althea were acting yesterday morning when she showed up at his office just as you were leaving. To quote Eddie, 'It was like being in a room with two people who couldn't wait for you to leave so they could tear each other's clothes off.'" He snickered. "Something you wanna share, Little Man?"

Damien shifted uncomfortably in the driver's seat. "Yeah," he grumbled irately. "Tell Balducci it's inappropriate to speculate and gossip about the personal lives of his agents."

Garrison laughed. "You told him you and Althea met for the first time on Friday night. You were at the club celebrating your birthday, weren't you? Is that where you met Althea?"

"Maybe."

Garrison chuckled, enjoying his brother's discomfiture. "Maybe I should be talking to the fellas instead. What do you think they'd tell me if I asked them about that night? Hmm?"

Damien said nothing, mentally kicking himself for letting it slip that he and Althea met on Friday night. He hadn't been thinking clearly because he was so shocked to see her again.

In an amused voice, Garrison said, "Don't worry, I won't pry. You and Althea can keep your secret, whatever it is. But I'd be lying if I didn't tell you what a pleasant surprise this is. In all these years, it never occurred to me or Imani that you and Althea might hook up one day. And considering what a shameless matchmaker my wife is, that's pretty amazing. I guess it never occurred to us because Althea lived all the way out in Seattle and, quite frankly, we didn't believe she'd ever return home."

Damien frowned. "Based on the way this case is going, maybe she shouldn't have."

"Maybe not." Garrison hummed a thoughtful note. "Tell you what. Why don't you and Althea come over for dinner on Thursday? I know you're both going to be pretty tied up with the investigation, but a few hours off one night isn't going to make or break the case."

"I don't know, man. If this is your way of playing matchmaker—"

"Actually, I was thinking this might give us the perfect opportunity to share our concerns about her involvement in the case."

Damien made a face as he turned onto his quiet, residential street. "I don't think she'd appreciate being ganged up on like that. She might feel like she's the victim of an intervention."

"In a way it is," Garrison said with quiet gravity. The soft murmur of a woman's voice could be heard in the background. Garrison's answer was muffled as he covered the mouthpiece with his hand.

He came back on the line a moment later, a smile in his voice. "My wife says it's time for me to come to bed."

Damien grinned. "I know what *that* means."

Garrison chuckled, low and wolfish. "Don't be jealous. Anyway, dinner at our house. Thursday night at seven. You and Althea be there. Besides, I have to give you the souvenir I brought back from San Antonio for India. Don't make me have to call her and tell her you're keeping her from receiving a gift."

Damien shook his head in mock disgust. "Blackmail, coming from an assistant director in the FBI. Tsk, tsk."

Garrison laughed. "Just bring your ass over here. Later."

"Later," Damien said.

No sooner had he disconnected than the phone rang again. His pulse kicked. He hoped it was Detective Mayhew, calling to tell him about a big break in the case. But one glance at the caller ID dashed that hope, while raising another.

"Hey," Althea said softly when he answered.

"Hey." His voice was without inflection.

"Are you at home?"

"Just pulled up."

"Oh." She hesitated uncertainly. "Listen, I wanted to apologize for what happened earlier. You were only expressing your concern for me, much like everyone else has been doing, and I was rude to you. What I said was uncalled for, and I'm sorry."

Damien waited a beat. "Okay."

"Okay what? Okay you accept my apology? Or okay whatever?"

"Okay, I accept your apology. No hard feelings."

"Good." Her relief came through the line. "We have to work closely together on a daily basis, and I think it would be counterproductive for us to be at odds with each other."

"Is that the only reason you apologized?" *What the hell are you doing?* his mind shouted. *Are you asking her if she meant that whole "one meaningless night" remark? Don't play yourself like that, man! Let it go before she starts thinking you care!*

Althea let out a slow, measured breath. "No, that's not the only reason I apologized. After you left the office earlier, I realized that certain things I said might have, uh, offended you. And, uh, that wasn't my intention. All right, maybe it was. But only because I was angry, and my aunt always taught me that you should never say things you might regret when you're angry." She paused. "Am I making any sense?"

Damien felt a smile tugging at his lips, but he kept his tone impassive. "Yeah, sure."

She hesitated again, and he imagined her frowning into the phone, wishing she could read his expression.

The silence stretched between them.

He patiently waited it out.

"I'm on my way home from the office," she volunteered.

"Yeah?"

"Yeah. I stayed late to catch up on some paperwork since I was out most of the day. I've got a few updates to share with you, and I thought we could go over the text message transcripts from Claire's cell phone, which I commandeered from Detective Mayhew as soon as the fax arrived from the phone company. There are pages and pages of them."

Damien frowned. "What about the MyDomain transcripts?"

"Tomorrow morning, I was promised. By nine A.M. our time, not theirs." Althea hesitated for a moment. "I was thinking about ordering a pizza when I get home, if you'd like to join me."

Damien went still. "Are you inviting me over for dinner?"

"A working dinner," she clarified. "We can work while we eat. Kill two birds with one stone."

He glanced at the dashboard clock. It was nine-thirty.

"Thanks for the offer," he said, "but I think I'll have to pass. It's been a long day, and we need to be up early."

"Oh. Of course." Her disappointment was palpable.

"I can call you back when I get inside the house and get settled, and you can give me your updates. I've got a couple of my own anyway."

"All right. That's fine. Talk to you then."

Damien clicked off, shoved the phone into his back

pocket, and cut off the ignition. But instead of climbing out of the SUV, he sat in the still darkness, staring through the windshield at his three-story brick townhouse with its manicured front lawn and neat, colorful flowerbeds planted and maintained by his mother. He'd bought the townhouse a year after the divorce, wanting to give India a nice place she could call her own whenever she stayed with him. He'd chosen a quiet, tree-lined suburb on the outskirts of Baltimore in a good school district—just in case Angelique ever changed her mind and decided that India belonged with him. He'd allowed his mother and Imani to paint and decorate, transforming his cold, empty bachelor pad into a warm, inviting home. But there was just one problem. The bright new décor declared to all visitors that this was a place meant for a family, and to Damien, the absence of one often served as a painful reminder of his failed marriage and his inability to retain custody of his daughter.

And now, as he sat alone in the SUV contemplating the dark, silent house, he thought about the three-day-old leftovers in his refrigerator, the cold emptiness of his large bed.

Before he could stop himself, he reached for his cell phone and dialed Althea's number. She answered halfway through the first ring, sounding a little breathless and—unless his ears were deceiving him—hopeful. "Yes?"

"I'm on my way."

Chapter 17

Althea had just stepped out of the shower when she heard the doorbell, signaling the arrival of Damien or the pizza delivery guy—neither of whom she'd expected for at least another fifteen minutes.

Hurriedly she threw on an old Stanford T-shirt and a pair of pink sweatpants with no underwear. Halfway to the front door, she caught a glimpse of her reflection in a wall mirror and realized she was still wearing her shower cap. She snatched it off her head and hastily combed her fingers through her hair before continuing to the door.

When she glanced through the peephole, no one was there.

Frowning, she unlocked the door and opened it enough to poke her head through. She peered up and down the corridor. It was silent and empty. Yet she felt a cold draft, a whisper across her skin, as if someone had just walked past.

Someone did, silly. Whoever rang your doorbell.

Shaking her head at herself, Althea ducked back inside her apartment and closed the door, sliding the deadbolt into place. Someone had probably wandered

onto the wrong floor and rang her doorbell by mistake,
she decided. The apartment building's twenty-four-
hour front desk attendant and intercom system were
supposed to alleviate security concerns by controlling
visitors' access to the property. But Althea had noticed
different people entering the building by following tenants inside, and none of them were ever stopped by the
attendant, whose nose was usually buried in a newspaper or a paperback novel. She'd been meaning to bring
this up to the building management, but she'd been
too preoccupied with the case to remember.

But suddenly she felt jittery, and she was reminded of
the cold sensation she'd felt yesterday evening when
she looked out her office window. She'd felt as if someone was lurking in the shadows of the parking lot,
staring up at her apartment. Watching her.

She'd promptly dismissed the feeling, telling herself
she was just edgy and out of sorts because of the kidnapping investigation, and because she'd been trying to
stave off dark, sinister thoughts about the past ever
since her plane touched down in Maryland. She didn't
believe someone evil had been watching her last night
any more than she believed that same person had just
rung her doorbell.

So why are your hands so clammy?

Frowning, Althea wiped her damp palms on her
sweatpants and started across the room to build a fire.
She'd just taken three steps when the intercom buzzed.
She let out a startled cry, nearly jumping out of her skin.

A moment later she swore under her breath, feeling
like an idiot. A paranoid idiot.

She retraced her steps to the door and pressed the
intercom button. "Yes?"

"It's me. Damien."

She mentally berated herself for the surge of relief

that swept through her at the sound of his deep voice. She buzzed him in, then rushed around picking up after herself. By the time he rang the doorbell, the living room was spotless and a sedate fire was crackling in the fireplace.

Her pulse quickened at the sight of him in her doorway. The five o'clock shadow he'd been sporting that morning had darkened, and his deep-set eyes were hooded, as if he'd been struggling to keep them open on the way over. He looked bone-tired, but that didn't detract from his handsomeness. If anything, Althea thought, he looked even sexier.

Stop it! You're not supposed to be noticing things like that! You made it perfectly clear to him today that you're not interested in sleeping with him again. But how in the world can you convince him of that if you can't even convince yourself?

Althea was so preoccupied with her thoughts that she didn't realize she was blocking the door until Damien arched an amused brow and drawled, "Are you going to leave me standing out here?"

An embarrassed flush stole across her cheeks. "Sorry," she muttered sheepishly, opening the door wider.

He stepped inside the apartment and cast an appreciative glance around. "Nice place," he murmured.

"Thanks." She didn't point out the obvious, that he'd been there less than five days ago. They both knew the *last* thing on his mind at the time had been her decorating skills.

"I brought drinks," he said, passing her a small plastic bag with a six-pack of beer inside. "I didn't know which brand you like."

"Heineken is great. Thank you." She started toward the kitchen, saying over her shoulder, "Where's your jacket? It's cold out there."

"I never wear coats unless it's the dead of winter."

Althea laughed. "What kind of policy is that?"

He shrugged those broad shoulders, flashing a wry grin. "I think it's a family trait. My brother Garrison is the same way."

"Then you and Garrison must have *stayed* sick growing up."

"Actually, we hardly ever got colds. Just ask my mom."

Inside the small kitchen, Althea set the bag on the counter and rummaged around a drawer until she located the bottle opener. As she opened their beers, she watched through the wide alcove as Damien wandered over to the fireplace to study the framed photographs on the mantel. Most were of her posing with her aunt and uncle, their arms around one another as they beamed into the camera. At her college graduation, at their thirtieth wedding anniversary celebration, standing in front of the pyramids during a summer trip to Egypt.

"You must be very close to your aunt and uncle," Damien remarked after several moments.

"I am," Althea said as she emerged from the kitchen. "They're the only parents I've ever known. I owe them everything."

Damien turned as she approached and handed him a beer. "I'm sure they don't see it that way. I'm sure if you asked them, they'd say you don't owe them a single thing. They'd probably say they're the ones who are grateful to have you in their lives."

Althea smiled softly at him, pleased by his perceptiveness. "You're right. That's *exactly* what they say to me every time I try to thank them for all they've done for me. I can barely get the words out before they're hushing me up, telling me that they have far more to be grateful for." She smiled again, shaking her head a little. "They're amazing people. Have you ever met them?"

"I haven't had the pleasure." Damien's mouth curved

ruefully. "To be honest with you, I'm a little intimidated. They think Garrison walks on water. I'm afraid I won't measure up."

Althea grinned. "Yeah, I can see how that might be a problem for you."

He chuckled. "Thanks for the reassurance."

"I'm just teasing you. Garrison saved my life. That makes him a hero in their book. Hell, I was even planning to name my firstborn after him." Smiling, she tilted her head to one side, regarding Damien thoughtfully for a moment. "But you know what? I honestly believe my aunt and uncle would like you just for who you are."

"You think so?"

"I know so. And why wouldn't they? You're a good man, Damien Wade."

"Thank you for saying that," he said softly.

"I meant every word."

They gazed at each other. The only sound in the room was the soft crackle and hiss of the logs burning on the grate.

With a supreme effort, Althea forced herself to look away, willing her pulse to return to normal. "The pizza should be here any minute," she announced offhandedly. "I'm starving. You?"

"Ravenous," Damien murmured, but the low, husky timbre of his voice made her wonder whether he was referring to food—or something else entirely.

She shivered.

Turning away, she walked over to the sofa and sat down. Damien remained by the fireplace, watching her through those dark, penetrating eyes as he slowly drank his beer.

Seeking to lighten the atmosphere—and neutralize the dangerous effect he was having on her—Althea smiled whimsically. "It just occurred to me that you're the original D-Wade. Did your friends used to call you that when you were growing up?"

Damien nodded, his lips curving in a half smile, as if he recognized her ploy for what it was. "They still do."

"So can I call you that, too?" she teased.

"That depends."

"On what?"

"On whether or not I consider you a friend."

She stared at him expectantly. "Do you?"

He lifted one shoulder in a lazy shrug. "I haven't decided."

"What?" she cried, pretending to take umbrage. "Do I have to pass some sort of test or something?"

He chuckled softly. "Maybe."

"Maybe!" Sucking her teeth, she flagged him off with a wave of her hand. "Whatever. Be that way then. I don't need to jump through hoops to be your friend, Damien Wade. I have *plenty* of friends, thank you very much. In case you haven't noticed, I happen to be a very likeable person."

His eyes danced with mirth. "Are you trying to convince me or yourself?"

Sputtering with indignation, Althea grabbed a small throw pillow off the sofa and hurled it at his head. Without missing a beat or spilling a drop of beer, he snapped the pillow out of the air, demonstrating razor-sharp reflexes obviously honed by years of practice.

Thoroughly impressed, Althea grinned and began clapping. "Good hands."

Damien shook his head at her, mouth twitching. "Just for future reference," he drawled, starting toward her, "you shouldn't throw flammable objects at someone standing in front of a fire. Remember—only *you* can prevent apartment fires."

Althea burst out laughing. "Yes, sir, Mr. Smokey Bear!"

Damien laughed.

The playful exchange was interrupted by the door-bell. Althea found herself resenting the intrusion, then called herself a damn fool for it.

"That must be the pizza," she said, starting to rise.

"I got it," Damien said, already striding toward the door before she could protest.

As he passed the sofa, he bopped her gently on the head with the pillow, drawing from her a loud, exaggerated, "Ouch!"

While he paid for the pizza, Althea retrieved paper plates and napkins from the kitchen.

As they sat down in the living room to eat, Damien said, almost too casually, "The delivery guy didn't seem to need your help getting into the building."

Althea made a pained face. "I know. I've been meaning to talk to the management about that. The building doesn't seem as secure as tenants are led to believe when they sign a lease."

Damien frowned with displeasure. "That front desk attendant seems more like window dressing. He barely glanced at me when I walked by. Assuming I was up to no good, he wouldn't even be able to ID me in a lineup. All visitors should have to sign in with him, otherwise he serves no purpose."

Althea, sensing a lecture coming on, said quickly and resolutely, "I'm going to call management first thing in the morning."

Damien searched her face as if trying to decide whether she really meant it or if she was just trying to pacify him in order to shut him up. After another moment he nodded tersely. "You do that."

Althea bristled at his bossy tone, biting back an urge to remind him of his earlier words to her. *I don't have time to hold your hand or look after you.*

The nerve! Was it any wonder she'd lashed out at him after hearing that?

But even in defending yourself, you were dishonest, her conscience pricked her. *You described your night together as meaningless, when you know damn well it was anything but that.*

But Damien didn't know that. And as far as she was concerned, he never would.

They ate for a few minutes in companionable silence before Damien, glancing around the room, asked idly, "How'd you get unpacked so quickly? Didn't you just arrive on Friday?"

Althea nodded, wiping a dab of pizza sauce from her chin. "When my stuff arrived from Seattle early last week, my aunt, along with some of her friends from church, came over and unpacked everything for me."

"That was very generous of them."

"I know. It was a wonderful homecoming surprise. I walked through the door, tired from a long flight, expecting to be greeted by the sight of moving boxes everywhere. You can imagine my shock—and utter relief—upon seeing that everything was already in place. I immediately called my aunt to thank her. She and my uncle were attending a political function in D.C., otherwise they would have picked me up from the airport. Anyway, by the time I finished thanking her, we were both blubbering on the phone like idiots." Althea laughed softly at the memory. "It was funny, because you could hear the president speaking in the background. When I tried to apologize to my aunt for interrupting, she just giggled and whispered, 'Baby, don't worry. He ain't saying nothing worthwhile anyway.'"

Damien chuckled, shaking his head. "I take it your aunt and uncle aren't exactly best friends with the president."

Althea snorted indelicately. "Let's just say they're both

looking forward to a new administration. As are a lot of people in this country."

"I'll drink to that," Damien said, and they clinked their beer bottles in a mock toast and drank.

After another moment, Damien slanted her a look of mild curiosity. "Do you think your uncle is going to run in four years?"

"Honestly?" Althea pursed her lips, contemplating her half-eaten slice of pepperoni pizza. "I think there's a very strong chance he will. My uncle is a visionary, whether he's dealing with our family or chairing a Senate committee. He loves this country more than anyone I know, and he has a lot of great ideas about restoring the economy and repairing our image abroad, among many other things."

Damien smiled lazily at her. "I take it by that glowing endorsement that you've already embraced the idea of being First Daughter."

Althea laughed. "I don't know about all that. For starters, I don't think I'd enjoy being shadowed by the Secret Service. I mean, can you just imagine me interviewing witnesses, going on raids and carrying out arrest warrants with some Secret Service agent looking over my shoulder?"

Damien grimaced, taking a swig of beer. "I see your point."

She slid him a teasing grin. "On the other hand, if my uncle did become president, *then* would you be my friend?"

Damien grinned, disarming her with those dimples. "Maybe."

Althea sputtered out a laugh, then punched him playfully on the shoulder.

After demolishing the large pizza, they cleared away their plates and got down to business. Althea listened as Damien told her about his visit to Patrick Farris's remote riverfront house in Solomon's Island.

"So Suzette Thorndike was his second wife?" she clarified.

Damien nodded. "His first wife passed away almost twenty years ago. Breast cancer. They had two sons, Kyle and Corbin. Kyle, the oldest, is an investment broker living in Virginia with his wife and two young children. But it's the other son—Corbin—that I'm particularly interested in. He's been in and out of work for the last ten years, which is why he often has to crash at his old man's place. The neighbor said he mostly keeps to himself, doesn't really interact with anyone apart from his father."

"A loner," Althea murmured. "Fits the profile."

Damien nodded. "That's what I thought, too. And his unstable employment history could point to financial trouble, which bolsters your blackmail theory. Suppose Farris and his son are in on it together. They both walk away with a sizeable chunk of Spencer Thorndike's fortune. Money problems solved."

"But what about the note? Why bother sending the note?"

"To throw us off. To make us think there's some psycho copycat out there, which changes the scope of our investigation. If we're not focusing on ransom as the kidnapper's motive, then that means we're not knocking on their door."

Althea frowned. "But they'd have to know we're exploring all angles, and considering who Claire's father is, ransom tops the list of possible motives. Which reminds me. I went to see Spencer Thorndike this afternoon to ask him some follow-up questions, and he informed me that he's offering a $500,000 reward for information leading to Claire's whereabouts. He's holding a press conference outside his home tomorrow morning to announce the reward."

Damien frowned. "Half a mil. The hotlines are going to be lit up with tips from the public—three times the amount of calls they're receiving now."

"Tell me about it. But on the bright side, maybe all we need is one legitimate tip to give us the break we so desperately need. But getting back to Farris. When does the neighbor expect him back?"

"Thursday afternoon. And I plan to be there to welcome him."

"I'm going with you. Maybe we could even do a little sightseeing while we're there, check out any vacant or abandoned buildings and warehouses in the area."

Damien nodded. "Sounds like a plan. So what did you ask Thorndike about?"

"Patrick Farris, for one. I wanted to find out if there was any love lost between the two men. Surprisingly, Thorndike didn't have too much to say about his wife's ex-husband. He said by the time he met Suzette, she'd already gotten over her divorce. Easier to do, I guess, when you make out like a fat cat in the divorce settlement," Althea added sardonically.

Damien chuckled. "Just couldn't resist, could you?"

Althea grinned. "You know it. Anyway, since Suzette and Farris didn't have any children together, they didn't have to deal with each other once the divorce was final. They were able to go their separate ways. When I asked Thorndike what he thought of his predecessor, he just shook his head and said it takes a pretty sick individual to molest his patients the way Farris did. So I asked him point-blank if he thought Farris could be responsible for Claire's disappearance. I could tell by the look on his face that the thought had never occurred to him. He asked me if we had any reason to believe Farris could be involved. I told him no, but we were exploring all possibilities, and given how acrimoniously Suzette's first marriage ended, naturally we had to consider her ex-husband a possible suspect."

"What did Suzette have to say about this?"

"She wasn't there. Thorndike said he was going to run the idea past her when she got home. I'd love to be a fly on the wall during that conversation, just to see Suzette's reaction. If she lets Farris off the hook too quickly, that's a red flag. Not that I said this to Thorndike, of course. I did, however, casually inquire about Suzette's family. Do you know what he said?"

Damien's mouth twitched. "No, but I assume you're going to tell me."

Althea made a face at him. "He said that he'd never met any of Suzette's family members. Her parents didn't approve of her leaving home at seventeen, so they pretty much disowned her. She hasn't had contact with her family in years." Althea paused. "I don't know about you, but I'm willing to bet there's more to the story than that. At the very least, I think Suzette is hiding something about her past."

"You may be right. I've got someone looking into it. He's actually down in Crisfield this week talking to Suzette's former friends, classmates, and neighbors, discreetly gathering as much information as he can. I hope he'll have something for me soon."

Althea nodded, satisfied. "Another reason I went to see Thorndike was to ask him about a summer job Claire had last year." She told Damien her theory about the kidnapper targeting one of Claire's mentors, just as Anthony Yusef had targeted Imani eight years ago.

"If our guy is following the same pattern," she posed, "then isn't it possible that someone close to Claire could be his next target?"

Damien frowned, absently stroking his stubbled chin as he mulled over the question. "I hadn't thought of that angle before, but you're right. It is possible. So, assuming this is a copycat crime, that would mean the mentor, not Claire, is the primary target."

Althea nodded. "Possibly. So if we identified the mentor, maybe we could come up with a new list of potential suspects—people who are connected to the mentor, someone who might have an ax to grind."

Damien's frown deepened. "Maybe, but it's a bit of a stretch, don't you think? I mean, would the mentor's enemy go to such extreme lengths to get revenge?"

Althea stared at him unblinkingly. "Anthony Yusef did."

Damien studied her for a moment but said nothing. He didn't have to. He knew she was right.

Althea continued, "I asked Thorndike if he could think of anyone Claire might consider a mentor. A teacher, a riding instructor, a former supervisor. Yes to the first, no to the other two. He said Claire's favorite teacher at school was Mr. Unger, her music appreciation instructor."

"But he's a man, so that doesn't fit the victim profile."

"Right. Thorndike also mentioned a congressional aide that Claire met two years ago during her brief stay with her mother. Courtney Reese, a twenty-seven-year-old congressional aide to Senator Rich Horton. Apparently Courtney and Madison Thorndike frequently work together on environmental legislation. During Claire's visit, her mother invited Courtney over for dinner, and the two girls hit it off right away. Thorndike says Claire really liked and admired Courtney. They e-mailed each other every now and then, and Claire even drove to the District on a few occasions to meet Courtney for lunch."

"Okay," Damien said, stretching out his long legs as he settled more comfortably on the sofa, "so we've potentially identified the mentor. Now what? Do we go to her and warn her that she may be in danger?"

"Why not?"

"What if we're wrong?"

Althea frowned. "But what if we're right? Don't you think she deserves to know that she could be the next target of the psycho who abducted Claire?"

"Of course. But we have to walk a fine line here, Althea. We don't have any proof that Courtney Reese is in danger."

Althea stared at him in disbelief. "We don't need *proof*. We have a note from the kidnapper, and we have a set of circumstances that are too similar to be coincidental. Why are you backtracking all of a sudden?"

Damien scowled. "I'm not backtracking. I'm just saying we shouldn't jump the gun on this. We can't go around warning people that their lives are in danger based on our suspicions and a set of circumstances that may or may not be coincidental. We need more proof; otherwise we're just creating a panic."

Althea blew out a breath and rubbed her hands over her face, her nerves stretched taut. "Maybe you're right," she conceded after a moment. "The last thing I want to do is compromise this investigation in any way."

"I know," Damien murmured.

"At the very least, I need to talk to Courtney Reese to find out what she may know about Claire and James Odem. If Claire didn't confide in her friends from school, maybe she confided in Courtney—someone she believed she could trust, someone whose opinion she really valued."

"It's worth a shot." Damien paused. "And maybe while you're at it, you could casually suggest to Courtney that she get a watchdog and invest in a security alarm if she doesn't already have one."

Althea snorted. "*Suggest?* Hell, I'll even buy them for her—the alarm and the dog." She gathered their empty beer bottles, rose from the sofa, and made her way to the kitchen. "Want another cold one?"

"No, thanks. I'm good. What did Thorndike say about Odem? I assume Mayhew had already spoken to him by the time you got there."

"Yeah. As you can imagine, Thorndike wasn't too happy about his teenage daughter cozying up to some stranger online. He blamed himself for not being more vigilant. He said he never made good on his threat to monitor her MyDomain page; he thought it was enough that she knew he had the password and could log in any time he wanted. But what good is a threat if you never follow up on it, right? Anyway, he was so upset he told me he was going to delete her page, but I asked him not to because I've been monitoring the comments that people have been leaving. You never know when the kidnapper might reach out again. Anyway, Mayhew didn't tell him everything about the evidence against Odem. So Thorndike doesn't know, for example, that Claire paid a P.I. to run a background check. Mayhew thinks we need to keep some details close to the vest."

Damien nodded. "I agree. Did you tell Thorndike about the note?"

"Yes," Althea answered grimly, placing their empty bottles in a plastic recycling bin and washing her hands at the sink. "I thought I'd have to call 911. He turned chalk white and started trembling so bad I was afraid he'd go into convulsions, poor guy. After he drank some water and regained his composure, he told me he didn't know what the note could mean. He didn't understand the significance of the proverb. But it shook him up pretty badly. I made him promise not to tell anyone but his wife about it."

"Good. I called Mayhew on my way to Solomon's Island and told him about the note as well."

"Is he going to keep it under wraps?" Althea asked, drying her hands on a red-and-white checkered dish cloth that matched the kitchen's color scheme.

"He will if he knows what's good for him," Damien said tersely.

"Let's hope so. He didn't mention it when I went back to the police station after leaving Thorndike's house. But then again, we didn't really have a chance to talk. His phone was ringing off the hook, and he was dealing with a million other things at once. When the secretary brought him the fax from the phone company, I pretty much took it and ran."

Damien chuckled. "He probably wouldn't have had a chance to go through the messages anytime soon anyway."

"That's what I figured. Are you sure you don't want anything else to drink? I've got a ton of bottled water in the fridge. Want one?"

"Yeah, that'd be good. Thanks."

Althea grabbed two bottled waters and left the kitchen. "Before I forget, I also stopped by Heather Warner's house. But I didn't get a chance to talk to her."

"Why not?" Damien asked, accepting one of the drinks.

"Her mother answered the door and told me Heather was sleeping. She'd stayed home from school today because she wasn't feeling well. Her mother said she's taking Claire's kidnapping pretty hard, not eating, barely sleeping. Perfectly understandable, considering that they're best friends."

Damien's eyes narrowed shrewdly on her face. "There's a *but* in there somewhere."

Althea shrugged as she rejoined him on the sofa. "I don't know. I just got this weird feeling that Heather's mother didn't *want* me to speak to her daughter. She kept saying that Heather had already been questioned twice by the police, and she'd told them everything she knew."

"But you think Heather is withholding something."

"I don't know." Althea bit her lip, tucking her legs beneath her on the sofa. "Maybe I'm letting my own experience cloud my perspective."

Damien watched her quietly, waiting for her to continue.

She hesitated, then said, "When I was kidnapped, my best friend at the time, Elizabeth Torres, wasn't entirely forthcoming with the police or your brother. She wasn't involved in my abduction, but she had a few skeletons of her own that she wanted to hide."

Damien said in a low murmur, "I remember hearing on the news that she had conspired with Julian Jerome, who was initially a suspect in the case. She admitted to Garrison that she'd once mentioned wanting you out of the way so she wouldn't have to compete with you anymore."

Althea nodded slowly. "She wanted to replace me as the student panelist for a big program being held at the university, and Professor Jerome wanted to discredit Imani by claiming she'd plagiarized his work. He and Elizabeth agreed to help each other achieve their warped little goals." She shook her head, amazed, even after all these years, by the twisted conspiracy plot that had come unraveled while she was being held captive by a madman. All because of jealousy and greed.

"I guess you never really know a person," she said sardonically. "If someone had told me back then that my best friend hated me so much she would sleep with my boyfriend and joke about wanting me to disappear, I wouldn't have believed it. But I was naive then, a little too trusting." Her lips curved in a brittle, mirthless smile. "I can tell you I don't have *that* problem anymore."

Damien gave her a soft, sympathetic smile. "I can see how you might find it hard to trust others. You were betrayed by your best friend and boyfriend, and kidnapped by someone you admired and respected, someone who was supposed to be an authority figure. They all let you down in the worst imaginable way, but that doesn't mean the rest of the world is out to get you."

"I know that," Althea said, a little too defensively. "Believe me, Dr. Parminter has helped me work through all those issues in therapy. All I was saying is that I've learned from that experience not to put anything past anyone, no matter how things may seem."

Damien smiled rucfully. "I guess that mind-set comes in handy in our line of work."

Althea grinned. "Are you kidding? It should be a prerequisite."

He smiled again, briefly. "Can I ask you a personal question?"

But she already knew what he was going to ask. "Why did I join the Bureau instead of becoming a doctor?"

He nodded. "I guess you get that a lot," he said ruefully.

She chuckled. "Not as much as I used to. But it's a legitimate question, especially for those who have known me all my life, who knew all I ever wanted to be was a doctor. Growing up all I ever talked about was traveling to impoverished countries and curing the poor and sick." She sighed heavily. "I had good intentions, and I probably would have stayed on that course if my life hadn't changed so drastically. But it did. *I* changed. I still wanted to help people, but not in the way I'd always envisioned.

"After surviving the abduction, I swore I would never be a victim again. I joined the FBI because I wanted to dedicate my life to stopping criminals like Anthony Yusef. If I can save just one girl's life, then I've already made a difference. And *that* is what gets me up every morning."

Damien was watching her quietly, his eyes soft with admiration and something else, something that made her breath catch.

"What about you?" she said, quickly turning the tables on him. "Why did you become an agent? And why didn't Garrison want you to join the Bureau?"

Damien chuckled. "The answer to the first question is that I've always wanted to be in law enforcement. Like you, I've always wanted to help people, and I happen to enjoy hunting criminals and saving lives. As for Garrison, he's always been the overprotective big brother. He loves being an agent, but let's face it. Over time the job takes a toll on you. There are days when it seems like fighting crime is an uphill battle, and the more you climb, the farther you have to go. Consoling the families of murder victims never gets easier, especially when that victim is a child. I've worked cases that gave me nightmares about my own daughter being brutally murdered." He grimaced, shaking his head. "Anyway, Garrison wanted to shelter me from all that. But once he realized how serious I was about joining the Bureau, he didn't stand in my way."

Althea smiled. "Smart man. I get the feeling that nothing stands in your way when you've made up your mind about something, Damien Wade."

He held her gaze. "You're right about that," he said softly.

Inexplicably, Althea's heart thumped.

She jumped up from the sofa. "Let me, uh, get those message transcripts."

She hurried down the hall to her study to retrieve the

text message transcripts from Claire's cell phone, which covered the last thirty days of activity. Returning to the living room, she divided the pile in half and passed Damien a stack of printouts.

"As you can see," she said, settling back down on the sofa, "Claire, like most teenagers, did a whole lot of text messaging. If there's any chance she confided in one of her friends or even hinted at her relationship with Odem, it's possible she did it via her cell phone. I know it's a long shot since it appears that she knew better than to make any calls to him with her phone, but it's worth investigating."

"I agree." Damien scanned the first page of the printout and frowned, muttering under his breath, "It's like trying to decipher a foreign language."

Grinning, Althea handed him another sheet of paper. "I took the liberty of downloading this handy little guide to understanding online chat acronyms, which I think you will find quite useful." She paused, then couldn't resist adding, "Dinosaur."

Damien laughed.

Chapter 18

Over the next hour, while the voice of Jill Scott crooned softly in the background, Damien and Althea pored through the private text messages of Claire Thorndike, messages that were never intended for adults—*strangers*—to view and dissect. As Damien went through the pages, he reminded himself that he was just doing his job, that finding the missing teenager took precedence over everything else. But he couldn't help feeling like he was eavesdropping on someone's private conversation or, worse, reading his daughter's diary behind her back. And the more he read, the more ancient he felt.

Claire spent an average of three hours a day sending text messages to her friends, starting first thing in the morning and continuing into the night, long after she should have gone to bed. She had a mild crush on her music appreciation teacher, who she thought was a major hottie. She gossiped about girls she hated and took stabs at her ex-boyfriend Josh Reed, citing his "puny dick" as one of the reasons she'd gotten over him so easily. She complained about PMS and monster cramps that made her want to "go effin postal" on everyone who crossed her path. She complained about boring teachers and bragged about acing hard tests that her friends had struggled with. She bemoaned the stupidity of Hollywood starlets who couldn't stay out of trouble with the law. And, most telling, she griped about her step-mother—aka THE GLDDGR. Claire believed Suzette Thorndike had only married her father for his money, and she resented Suzette's "lame" attempts to befriend her. Her contempt for her stepmother was so fierce that Damien could only wonder whether Spencer Thorndike had deliberately lied when he told them that his wife and daughter had mended their relationship. Either he'd lied or he was in serious denial.

When Damien shared this observation with Althea, she chuckled dryly and said, "I told you. And my guess is that Suzette wouldn't have too many flattering things to say about her stepdaughter if we went through *her* text messages."

"Probably not. Anything about Odem yet?"

"Not yet. Is it just me or does it seem like Claire and Heather had a very shallow friendship?"

Damien chuckled. "You're getting old, Althea," he teased, although he agreed with her assessment.

"Maybe I am," she muttered. "I mean, I realize that this may not be the medium for sharing deep, personal thoughts and feelings, but there doesn't seem to be any real substance here at all. Why spend so many hours text messaging each other just to essentially shoot the breeze?"

"Isn't that the point?"

"I guess." Althea grimaced. "God, I've never felt so old in my life."

Damien grinned. "Join the club. It's the job. It ages you more than you think. Anyway, maybe Claire and Heather had more, ah, substantive conversations in person."

"I hope so."

Silence lapsed between them again as they returned

to reading. Just when Damien began to wonder if they were searching for a nonexistent needle in a haystack, he came across a conversation between Claire and Courtney Reese. It was dated September 26, starting at 12:34 P.M.

CLAIRE: wu? (What's up?)

COURTNEY: hey u. working on speech. need mental break. wrud? (What are you doing?)

CLAIRE: at lunch. ?4u. (I have a question for you.)

COURTNEY: k

CLAIRE: have u ever been with a black guy?

COURTNEY: umm . . .

CLAIRE: tmi? (Too much information?)

COURTNEY: lol

CLAIRE: sry (Sorry)

COURTNEY: np (No problem) u really wanna know?

CLAIRE: vm (Very much)

COURTNEY: yes

CLAIRE: yarly? (Ya, really?)

COURTNEY: really

CLAIRE: wh5! (Who, what, when, where, why)

COURTNEY: lol. can't say. he's really important . . . and married.

CLAIRE: gtfo! (Get the fuck out) is he a senator?

COURTNEY: really can't say. back 2 u. why did u ask?

CLAIRE: i met someone online.

COURTNEY: a black guy?

CLAIRE: yeah. a surgeon. i really like him.

COURTNEY: is he married?

CLAIRE: nw (No way)

COURTNEY: how do u know?

CLAIRE: hired pi

COURTNEY: omg! r u serious?

CLAIRE: had to make sure he wasn't schizo or anything

COURTNEY: r u gonna meet him?

CLAIRE: yeah. next friday. my dad and the glddgr will be in colorado

COURTNEY: idk . . . (I don't know)

CLAIRE: don't worry. it's cool. he's amazing. he even offered to meet in public, but i said no. my house is more private.

COURTNEY: are u gonna . . . ?

CLAIRE: hell yeah!

COURTNEY: lmao. cb! (Laughing my ass off. Crazy bitch.)

CLAIRE: is it true what they say about black guys?

COURTNEY: guess u'll find out soon enough

CLAIRE: lol. bgwm (Be gentle with me.)

COURTNEY: lmao. ig2r. bib. cm later. (I got to run. Boss is back. Call me later.)

CLAIRE: l8r (Later)

"More evidence that the son of a bitch is lying to us," Damien muttered darkly.

Althea glanced up quickly from her printout, her expression hopeful. "What? Did you find something?"

Nodding, he passed the page to her, then watched as she read the conversation between Claire and Courtney Reese with an air of mounting excitement.

"Got him," she declared triumphantly.

Damien shook his head grimly. "Not quite."

Althea frowned. "What do you mean? We've got proof that Odem was planning to meet her!"

"No, what we've *got* is her word against his." Damien sat forward intently. "Look, you and I both know that Odem is lying through his damn teeth, but unless we can prove it beyond a reasonable doubt, he can pretty much stick to his story about Claire being delusional and obsessed with him. If we show him that text message, he'll just say she was lying, that he never agreed to meet her in person. And his lawyer will back him up. Like I said, it's her word against his."

Althea scowled, glaring at the page she held. "Damn it. That's why we really need those MyDomain message transcripts, to see if he misrepresented anything."

"What we need," Damien countered, "are the messages they sent to each other via the secret e-mail account. We need the smoking gun, the irrefutable proof that he agreed to meet her at her house on the night she disappeared. And even with those messages, Odem can always backtrack and claim that, yeah, he was going to meet her, but at the last minute he changed his mind. Short of placing him at the scene on the night in question, we're going to have a helluva time making the charges stick against a respected neurosurgeon with no priors."

"So does that mean we shouldn't arrest him at all?" Althea demanded, her dark eyes flashing with outrage.

"Of course not. If we ever get our hands on those secret messages, we're hauling him in and charging him, no questions asked."

Impatiently Althea shoved a hunk of hair out of her eyes and heaved a sigh of frustration. "This guy is the closest thing we've got to a suspect," she said bitterly, "and there's nothing we can do about it."

"Not yet," Damien murmured, understanding her frustration, the sense of urgency that fueled her anger. He felt the same way, but he knew they couldn't let it get the best of them, or they'd lose focus. "We have to be patient."

"Easier said than done," Althea snarled. "A young girl is missing, and God only knows what's being done to her."

Damien said nothing. He probed her dark, tumultuous eyes, wondering if she was remembering her own horrifying ordeal.

Swallowing hard, she averted her gaze, jerking her chin toward the printout in his hand. "Find anything else?"

Damien scanned the few remaining pages and shook his head. "Just more messages between Claire and her friends. She and Courtney must have continued their conversation over the phone."

Althea nodded, setting her own stack of pages on the antique sofa table behind them. Unbidden, Damien's mind was filled with vividly erotic images of what they had done on that table, images of her long, luscious legs wrapped around his hips as he pounded into her. Just thinking about it made him hard.

Damn. And he'd been doing so well, too.

When he arrived at the apartment, he'd forced himself to ignore the way her snug T-shirt outlined the firm, ripe swell of her breasts, the way her sweatpants molded the lush roundness of her bottom. Even the sight of her slender bare feet, the toenails painted a deep red, had threatened his self-control. But he'd kept himself in check, kept his mind on the case.

Now he felt his concentration slipping a little. It had been a long day, and Althea's tantalizing nearness on the sofa, combined with the cozy fire and the soft music playing in the background, didn't help matters any.

It was time for him to leave.

But before he could rise from the sofa, Althea said, "Can I ask you a somewhat personal question?"

Damien hesitated. "Go for it."

"Does it bother you . . . You know, reading something like that, being reminded of that whole stereotype . . ."

He just stared at her, unblinking.

"You know," she prompted, nervously twisting her hands on her lap, looking like she suddenly regretted bringing up the subject. "You *know*," she repeated, sounding just a touch flustered.

Suppressing a grin, Damien leaned back slowly and spread his arms across the back of the sofa, posturing like he had all the time in the world. "I don't know what you're asking me, Althea," he drawled, enjoying himself immensely. "You're gonna have to be more specific."

She gave him an aggrieved look. "I'm talking about the stereotype about black men."

"There are a lot of stereotypes about black men. Which one, in particular, are you referring to?"

She glared balefully at him. "The one that Claire and Courtney were talking about. The one about black men having, uh, being, you know—"

He arched an amused brow. "Hung like horses?"

He stared at Althea, marveling at the deep flush that spread across her cheekbones. He could hardly believe the blushing woman before him was the same one who'd boldly stepped to him at the club, invited him back to her apartment, then spent the night doing unspeakable things to him and with him.

"You know very well that's what I was talking about," she grumbled.

Damien flashed a crooked grin. "I wanted to make you sweat a little. Now I can't even remember the original question."

Althea rolled her eyes in exasperation. "I asked you if the stereotype bothers you. When I read Claire's question to Courtney, *I* was a little offended. I wondered if you were, too."

"Do you think I should be?"

"I don't know. It's not for me to say how you should or shouldn't feel."

"Why were *you* offended?"

"Why? Well, because I find most stereotypes—especially stereotypes about my people—vulgar and offensive."

"Yes, but do you think there's any truth to this one?"

"I—" She met his wicked gaze, then dropped her eyes and blushed furiously.

Damien threw back his head and roared with laughter.

"I almost walked right into that one," Althea muttered, a sheepish smile tugging at the corners of her mouth.

Grinning and shaking his head, Damien rose from the sofa and grabbed his car keys off the coffee table. "It's getting late. I'd better go since we have to be up early."

Althea walked him to the door. "Thanks for coming over. And thanks for dinner, even though it was supposed to be on me."

He turned at the door and smiled down at her.

She smiled back.

He forgot what he was about to say.

They gazed at each other.

He started to lower his head. He heard her breath catch. Her lips parted slightly, as if she meant to tell him no. Or so he thought at first. But as he leaned closer, her sooty lashes fluttered and her eyelids drifted shut. He paused for a moment, his gaze roaming across her upturned face, temptation pumping through his veins like a potent drug.

At the last second he brushed a light kiss across her forehead and murmured, "Lock up."

Her eyelids snapped open and she stared up at him, confusion and embarrassment mirrored in her dark eyes before she nodded wordlessly.

And for the second time in less than a week, Damien walked out of her apartment and started down the long corridor, wondering what would have happened if he'd kissed her, wondering how far he could have gone before she stopped him. *If* she stopped him.

As he rode the elevator down to the lobby and stepped out into the cold night, he was so preoccupied with his thoughts that he didn't notice the pair of eyes hidden in the shadows, following his every move.

* * *

He watched Damien Wade make his way to the black SUV parked near the front of the building and climb inside, fury boiling his blood, settling like a red haze over his vision.

Fucking bastard!

Once again, the FBI agent had intruded upon *his* time with Althea!

After following her home from the office, he'd looked forward to spending at least one hour spying on her from his nightly hiding place. Dressed in one of his elaborate disguises—which allowed him to change his hair, eye color, facial features, height, weight, even race— he'd entered the apartment building and hung around for a while, as he'd done on numerous occasions, just to prove that he could. No one recognized him. No one gave him a passing glance. He was a chameleon. Unable to resist, he'd taken the elevator to Althea's floor and rang her doorbell. He'd waited, almost dizzy with anticipation, the thrill of the chase. He'd wanted her to look into his eyes and not recognize him, to smile politely and tell him he was on the wrong floor. But when she didn't come to the door, he realized that she might be taking a shower, as she often did after a long day. He was tempted, so very tempted, to sneak inside and watch her bathe—he could have if he wanted to—but he decided not to take such a risk. Once was sufficient.

And soon enough he would have her all to himself.

But shortly after he returned to the parking lot to begin his nightly ritual, Damien Wade had shown up. And this time he hadn't stayed in his SUV. He'd disappeared inside the building as if he had every right to be there, and he'd remained inside her apartment for more than *two* hours! Long enough to work his charm, to seduce her, to remove her clothes, to run his filthy hands over her body and mount her like an animal in heat.

Rage blazed a fiery path through him at the thought of Althea—*his* Althea—lying with another man and giving herself to him with reckless abandon.

Not her.

Not his brave, beautiful Althea.

Didn't she know she belonged to *him?* Didn't she know there could be no one but him for her?

His pulse throbbed, pounding through his brain like a jackhammer. He thought of the many diabolical ways he could get revenge against Wade for taking what didn't belong to him. How he would have loved to break into his SUV, to hide in the cold darkness until the agent emerged from the building, clothes rumpled, smelling of sex and *her.* How he would have loved to meet his gaze in the rearview mirror, to see the terror in Wade's eyes before he calmly sliced his throat from ear to ear.

Or maybe he would kidnap the agent's eleven-year-old daughter instead. A pretty little thing with an infectious smile and bright, intuitive eyes. He could get to her so easily. He could snatch her off the sidewalk as she walked the short block from her bus stop to her grandmother's house after school. All it took was one crank phone call to the old woman's house, a temporary diversion that would detain her inside while he grabbed her granddaughter. Or he could simply take India from her apartment on a Friday night when she was home alone while her whore of a mother was out partying. If Wade only knew how vulnerable his precious little girl was. Oh, to see the sheer anguish on his face when they discovered her missing, to behold the rage that would sweep through him like a hurricane. When he'd finished lashing out at his ex-wife for being so selfish and irresponsible, he would blame himself for not doing a better job of keeping his own child safe. And the guilt would ravage his soul and slowly eat him alive.

What better revenge could there be?

But, no, as tempting as it was, he could not deviate from his plan. Not now. Patience was the key. Patience, diligence, and cunning.

Besides, now that he thought about it some more, he realized that Wade had not emerged from the building looking like a man who had just satisfied his sexual urges. He'd looked distracted, even unsettled.

Had Althea rejected his advances? Had she sent the bastard packing?

A slow, knowing smile crept across his face. Of course she had. She was way too smart to fall for Damien Wade's dark good looks and cocky swagger. She'd learned from past experience that she couldn't trust a handsome face and a charming smile. And she knew better than to give herself to another man, when *he* was the only one who held her destiny.

He never should have doubted her.

Taking a deep breath, he smiled again, and felt much calmer. In control. Which was where he needed to be.

It was time for him to pay a visit to the other woman who would help him achieve his ultimate goal. The woman who was an integral part of the unveiling of his masterpiece.

With his purpose in mind, he started the car and headed toward his new destination.

Chapter 19

Suzette Thorndike's hand trembled violently as she lifted a cigarette to her mouth and took a deep drag of nicotine. She held it in her lungs for a moment, then exhaled on a long, shaky breath, sending a plume of smoke into the cold night sky.

She'd had to wait until her husband went to bed before she snuck out to the terrace to have a smoke. Spencer hated her "filthy addiction" and had been urging her to quit ever since they got married. Although Suzette had tried several times—chewing nicotine gums, using the patch, switching to different cigarette brands with increasingly lower levels of nicotine before turning to herbal and homeopathic remedies—nothing had worked. She'd even undergone hours of aversion therapy at a posh private clinic outside Baltimore, but thousands of dollars later, she still craved the taste of nicotine. She'd been smoking ever since she was fourteen years old. Old habits died hard.

Besides, she resented Spencer's constant criticism of what he called her "pathetic weakness" for cigarettes. Did she criticize *him* for some of his unscrupulous business practices, the shady land deals he'd made that

had caused many families to lose their homes? Did
she criticize him for being such a workaholic that he
couldn't go to the bathroom, let alone go on vacation,
without taking his damn Bluetooth phone? Or did she,
for that matter, criticize his permissive parenting style
or his insistence upon spoiling his daughter rotten?

No!

She never, ever criticized Spencer. In fact, she'd spent
the last three years proving to him just what a loving,
supportive wife she could be. She tolerated Claire's bla-
tantly disrespectful attitude toward her, telling herself it
would be unfair to ask Spencer to choose between his
wife and his daughter, knowing he would never take her
side anyway. She kept herself in excellent shape so he
could wear her proudly on his arm wherever they went.
She satisfied his every sexual whim, from the tame to the
outrageously kinky, even when she found herself secretly wondering whether he was fantasizing about her
or his beautiful daughter.

She'd been a damn good wife to Spencer Thorndike.
Yet there she was, freezing her ass off in the cold just so
he wouldn't know she'd had a smoke. Damn it, she
shouldn't have to sneak around in her own home just
to get some stress relief. Didn't he understand that she
was supposedly as stressed out as he was over Claire's
abduction?

Didn't he know that keeping up appearances could
take a serious toll on one's health, mentally and
physically?

With a cold, narrow smile, Suzette blew out a jet
stream of smoke through her nostrils and watched it dis-
sipate into the gloom. Her craving for nicotine wasn't
the only thing that had driven her outdoors on that
dark, wintry night. She'd needed a moment of privacy,
an escape from the interlopers who had commandeered

the house over the last forty-eight hours. She never thought she'd live to see the day that she would feel claustrophobic in a nine-bedroom mansion, but that's precisely how she felt. Suffocated. Invaded. By the police officers huddled around the phone in anticipation of a ransom demand. By the endless procession of visitors—friends from their insulated little community, Spencer's family members, his colleagues and business associates who dragged their wives along to make meaningless small talk with Suzette in an obvious attempt to get her mind off the crisis. And one could not forget the constant barrage of reporters camped out at the gate to the property, waiting for any scrap of news. Waiting for her, or anyone else remotely connected to the case, to emerge from the house so they could pounce with their questions. *Is it true that the kidnapper took the time to de-stage the crime scene? Is it true that Claire might have known her abductor and unwittingly invited him into her home? Can you comment on speculation that Claire's disappearance may be linked to the Pritchard abduction eight years ago?*

Suzette shuddered, chilled by the thought of how easily information could be obtained. How easily long-buried secrets could be exposed.

It was this terrible fear that had plagued her for the last eleven years, eating away at her conscience like the deadliest of tumors. She'd worked so hard to put the past behind her, to erase all traces of the person she'd once been, the unspeakable things she had done. And then one day while snooping around in Claire's bedroom, she'd stumbled upon something that made all her fears and nightmares coalesce into a moment of sheer, blinding panic.

At the bottom of Claire's lingerie drawer, she'd found a receipt issued by Charm City Investigations.

And that was when she realized that the unthinkable had happened.

Claire, who'd never made any secret of her hatred and distrust of Suzette, had hired a private investigator to dig up her stepmother's skeletons.

Suddenly the pieces of the puzzle fell into place.

Claire's secrecy over the last month.

The strange package that arrived in the mail one day from an unknown sender.

Her increasing hostility toward Suzette, the way she'd often looked at her as if she knew something Suzette did not.

Suddenly everything made sense. Claire intended to use Suzette's past sins against her. If Spencer learned the shameful truth about his wife, he would divorce her faster than her parents had disowned her.

She couldn't let that happen. She couldn't lose her husband, the mansion, the respectability and prestige, everything she'd worked so hard for.

Standing in the middle of her stepdaughter's bedroom that afternoon, Suzette had been seized by a blinding rage, a rage unlike anything she'd ever felt before.

Claire Thorndike had everything. A closet overflowing with designer clothes, shoes, and handbags. The latest and greatest gadgets—an iPhone, an iPod touch, a state-of-the-art computer and laptop. A chauffeur at the ready whenever she didn't feel like driving her $60,000 car. A household staff that catered to her every need. An overindulgent father who did the same. Whatever Claire wanted she got, no matter how outrageous the request. Last year when she decided she wanted bigger tits, Spencer didn't hesitate to shell out $15,000 for her breast implants. For her sweet sixteen birthday, he'd hired her favorite singer to perform at her party, an extravagant affair held on the grounds of the estate and attended by more than one hundred teenagers.

Ungrateful bitch, Suzette had fumed as she stood in her stepdaughter's bedroom three weeks ago. Claire would never know what it was like to be dirt poor, to struggle to stay awake in class because she'd worked a late shift at the mini-mart the night before just to help her parents make ends meet. Claire would never know what it was like to go to bed hungry because her four younger siblings had eaten her portion of dinner before she came home. And Claire would never know the pain and humiliation of having to share underwear with her younger sister and going to school dressed in raggedy hand-me-downs donated by local charities.

Claire had more than any girl could ever ask for, yet it *still* wasn't enough. She wouldn't be satisfied until she had her father's undivided love and attention. And in order to get that, she had to remove the only obstacle standing in her way: her stepmother.

The joke's on you, little girl, Suzette mused to herself now, suffering a pang of guilt when she remembered the relief she'd felt upon returning home on Sunday and discovering that Claire had been abducted.

No amount of acting classes or community theater experience could have prepared Suzette for the performance she would give that day, tearing through the house shrieking Claire's name before falling apart in Spencer's arms. She had sobbed hysterically and railed at God just as angrily and bitterly as her anguished husband, repeating the theatrics for the benefit of the police officers who arrived shortly afterward to take their statements. And she'd made a show of dutifully taking the sedatives provided by the family physician, only to spit the pills into a wad of Kleenex when no one was looking.

Lying in bed with her husband that first night, she'd kissed his tears away and assured him that Claire would be found and returned home safely, even though she knew there was a very strong chance that his daughter was already dead.

She was counting on it.

Because if Claire somehow survived this ordeal and made her way back home, Suzette would be ruined. And she couldn't let that happen.

She would do whatever it took to keep her dark secret buried in the past.

Even if it meant selling her soul to the devil.

Wednesday, October 8
Day 6

Althea was in a dark room illuminated by candles. They were everywhere, glowing softly, casting unearthly shadows on the walls. She was lying on an unfamiliar bed, her arms stretched taut above her head, her wrists tied to the center bedpost. She was naked, exposed. Vulnerable. She couldn't fight. She couldn't escape. But she didn't feel fear. She felt anticipation. Desire.

Damien was kneeling between her legs. He lowered his dark head to her breast, licking her nipple before dragging his mouth lower, moving slowly and sensually across her belly. She moaned and arched her body toward him, swept away on the racing tide of her pulse. She couldn't fight. She couldn't escape. And she didn't want to.

His tongue snaked out, touching her clitoris. Heat shot through her veins. Her mouth opened on a silent cry.

Then his head lifted, and she stared into the cruelly smiling face of James Odem.

Althea jerked awake, gasping and choking.

The sheets were tangled around her legs. She kicked out at them, struggling to free herself. The T-shirt she'd worn to bed was soaked through with sweat. She sat up quickly, nausea churning in her stomach.

Heart pounding, she checked the alarm clock. The glowing numbers burned into her retina: 4:20.

Same as yesterday.

She shuddered.

Dragging herself out of bed, she stumbled into the bathroom and splashed cold water on her face, over and over again, trying to wash the vivid images out of her memory. *All* of them.

Leaving the bathroom, she peeled off the soaked T-shirt and tossed it in the hamper. She quickly pulled on her workout clothes and went down the hall to her office, which doubled as her exercise room.

As she went through her warm-up and stretching routine, she thought about the dream. She'd gone to sleep last night thinking about Damien, mentally re-playing that embarrassing moment when she'd walked him to the door and he leaned down to kiss her. She'd opened her mouth to refuse him, but no words would come forth, because she realized that she *wanted* him to kiss her. Against her will, against her better judgment. She'd closed her eyes, anticipating the warmth of his soft, sensuous lips. But when he planted a brotherly kiss on her forehead, she was mortified to realize that was all he had ever intended to do. When she saw the know-ing gleam in his eyes, she had prayed for the floor to open up and swallow her whole.

She was still berating herself when she went to bed two hours later. But gradually the recriminations had evolved into *what ifs*. What if Damien had kissed her the way she'd wanted to be kissed? What if he'd backed her against the door and thrust his tongue into her mouth? Would she have eventually stopped him? Or would she have begged him to carry her into the bedroom and make love to her?

She'd drifted off to sleep with those questions swirling in her mind, her body humming with arousal. What should have been nothing more than a steamy, perfectly harmless dream had ended in a nightmare.

But this time, instead of the face of her captor, she had seen James Odem.

What did that mean?

You watched his interrogation at the police station, and ever since then you've been thinking about him, trying to determine if he's responsible for abducting Claire. It's only natural that he'd work his way into your subconscious.

Grimacing, Althea hooked her feet into the straps on the incline board and started her sit-ups. She did seventy-five every day, morning or evening, whether or not she felt like it. Back in Seattle she'd also run three miles a day four times a week, a schedule she knew she would have to resume as soon as possible. The workout was necessary if she expected to compete in the male-dominated world of law enforcement, where her gender was still viewed by many as a liability. But being a woman was one thing. Being a weakling was another. Althea had survived sixteen grueling weeks of physical training at the Academy because she'd learned—not a moment too soon— that no one was going to give her a pass just because she was a member of the "weaker sex." She had been taunted, bullied and singled out by tyrannical instructors determined to wash out female applicants from the program. It was pure hell, and some days she'd questioned the wisdom of her decision to drop out of medical school, which, in comparison to the Academy, had seemed like a cakewalk. But she'd survived, proving she was no featherweight.

More than anything, Althea knew that being in top physical shape might one day save her life. Which was also why she regularly practiced her shooting at the firing range. She had to be prepared for anything.

She counted off her last sit-up and climbed off the incline board, every muscle in her abdomen burning. Time to hit the jogging trail.

But as she was about to leave the room, her gaze was drawn to the tall cherry bookcase in the corner. At the very bottom, on the last shelf, was an empty space where a book had been.

Althea froze, the sweat turning cold on her skin.

Fine hairs rising on the back of her neck, she slowly walked over to the bookcase and crouched down.

A book was missing.

But how was that possible?

She scanned the other titles in the bookcase. Her reading collection encompassed everything from popular African-American fiction to medical tomes she'd kept just in case she ever decided to return to medical school. In Seattle the books had been alphabetically arranged by category, but her aunt and her friends wouldn't have known that. Reorganizing the bookcase was one of the projects Althea had been meaning to tackle but hadn't gotten around to yet. As a result, it was hard for her to tell which title was missing.

Maybe her aunt had borrowed the book and forgot to mention it to her. Why not? They shared the same taste in literature and used to swap books all the time. Aunt Bobbi probably came across a novel that interested her and decided to check it out. All Althea had to do was call her and ask.

But why hadn't she noticed the empty space on the shelf before?

You've only spent a few hours in this room since you moved in. You haven't given the bookcase more than a passing glance.

But she would have noticed the missing book before now. She definitely would have noticed it last night after she completed her sit-ups, just as she had now.

Wouldn't she?

Althea shivered as a chilling idea struck her.

Someone had been inside her apartment. Sometime in the middle of the night. While she was sleeping.

Impossible. She wasn't a deep sleeper, never had been. She would have heard an intruder sneaking into her apartment. Because that was the very thing she feared, she slept with one eye open and a 9mm tucked beneath her pillow.

But why would someone break into your apartment to steal a book?

The line from the note whispered through her mind. *When the music changes, so does the dance.*

Was there a connection between the missing book and the kidnapper's eerie message? She didn't have a book of African proverbs, but maybe the quote had appeared in one of her novels.

Suddenly Althea sensed a tickle of cold breath against her skin, as if she weren't alone in the room. She looked over her shoulder but saw nothing. She swallowed hard, then slowly straightened from her crouching position and turned toward the open doorway.

Her muscles were rigid. She held her breath, listening.

And then she heard it. A faint noise down the hallway. A whisper of sound in the utter stillness of the apartment.

Her diaphragm slammed hard against her lungs.

Galvanized into action, she raced across the room and shoved the door closed, turning the lock in place.

Next she ran to the desk and yanked open the bottom drawer, half afraid to find it empty.

Her knees almost buckled with relief when she saw the .32 caliber she'd stashed there when she moved in. She grabbed the pistol, cocked the hammer, and silently approached the door. She flattened herself against the wall beside it, heart thudding in her chest. Her breathing was shallow as she strained to hear if someone was on the other side.

Whomever it was would be in for a rude awakening if he tried to break into the room, she vowed. She had a fistful of firepower and she wasn't afraid to use it.

She thought about her cell phone on the nightstand in her bedroom, and wished like hell she'd had the foresight to install a phone in her office.

She waited, air stalled painfully in her lungs, ears straining to pick up the slightest sound from the other side of the door.

But there was nothing but silence.

Options raced through her mind. She couldn't hide in the room forever. She and Damien were supposed to attend the task force meeting at eight-thirty A.M. If she didn't show up, he would get worried and come looking for her. But that was three hours from now, and suddenly, the idea of being trapped like a prisoner in her own home pissed her off. Damn it, she'd done enough running and hiding over the last eight years.

Enough is enough!

It was time to confront the intruder.

Decision made, Althea counted to five, quietly unlocked the door, then threw it open.

The hallway was empty.

Leading with her pistol, she stepped carefully from the room, sweeping right, then left.

No intruder jumped out at her.

Pulse hammering, she checked the powder room, the kitchen, and the living room. The front door was locked, the deadbolt secure. None of the windows had been tampered with.

She crept down the corridor to her bedroom. She looked under the bed, inside the walk-in closet and the bathroom.

Only then did she let out the breath she had been holding.

The apartment was empty.

Maybe you were imagining things, she told herself. *Maybe what you heard was a rush of wind against the windows, or the heat kicking on. Just because you heard a noise doesn't mean someone was inside your apartment.*

But there was still the matter of the missing book. She *definitely* hadn't imagined the empty space on the bookcase.

Althea glanced at the alarm clock. It was five-thirty, too early to call her aunt to ask about the book. She'd have to wait a few more hours.

In the meantime, her nerves were too shattered to go back to sleep, and the idea of removing her clothes and taking a shower suddenly evoked images of the famous shower scene in *Psycho.*

She shuddered. She'd have to get dressed somewhere else.

Damien's house.

Instead of meeting him at the old fire hall, as planned, she could head over to his place now, and they could ride to the task force meeting together. She hoped he wouldn't mind her showing up on his doorstep at six o'clock in the morning.

Plan set, Althea crossed to the dresser and snatched a fistful of clean underwear before hurrying to the closet and grabbing a pair of jeans and a sweater.

As she left the apartment a few minutes later, she couldn't dismiss the sense of foreboding that whispered across her skin, invading her senses like icy fingers of dread.

She hoped to God her aunt had borrowed the missing book.

The alternative was too chilling to contemplate.

Chapter 20

Damien was having the most intensely erotic dream.

Althea was lying beneath him, her dark hair fanned out across his pillow, her head flung back and her eyes closed as he stroked deep inside her. Her long legs were locked around his thrusting hips, her nails raking his back. Her desperate cries and moans swarmed in his blood, urging him harder and faster until a thick sheen of sweat covered their bodies and dripped from his forehead, into his eyes. She felt incredible, sublime. He couldn't get enough of her.

But something was wrong.

It pulled at the edges of his mind, dragging him toward consciousness. He groaned, resenting the intrusion, wanting to stay buried in Althea's exquisite heat for as long as he could.

But something wasn't right, and as he slowly came awake, he realized with a jolt what it was.

Someone was on top of him, straddling him through the comforter. Kissing his neck, his jaw. Moving toward his mouth.

His eyes flew open, and he found himself staring into

Angelique's innocently smiling face. His muscles went rigid with shock. Rage swept through him.

"What the fuck do you think you're doing?" he demanded.

She giggled naughtily, clamping her hand over his mouth. "Shhh! India will hear you."

Damien slapped her hand away and bolted upright, violently dislodging her from his lap. She sprawled on the other side of the bed and started laughing.

He reached across the nightstand and angrily snapped on the lamp, then turned to glare at her. "What the hell are you doing here?"

Instead of answering, Angelique folded her hands behind her head and closed her eyes with a soft, contented purr. "Mmm. I had forgotten how good it feels to lie in the same bed with you."

Damien was sorely tempted to shove her out of his bed, but his mother had always taught him and his brothers never to lay a hand on a woman. *Especially* not now, when he was feeling decidedly violent.

Angelique opened her eyes and looked at him. "You must have forgotten that I'm going to a conference in Orlando this week and you're supposed to be keeping India. My flight leaves in two hours."

"Bullshit," Damien growled. "I wouldn't have forgotten something like that. And you didn't say a damn thing yesterday morning when I saw you."

Angelique made a sour face. "Oh, yes, at the café. You were snuggled up with little what's-her-name. The Kerry Washington look-alike." Turning onto her side, she pinned him with a direct look. "Are you screwing her, Damien?"

"None of your damn business." He threw back the covers and swung his legs over the side of the bed before remembering that he was buck naked. Damn it. He was so exhausted by the time he came home last night that he'd taken a quick shower and crawled into bed without bothering to put on shorts. He rarely slept in the nude, because he always wanted to be prepared for an emergency. Which also explained the presence of the Glock beneath his pillow. Angelique was so damn lucky he hadn't mistaken her for an intruder when he first woke up.

Not that any sane intruder would have taken the time to crawl into bed with you, he thought darkly.

He scowled at Angelique over his shoulder. "What happened? Your parents pull another one of their disappearing acts?"

She huffed out an indignant breath. "You don't have to say it like that."

"Did they or did they not back out of keeping India this week?"

"Yes," she snapped. "They were supposed to keep her for me, but they called last night and told me they wouldn't be able to."

"Of course," Damien said caustically. "What else is new?"

"Don't you dare start on my parents," Angelique warned. "They love our daughter just as much as your family does!"

He snorted rudely. "They sure as hell have a funny way of showing it."

"All right! Fine! They couldn't watch India for me. We've already established that. But what's the problem, Damien? She's *your* child! You're *supposed* to keep her if I'm unable to. But now I'm getting the feeling that you don't want her here." Her tone turned coldly mocking. "What's the matter, baby? Afraid your eleven-year-old daughter is gonna put a cramp in your lifestyle? Afraid you won't be able to invite little what's-her-name over for late-night booty calls?"

Damien whirled on her, his eyes blazing with lethal fury. "Don't even try it! You know damn well I've never had a problem keeping my daughter. If it were up to me, she would stay here permanently!"

Angelique glared at him but said nothing.

"And by the way," he growled, "I don't appreciate waking up in the middle of the damn night to find my *ex-wife* lying on top of me. What part of 'Stay the hell out of my bedroom' are you having a problem understanding?"

She sniffed haughtily, tossing her dark hair over one shoulder. "It's not my fault you never turn on your alarm. And it's certainly not my fault you've become such a heavy sleeper you didn't even hear me and India coming into the house." She smirked, deliberately lowering her gaze to the covers bunched around his waist. "That must have been one helluva dream you were having. You were hard as a rock when I climbed on top of you." She paused, a malicious gleam filling her eyes. "Or maybe that was *after* I climbed on top of you."

Damien raked her with a contemptuous look. "Don't flatter yourself. Believe me, any hard-on I had went south the moment I realized you were in bed with me. Jumping into a frozen lake couldn't have done the trick faster."

Her cheeks flamed with humiliation. Recovering her composure, she sneered, "If you're having to settle for pathetic adolescent wet dreams, you must not be getting any."

Damien barked out a mirthless laugh. "And if *you're* having to settle for humping unconscious men, *you* must not be getting any."

Her face contorted with rage. "Fuck you, Damien!" she shrieked.

"No, thanks. Eight years were more than enough for me."

Angelique grabbed one of his pillows, but before she

could launch it at him, the doorbell rang downstairs.
He glanced at the alarm clock. It was barely six A.M.

A few moments later, India called, "Daddy! There's a
lady here to see you!"

A lady . . . ?

Althea. It had to be.

Shit!

"Well, well, well," Angelique drawled. "So much for
late-night booty calls."

Ignoring her, Damien lurched from the bed and
strode across the room to the closet, feeling the heat of
her hungry gaze on his bare ass. This time he didn't
give a damn.

He stepped into the closet and quickly tugged on a
pair of jeans. When he emerged, Angelique was standing
beside the bed, hurriedly combing her fingers through
her hair and straightening her clothes.

He sent her a dark look, then strode past her and
out of the room. He was halfway down the stairs when
he realized he'd forgotten to put on a shirt. But it was
too late.

Althea was standing in the foyer, a black tote slung
over her shoulder. Her hair looked like it had been
scraped back hastily into a ponytail. Her long, glorious
legs were bare beneath her belted cashmere trench,
and she wore a pair of sneakers.

As he descended the staircase, her dark eyes lifted
to his face as if in slow motion. The beginnings of a soft,
apologetic smile touched her mouth.

It faded a moment later.

He soon realized why.

Angelique was trailing him down the stairs. When he
glanced over his shoulder at her, he saw that her hair
was tousled and she'd unbuttoned her shirt to reveal an
ample amount of cleavage. And then he glanced down

at himself— at his bare chest and his unsnapped fly—
and inwardly groaned. He didn't have to see the stunned
look on Althea's face to know what conclusion she had
reached, nor could he blame her.

If he could have strangled Angelique without leaving
their daughter scarred for life, he would have.

Gladly.

When Althea set out for Damien's house that morning, she had no idea what surprises were in store for her.

The first surprise came when his daughter answered
the door, looking at Althea as if she were a vagrant who
had wandered off the street and somehow found her
way into the quiet, tree-lined neighborhood with manicured green lawns and lovely brick townhouses.

"Uh, hello," Althea said, belatedly realizing that her
unkempt appearance probably didn't help her cause.
She offered a friendly smile. "You must be India."

The girl's thick-lashed dark eyes, so much like her
father's, narrowed suspiciously on Althea's face. "Who
are you?"

"My name is Althea Pritchard. I work with your father."

India just looked at her.

Althea shifted from one foot to another. "Is he here?"

India hesitated, then called over her shoulder, "Daddy!
There's a lady here to see you!"

"Thanks," Althea murmured.

India's gaze returned to her, and after a moment she said
reluctantly, "It's cold outside, so I guess you can come in."

Not the most welcoming invitation she'd ever received,
Althea mused, but at least the girl hadn't slammed the
door in her face.

She stepped into the wide foyer and swept an appreciative glance around, taking in the two-story ceiling,

beautifully painted walls, and gleaming hardwood floors. The second surprise of the morning: Damien did not live in a typical bachelor pad, as she'd expected. This place could have easily doubled as a model home.

"My dad wasn't up yet," India informed Althea. There was no mistaking the hint of reproach in her voice.

Althea smiled easily. "I know it's early. I wouldn't have come if it wasn't really important."

India frowned, folding her skinny arms across her chest and openly staring at Althea, who calmly returned her appraisal. The girl wore a purple Bobby Jack hoodie, Baby Phat jeans, and—unless Althea's eyes were deceiving her—a soft shade of pink lipstick. Her curly black hair had grown longer since the photo in Damien's wallet was taken. It was parted neatly down the center and hung past her shoulders. Althea marveled that Damien, whose brutally masculine features took her breath away, could produce the feminine equivalent of himself in the beautiful little girl who stood before her.

At that moment, her gaze was drawn to the staircase, where the man in question had appeared.

Her breath caught in her throat at the sight of Damien's magnificent bare chest, with those impossibly broad shoulders; hard, sculpted muscles; and washboard stomach. Dark jeans hung dangerously low on his lean hips and clung to his powerful thighs as he descended the stairs.

When their eyes met, Althea smiled wanly and opened her mouth to apologize for showing up at his house so early. Both the smile and the apology died on her lips at the sight of Angelique Navarro coming down the stairs behind him. With her dark hair mussed and her shirt unbuttoned, it was perfectly clear what she and Damien had been doing before Althea arrived.

Angelique met her stunned gaze with a cool, triumphant gleam in her eyes.

Althea swallowed and looked away, cursing the stab of jealousy that sliced through her heart. She had no reason to be jealous. What Damien did with his ex-wife, or any other woman, was none of her business.

She found herself shrinking against the wall as Damien reached the landing and came toward the front door, his gaze on hers. "I, uh, I'm sorry for coming over this early," she said quickly. "I-I didn't mean to interrupt anything."

"Nah, you're fine." He kissed the top of his daughter's head, murmuring softly, "Hey, baby girl. How you doing?"

India beamed up at him. "Hi, Daddy! Were you surprised to see me and Mom?"

He affectionately tweaked her pert nose. "You could say that. But you know I'm always happy to see you."

She gave him an adoring grin. "Guess what? I'm going to make you breakfast. Blueberry pancakes, just like Grandma taught me. She said you used to love them when you were a little boy."

"I sure did. Used to ask for them every morning."

"That's what Grandma told me. So she showed me how to make them so you can have blueberry pancakes whenever I stay with you."

"That's great, sweetheart. But I don't have any blueberries."

"Don't worry, Daddy. I brought some!"

He smiled. "Good looking out." Eyes narrowing, he cupped her chin in his big hand and gently angled her face toward the ceiling light. "My eyesight must be getting bad, baby girl. It looks like you're wearing lipstick, but that *can't* be right, since we agreed you can't wear makeup until you're sixteen."

India gulped visibly. "M-Mom said it was okay."

"Did she now?" Damien's voice was remarkably mild. "Mom must be getting old, too. That's probably why she forgot our agreement. Why don't you go wash off the lipstick, then you can get started on those pancakes. My mouth is watering just thinking about them."

"Okay, Daddy!"

Damien watched his daughter take off down the hall to the powder room before his eyes met Angelique's, who'd witnessed the entire exchange from where she stood at the bottom of the staircase. He gave her a look that said he would deal with her later, when they had more privacy. Her eyes glinted with subtle challenge.

Althea had never felt more like an interloper than she did at that moment. Clearing her throat, she edged toward the door. "Look, I should probably go. I didn't mean to—"

Damien turned, capturing her wrist to halt her retreat. Heat flooded her veins at his touch, and she silently cursed her body's traitorous reaction to him.

When is he going to put on a damn shirt?

"You're not going anywhere," he said, a gentle but firm command.

She tugged her wrist free. "Damien—"

Those dark, probing eyes searched her face. "Is everything okay?"

She bobbed her head quickly. Too quickly. "Of course. I just thought since we're going to the same place this morning, we could commute together. You know, save gas, save the environment."

His eyes narrowed on hers. He wasn't buying it for a second.

Neither, apparently, was Angelique. She snorted, then muttered under her breath, loud enough for Althea to hear, "Yeah, right."

Althea bristled, her hand curling into a tight fist at her side.

Damien threw a dark frown over his shoulder. "Don't you have a plane to catch?"

"BWI is only twenty minutes away," Angelique pointed out. "I've got plenty of time. Besides, I want to spend as much time as possible with our daughter before I leave."

Damien clenched his jaw. "Then why don't you join her in the kitchen?" he suggested.

Angelique wavered, then shrugged and started toward the kitchen. Halfway down the hall she turned, her lips twisting in a venomous smile as she looked Althea up and down, from her messy ponytail to her beat-up sneakers. "By the way, girl, that's quite an interesting look you're sporting this morning. I didn't realize the Bureau had lowered its dress code."

Althea smiled narrowly. "Oh, they haven't, sweetie, but thanks for your concern. By the way, you might want to button up your shirt before you reach the airport. Wouldn't want those airport screeners thinking you actually *want* to be strip-searched." She paused. "Unless, of course, you do."

Angelique's face pinched with fury. "You b— "

"Angelique." Damien's tone was flat, hard. "Inside the kitchen. *Now.*"

After skewering Althea with a glare that promised retribution, the other woman turned and stormed off down the hall.

Left alone with Damien, Althea gave him a rueful look. "Sorry about that. I probably should have taken the high road, but after the morning I've had, I'm not in a very charitable mood."

His gaze sharpened on her face. "What the hell happened?"

She shook her head. "It's probably nothing," she

muttered irritably, pinching the bridge of her nose as a headache threatened. *Damn intruders. Damn ex-wives.*

Damien scowled. "Let me be the judge of that."

"All right, but would you mind if I tell you after I've had a shower? I got up to work out this morning, and I'm pretty funky."

"You wanna take a shower over here?" He sounded surprised.

"If it's okay with you."

"Of course. You can use the guest bathroom. Third door on your right. The spare towels are in the closet. When you're finished, you can get dressed in the guest bedroom—it's right beside the bathroom."

"Great," Althea said, starting up the stairs. "Thanks a lot. I really appreciate it."

"No problem."

When she had reached the second floor, she glanced down and saw Damien still standing at the bottom of the staircase, gazing up at her with an indecipherable expression.

She gave him a teasing grin. "Don't worry. I won't steal anything. Not that I won't be tempted, though. You have a beautiful home."

His answering smile was somewhat distracted. "You're eating breakfast with us."

She arched a brow. "Was that an invitation or an order?"

He flashed a crooked grin. "A little of both."

"In that case," Althea drawled, "you'd better get in there and supervise the cooking. I'm afraid Angelique might poison one of the pancakes and feed it to me. And after everything I've survived, I'm not about to be taken out by a vindictive ex-wife."

Damien chuckled as he started away. "We definitely can't have that."

* * *

Twenty minutes later, Althea, freshly showered and dressed in a V-neck sweater and boot-cut jeans, made her way downstairs. Passing the spacious living room, she took in the tasteful contemporary furnishings and oil on canvas paintings that captured a mosaic of themes, from wildly lush African landscapes to a jazz quartet taking center stage in a smoky Harlem club.

Spotting a row of framed photographs on the fireplace mantel, Althea, unable to resist, wandered over for a closer inspection. Predictably, most of the photos were of India, chronicling her growth from an adorably chubby infant to a pigtailed gymnast sporting a wide, gap-toothed smile as she held up a silver medal. Althea's heart melted at a photograph of Damien cradling his baby daughter in his arms, his dark eyes shining with the love and wonderment of a proud new father. A beautiful sepia-toned portrait, taken more recently, revealed father and daughter lying on opposite ends of each other, shoulder to shoulder, their heads bent together as they gazed up at the camera with meditative expressions, an effect ruined by the laughing mischief twinkling in their eyes.

When Althea's gaze landed on an old photo of Damien and his older brothers, she grinned and whistled softly under her breath. With their rich mahogany skin, piercing dark eyes, and strong, chiseled features, the Wade brothers were the epitome of a triple threat. With muscles flexing in sleeveless white undershirts and wearing Timberland boots and baggy khaki pants that hung low off their waists, Damien and Garrison stood with their legs braced apart and their arms folded, while oldest brother Reginald slouched on a chair in the middle, wearing the bored, superior expression of a king. The picture could have easily graced the cover of *Essence* under the heading "Too Much Fineness in One Family."

Chuckling softly to herself, Althea forced herself to step away from the mantel before she yielded to temptation and snatched the photograph—as well as the sepia-toned one with Damien and India.

As she neared the kitchen, drawn by the wonderful aroma of fresh blueberry pancakes, she could hear hip-hop music interspersed with laughter—the low, husky rumble of Damien's laughter mingled with India's girlish giggles. Althea hesitated, wondering if she should just wait in the living room until breakfast was ready. She didn't want to intrude upon Damien's time with his daughter.

And don't forget his ex-wife, who just tumbled out of his bed before you arrived.

Althea was the outsider, and as such, Angelique would do everything in her power to make sure she didn't forget her place.

Another burst of laughter spilled from the kitchen. Hopelessly intrigued, Althea continued walking until she reached the doorway. The sight that greeted her brought a wide, startled grin to her face.

India and Damien, who had finally put on a T-shirt, were doing the Soulja Boy to the hit song "Crank That," which was blasting from a built-in speaker on the wall. Althea didn't know what shocked her more. The fact that Damien actually knew the steps to the popular dance or that he looked so good—so natural—executing them. They'd only slow danced at the club, but watching him shuffle and move across the floor as he did the Soulja Boy, Althea realized he might have put her to shame that night, and she considered herself a pretty good dancer.

She couldn't help wondering just how many other surprises Damien Wade had up his sleeve.

India was the first to notice Althea standing in the doorway. She froze midstep, cupping her hand over her mouth as if she'd been caught misbehaving. Althea grinned and winked at her, and the girl's dark eyes twinkled with merriment.

"Um, Daddy," she said over the loud music. "I, uh, think we have company."

She pointed toward the doorway, and Damien turned his head. When he saw Althea, his face broke into a boyishly dazzling grin that made her heart catch.

And just like that, she realized how easily she could fall for this man.

Oh God. Please help me.

"Hey, Pritchard," Damien called, not missing a step. "Stop holding up the wall and come dance with us."

She laughed. "Uh, no, thanks. The two of you seem to be doing just fine."

"Ah, come on, girl," he cajoled, straightening from a move and sauntering toward her with his hand outstretched. "Don't be such a spoilsport."

Althea laughed and shook her head, skirting around the center island to evade him. He was quick, but she was quicker. Once when he almost caught her, she let out a squeal that made him laugh.

Leaning against the massive stainless steel refrigerator, India, watching their antics, doubled over giggling.

As the song ended, Damien gave up the chase and walked over to the wall to turn off the speakers. "You're no fun," he grumbled good-naturedly.

Althea laughed in protest. "Hey, that's not fair! I don't know the steps to the Soulja Boy. I would have looked like an idiot trying to keep up with you guys."

He chuckled. "India and I could have taught you. That's how I learned last year. Right, baby girl?"

India nodded vigorously. "Daddy learned really fast," she told Althea proudly. "But he's already a great dancer. All my friends think so, too. Did you know my dad could dance, Ms. Pritchard?"

Meeting Damien's amused gaze, Althea murmured, "Oh, I knew he had some moves."

His mouth curved in a wicked grin, and he winked at her.

"It's time to eat!" India announced, carrying a platter piled high with blueberry pancakes over to the round oak breakfast table.

"Your pancakes look amazing, India," Althea said with warm sincerity. "They came out perfectly."

India beamed with pleasure, and Damien mouthed over her head to Althea, *Thank you.*

She shrugged, eyeing him curiously before mouthing back, *I meant it.*

I know.

They smiled at each other.

It was only then that Althea realized Angelique was nowhere in sight. The other woman must have left for the airport while Althea was in the shower, a thought that brought her a wave of relief. She was a tough cookie and could hold her own in any verbal sparring match, but she simply wasn't in the mood that morning to fend off Angelique's barbed attacks. And she honestly didn't think she could have handled watching Damien and Angelique exchange intimate looks over the breakfast table. It was one thing to *suspect* they'd slept together before her arrival; it was quite another to have it thrown in her face.

Althea helped Damien and India set the table, and as they sat down to eat, she told herself she was crazy for enjoying the sense of togetherness. It felt natural to be sitting there, in the large sunny kitchen, sharing the first meal of the day with Damien and his daughter. It felt . . . right.

Don't go there, her conscience warned. *That's some dangerous territory you're venturing into. You've already established all the reasons you can't become involved with Damien Wade. And for all you know, he might not be over his ex-wife. If they're still sleeping together, there's a very real chance they might get back together. You don't want to get caught in the middle of that. Don't let yourself get hurt!*

"Something wrong with the pancakes, Ms. Pritchard?"

Snapping to attention, Althea realized that India and Damien were staring at her with identical expressions of concern.

Shaking her head, she ate a forkful of pancake and sighed with pleasure. "They're absolutely delicious, India. Just as I thought they would be."

"I second that," Damien agreed, smiling at his blushing daughter. "They're even better than Grandma's."

India's eyes lit up. "Really?"

"Yeah." He gave her a conspiratorial wink. "But that's just between us. Don't wanna hurt Grandma's feelings, know what I mean?"

India grinned, nodding wisely. "Gotcha."

At Damien's prompting, she launched into a humorous account of Rosemary Wade's indignation at Thanksgiving dinner last year when she was told that Imani's sweet potato pie was *almost* as good as hers. Althea listened and laughed, allowing herself a temporary reprieve from thoughts of missing books, sadistic predators who kidnapped innocent girls, and things that went bump in the night.

Chapter 21

"She's a great kid," Althea said to Damien an hour later after they dropped India off at the East Baltimore middle school she attended.

"She is," Damien said, a note of deep pride in his voice as he pointed the truck north. "She's the most incredible thing that ever happened to me."

Althea smiled gently. "She adores you. She thinks you walk on water. You know that, don't you?"

Damien chuckled wryly. "Then she's in for a rude awakening."

Althea laughed. "Oh, I don't know about that. You're a pretty cool dad, D-Wade. I can't think of too many fathers who do the Soulja Boy with their kids. Even if you *did* totally bust her on the lipstick."

He grimaced. "Her mother knows better."

Resisting the temptation to take sides, to take *his* side, Althea said diplomatically, "I guess parents never agree on everything."

"You got that right," Damien muttered under his breath.

Althea said nothing, but there were so many questions racing through her mind. Why did he and Angelique split up? How long had they been divorced? How had he coped with losing custody of India? What kind of relationship did he and Angelique now have? Were they friends with benefits? Did they argue passionately one moment, then tumble into bed the very next? Were they thinking about getting back together?

None of your business, to all of the above.

"What happened at your apartment this morning?" Damien asked, breaking into her tortured musings.

Welcoming the opportunity to segue from one unpleasant topic to another, Althea told Damien about the missing book and her suspicion that an intruder had been inside her apartment sometime yesterday. As she recounted her nerve-racking encounter that morning, Damien's jaw hardened and his hands tightened on the steering wheel until his knuckles protruded.

Too late, Althea realized her mistake in confiding in him. Now she'd never be able to convince him she didn't need protecting. *Damn it!*

She immediately began damage control. "I was probably just hearing things, noise from outside or another apartment. I was on edge, jumpy. It's possible my mind was playing tricks on me. The locks were secured, and I live on the fourth floor of a high rise building. There's no way someone could have scaled the window, definitely not without being seen. In fact, the more I think about it, the more unlikely it seems that there was an intruder."

Damien kept his gaze trained ahead, a solitary muscle ticking in his jaw. She could feel the tension radiating from his body, and she knew he was fighting to keep his temper in check.

When he spoke, his voice was deceptively calm. "I saw an alarm panel when I was at your apartment last night. Is it activated?"

"No, but I already called the security company and

left a message. If I don't hear back from them by noon, I'm calling again to have someone come out this week."

Damien inclined his head coolly. "And what about the missing book?"

Althea glanced at the clock on the dashboard. It was seven-forty. "I was waiting until nine to call my aunt. She and my uncle panic whenever I call late at night or early in the morning. I don't want to get their blood pressure up for nothing."

"You're not going to be available at nine," Damien reminded her in that same mild, implacable tone. "And depending on how the rest of the day goes, it may be hours before you have a chance to call her—if you remember. So why don't you just do it now?"

It was posed as a suggestion, even though Althea knew it was anything but.

Conceding the logic of his explanation, she dug her cell phone out of her purse and pressed the button to speed-dial her aunt and uncle.

Barbara Pritchard answered halfway through the first ring, sounding alert and worried. "Hey, baby. Is everything all right?"

I told you, Althea mouthed to Damien, who was watching her instead of the road.

"I'm fine, Aunt Bobbi," Althea quickly reassured her. "I hope I didn't wake you."

"Not at all. I was just about to get dressed and run some errands, and your uncle is on his way to the Hill. She's fine," Barbara murmured to someone in the background, and Althea could imagine her uncle hovering nearby with an anxious look on his face.

"Good morning, Uncle Louie," she called into the phone, smiling.

Sure enough, he called back, "Morning, baby!"

"Are you sure everything is okay, Althea?" Barbara

pressed. "You know your uncle and I have been worried sick about you ever since that girl went missing. They were saying on the news last night that this kidnapping might have something to do with what happened to you."

Althea inwardly groaned. She should have known it wouldn't take the media long to make the connection. "They're just speculating, Aunt Bobbi. We don't know for sure that there's a correlation between the two cases."

"We certainly hope not." Her aunt didn't sound too convinced. "Your uncle spoke to Garrison Wade yesterday, and Garrison told him he's hiring a bodyguard for Imani and the children until this is over. We'd like to do the same for you, if you'd let us."

"You both mean well, but that really won't be necessary, Aunt Bobbi. I can take care of myself," she said, pretending not to notice Damien scowling. "Don't worry."

"That's easier said than done. I don't have to tell you how devastated we would be if anything happened to you again."

"I know," Althea murmured.

Barbara heaved a sigh. "Will you at least consider moving back home for a while? I know the commute from Georgetown to Baltimore would be a little long, but at least you'd be safe here with us."

"I—" Althea broke off as Damien abruptly switched lanes, pinning her against the passenger door as he veered around another vehicle. This time she scowled at him, and he grumbled a sheepish apology.

"Althea?"

"Sorry about that. Crazy Maryland drivers," she muttered, glaring pointedly at Damien. "As I was about to say, as much as I'd love to see you and Uncle Louie more often, I can't move back home. I need to be close to my job."

"Well, at least give it some thought. Will you do that for us?"

"I will," Althea lied. "Oh, before I forget, Aunt Bobbi. Did you happen to borrow one of my books on Friday?"

"One of your books?" Barbara sounded puzzled.

Althea's heart sank. Her aunt didn't have a clue what she was talking about. "Yeah. From the bookcase in my office."

"No. I didn't borrow a book. I can ask the ladies from church who helped me unpack your things, but I'm sure none of them took it. Not without asking first. Are you telling me one of your books is missing?"

"I probably just misplaced it," Althea said, feeling the weight of Damien's hawklike gaze on her face. Dread settled in the pit of her stomach. Her mind was spinning.

"Listen, I have to run, Aunt Bobbi."

"All right. Oh, wait! Your uncle wants to know if you're free to meet him for lunch this afternoon. He's got a two-hour midday break between sessions."

Althea groaned softly. "I'd love to meet him for lunch, but I can't. My day's going to be pretty full. But tell him I want a rain check."

"I'll do that. And Althea?"

"Hmm?"

Barbara hesitated. "You be careful."

"Yes, ma'am."

Althea snapped the phone shut and shoved it back inside her purse with hands that trembled slightly.

Damien noticed.

He stared at her, his eyes hooded, his expression grim. "We can't ignore it," he said in a low, flat voice.

"I know." Althea let out a long, measured sigh. "But I can't focus on it right now. This case isn't about me. It's about Claire. And until we find her and bring her home safely, nothing else matters."

Damien looked like he wanted to argue, but he said nothing.

Her lie hung in the tense silence between them. *This case isn't about me.*

Althea wanted to believe it was true, but she knew better.

And so did Damien.

Organized chaos greeted them when they arrived at the old fire hall on Reisterstown Road in North Baltimore.

As Althea and Damien entered the building, they passed a group of volunteers headed out the door, armed with flyers that provided Claire's photo and vital statistics. The flyers would be distributed all over the community—papered across storefront windows, stuck on bulletin boards, stapled to light poles, tucked under windshield wipers, passed along to people on the street. The hotline telephones, temporarily housed at the police station, had been set up on a long bank of conference tables in a far corner. Even at that early hour, the phones were already manned and busy; the number of incoming calls and tips was expected to quadruple once Spencer Thorndike announced the $500,000 reward later that morning. Copy and fax machines lined one wall where, at a nearby table, volunteers stacked flyers in neat piles and ran off additional copies as necessary. Office supplies donated by local businesses—envelopes, staplers, stamps, and boxes of rubber bands—littered every available surface of the tables.

The hall was overflowing with law enforcement officers, volunteers from the community, and those who had been lured by their curiosity and morbid fascination with the high-profile case. There were reporters, photographers, and cameramen from newspapers and radio and television stations around the entire metropolitan region—which encompassed Maryland, Virginia, and Washington. They prowled around filming footage of the volunteer efforts while trolling for a scoop, an exclusive, an angle none of their competitors had. They interviewed concerned citizens who expressed fear, shock, and outrage that such a heinous crime could have struck the quaint, insulated community of Mount Washington, where teenage girls were supposed to be safe at all times, especially in their homes. These sound bites would be aired and reaired ad nauseum on evening broadcasts, along with video montages of the bright, beautiful heiress who had seemingly vanished into thin air.

"I'm gonna go talk to Detective Mayhew before the meeting begins," Damien said, briefly touching Althea's arm before moving off, threading his way easily through the throng of bodies.

Althea watched him go, then continued scanning the crowded room in search of two particular individuals. She saw a number of teenagers that could only be Claire's classmates. Some were making good use of their time, while others loitered around and congregated in small groups, laughing and enjoying the day off from school.

Althea eventually spied Heather Warner, whom she recognized from her MyDomain page. The cute, petite blonde wearing black leggings and an oversize cardigan sweater stood behind a table serving hot coffee and doughnuts donated by a local bakery. As Althea watched, a tall, good-looking kid with dark hair and a trim, athletic build sauntered over to the table and struck up a conversation with Heather. Althea recognized the newcomer as Josh Reed.

Josh, who had traded insults with Claire just a week before she disappeared.

Josh, who had hired an attorney and now refused to speak to the police.

Althea stood there for a moment watching him and Heather, studying their interaction with each other, reading their body language. Heather seemed annoyed with him, rolling her eyes and shaking her head in barely concealed disgust. Josh seemed unperturbed by her rancor, snagging two doughnuts from the tray and laughing when she rebuked him.

Deciding she'd seen enough, Althea made her move, cutting a path through the crowd to reach the table near the back. As she approached, Josh glanced up, his dark eyes widening in startled recognition before he quickly averted his gaze.

Althea frowned to herself. How had he recognized her? Neither she nor Damien had appeared in the news in connection to the kidnapping investigation. And even if Josh had seen an old photograph of her, she had changed a lot over the last eight years. Even Keren and Kimberly, her best friends from high school, had done a double take when they saw her on Friday for the first time in years. And none of the reporters milling around the room had recognized her, and some of them had covered her abduction extensively.

But somehow Josh Reed knew who she was.

In contrast, Heather Warner greeted Althea with a friendly, vacant smile that held no trace of recognition. "Good morning. Would you like some coffee?"

Althea smiled. "Sure, that'd be great. Thanks." Out of the corner of her eye, she could see Josh fidgeting with a bracelet on his wrist, looking everywhere but at her. She silently counted to five.

On cue, he mumbled, "I'll, uh, catch you later, Heather."

Althea turned as he started away. "Leaving so soon, Mr. Reed? I was hoping to have a moment of your time."

He shook his head jerkily. "Sorry. My lawyer said I'm not supposed to talk to the authorities. That includes feds."

So he *did* know who she was.

"Why are you hiding behind a lawyer, Mr. Reed?" Althea asked mildly.

He walked faster, not looking back.

"Well," Althea said, turning back to Heather, who was staring curiously at her.

She passed Althea a steaming cup of coffee. "He's been acting weird ever since Claire went missing. But I guess we all have. Are you an FBI agent?"

Althea nodded, flashing her creds with a practiced flick of her wrist. "Althea Pritchard."

The girl's blue eyes narrowed shrewdly on her face. "You came to my house yesterday."

"Yes, I did. I wanted to ask you some questions about Claire."

"That's what my mom told me. But I already spoke to the police, so I'm not sure how much—" She paused to serve coffee to a volunteer who had wandered over.

"Here, let me help you." Althea set down her own cup, then rounded the table to stand beside the teenager in front of an industrial-sized coffee machine. "Why don't we just fill some cups and leave them on the table?"

"I was doing that at first, but I heard a few people complaining that the coffee was cold."

"Ingrates," Althea grumbled.

Heather grinned. "It's no big deal. It was a madhouse when I first got here, but it's trickled off since then." She shrugged. "I used to work at Starbucks. This is tame in comparison. Besides, someone's supposed to relieve me in a few minutes so I can go out with the search team."

Althea nodded. "It's nice of you to come out here so early and help with the volunteer efforts."

"It's the least I can do. She was my best friend." Heather shook her head, closing her eyes for a moment. "God, I keep doing that," she whispered, emotion clogging her voice. "I keep referring to her in the past tense. *Was.* Like she's already dead."

"Do you think she is?" Althea asked quietly.

Heather's blue eyes clouded. "I don't know. I hope not." She swallowed hard. "But I keep having these horrible dreams. They seem so *real.*"

Blinking back tears, she grabbed a paper towel and busied herself wiping a ring of coffee off the table.

Althea watched her sympathetically for a moment. "How long have you and Claire been friends?" she asked, deciding to start with the easy questions first.

Heather sniffed. "Forever. We grew up together, went to the same schools. She was like my sister." She groaned. "God, there I go again."

"It's all right," Althea said gently. "Just because you use past tense doesn't mean you think Claire is dead."

"But she probably is, isn't she? I mean, she's been missing for almost a week now. In most cases, kidnapped people don't come back after they've been gone that long. Am I right?"

Althea pursed her lips, trying to think of the best way to reassure Heather without misleading or patronizing her. "It's true that the odds against finding a missing person increase the longer they're gone," she said carefully, "but that doesn't mean we should give up hope. We just have to keep praying and doing the best we can to help find Claire."

Heather nodded slowly. "I knew something was wrong. I kept calling her all weekend, but she wouldn't answer her cell phone. I even tried calling the house, but no one answered. Finally I just gave up and figured she'd gone to hang out at her mother's place." She shook her head, looking guilty and miserable. "Maybe if I'd driven over to the house and saw her car sitting there, I would have realized something was wrong, and I could have called the police."

"You can't blame yourself, Heather," Althea said softly. "You had no way of knowing Claire was in danger."

"I know," the girl mumbled, her eyes downcast. "That's what my parents keep telling me. But it doesn't make me feel any better. I just wish there was something I could do."

"Actually," Althea murmured, "there is."

Heather lifted her head, meeting her gaze. Her expression was suddenly wary.

"If you know *anything* that might give us a clue into Claire's whereabouts, you have to tell us, Heather. Anything at all. No matter how small or insignificant it may seem to you."

"I already told the police I didn't know Claire was planning to meet someone on Friday night. She didn't tell me anything about that, I swear."

"So she never told you about the man she met online through MyDomain?"

Heather shook her head emphatically. "Oh, I saw a few of the comments they left on each other's pages, but I didn't think anything of it. Claire said he was just some guy who was helping her with her music appreciation class. She said he was nice, really smart, and that was it. I didn't know she was planning to meet him in person."

Althea searched her face and realized that the girl was telling the truth. "Why do you think Claire kept something like that from you?" she gently probed.

Heather shrugged, looking aggrieved. "I don't know. Maybe she thought I would make fun of her, because he's older. She's been really sensitive ever since she and

Josh broke up. A lot of girls talked about her behind her back, saying Josh played her with Brandi. He really humiliated her."

Althea nodded, understanding all too well what Claire must have gone through. "So maybe that's why she kept her online friend a secret," she speculated. "She didn't want anyone at school to find out she was hooking up with an older man because she'd already been embarrassed by Josh cheating on her."

"I guess so. But she should have known I wouldn't tell anyone. She should have known she could trust me." There was unmistakable hurt in Heather's voice. Hurt and betrayal.

Her lips twisted bitterly. "I'm sure she had no problem telling Courtney though."

Althea studied her for a moment. "Do you have a problem with her friendship with Courtney?"

"No."

Lie, Althea thought.

She waited patiently, and after a prolonged moment Heather blurted, "It's just that she was always bragging about how cool Courtney is, how smart and sophisticated. Courtney could do no wrong. I got sick of hearing about her."

"That's understandable," Althea murmured. "Courtney's on a different wavelength. She's twenty-seven years old, she has her own place. A career. I can see how you would find it frustrating to have to compete with that. I'm sure Claire never meant to make you feel that way."

Heather sniffed, blinking back angry tears. "Well, she did."

They were interrupted by two volunteers who walked up, helping themselves to glazed doughnuts while Althea filled two cups of coffee. She served them quickly and sent them on their way, not wanting to lose ground with Heather.

"Where were some of the places you and Claire liked to hang out after school and on the weekends?"

Heather shrugged, bending to retrieve more Styrofoam cups from under the table. "The mall, I guess. Sometimes the park, to talk in private. But we hung out at her house a lot, went horseback riding and swimming in the lake."

"You didn't hang out at any coffee shops or Internet cafés?"

Heather frowned. "No. Why?"

"I'm just trying to find out where Claire liked to spend her time. It's possible that whoever took her may have seen her somewhere and followed her home."

Heather paled. "That's scary," she whispered.

"Yes, it is. But it happens, unfortunately." Althea glanced up and saw Damien standing across the room, deep in conversation with Detective Mayhew and his partner, an attractive, thirty-something black man with a trim mustache and a stocky build.

Althea stole a peek at her watch and saw that it was eight-fifteen. The task force meeting would be starting soon, and the teams of volunteers would be heading out into the cold for the ground search. She didn't have much more time with Heather.

She turned back to the girl. "You mentioned earlier that Josh had been acting weird ever since Claire went missing. What did you mean by that?"

Heather shrugged. "I don't know. In school on Monday he was really upbeat, even though everyone already knew what had happened to Claire. He was acting goofy in class—even goofier than usual. Cracking silly jokes, laughing at the dumbest things. Just weird."

"Are you saying he seemed almost *happy* that Claire had been kidnapped?" Althea asked.

Heather's alarmed gaze shot to her face. "I didn't say that. Josh may be an asshole, but I don't think he'd want anything bad to happen to Claire. He was still hoping they would get back together. He used to beg me to talk to her about giving him a second chance. But that wasn't gonna happen."

"Because Claire didn't want him back."

"No way. She despised him. After they broke up, she told me she didn't know what she saw in him in the first place." The girl shrugged dismissively. "I always thought she could do better than a dumb jock anyway."

Althea said nothing, wondering what lengths Josh Reed would go to convince Claire to take him back. Had he resorted to violence? If so, wouldn't he have the sense to at least *pretend* to be distraught over her disappearance?

But then again, Heather *had* called him a dumb jock.

Switching gears for the sake of time, Althea said, "I got the feeling, from talking to Mr. and Mrs. Thorndike, that Claire and her stepmother didn't always get along so well."

Heather snorted. "That's an understatement. They *never* got along."

"Why?"

"They hated each other's guts. Claire thought Suzette was a slut, white trash. Suzette thought Claire was a selfish, spoiled brat." Heather made a pained face. "I guess they were both right, to an extent."

Althea smiled a little. "Why did Claire think such terrible things about Suzette? Because she grew up poor?"

"Well, yeah, but that's not the only reason," Heather hastened to add, not wanting to sound like a snob. "She had other reasons, too."

"Like what?"

Heather hesitated, her expression turning veiled.

"Remember what I said," Althea prompted gently. "Nothing is too small or insignificant."

Heather bit her bottom lip, then blurted, "Claire found out three months ago that Suzette slept with her stepson when she was married to her first husband."

"Which stepson?" Althea asked evenly, feeling like she'd hit the mother lode of dirt—and possibly a lead.

"The younger one. Corbin, I think. He was sleeping with Suzette practically the whole time she was married to his father."

"I see. And how did Claire find out?"

"She accidentally overheard them talking on the phone. She says Corbin called Suzette one day out of the blue, and Suzette seemed really angry and upset." Heather frowned. "Claire thinks he was trying to blackmail her."

Chapter 22

The task force chose a small community room down the hall from the main volunteer station for their war room. It was far enough away from the noisy hub of activity to afford them privacy, and it was already equipped with a conference table that accommodated the seven members of the team, which included Baltimore Police Commissioner Frederick Bell, Detective Mayhew and his partner Curt Johnson, Sheriff R. Jay Fisher, an assistant state's attorney, and Althea and Damien, representing the Bureau.

Althea was the last to arrive to the meeting. When she appeared in the doorway, murmured conversations died, the rustle of paper ceased, cell phones went silent. Six pairs of eyes latched onto her.

She hesitated for a moment, heat crawling up her neck and seeping across her face. Not only was she the only woman in the room, she was also the only one who'd ever been kidnapped, held captive for weeks, presumed for dead.

And, suddenly, for the first time ever, Althea realized how her ordeal could actually be an advantage to her. She'd survived the most harrowing experience of her life and come out stronger, tougher. Battle-tested. Everyone here knew who she was and what she had been through. No one could question her resolve, her intestinal fortitude.

No one could question her cojones.

Straightening her back, squaring her shoulders, and lifting her chin, Althea strode confidently and purposefully into the room. *I am strong. I am invincible. I am woman, hear me—*

Damien rose from the table and pulled out her chair, ruining the moment.

Althea muttered her thanks and sat down, making a mental note to chew him out when the meeting was over. *Damn him and his chivalry!*

Once the formal introductions had been dispensed, the meeting got under way. Seated at the head of the conference table was Commissioner Bell, who had assembled the task force. A tall, lean man in his late fifties with a ruddy complexion, aristocratic features, and neatly trimmed silver hair, Bell possessed the polished veneer that the mayor had sought in a candidate who would bolster the BPD's public image.

He wasted no time grabbing the reins. "I'm sure I don't have to tell any of you the tremendous pressure we're under to find Claire Thorndike and apprehend her abductor," he began intently, looking at everyone in turn. "The phones in my office are ringing off the hook from reporters and concerned citizens. I've got the mayor breathing down my neck every hour on the hour, wanting to know if we have any viable leads or suspects. The daughter of a prominent businessman has vanished without a trace. People start thinking if it could happen to someone like her, it could happen to anyone. That creates mass hysteria, an environment of fear, and one thing we don't need in a city with our high crime rate is *more* fear."

He swept another glance around the table, as if daring anyone to contradict him. When he encountered stoic silence, he said, "So what have we got so far? Give me something to work with, something I can take back to the mayor before the candlelight vigil scheduled for Friday evening."

Looking like he'd rather not, Detective Mayhew stepped up to bat. "Right now we're pursuing a number of different angles and motives for this crime. One of our theories is that a disgruntled former employee or contractor took Claire as a way of getting back at her father. Thorndike's secretary provided a complete list of everyone who has ever worked for or with him, so we're running the names through the system, conducting interviews, and sitting down with Thorndike to go through the list and basically identify anyone who may have despised him enough to go after his kid."

The commissioner frowned. "That's no small undertaking. Thorndike has employed hundreds of people and has probably made twice as many enemies."

Mayhew snorted. "Tell me about it. But so far no one is standing out as being particularly vindictive toward him. We're also going through a list of people who have had access to his property over the last sixty days. Again, no small task. The Thorndikes have thrown three dinner parties in the last two months. More than eighty people attended each party, but here's the kicker: It was a different guest list for each one."

There were collective groans around the table.

Bell scowled, undoubtedly realizing that zeroing in on a suspect wouldn't be as simple or speedy as he would have liked, as his *boss* would have liked. In any large metropolitan police department, the commissioner or chief

was an administrator, a spokesman, a politician. Frederick
Bell was no exception. He didn't understand the sheer
amount of legwork that went into a criminal investigation, and any memories he had of being in the trenches
and doing actual police work had long since faded as he
climbed through the ranks, scratching and clawing his
way to the top of the food chain.

"What about teachers at Claire's high school? Former
employees?" he demanded.

Mayhew answered, "We got our hands on a list of employees fired from the school within the last six months.
We found a janitor convicted of felony check fraud who
lied about his record on his application, but other than
that, everyone checked out. No red flags on any of the
current staff, either. And we've finished going through
Claire's computer. Other than the bookmarked site that
led us to the P.I. she hired, we didn't find anything else
useful."

Bell asked, "What about this surgeon you interro-
gated yesterday? The media's been buzzing about him
all morning."

Mayhew traded grim looks with Damien.

"Odem's a slippery bastard," Damien said darkly. "We
know he's lying about the extent of his online relationship with Claire, but without proof that he was there on
the night she disappeared, our hands are tied. As his
lawyer pointed out on the news this morning, Odem's
got no priors and he's been nothing but a model citizen.
Hell, he saves lives every day."

Althea interjected, "But if we can at least prove that
he was planning to meet Claire in person that night, we
have grounds for arresting him. If for nothing more
than giving a false statement."

"Agreed," Bell said with a brisk nod, obviously pleased

at the prospect of having someone in custody. "You get that proof, you arrest him."

Althea nodded. "The message transcripts between him and Claire should be on my desk when I get back to the office. If Odem provided any conflicting information, we've got him. Who knows? If we rattle his cage hard enough, maybe we can get a confession out of him."

Mayhew snorted. "Hope springs eternal."

"You got a tail on him, right?" the sheriff asked.

"Yeah, and at this point we stand a better chance of him leading our guy to a secret hiding place than confessing to the crime."

"He knows he's being followed," Damien said. "So he's not going to go anywhere or do anything that would draw suspicion. Hospital, then home. Hospital, then back home. That's going to be his new routine."

There were nods of agreement around the table.

Detective Johnson grumbled, "I don't like that Reed kid running around here, thumbing his nose at us while hiding behind his damn lawyer."

Bell lifted his shoulders in a negligent shrug. "It's a free country. Mr. Reed is welcome to show up here to help with the search efforts if he so chooses."

"Yeah," Mayhew muttered under his breath, "even if *he* might be the reason we're having a damn search in the first place."

Bell frowned. "Just because the boy forgot to mention e-mailing Claire a week before she disappeared doesn't mean he kidnapped her, Detective. In our urgency to identify a suspect, let's resist the temptation to go on a witch hunt."

In the ensuing silence, Althea made a mental note to find out whether the commissioner and Josh Reed's father, a wealthy industrialist, belonged to the same country club.

Mayhew continued, "We're also looking closely at Suzette Thorndike's ex-husband, a retired physician named Patrick Farris. He and Suzette split up a few years ago, and she made out like a bandit in the divorce settlement."

Bell looked intrigued. "You think he kidnapped Claire to get back at his ex-wife?"

The detective hitched his chin toward Althea. "Why don't you explain the theory, Pritchard, since it was yours?"

Althea hesitated. She had decided to wait until after the meeting to tell Damien what she'd just learned about Suzette Thorndike. Although the task force had been assembled for the purpose of sharing—not withholding—information, the reality was that anyone seated at this table could be responsible for the leaks to the press. While she trusted Damien implicitly, she didn't know the others well enough to say the same, and she didn't want to risk tipping off Suzette Thorndike before she had a chance to talk to her. Which she intended to do as soon as possible.

But Mayhew had put her on the spot, so she'd have to give them something. In a carefully measured voice, she said, "I think it's possible that Farris may be blackmailing Suzette Thorndike for ransom in order to recoup some of the money he lost in the divorce settlement."

The commissioner's eyes bulged. "*What?* Are you suggesting that Spencer Thorndike's *wife* may be involved in his daughter's abduction? Is that what you're telling me?"

Althea didn't flinch at the shocked outrage in his voice. "I think it's possible."

"Based on what?"

"Based on the fact that we never rule out parents as suspects when a child goes missing," Damien intervened, calm and implacable. "The reality is that Patrick

Farris has motive for going after his ex-wife any way he can. Before their divorce, he was sued for malpractice by five of his former patients who accused him of sexual misconduct. The lawsuit cost him everything—his practice, his medical license, his reputation, and then his marriage. On top of that, he has a criminal record. Last year he was charged with three counts of aggravated sexual assault. I think we can all agree that kidnapping Claire Thorndike would demonstrate a pattern of escalating violence, which fits the profile of the perpetrator we're looking for."

The room fell silent.

Bell pursed his lips, looking grim. "All right. I agree. Farris is a very strong suspect. But I'd rather assume he's working on his own, rather than conspiring with Suzette Thorndike."

Because that scenario is more politically expedient, Althea thought cynically. Bell was a smart politician who understood the ramifications involved in accusing the wife of a prominent businessman of kidnapping. Spencer Thorndike was one of the richest, most powerful men in the tri-state area, which meant he could make it very difficult for the commissioner to keep his job if he chose to do so. Bell knew that going after Suzette Thorndike was a surefire way to turn her husband into a formidable enemy.

"Have you questioned Farris yet?" Bell asked Damien.

"Not yet. He's visiting his oldest son and daughter-in-law in Virginia this week. Our agents in Richmond are staking out the house, but so far they haven't observed any suspicious activity. Farris is supposed to return home tomorrow. His neighbor promised to call and let me know when he arrives."

"Where does he live?"

"Solomon's Island. Agent Pritchard and I will be

checking out any abandoned buildings and warehouses in the area and conducting surveillance on Farris's home to see where he goes and what he comes back with. Then we're going to pay him a friendly little visit."

Bell nodded in satisfaction. "That sounds like a solid plan. The task force can reconvene on Friday to find out what, if anything, the two of you learned. I'm familiar with Solomon's Island. Pretty little fishing village, but very remote. Farris could have a stash of bodies in an old boathouse and we would be none the wiser." He glanced at his expensive watch. "I'm afraid we have to wrap this up. I have a meeting at the mayor's office, and then we're heading over to the Thorndike estate for the reward announcement."

Meeting adjourned, everyone pushed back their chairs and stood, filing purposefully out of the room. Only Althea and Damien hung back.

"Mayhew didn't bring up the note," she said, keeping her voice low in case someone was lingering by the door.

"I know. We spoke before the meeting, and I asked him not to. The less people who know about it, the less we have to worry about it being leaked to the media. He agreed, and so did his partner."

"Detective Johnson? Can we trust him?"

Damien nodded. "I've served on different task forces with him before. He's a good cop."

"He didn't have much to say during the meeting," Althea observed.

Damien made a face. "That's because he thinks Bell is an opportunistic asshole. An opinion shared by many, I might add."

Althea chuckled dryly. "Gee, I wonder why."

Damien smiled, lazily searching her face. "What aren't you telling me?"

Her eyes widened in surprise. "How did you know?"

"I know you better than you think, Miss Pritchard."

What a scary thought.

Shoving *that* thought aside, Althea said, "I was talking to Heather Warner before the meeting, and she had the most interesting news to impart. It seems that three months ago, Claire found out that her stepmother had an affair with Corbin Farris when she was married to his father."

"Are you serious?"

"As a heart attack. Apparently Corbin called Suzette one day and threatened to tell her husband about the affair. Claire overheard enough of the conversation to reach the conclusion that Corbin was trying to blackmail her, but the housekeeper caught her eavesdropping and shooed her away before she could hear the rest."

Damien frowned. "That's pretty compelling, but it's not a strong-enough motive for Suzette to agree to the kidnapping plot. I doubt that Spencer would have divorced her if he found out she cheated on her first husband with his own son. It might anger or disgust him, maybe even cause him to question her judgment. But would he actually divorce her over something that happened before he met her, especially considering that her first husband wasn't exactly a model of virtue himself?"

"I asked myself the same thing. That's why I suspect Corbin knows plenty more about Suzette Cahill Thorndike. If they were lovers, she might have confided in him about her past. He obviously believed he had enough dirt on her when he called her that day."

Damien nodded. "I think you're right."

"Where *is* Corbin? Is he visiting his brother in Virginia, too?"

"The folks in Richmond haven't seen him yet. They've observed Patrick and Kyle Farris, along with his wife and two children, entering and leaving the house. But no sign of Corbin. His last known address is his father's house in Solomon's Island. But he wasn't there yesterday when I showed up. There were no cars in the driveway, and according to the neighbor, no one was home."

"That *he* knows of." Althea stared at Damien. "Are you thinking what I'm thinking?"

"That we need to make a trip out there tonight instead of waiting until tomorrow? Yeah."

"We can spend a couple of hours tonight sitting on the house, then go back tomorrow to do the rest of the stuff when Patrick Farris comes home."

Damien nodded. "That works. But I need to drop India off at my mother's house first."

"That's right. I'm sorry. I forgot India is staying with you this week." She bit her lip, feeling guilty for taking him away from his daughter. "Maybe I could just—"

"Hell, no." The steely edge of his voice cut her suggestion short. "You're not going out there by yourself. I'm going with you, or you're not going at all."

She frowned, but before she could open her mouth to protest his heavy-handedness, his cell phone trilled. Giving her a look that said the discussion was over, he dug his phone out of his back pocket and clipped, "Wade."

Once Althea realized the call pertained to another case he was working on, she left the room and headed down the hall toward the main area.

Although many volunteers were out with the search teams, the room was still crowded, buzzing with conversation and the steady flow of foot traffic. As Althea stood there surveying the chaotic harmony, her gaze was drawn to the entrance, where a small group of reporters had gathered. Camera bulbs were flashing, and an air of hushed excitement swept through the room.

Intrigued, Althea wandered closer to find out what on earth was going on.

Suddenly she froze.

A tall, dark-skinned man with a gleaming bald head sporting dark sunglasses and a trademark swagger stepped through the doorway.

Althea thought her eyes were deceiving her, although deep down inside she had known, with an almost fatalistic sense of inevitability, that he would come looking for her.

Malik Toomer.

Her college sweetheart.

The man she once thought she would marry.

And just like that, memories assailed her.

Coming out of college, Malik Toomer was the fifth overall pick in the NBA draft, signing a multimillion-dollar contract with the Chicago Bulls and netting a lucrative deal with Nike. But after two disappointing seasons in the Windy City, Malik was traded to the Washington Wizards, where his stats improved slightly and he was credited with leading the team into the playoffs for the first time in years. Still, his poor career shooting percentage served as fodder for his critics, who bemoaned the fact that the promising young shooting guard who'd dazzled recruiters in college had not lived up to his potential in the pros.

But his fans adored him. He was a local success story, a hometown hero who'd risen above abject poverty and the crime and violence that had claimed the lives of too many of his childhood friends. He'd not only defied the odds by graduating from college but made it into the elite ranks of the NBA. He was a multimillionaire who'd bought his struggling single mother a mansion in the exclusive enclave of Potomac, Maryland, not far from his own sprawling estate. He promoted drug abuse prevention programs through public service ads that aired on local television, he coached inner-city youth during the summers, and he served turkey dinners to the homeless during the holidays.

Despite what had transpired between them nearly eight years ago, Althea knew, at heart, that Malik Toomer was a good person.

The moment he entered the building he was swarmed by reporters and cheering fans. More camera bulbs went off. Microphones were shoved in his face. Questions were fired at him in rapid succession, shouted to be heard above the rest.

"Malik! Malik! Are you here to help with the search efforts?"

"Malik, does Claire Thorndike's disappearance bring back painful memories of the time your girlfriend was kidnapped in college?"

"Malik, have you had an opportunity to speak to Althea Pritchard since she returned to the area? We understand she's now working at the Baltimore FBI field office, although the Bureau won't confirm those reports."

"Malik, are the Wizards going to make it out of the first round of playoffs this year?"

He smiled, his teeth startlingly white against his smooth dark skin, his eyes concealed behind the mirrored sunglasses as he obligingly signed a few autographs. "Hey, guys. Chill a little bit. I'm not here to hold a press conference. I didn't come here to talk about basketball or myself."

"Then why are you here, Malik?"

He flashed a small, enigmatic smile. "To handle some unfinished business."

The press hounds began buzzing with speculation. As Malik swept a look around the packed room, Althea lowered her head and turned away, becoming absorbed in an inspection of an old firemen's poster on the opposite wall. She seriously considered slipping through the crowd and ducking quietly out of the building. But she knew she couldn't do that. Malik had already called her aunt and uncle to ask for her phone number, and now he'd shown up there. It was clear he meant to track her down, whether or not she wanted to be found.

Lifting her head, she discreetly scanned the room. Where the hell was Damien?

"Althea?"

Her shoulders stiffened. She'd run out of time. Damn it.

Taking a deep, steadying breath, she arranged the muscles in her face into a friendly smile and turned to face her past.

"Hello, Malik."

Removing his designer sunglasses, Malik Toomer, towering over Althea at six foot six, gave her a slow, appreciative once-over. A huge, delighted grin swept across his boyishly handsome face. "It *is* you! Damn, girl, I hardly recognized you. You look incredible! Not that I'm saying you weren't beautiful before," he hastened to clarify himself.

A wry smile tugged at Althea's lips. "I know what you meant. I—"

They both turned as a flash strobe went off. Althea inwardly groaned, realizing that the reporters and cameramen had followed Malik over to where she stood. Her cover, such as it was, had been officially blown.

The questions came at her like flying shrapnel from an explosion.

"Miss Pritchard, we've been trying to reach you for comment on the kidnapping investigation! Do you think Claire Thorndike's disappearance is linked in any way to your abduction?"

"Miss Pritchard, do you think this is a copycat?"

"Miss Pritchard, do you think you're in danger?"

Scowling, Althea grabbed Malik's hand and pushed her way through the crowd, leading him down the hall toward the war room. The reporters charged after them, still firing questions, but they were stopped short by a pair of unsmiling police officers posted at the entrance to the hallway.

"No unauthorized personnel beyond this point," the officers warned the reporters, who grumbled in protest before turning and shuffling away, no doubt lamenting their missed opportunity for a scoop.

Realizing that Damien might still be on his cell phone in the war room, Althea hung a quick left and led Malik into the small area where a row of old vending machines lined the wall.

"Sorry about that," Malik said with a sheepish grin. "I didn't mean to lead the wolves right to your door."

Althea grimaced. "I've been trying to keep a low profile for days, but somehow the story got leaked to the press that I was back in town. Apparently an article was printed in one of the local newspapers a week before I even arrived."

"I didn't know about the article. I heard through the grapevine that you were coming back. A friend of a friend from college called to let me know." His big brown eyes softened, roaming across her face. "I won't lie, Althea. I was very excited to hear you'd be coming back home. I've been wanting to see you for a long time. When I heard on the news that this volunteer center was opening to the public today, I took a chance that you might be here. I'm glad I did."

Althea heaved a deep sigh. "Malik—"

"I *hate* the way things ended between us," he rushed on earnestly. "I hated knowing how much I hurt you. You didn't deserve that, not after everything you'd been through."

"Malik," Althea said in a carefully measured voice. "You don't have to apologize again. We said all we needed to say to each other when we *both* agreed to go our separate ways."

He frowned. "I don't remember having much of a choice in the matter. You told me you were breaking up with me, spelled out your reasons, and that was pretty much the end of it. No matter what *I* said, you weren't trying to hear it."

Althea narrowed her eyes coolly. "*If* your version of events is true—and that's highly debatable—then what makes you think anything has changed? Because all these years have passed?"

"Well, yeah. We're both older now, more mature. And I *know* you, Althea. You've never been the type of person to hold a grudge against anyone."

She said nothing.

He took a small step toward her with a pleading expression. "I've had almost eight years to think about what I did, how I let you down. It's been eating me up inside. I honestly think that's why my game on the court hasn't been what it should be."

Althea sputtered out a laugh, staring at him in disbelief. "Is *that* why you're here? To clear your conscience so you can play better basketball?"

"Of course not! Damn, Althea, you know it ain't like that! I'm here because I miss you, because I miss our friendship. Because I want you to give me another chance."

Seeing the refusal in her eyes, he continued beseechingly, "You know I never wanted your friend Elizabeth. I meet skeezers like her every time I'm on the road. They hang around the locker room after games, they slip their numbers and their panties in our pockets, they sneak into our hotel rooms and push up on us at the clubs."

Althea let out a brittle, mirthless chuckle. "Congratulations. You must be in testosterone heaven."

Malik scowled. "The point I'm trying to make is that the Elizabeth Torreses of the world are a dime a dozen, and I knew that even back then."

Althea snorted. "It sure as hell didn't stop you from sleeping with her. Over, and over, and over again."

"I made a mistake!"

"No, Malik. The first time might have been a 'mistake.' After that you just didn't give a damn."

"That's not true! I felt horrible about what I did!"

Althea smiled mockingly. "But you just couldn't help yourself, could you? Elizabeth was just too beautiful for you to resist. You were like an addict, so far gone you even lied to the police about the number of times you slept with her." She paused, striking a thoughtful pose. "You know, I heard she's doing time in Upper Marlboro for grand larceny. If you ever get tired of those groupies, I'm sure you and Elizabeth could arrange some conjugal visits."

If Malik weren't so dark-skinned she would have sworn he turned beet red. He looked so wounded she immediately felt a sharp pang of guilt for her caustic words.

She blew out a ragged breath, scraping her hand through her hair. "I'm sorry," she murmured. "That was uncalled for. Not only that, but it smacks of bitterness, and believe it or not, Malik, I'm not angry at you anymore."

"Coulda fooled me," he mumbled.

Althea chuckled grimly. "Okay. Maybe I am a *little* angry, but believe me when I tell you it's not keeping me up at night. Not anymore. I've moved on with my life, Malik. We were friends before we started dating, and a part of me will always care for you. But the one thing I've learned over the years is that it's unhealthy to stay in the past. It's unhealthy *and* dangerous. I'm not interested in rekindling our relationship, Malik. I'm sorry you came all the way out here."

He spread his big hands in a gesture of supplication. "Will you at least have dinner with me?"

She gave him an exasperated look. "What would be the point?"

"To catch up on old times. Come on, Althea," he cajoled, giving her his most charming smile, the smile that once melted her into losing her virginity to him. "We can go anywhere you want, and I mean *anywhere*. I've got a private jet stocked with all the Cristal and Moët you could ever want. We can fly to the Caribbean, Mexico, even *Paris* if you want."

Althea couldn't help but laugh. "Hello? In case you haven't noticed, I'm in the middle of a kidnapping investigation here. I can't just take off and go flying around the world with you!"

"Come on, girl. You know you want to." When Malik turned his head at a certain angle, a diamond stud in his right earlobe caught and reflected the overhead lights, twinkling in tandem with his megawatt smile.

He reached for her and she backed away, holding up her hands. He heaved a sigh of frustration. "At least let me give you my number in case you change your mind about dinner. Or about anything else."

"I won't," Althea vowed, but he was already reaching inside his black leather jacket and pulling out a business card.

"Got a pen?"

She gave him a look. "No."

Chuckling, he patted his pockets, then retrieved a fancy ballpoint. "Here's my cell phone number," he said, scribbling on the back of the card. "You can reach me anytime. Well, unless I'm in the middle of a game, then obviously I'm not available. But just leave a message, and I swear I'll call you back as soon as the buzzer hits double zeroes."

Althea shook her head in exasperation as he pressed the card into her hand and folded her fingers around it. "Malik—"

"I've been looking for you."

Althea glanced up quickly.

Damien stood in the entryway watching her and Malik with a dark, impenetrable expression. Inexplicably, her heart thudded.

She quickly performed the introductions. "Malik, I'd like you to meet Special Agent Damien Wade. Damien, this is—"

"I know who he is." Damien inclined his head coolly toward Malik. "Nice to meet you."

"Yeah. Likewise." Malik divided a speculative look between Althea and Damien. "So the two of you work together?"

"Yes," Althea answered, shooting a glance at Damien. "And as a matter of fact, we need to be getting back to the office. We have a lot of work to do."

Malik nodded, looking disappointed. "I understand."

"It was, uh, good to see you again, Malik. Good luck on the season."

"Thanks. I'd love to see you at one of the games. You have my number—call me if you ever want any tickets."

Althea nodded as she started away, following Damien out of the vending area.

"Althea?"

She turned back, one brow arched inquisitively.

Malik was smiling softly. "You haven't seen the last of me."

Althea felt, rather than saw, Damien stiffen beside her.

She forced a dry, humorless laugh. "Be careful, Malik. I'm an FBI agent now, so you can't go around saying things to me that might make you sound like a stalker."

"My partner's right, Toomer," Damien said, deceptively soft. "Watch what you say."

Malik held his gaze for a long, tense moment. Then he shrugged, winking at Althea. "My bad."

Chapter 23

When Damien and Althea returned to the office, the fax they had been waiting for was lying on her desk. Before Althea could pick it up, Damien reached around her and snatched it away.

"Hey!" she protested. "That was addressed to me!"

In the cubicle beside her, another agent—a young Hispanic man named Anival Gonzalez—was talking quietly on the phone. He shot Althea a dirty look and put his finger to his lips.

"Sorry, Ani," Althea muttered, following Damien down the aisle to his cubicle on the opposite end of the bull pen. "That was my fax, Wade."

Without breaking stride, Damien said, "My case. My fax."

"*What?* What's that supposed to mean?"

Reaching his cubicle—seniority had afforded him one of the largest cubicles of the twelve agents assigned to the VCMO squad—Damien sat at his cluttered desk and grabbed the phone receiver to check his voice mail messages.

When Althea tried to grab the printout from his hand, he held it out of her reach. Scowling, she plunked down in the visitor chair, impatiently folded her arms, and glared daggers into him.

Winking at her, Damien slid his chair all the way back against the far wall of the cubicle and stretched out one leg, a negligent pose that masked the tension and anger that had been running through his veins ever since they left the fire hall.

Something had come over him when he stumbled upon Althea and Malik Toomer in the vending area. Damien had been searching all over the building for her and had even started to worry until a police officer tapped him on the shoulder and told him that Althea had taken Malik Toomer into the back to get away from reporters. As Damien neared the vending area, he'd overheard the basketball star promising to fly Althea to exotic locales aboard his private jet. Althea had laughingly turned him down, citing her involvement in the kidnapping investigation. But Damien had heard a note of something in her voice—temptation, regret—that made his gut clench. When he reached them and found Toomer holding her hand, he'd been seized by a vicious urge to march across the room and slam his fist into the other man's face, felling him like a tree. It didn't matter that Toomer had a good three inches on him. Growing up in one of the roughest neighborhoods in East Baltimore, Damien had spent his childhood fighting kids who were bigger and stronger, and he'd held his own. Toomer, who was skinny, would be no match for Damien, especially with so much rage fueling him.

The thought of Althea having dinner with her old boyfriend—let alone boarding a private jet with him for a romantic getaway—struck Damien hard, awakening feelings of jealousy and protectiveness he would have denied possessing just a week earlier. He'd never felt this territorial over any woman before, not even his own wife, and with her wild, partying ways, Angelique had given him *plenty* of reasons to be jealous. But not even the fury he'd felt when he suspected her of cheating could compare to the turbulent emotions roiling through him now. His possessiveness toward Althea was totally out of proportion to the short amount of time he'd known her, yet he couldn't seem to rein it in.

Althea had spent the ride back to the office making calls on her cell phone, leaving Damien to stew in his own juices, a potent blend of anger and confusion.

He'd taken perverse satisfaction in making *her* angry when he snatched the fax off her desk. Which was part of the reason he'd done it. To get back at her a little, petty though it was.

While he listened to a series of voice mail messages, he watched her. She was beautiful, innocently provocative as she tugged her lush bottom lip between her teeth and crossed her long, shapely legs covered in stretch denim. Even the way she was glaring at him through those dark, sultry eyes turned him on.

And he couldn't have her—except in his dreams.

Damien scowled to himself.

Maybe Angelique was right. Maybe he *was* pathetic.

Ruthlessly shoving the thought aside, he finished listening to his voice mail messages and hung up the phone.

Althea pounced. "What was that crack you made about 'My case. My fax'? I thought you told me you don't play power games."

Damien shrugged. "So I lied." He grabbed a pen and stood with the printout in his hand. "Come on. Let's grab the conference room, and we can go over the transcripts together."

She muttered something unintelligible under her breath as she followed him out of the cubicle.

Once inside the conference room, they sat at the table and divided the pages. Damien took the messages sent by James Odem, while Althea took Claire's messages. To make the task easier, they decided to read aloud to each other, in chronological order.

As Odem had stated during the interrogation, Claire made the first contact on Sunday, September 7, leaving a friendly comment on his profile page about how much she'd enjoyed learning about John Coltrane and sampling his music. Odem had promptly responded, thanking her for the feedback and encouraging her to visit the page often for updates and new music downloads.

"Innocent enough," Althea remarked when they'd finished reading the first message exchange.

Damien grunted noncommittally.

But as they continued reading, it became apparent that James Odem had been telling the truth about the way his online relationship with Claire had unfolded. They spoke about music, their favorite places and restaurants in Baltimore, and the most interesting countries they had ever visited, both delighted to discover how well traveled the other person was. Claire talked about her classes and shared her goal of becoming a doctor, and Odem offered a wealth of advice about preparing for medical school and choosing a specialty. All perfectly harmless. Innocent.

Until Claire began to divulge more personal information about herself. And then the conversations took on a slightly different tone. Flirtatious, edgy.

Althea read aloud, "'I'm not embarrassed to tell people I've had my boobs done. I think the surgeons did an amazing job. I wonder if you'd be impressed with their work. You know, professionally speaking.'"

Damien said, "Odem wrote back: 'Don't tempt me. LOL.'"

"'Are you tempted?'"

"'I'd have to be crazy not to be.'"

"'Hmm. What else tempts you?'"

"'Nothing I should be telling a seventeen-year-old girl. LOL.'"

"'LOL. I've been thinking how much I would enjoy a tour of the new surgery wing at Mercy Harbor. Maybe that would help me decide on a specialty. Do you give tours, Dr. Odem?'"

"'Of course. I squeeze in as many as I can between surgeries.'"

"'Sorry. Guess that was a dumb question.'"

"'The first one you've asked so far. LOL. But, seriously, your dad has donated a boatload of money to the hospital. I'm sure he could arrange a private tour for you.'"

The next day, Claire responded: "'LMIRL.'"

"'I'm going to show my age here, Claire. What did your last message mean?'"

"'LOL. Sorry. I said let's meet in real life. I think you're a really nice guy and cool to talk to. I thought it would be great if we got together sometime.'"

Damien read Odem's response: "'I'm not sure that's such a good idea.'"

"'Okay. Forget it. Sorry I asked.'"

"'I hope you're not mad. I didn't mean to offend you.'"

"'It's cool. We don't have to meet.'"

Two days passed with no e-mail communication. And then on September 17, Odem sent a message. But there must have been a glitch on the server, because the content was scrambled.

Althea glanced up from her printout, frowning at Damien. "What do you mean 'scrambled'?"

Damien slid the sheet over for her inspection. Her

frown deepened as she studied the message. "It looks like gibberish. The JavaScript must have gotten corrupted or something."

Damien flipped through the remaining pages. "None of the other messages are like that."

Althea quickly checked her printout. "Neither are mine." Again she frowned. "It looks like they didn't correspond too much after that. They exchanged, what, four or five messages after that. I see where she responded to his message about the Coltrane song 'Equinox.' She downloaded it, as he recommended, and wrote back to tell him she really liked it. Over the next two weeks, they reverted back to sharing generalities and making small talk." She glanced up at Damien. "Do you think that's because Claire's feelings were hurt because he turned down her invitation to meet in person?"

Damien shook his head, bent over the scrambled message. "No, I think it's because they were already e-mailing each other through a different account."

"What did he say to her on that last message? The one he sent on October 2—the day before she disappeared?"

Damien glanced at the last page and muttered distractedly, "'Hope you enjoy the program at Johns Hopkins. Hope it's very informative.'"

Althea hummed a thoughtful note, turning possibilities over in her mind.

But Damien had returned his attention to the scrambled message. As he scrutinized the jumbled script, his nerve endings tightened and his skin prickled the way it did whenever he sensed he was onto something.

And suddenly he knew why.

"It's a code," he announced, his voice shattering the silence of the room.

Althea stared at him. "What?"

"He sent her an encrypted message. You've heard of e-mail cryptography, right?"

"Yeah. That's where you send encrypted messages to specific users."

"Right. Most e-mail cryptography uses a digital certificate system where a computer generates two keys—a public key and a private key. Either of these can be used to scramble information. The keys are opposite; anything scrambled with a public key can only be unscrambled with a private key, and vice versa. When you set up e-mail crypto, you have your computer generate a public and private key. You can give out the public key to anyone you want, say through your Web site, but you keep the private key and protect it with a strong password. So if you want to send me a message, and you want to make sure only *I* can read it, you use my public key to scramble the message."

Althea nodded slowly, her lips pursed. "I'm following you."

Damien continued, "Social networking sites like MyDomain aren't set up to support cryptography programs, for safety reasons. So Odem had to basically mimic the technology by creating his own scrambled message to Claire. To the naked eye it just looks like corrupted JavaScript, like what you might see in a spam e-mail. But if you look closely, you see that there's a keystroke pattern. Six symbols followed by three numbers and then a letter, and so on. A bit amateurish, but my guess is that he kept it simple enough for Claire to understand, but maybe not her father if he was snooping through her messages."

Looking intrigued, Althea slid her chair closer, pulling up beside Damien. He laid the page on the table between them, reached for his pen, and began circling all the letters contained in the message.

When he'd finished, a note emerged: *Open a private e-mail account so we can talk more freely. I'm at braindoc08-@gmail.com.*

"Son of a bitch," Althea breathed. "So *that's* how he did it."

Damien nodded, his lips curved in a grim parody of a smile. "I don't know whether to be amused or insulted that while he assumed a seventeen-year-old girl would be able to solve his little riddle, he didn't think we could. He obviously doesn't have a very high opinion of those in law enforcement."

Althea gave a wry laugh. "He's a brain surgeon. He probably doesn't have a very high opinion of *anyone*. But this time the joke's on him. We've got him dead to rights on knowingly and willfully making a false statement to police. He lied to you about not exchanging e-mail addresses with Claire. What else is he lying about?"

"That's a damn good question." Damien shoved back his chair and surged to his feet. "I'm calling Mayhew right now. I think it's time we make a little trip to Mercy Harbor to get reacquainted with the good doctor."

After Damien left to meet Detective Mayhew at the police station, Althea returned to her desk and got on the Internet. She pulled up the Web site for the U.S. Senate, a site she'd already bookmarked, and accessed the home page for Republican Senator Rich Horton. Typical of most senators' sites, there were links for constituent services, congressional issues relevant to the senator, news and press releases, a biography page, and a page dedicated to highlighting his home state of Tennessee. Althea went to the photo gallery and scrolled through images of the white-haired senator posing with the president and various foreign dignitaries and prominent businessmen until she found what she was looking for. A photo of Horton flanked by his congressional aides on the steps of the Dirksen Senate Office Building in Washington, D.C. Althea didn't need the caption below the picture to identify Courtney Reese; she was the only female in the group.

Althea studied her for a moment, surprised to realize that Courtney was biracial, with pale honey-toned skin, large hazel eyes, generous lips and dark, shoulder-length hair that had the telltale wavy thickness of a person of African-American descent. She looked smart and successful in a pinstriped navy skirt suit and Dolce & Gabbana peep-toe pumps.

Why, Althea wondered idly, had Claire asked Courtney Reese about being with a black man when it was clear that at least one of Courtney's parents was black? Why hadn't Courtney been offended by the question?

Just because she may be half-black doesn't mean she dates black men, Althea reminded herself.

She returned to the home page and jotted down the phone number to Senator Horton's office. She'd decided to call Courtney Reese in lieu of showing up on Capitol Hill unannounced. It would take Althea more than an hour to reach the District, and with her busy schedule, she didn't want to take a chance on driving all the way out there, only to be told that Courtney was in meetings all day.

When a secretary answered the phone, Althea asked for Courtney Reese and was told that the congressional aide was unavailable at the moment.

"This is Special Agent Althea Pritchard, with the FBI. It's very important that I speak to Ms. Reese."

The secretary hesitated. "Please hold."

Althea was transferred to another line. A moment

later a young woman answered in brisk, cultured tones, "This is Courtney Reese."

Althea suddenly realized she hadn't finalized what she was going to say to Courtney. She'd have to wing it. "Hello, Ms. Reese. My name is Althea Pritchard, and I'm with—"

"I know who you are. You're Senator Pritchard's niece."

"Yes." Althea paused, wondering if she'd only imagined the note of cool reserve in the other woman's voice. "Do you know my uncle?"

"I've worked with him on different legislation, and I've heard him speak very fondly of you before. What can I do for you, Ms. Pritchard?"

"I'm investigating Claire Thorndike's abduction, and I wanted to ask you a few questions. I understand that you and Claire were friends?"

"That's right. I met her through her mother, Madison Thorndike. Claire's a wonderful girl. I was very sorry to hear what happened to her. We're all praying for her safe return."

"We're doing everything we can to find her," Althea said. "Which is why I'm calling you. I was hoping you might be able to tell me what you know about Claire's relationship with James Odem."

"The man she met online?"

"Yes. Through MyDomain."

"Do you think *he* kidnapped her?"

"We're considering all possibilities," Althea said neutrally.

On the other end, Courtney expelled a long, shaky breath. "I knew it was a bad idea for her to meet that guy. She sent me a text message a couple of weeks ago, then called me later to fill me in on the details. I didn't like the way she was sneaking around to talk to him. He had her open a new e-mail account so they could 'talk dirty to each other' as much as they wanted."

"Is that what he said or she said?"

"That's what *he* said to her. He wouldn't let her e-mail or IM him from home, and he absolutely refused to give her his home or cell phone number. It didn't sound right to me. It sounded suspicious. I kept asking her if he was married, but she said no."

"You said she was sneaking around to talk to him. Did she tell you where she was e-mailing him?"

"She went to the public library."

"Which one?" Althea demanded, trying to keep the excitement out of her voice. She had to call Damien.

"The one closest to her home, I believe. She goes there pretty often to check out books for school projects. But she told me that whenever she went to the library to e-mail that doctor, she'd wear a baseball cap and dark sunglasses, sometimes even a wig, just so the librarians wouldn't recognize her." Courtney sounded angry and exasperated. "All that cloak-and-dagger nonsense was exciting to her, like she was having one big adventure. I half jokingly told her that was the problem with spoiled, white, rich kids living out in the boonies—too much damn time on their hands to get into trouble. Anyway, I made it clear to Claire that I didn't think it was a good idea for her to meet that guy, but she insisted it was okay. She kept saying how nice he was, how smart and successful. And he passed the background check, so that put her mind at ease."

"When was the last time you spoke to Claire?"

"Wednesday. October 1. I called to ask her whether she still planned to go through with the date. She said yes and told me not to worry, that she would be okay." Courtney gave a short, bitter laugh. "Little did she know."

Althea said quietly, "Did she tell you whether they were planning to go out anywhere?"

"No. They were having dinner at the house. She had a very romantic evening planned."

Althea thought about the sterilized crime scene that had greeted Spencer and Suzette Thorndike when they returned home. *De-staged*, as Damien had put it. How far had James Odem gone to cover his tracks?

"Ms. Pritchard? I'm sorry, but I have to run to an oversight hearing on the Hill."

"Of course. Thank you for taking the time to answer my questions, Ms. Reese. You've been very helpful. Oh, and one more thing?"

"Yes?" A note of wariness had crept into Courtney's voice.

Althea hesitated, choosing her next words very carefully, "We're telling all of Claire's friends to be extra careful as they go about their daily routines. Until we've apprehended Claire's kidnapper, we can't eliminate the possibility that anyone who knew her could be in danger as well—especially if the suspect saw Claire while she was out somewhere with friends. If you don't already have a security alarm, I strongly suggest you get one."

There was silence on the other end. Then, "Are you trying to frighten me, Agent Pritchard?"

Althea frowned. "I just want you to be safe, Ms. Reese."

"Thanks for your concern. Good-bye, Ms. Pritchard." There was a loud click as she disconnected.

Althea slowly hung up, feeling strangely unsettled. Almost from the moment Courtney Reese got on the phone, Althea had sensed something odd in her voice, something akin to resentment. Hostility. But that was ridiculous. Courtney had no reason to resent Althea. She didn't even know her. But she knew her uncle. And suddenly everything made sense. Courtney worked for a Republican senator who, if Althea remembered correctly, served on the Senate Armed Services Committee with Louis Pritchard. It was possible that the two men had butted heads over matters of national security and defense authorization requests, but that was the nature of politics. Politicians butted heads, especially when they were seated on opposite sides of the aisle. If Courtney Reese didn't understand that, if she held a grudge against every senator who'd ever opposed her boss, then maybe she belonged in a different line of work.

Making a mental note to ask her uncle about his relationship with Senator Horton, Althea quickly dialed Damien's cell phone, eager to tell him about her conversation with Courtney before he and Mayhew arrived at Mercy Harbor Hospital to arrest James Odem. But after four rings, her call was transferred to voice mail, and Damien's deep baritone instructed callers to leave a brief message. She complied, thinking irritably that the man's voice could sound sinful even on a simple voice mail prompt.

After hanging up, she dialed Suzette Thorndike's cell. They had agreed to reach the Thorndikes on their cell phones and keep the house line free in case the kidnapper called to make a ransom demand. Althea had decided to question Suzette about her alleged affair with Corbin Farris, but she wanted to speak to her privately. She knew there was no chance of Suzette confessing to anything if her husband was around, so Althea planned to ask the woman to meet her somewhere.

But once again, her call was kicked to voice mail. She considered, then decided against leaving a message. No sense in giving Suzette *too* much time to get her story together. She'd try her again later.

Althea swiveled back to her computer and Googled a list of public libraries in the Mount Washington area.

She mapped the location closest to the Thorndike estate, jotted down the address, then headed down to the lab to recruit one of the forensic examiners to accompany her to the library.

Suzette Thorndike stifled a scream as Josh Reed rammed her against the bathroom door, his hips pumping furiously as he thrust into her.

"Hurry," she whispered breathlessly, tightening her legs around his hips. "We have to hurry!"

"I know," he muttered, his voice muffled against her throat as he alternately bit and kissed her, sending shivers of erotic pleasure down her spine.

She grabbed his tight little butt and he groaned and thrust faster, pounding her so hard against the door it rattled in its frame.

But Suzette wasn't worried about being overheard. For the first time in days, the house was empty.

Upon learning that the police had arrested a suspect in Claire's disappearance, Spencer had taken off for the police station, along with his hysterical ex-wife Madison, who'd just flown in from Scotland and had taken a cab straight to the estate. Their cook was not scheduled to arrive until later, the butler was out with the flu, and Suzette had sent the housekeeper on several errands, accompanied by the driver. Suzette had even talked the bleary-eyed police officer on phone duty into taking a thirty-minute lunch break, assuring him it would be their little secret.

And then she'd snuck Josh Reed through the back door and upstairs to the master bathroom for a long-overdue quickie.

He lifted his head now and kissed her hard, rough the way she liked it. He plunged his tongue into her mouth and she sucked it greedily, tasting cherry-flavored candy that reminded her she was being fucked by a high school boy.

But robbing the cradle had never felt so good.

The bathroom was filled with harsh animal pants and the solid, rhythmic thud of body against body. Her cell phone rang somewhere inside the bedroom, but she didn't care. Josh gripped her bottom, spreading her cheeks wide as he slammed into her. Her heart hammered. A delicious heat spread through her loins. A moment later, she dug her manicured nails into his back as she let go with a long, violent shudder.

After three hard strokes Josh closed his eyes and stiffened against her, his cock throbbing inside her as he came forcefully. Suzette clamped a hand over his mouth to smother his loud groan—just in case the cop had returned early.

When their ragged breathing had returned to normal, Josh eased back from her, lowering her feet to the floor. Suzette smoothed her silk skirt down over her thighs as he peeled off his condom and dropped it into the toilet, then raised the lid to take a piss.

She surveyed him in the mirror as she straightened her mussed hair and checked her makeup. She'd once overheard her stepdaughter complaining to her best friend about the size of Josh's dick. While Suzette agreed it wasn't the biggest thing she'd ever worked with, the boy definitely knew what to do with it. In the three months they'd been sleeping together, he'd never failed to give Suzette an orgasm—something she couldn't say about her own husband.

Josh flushed the toilet and came up behind her, wrapping his arms around her waist and brushing her long hair aside to kiss the nape of her neck. Suzette gave a low, throaty purr of contentment, feeling the swell of his erection against her backside. Yet another advantage to having an affair with a high school teenager. No Viagra necessary.

"Not that it isn't tempting," she murmured as he slowly and sensually ground his pelvis against her, "but we're almost out of time."

He groaned softly in protest as she stepped out of his embrace and moved to sit on the edge of the whirlpool bathtub, one of the many places they'd christened when they first started sleeping together.

As if it were yesterday, Suzette remembered the lazy summer afternoon the young, hunky jock had shown up at the mansion looking for Claire, hoping to get a terrible secret off his chest. When Suzette told him that Claire was spending the week in Cabo San Lucas with some friends—a trip she'd apparently failed to mention to her own boyfriend—Josh looked so crestfallen that Suzette took pity on him and invited him inside for lemonade and scones. She'd listened sympathetically while he poured out his heart to her, confiding his deep regret over the way he'd cheated on Claire with a popular cheerleader at school. She'd patted his hand comfortingly and reassured him that he wasn't a horrible person, that people made mistakes and no one was perfect. She'd even subtly suggested that Claire was to blame for his infidelity. Maybe if Claire had been less self-absorbed and more attuned to his needs, Suzette noted, she would have realized how unhappy he was before it was too late.

By his third glass of lemonade, Josh was feeling a lot better about himself and the state of his troubled relationship with Claire. Suzette graciously promised to keep his secret until he was ready to come clean to Claire, and he shyly mumbled his gratitude.

She was in the middle of giving his hand another reassuring squeeze when their gazes locked.

And in that moment, she knew they were going to become lovers.

Just as she and her former stepson had.

As she walked Josh to the door that afternoon, she casually mentioned that her husband was leaving for a business trip the following day, and she planned to give the household servants the day off to spend with their families, which they always appreciated.

Just as she'd anticipated, Josh showed up the next day. They fucked so many times Suzette lost count. By the time he snuck out of the house late that night, she was hooked.

They had been sneaking around ever since. Neither her husband nor stepdaughter had the slightest clue, and Suzette intended to keep it that way.

She watched now as Josh leaned back against the marble counter and folded his arms across his lean chest. He had a swimmer's physique—trim, lithe, and athletic. *She* definitely benefited from the incredible stamina he'd developed from his rigorous training regimen—120 laps twice a day, six days a week. No exceptions.

"What did you want to tell me?" Suzette prompted, glancing at her platinum diamond-encrusted Cartier wristwatch. The police officer would be returning in fifteen minutes to resume watching the phone. She needed to hurry and get Josh out of the house.

"That FBI agent was at the volunteer center this morning," Josh said, looking none too pleased.

Suzette stared at him. "Which one? Mr. Tall, Dark, and Handsome—or the woman?"

"Both. But it was the woman who went over to talk to Heather." He frowned. "I was watching them the whole time. I think Heather told her something."

Suzette felt a cold dagger of fear pierce her heart. She swallowed convulsively. "How do you know that?"

Josh smirked. "I've known Heather since kindergarten. There's a look she gets on her face whenever she's telling something she thinks she shouldn't be. She had that look when she was talking to the FBI agent this morning."

Feeling slightly nauseated, Suzette rose from the corner of the bathtub and began pacing up and down the custom tile floor, her mind spinning.

Josh watched her in wary silence, knowing what was at stake for her. It was he who'd told her that Claire had overheard Suzette's conversation with Corbin Farris that fateful afternoon when he called her, threatening to expose all her dirty secrets if she didn't give him what he wanted.

Days before they broke up, Claire had told Josh all about the scandalous argument she'd "accidentally" overheard between her stepmother and former stepson, which Josh later shared with Suzette when she mentioned the receipt she'd found in her stepdaughter's bedroom. According to Josh, Claire's eavesdropping had been interrupted by the housekeeper, which prevented her from learning the full extent of the trouble her stepmother was in. But her curiosity had been piqued. Which would explain why she had decided to hire a private investigator to dig into Suzette's past, to see what other skeletons she could unearth. *Spiteful little bitch.*

Josh said, "I wanted you to know so you could be prepared in case that FBI chick comes knocking on your door."

Suzette nodded distractedly. "Thank you, Josh. You did the right thing. I appreciate the heads-up."

He hesitated, his dark eyes concerned. "Is there anything I can do?"

She stopped pacing and looked at him. She marveled that this good-looking All-American teenager—this boy who had been born into wealth and privilege and who would never know the poverty and blind desperation that had characterized Suzette's upbringing—had proven that he would do anything for her.

Even break the law.

A soft, tender smile curved her lips. She walked over to him and gently laid her palm against his smooth, clean-shaven cheek. "You've already done more than enough for me," she whispered. "But if I need another favor, it's good to know I can count on you."

He leaned down and kissed her, and she let herself savor his taste, his youth, his innocence, all the while wondering if she'd ever known a moment of innocence in her own life.

Minutes after Josh left, sneaking out the same way he'd entered, the cop returned from his lunch break. As he resumed his vigil by the phone, Suzette eyed it just as anxiously, praying for an outcome that would have horrified the police officer.

Chapter 24

News of James Odem's arrest hit the airwaves by noon. He was charged with one count of making a false statement and unceremoniously thrown into the slammer. It wasn't a long stay, however. Preston Gallagher, his high-priced attorney, arrived within minutes, blustering about miscarriages of justice and the egregious violation of his client's rights. After two hours of interrogation, Odem maintained his innocence in Claire Thorndike's abduction. With his lawyer at his side, acting as buffer and shield, the surgeon admitted to lying about the extent of his online relationship with Claire because he was embarrassed, but he refused to elaborate on anything and he denied being at the Thorndike estate on the night she disappeared. No matter how hard Damien and Mayhew tried to rattle his cage—a task further complicated by his lawyer's constant objections—Odem remained calm and implacable, watching Damien with a look of smug triumph.

Mr. Cool. Mr. Untouchable.

Within two hours of being arrested, Odem was released on bail. Outside the downtown police station, his attorney delivered a blistering statement to the reporters gathered, accusing the Baltimore Police Department and the Federal Bureau of Investigation of manufacturing a bogus case against his client in their blind desperation to apprehend a suspect in Claire's kidnapping.

Acknowledging that the missing teenager's abduction was "a heinous crime and a parent's worst nightmare," he urged the public not to rush to judgment in presuming his client guilty. He reminded the viewing audience that *Dr.* James Odem was an exemplary citizen with no criminal history, an esteemed neurosurgeon who had dedicated his life to the advancement of medicine.

"This is a man whose gifted hands have saved countless lives," Gallagher declared in the theatrical voice of an orator. "He could not—*would* not—use those same hands to harm an innocent young girl!"

Damien was still gnashing his back teeth and seething with disgust as he pulled into the parking lot of his daughter's middle school at three-fifteen. His frustration with the stalled investigation was mounting dangerously. Claire Thorndike had now been missing for five days, and with the exception of James Odem, they had no solid leads or suspects to sneeze at. Not even the discovery of the library computer Claire had likely used to secretly correspond with Odem was enough to keep him in custody. Odem had stolen Althea's thunder when he readily admitted to encouraging Claire to open a separate e-mail account so they could communicate away from prying eyes. It would be hours before the Bureau's forensic examiner finished going through the confiscated hard drive, but Damien doubted that the e-mail files would yield the incriminating evidence they needed to nail the son of a bitch.

They needed a break in the investigation soon. Like yesterday.

When his cell phone rang, he snatched it up and growled, "Wade."

"Wade, this is Agent Brewster in Richmond. Tough break about Odem, but I've got some news that might cheer you up. I just left the post office where the letter was mailed from. One of the employees, who's been off until today, positively ID'd Corbin Farris from the driver's license photo. She said he was definitely there on Saturday morning."

Damien straightened in the driver's seat, his muscles tightening. "Is she sure?"

"Yep. Apparently she's got a knack for remembering faces—all of her coworkers vouched for that. Anyway, I'm not sure how helpful this is to you. It's not as if she remembered specifically what he mailed, and she couldn't find his credit card in the system to trace the transaction. But it's a start."

"A damn good start," Damien agreed. "Still no sighting of Farris?"

"Unfortunately not. But we're still sitting on the house. The old man is still there, doting on his grandchildren, pushing his grandson on the swing set, and tossing the ole baseball with him." Brewster snorted. "I sure hope to God *he's* not your guy."

Damien gave a short, grim laugh. "Can't rule him out. Not with his priors." He thanked Agent Brewster for following up on the lead, then hung up and called Althea.

She had gone home to meet the security alarm technician, whose only available timeslot was this afternoon. After today the company was booked solid through the end of next week. When Althea had balked at taking today's appointment, citing her busy schedule, all it took was one look from Damien to make her change her mind.

He'd wanted to accompany her to her apartment that afternoon, not wanting her to be alone there for a single moment, but he'd promised India that he would pick her up from school, and he was already feeling guilty about having to leave her at his mother's house overnight while he and Althea went on their stakeout.

When she answered her cell phone, he could hear female voices and laughter in the background. "Hey," Althea said, and he foolishly wished the smile he heard in her voice was for him, and not because she'd been laughing at a joke before she picked up the phone.

"Hey, yourself. Has the security guy arrived yet?"

"Not yet. But you'll be happy to know that I'm not alone. My friends, Keren and Kimberly, are here with me. They've been trying to get in touch with me all week. When I told them about my appointment this afternoon, they took off early from work and headed over here to wait with me." She chuckled wryly. "They said if this is the only way they can spend some time with me, they'll take what they can get."

Damien smiled. "Good. I'm glad to hear it. Hey, listen. Brewster just called me from Richmond."

When he had finished relaying what the agent had told him, Althea said, a note of excitement in her voice, "I bet you anything Corbin is hiding out at his father's house in Solomon's Island."

"You could be right. Guess we'll find out tonight."

"I hope so. We need a lucky break. Oh, that's the doorbell. See you in a few hours."

"Bye, Damien!" a chorus of female voices cooed in the background.

Damien chuckled and flipped the phone shut just as the school's dismissal bell rang. A few minutes later a swarm of noisy adolescents, shepherded by two teachers, erupted from the old brick building, spilling through the double glass doors and charging toward school buses lined at the curb or cars parked in the designated pick-up zone.

His cell phone rang again and he answered, keeping an eye out for India as he gave Mayhew a quick update on Corbin Farris, then listened to the detective gripe about Spencer and Madison Thorndike, who had hung around the police station long after Odem was released, demanding to know why the only suspect in their daughter's kidnapping was not spending the night in jail.

Damien smiled suddenly, his spirits lifting as he watched his daughter emerge from the building, flanked by two of her best friends. He wracked his brain for a moment before retrieving their names—Dominique and Janay.

As he watched, the girls waved at India and headed off to their bus, and India scanned the crowded parking lot before spotting Damien. Her face lit up, but before she could step off the curb, a tall, heavyset white man wearing a brown porkpie hat and a brown wool coat approached her.

Damien's smile faded. The muscles in the back of his neck instinctively tightened. He muttered something to Mayhew and disconnected, carelessly tossing aside the cell phone.

India eyed the stranger warily as he asked her a question. She shook her head and said something Damien couldn't make out.

Slowly the man lifted his head and looked straight in Damien's direction.

A chill ran through him.

Before he knew it, he was out of the SUV and charging across the big parking lot, his mouth dry, his heart thudding with fear. A horn blared at him as he bolted out in front of a car, causing the driver to slam on her brakes. He hardly noticed, his gaze focused on his daughter and the strange man standing beside her.

Damn it, where are the teachers!

"India!" he called.

He swore savagely as a blue Mercury Mountaineer suddenly pulled out in front of him, cutting his daughter from his line of sight. He raced around the truck impatiently, adrenaline surging through his veins, pulse pounding in his ears, throat locked with panic.

By the time he neared the front entrance, wending his way through a row of idling school buses, the stranger was gone. Vanished into thin air.

Damien reached India, hauled her into his arms, and crushed her against him.

"Hey, Daddy!" she greeted him, cheerfully oblivious, her voice muffled against his midsection as she wrapped her little arms around him and hugged him back.

"Hey, sweetheart," he said hoarsely. As he drew back from her, his sharp, searching gaze swept the crowded parking lot before returning to his daughter. "Who was that man you were talking to?"

India shrugged dispassionately. "I don't know. He asked me if I knew a girl named Lynette. He said he was her father and he was looking for her. I told him I didn't know anyone by that name." She eyed her father curiously. "Are you okay, Daddy?"

"Yeah," Damien lied, still shaken. "I just don't like seeing you talking to strangers. You know the rules."

"I know, but he caught me by surprise."

You and me both, kiddo.

Damien lifted his head and looked around again, encountering the speculative gaze of a teacher who had witnessed his mad sprint across the parking lot. She stood less than ten feet away, directing students to their buses. The principal stood in the doorway, smiling as a procession of laughing children filed past her and out of the building. When she caught Damien's eye, her smile widened with pleasure and she waved.

"Hello, Mr. Wade! It's good to see you again!"

Damien inclined his head with a brief smile. As he turned away, he told himself that India had never been in any danger. He'd let his jagged nerves get the best of him.

Yet he couldn't shake the whisper of unease that had crawled down his spine when he saw the stranger talking to India. And he couldn't dismiss the chill of foreboding that lanced through his heart when the man lifted his head and looked right at him. As if he already knew exactly where Damien was parked.

Frowning, Damien took his daughter's small hand and murmured, "Come on, let's go."

Once they were inside the SUV and heading away from the middle school, India asked, "Where's Ms. Pritchard?"

"She had to go home for a while."

"Oh." India turned her head to stare out the window, but Damien could sense that she wanted to say more.

He waited.

Finally she spoke. "You like her."

Damien slanted her an amused look. "How can you tell?"

"The way you were looking at her this morning. The way you chased her around the kitchen." India sighed, a sound of long-suffering. "You reminded me of the way boys at school act when they like a girl."

Damien laughed. "That bad, huh?"

She turned her head to grin at him. "It wasn't bad. It was just, well, funny. I've never seen you like that before." She paused, frowning. "Not even with Mom."

Damien said nothing. He saw no point in denying it.

After another moment, India said sagely, "But you don't have to worry. 'Cause she likes you, too."

Damien chuckled, his heart giving an irrational little leap. "You think so, huh?"

"Definitely. I saw the way she was staring at you when she thought you weren't looking. She definitely has a thing for you, Daddy."

Damien's mind flashed on last night, and the way Althea had closed her eyes in anticipation when she thought he was going to kiss her.

And then he remembered the scene he'd stumbled upon between her and Malik Toomer that morning, and he scowled.

"It's okay if you decide to marry her."

Damien choked out a laugh. "*What?* How'd we jump from liking to marriage?"

"I'm just saying. It would be okay with me if you wanted to marry her. Remember how I told you the other night that you needed a wife?"

Damien nodded.

"Well, if you really like Ms. Pritchard, you should marry her."

He smiled. "I wish it were that simple, baby girl."

"Why isn't it?"

"Because grown-ups make things a lot more complicated than they sometimes have to be," he said softly, half to himself.

India fell silent, contemplating his words.

Damien gave her a sidelong glance. "What did *you* think of Ms. Pritchard?"

"She seems nice. Smart. Tough, too. I liked her." She turned her head to stare out the window at the passing streets of East Baltimore. "I used to wish you and Mom would get back together, but more and more I don't think that's such a good idea." She hesitated, gnawing her bottom lip. "I heard you arguing this morning."

Damien winced, remembering the coarse, angry barbs he and Angelique had exchanged in his bedroom. "Sweetheart, I'm—"

"It's okay. I was downstairs, so I didn't hear *what* you said. I just heard your raised voices." She gazed at him with those big dark eyes that were too intuitive for her years. "I think you were right," she said solemnly.

"About what?"

"You and Mom are better off apart from each other than you are together."

Damien hesitated, then reached over and gently brushed his knuckle across her cheek. "You hungry? I thought we could stop at Fuddruckers on our way to Grandma's, for old times' sake."

Her expression brightened. "Cheeseburgers! Yum! I could eat a—" She broke off abruptly, frowning in confusion. "Wait a minute. Why are you dropping me off at Grandma's? I thought we were going home? To *your* house?"

Damien felt a fresh stab of guilt. "Not tonight, baby girl. I'm sorry. I have to work late."

Her frown deepened. "Are you doing another stakeout?"

He nodded. "We're trying to find out who took Claire Thorndike, the girl who's been missing. I know you're disappointed, sweetheart, but I promise to make it up to you."

India cast her eyes downward. "Will you be home tomorrow night?"

His heart constricted. "I'm going to try my best."

After a prolonged moment of silence, India heaved a sigh of resignation. "Okay."

"Okay?"

She nodded somberly. "If I were missing, I would

want everyone to do their best to find me. That means daddies, too."

Damien smiled tenderly at his daughter. "I know Claire would appreciate the sacrifice you're making for her, baby girl."

"She probably would." India paused, then added thoughtfully, "I hope you find her soon, so she can thank me."

Damien's answering laughter was bittersweet.

Chapter 25

The idyllic, picturesque fishing hamlet of Solomon's Island was nestled between the Patuxent River and the Chesapeake Bay in Calvert County, Maryland. It was after nightfall by the time Althea and Damien crept into town, driving through quiet streets where lights glowed invitingly in the windows of quaint Victorian houses and cozy B and Bs. Merchants had closed their storefront shops and headed off to home and hearth, fishermen had unloaded the day's catches and docked their boats for the night, and tourists had retreated to their warm lodgings.

Patrick Farris lived on a remote oasis along the river, in a white clapboard house with blue shutters that backed to the water. Across the bank, hidden behind a cluster of live oaks that would not lose their thick leaves for another five weeks, Althea and Damien sat in a dark, nondescript sedan, their binoculars trained on the darkened house across the river. They had been there for more than two hours, and so far there had been no movement inside the house or around the property, and the driveway remained empty.

"Where are you hiding, Corbin Farris?" Althea muttered half to herself. "More to the point, *why* are you hiding?"

Beside her, Damien said nothing as he shifted slightly in the driver's seat. His legs were so long he'd had to push the seat back as far as it would go, and it still didn't seem like he had enough room.

"Maybe he won't show," Althea speculated. "Maybe he knows we're onto him."

"Maybe," Damien murmured.

Slowly lowering her binoculars, Althea said, "I've been thinking about another angle involving Corbin. What if he's not blackmailing Suzette Thorndike? What if he wants something other than money from her?"

"Like what?"

"Well, if they were lovers, maybe he fell in love with her. Maybe he became obsessed with her, and that's why she ended the affair. Maybe the phone conversation Claire overheard was Corbin trying to coerce Suzette into resuming their relationship. When she refused, he became angry and decided to kidnap Claire."

"Why take Claire? Why not Suzette?"

"Because Suzette rejected him. And maybe in his warped little mind, Claire represents the Suzette he met ten years ago. She married Patrick Farris when she was eighteen years old. Claire's almost eighteen, and you and I have already noted that she's practically the spitting image of Suzette. So maybe Corbin decided if he couldn't have Suzette, he'd take the next best thing. Maybe he's twisted enough to think he can somehow make Claire fall in love with him."

"And if he can't," Damien muttered grimly, "then God help her."

Althea said nothing. A fine chill swept through her at the thought of the young girl—alone, terrified, at the complete mercy of a dangerous madman obsessed with her stepmother. What would he do to Claire if she refused him? If she showed fear or revulsion? Would he become so enraged that he would rape her, torture her? Kill her?

Or had he already done those things?

She shuddered at the unspeakable thought, drawing Damien's gaze to her. "Are you cold? I can turn up the heat."

She shook her head, staring out the window. "I'm fine."

A sliver of moon could be glimpsed through thick clouds that rolled across the night sky. Fog skimmed off the surface of the water and floated past like ghosts. There were several boats docked at piers up and down the river, belonging to the inhabitants of the small clapboard houses that rimmed the bay. The chilly night air had grown heavy with a thick mist that threatened to become rain. Althea hoped it wouldn't rain. It would be hard to continue surveillance on the dark house with sheets of water sluicing down the windshield, decreasing visibility.

Setting aside his binoculars, Damien reached for his thermos and unscrewed the lid. The strong, fragrant aroma of hot coffee filled the interior of the car. He took a long sip. "Have you figured out which of your books is missing?"

Althea shook her head. "I'm going to set aside some time tomorrow evening to rearrange the bookcase. There are hundreds of books, most of which I haven't read in years. I can't tell what was taken, whether it was fiction or nonfiction." She lifted the binoculars to her face again. "Maybe I'm wrong. Maybe there *isn't* a book missing. Maybe it just looked like there was an empty space on the shelf now that the books are arranged differently."

She didn't have to see Damien's face to know he was

scowling at her. "You need to take this more seriously," he growled.

"I am. Believe me, the idea of someone skulking around my apartment when I wasn't home or sometime in the middle of the night is nothing to take lightly. But the more I think about it, the more unlikely it seems. As I already told you, I checked the front door and windows; the locks were in place and there was no sign of forced entry. The only way someone could have gotten inside my apartment without my knowledge is if he—or she—had a key. And I just don't see how that's possible."

"Anything's possible," Damien muttered darkly. "Have you spoken to the building management about the shoddy security?"

"Yes. I called them this afternoon, and I was assured that they're handling the matter and will be speaking to the front desk attendant about doing a better job of enforcing security. Apparently they've also received some complaints about people's cars getting broken into in the parking lot. Anyway, you'll be happy to know that all visitors to the building will have to sign in from now on."

Damien nodded shortly. "Glad to hear it."

Althea leaned back on the headrest, her mouth curving in a soft little smile as she gazed at him. "Despite the impression I may have given you, Mr. Wade, I do appreciate your concern for me. I don't want you to think I'm an ingrate."

"Too late."

She laughed. "You're so mean!"

His lips twitched. "I've been called worse."

"Not by anyone at the office, I'll bet. Everyone seems to adore you. I think the office service manager has a serious crush on you. Have you noticed the way she stares at you whenever she sees you coming down the hall?"

Damien chuckled. "Don't be jealous."

Althea rolled her eyes. "Yeah, right. I'm just burning up with jealousy. It's so bad I can't even see straight." Unbidden, her mind conjured an image of Angelique trailing Damien down the stairs, her hair tousled and her shirt unbuttoned. Althea's imagination rewound like a videotape, and she saw the couple lying naked in the rumpled king-size bed she'd glimpsed on her way to the guest bathroom. She saw Angelique kissing Damien, touching his sculpted bare chest as he slowly lowered his body over hers and—

Althea turned toward the window and squeezed her eyes shut, as if to block out the image. *It's bad enough that you can't have him. Why torture yourself imagining him with his ex-wife, or any other woman!*

"So what's the story with you and Toomer?"

Althea's eyes flew open. She whipped her head around and stared at Damien. "*Excuse* me?"

He stared back at her, unblinking. "I don't think I stuttered. What's up with you and Malik Toomer?"

"What kind of question is that?"

He just looked at her. The directness of his gaze set her pulse racing.

She forced a laugh that sounded strangled to her own ears. "With all due respect, Damien, I really don't think that's any of your business. Besides, you don't see *me* asking you about your ex-wife, who you're apparently still screwing!"

The moment the angry words were out of her mouth, she wished she could snatch them back. She could tell by the smoldering gleam in Damien's dark eyes that she'd said too much. Revealed too much.

"You think I'm sleeping with Angelique?" he inquired silkily.

She gave a dismissive shrug. "It's none of my business. I don't care."

"Liar."

Her cheeks flushing, Althea picked up her binoculars to resume watching the house. But before she could lift it to her face, Damien reached over and snatched it out of her hand.

Her temper flared. "Hey! I'm trying to *work* here! And that's the second time today you've snatched something out of my hand. I'm getting sick and tired—"

"I saw the look on your face this morning when you saw Angelique coming down the stairs behind me," Damien said huskily, searing her with his dark, intense gaze. "I was afraid to interpret it as jealousy, and you played it off so well. But just now," he said, shaking his head slowly, "you didn't do such a good job. Don't tell me you don't care whether or not I'm sleeping with Angelique, because I know better. And so do you."

Althea's heart was hammering painfully against her rib cage, as if she'd just completed a marathon. She moistened her dry lips with the tip of her tongue and watched Damien's heavy-lidded eyes follow the innocent gesture. Her belly quivered in response. The air between them crackled with sexual tension. If a bolt of lightning had struck anywhere *near* the car at that moment, they both would have gone up in flames.

Forcing herself to break eye contact with him, she passed a trembling hand over her hair and dragged in a deep lungful of air.

"This is crazy," she muttered under her breath, glaring out the window. "We're supposed to be concentrating on the case, not our libidos."

"I want to find Claire and nail the son of a bitch who took her just as much as you do," Damien said in a low voice. "But I'm human, and I'd be lying to you if I said

I haven't thought about making love to you at least once since we've been sitting out here. I'd be lying if I told you I haven't been trying to ignore the teasing scent of your perfume, the smell of your hair, how incredible your legs look in those jeans."

Althea swallowed, her nipples hardening beneath her sweater. "Damien—"

"And just so you know, that jealousy thing goes both ways. The only thing that kept me from killing Toomer this morning was the knowledge that the place was crawling with cops and innocent bystanders."

Althea turned from the window to stare at him, her eyes wide with shock. "You . . . you were jealous of Malik?"

"Burning up with it," Damien said grimly, echoing her earlier words. "It was so bad I couldn't even see straight."

Althea shook her head at him, bemused. "No wonder you were so quiet on the way back to the office. I just thought you had a lot on your mind."

"I did. I was plotting what I was going to do to Toomer the next time I ran into him."

Althea felt the ghost of a smile tugging at her mouth. "You're crazy, you know that?"

He chuckled ruefully. "Tell me something I don't know."

She hesitated, biting her bottom lip. "Okay. Here's something you don't know. There's nothing going on between me and Malik. He asked me out to dinner. I turned him down. End of story."

Damien gave her a long, probing look. "You're not thinking about taking him back?"

She held his gaze. "No."

"That's good," he said softly. "That's very good."

Althea waited. When he said nothing more, she arched a brow. "Well?"

"Well, what?"

She hesitated, but her curiosity got the best of her. "Are you thinking about reconciling with Angelique?"

His eyes glinted with mischief. "I thought you said you don't care?"

"Maybe I lied."

One dubious brow sketched upward. "Maybe?"

"All right. I lied. I care. There. Are you happy?"

His gaze roamed across her face. "Why do you care?"

She huffed out an impatient breath. "I don't know. I just do. Are you getting back with her or not?"

He held her stare a moment longer, then shook his head. "No. We're not getting back together. And what you saw this morning wasn't what it looked like. Far from it."

A wave of relief swept through Althea, and she called herself a damn fool. "But she wants to, doesn't she?"

Damien made a face. "Angelique wants a lot of things she can't have."

Althea knew she should just drop the subject, but she couldn't stop herself from asking gently, "What happened between the two of you? Why did you split up?"

His mouth hardened. His eyes went flat and cold. "It's a long story," he muttered, passing her binoculars back, signaling to her that the conversation was over.

But Althea wasn't to be put off so easily. "You started this," she reminded him, turning partially in the seat to face him.

"And now I'm finishing it," he growled.

She just looked at him, undaunted.

He turned away and peered through his binoculars for a moment. Even in the shadowy darkness, Althea could see a telltale muscle pulsing in his jaw.

After a long, tense moment, he lowered the binoculars and heaved a resigned sigh. "We met during our junior year in college. After we'd been dating for a while, Angelique got pregnant. It wasn't what either of us wanted, but we'd both been raised to value human life, so getting an abortion was out of the question. After India was born, Angelique dropped out of school and moved in with her parents. But I didn't want her to shoulder the burden of trying to raise our child alone, so I dropped out and got a full-time job to take care of her and the baby. We had our own place for a while, but Angelique missed the creature comforts of home."

"In other words," Althea said wryly, "she missed being spoiled by her parents."

Damien grimaced. "Basically. I couldn't compete with what they could give her. After she moved back home, I pretty much did the same thing. I moved in with my mom to save money so I could go back to college. India stayed with me most of the time, because quite frankly, motherhood wasn't high on Angelique's list of priorities. My mom had retired from teaching, so she was able to keep India for me while I went to work and school. I don't know what I would have done without her. She was a godsend—she still is. She keeps India every day after school until Angelique gets off from work. She helps her with her homework, does school projects with her, and makes sure India eats a balanced dinner before Angelique picks her up. My mom adores India, and the feeling is mutual.

"Still, I always wanted to give my daughter a stable home life, a family with a mother and father in the picture. After I graduated from college and joined the Bureau, Angelique decided we should get married. I had my reservations, but Angelique swore to me she'd sowed her wild oats and was ready to settle down. I thought I was doing what was best for India, and hell, I wanted what my brothers had, what Garrison and Imani had." A shadow of cynicism curved Damien's mouth. "I should have known better. Angelique and I didn't have that magic, that powerful connection my brothers have with their wives. We never did. We had great sex, and toward the end of our marriage, even that went by the wayside."

"How long were you married?" Althea asked quietly.

"Two years. Two of the longest damn years of my life. In the beginning Angelique tried her best to be a good little wife, and I tried my best to pretend we could be a real family, but we both knew we were deceiving ourselves. After a while she gave up all pretenses and started hanging out every night with her friends. We were constantly arguing, not sleeping together." He shook his head, his lips twisting bitterly at the memory. "The final straw for me was when I found a man's number in her purse one day when I was looking for India's health insurance card. I'd always suspected Angelique was cheating on me, but I'd never found any proof. When I confronted her about the phone number, she started crying and insisting that nothing had happened, he was just some pushy guy she'd met at the club. I actually believed her, but I realized right then and there that I didn't want to live like that. I didn't want to become some jealous, insecure husband who was always snooping in his wife's purse just to make sure she wasn't having an affair. I couldn't live like that, and I didn't want our daughter subjected to a marriage like that. So I told Angelique I wanted a divorce, and the rest is history."

"I'm sorry," Althea murmured.

He shook his head. "Don't feel sorry for me. I didn't share those things with you because I wanted your pity or concern. I wasn't a victim. I knew what I was getting myself into when I married Angelique. And she wasn't entirely to blame for what happened. There are always two sides to every story, and I'm sure if you talked to Angelique, she could tell you how I failed her as a husband."

"Doesn't mean I'd believe her," Althea muttered.

Damien chuckled softly. "That's because you're not being objective."

"No, probably not." She hesitated. "It must have been very difficult for you to lose custody of India."

He nodded, pain flitting across his face. "It was one of the worst days of my life," he admitted quietly. "But in a way I was prepared for that outcome. I'd done my research, read the statistics, and I knew that this particular family court judge had a track record of ruling in the mother's favor unless there was clear-cut evidence of abuse or neglect, and even then it had to be a long history."

Althea nodded. "I've heard that happens a lot, unfortunately. But that was, what, six years ago? Have you ever thought about appealing the judge's decision?"

"Just about every day," Damien said, looking grim. "But after that first custody battle, I swore I'd never put India through anything like that again. It not only brought out the worst in me and Angelique, but it pitted our families against one another in the worst possible way. So, yeah, I'd like nothing more than to have full custody of India, but not if it means subjecting her to another long, bitter custody dispute."

"I understand," Althea said with quiet sympathy.

Damien looked at her. "Yeah," he murmured. "Somehow I think you do."

They stared at each other. Not for the first time, Althea felt an inner stirring, felt something shifting and stretching inside her. She'd only known this man for *six* days, yet she'd never felt more intrinsically connected to another human being.

And she could tell, by the way Damien was staring at her, that he felt it, too.

"Althea—"

She would never know what he was about to say, for at that moment, the soft glow of headlights cutting through the darkness snared their attention.

They looked across the riverbank in time to see a dark car pull into the driveway of Patrick Farris's house.

The headlights went out.

Althea and Damien quickly raised their binoculars, but all they could make out was the shadowy silhouette of a man's head and broad shoulders. The figure sat behind the wheel, silent and unmoving.

And then, suddenly, the car lurched into reverse, shooting out of the driveway.

"*Shit,*" Damien growled, tossing aside his binoculars.

Althea's pulse pounded as he cranked the ignition, backed up sharply, and gunned the accelerator, plunging headlong into the night.

And for the first time, she uttered not a word of complaint about his aggressive driving skills.

Chapter 26

But it didn't matter.

By the time they reached the other side of the bank in hot pursuit of the mystery driver, they were too late. The other car was nowhere in sight.

The narrow two-lane road was empty and dark, a lonely stretch of asphalt flanked on either side by the silent river. Damien continued down the road for a while, turning down quiet side streets lined with Cape Cods and quaint saltbox houses shaded by big, leafy trees. As they drove past, they peered inside parked cars and scanned the tidy lawns for signs of movement before giving up and heading back to Patrick Farris's neighborhood.

Killing their headlights, they crept along the winding, deserted road that ran parallel to the river, driving past the other waterfront homes shrouded in darkness and mist.

There was no sign of Corbin Farris.

Cursing a blue streak, Damien pounded his fist against the steering wheel in frustration.

"He must have seen us," Althea said, equally frustrated. "But *how?* We had the perfect hiding place behind those trees."

"Obviously not," Damien muttered. "Besides, we were too far away."

"We couldn't get any closer to the house, or he *definitely* would have made us."

Damien said nothing. He knew she was right.

The rain had finally begun to fall, a cold, steady drizzle that would, at any moment, become a deluge. Damien returned to Patrick Farris's house and parked at the end of the driveway. He and Althea grabbed flashlights and climbed out of the car.

Heedless of the rain, they started purposefully across the lawn and made their way up to the small white clapboard. Weapons at the ready, they separated and circled the house, shining their flashlights through windows, listening for anything out of place. Althea tried the back door, knowing she wouldn't be lucky enough to find it unlocked, knowing they couldn't enter without a search warrant anyway.

They walked the length of the backyard, which sloped down to meet the river. The rain had worsened, coming down in frigid, driving sheets that plastered her hair to her scalp and soaked her trench coat.

"Let's go!" Damien called, grabbing her hand. Together they ran back to the car and climbed inside.

Shivering uncontrollably, Althea smoothed her wet hair off her face and grumbled, "This just hasn't been our day, has it?"

"Tell me about it," Damien muttered, turning up the heat and chafing his hands together. Rainwater clung to his thick black lashes and dripped off his nose.

Althea reached inside the glove compartment and grabbed a handful of clean napkins from Wendy's, and she and Damien mopped at their faces. Their clothing was a lost cause.

"Now what?" she asked.

"Well, we could stay out here to wait for Farris to make another appearance, but I think we both know there's a snowball's chance in hell of that happening."

Althea snorted. "No kidding. Now that he knows we're onto him, he won't be coming back here anytime soon. At least not anytime tonight."

Damien nodded. "As soon as it's daylight, I'd like to drive around checking any vacant buildings and warehouses, maybe even some old lighthouses. We should stop somewhere and get a map and ask one of the locals to point us in the right direction, since they're more familiar with the area than we are."

Althea nodded, chilled to the bone. The idea of sitting around for hours in soaking wet clothes held no appeal whatsoever.

Damien must have shared the sentiment. "In the meantime," he said, starting the car and flipping on the windshield wipers, "I say we find the nearest motel, get out of these wet clothes, and maybe grab a few hours of shut-eye. What do you think?"

Althea groaned. "I think that's the best idea I've heard all day," she declared.

They headed back to the main road, which took them back into town. They stopped at the first place they came to, a quaint bed and breakfast situated on the tree-lined banks of a scenic waterway identified as Back Creek. The friendly innkeeper took one look at their sodden clothes and informed them that they were in luck. There was one more room available for the night.

Relieved, Althea and Damien grinned at each other. It was the first good news they had received all day.

They were shown to a small, cozy room with a charming French country décor, a comfy-looking bed and sofa, and a gas fireplace, which the innkeeper graciously stoked for them. Not bothering to correct his assumption that they were a couple, Althea and Damien patiently listened as the man gushed over a list of the inn's amenities, which included breathtaking waterfront views, picturesque botanical gardens, private baths for every room, and a hearty country breakfast to be served promptly at seven A.M. tomorrow. He encouraged them to take a leisurely walk down to the nearby shops and boutiques after breakfast, and recommended a lovely little restaurant where they could watch the sun set over the bay and enjoy a romantic stroll along the pier.

Before leaving the room, he presented them with a complimentary bottle of champagne and a gift basket filled with a colorful assortment of cheese, crackers, sausages, fresh fruit, and canned preserves.

"I hope you will enjoy your stay with us," he told them with a conspiratorial smile as he gracefully bowed out of the room.

When the door closed behind him, Althea and Damien stood across the length of the room from each other for a brief, awkward moment.

"Well," said Althea. "He certainly knows the meaning of the word *hospitality*."

"You think?"

They grinned at each other, and the awkward moment passed.

"I call the bed," Althea announced.

Damien inclined his head, mouth twitching. "Of course."

She started for the bathroom. "I think I'll take a hot shower, try to put some feeling back into my extremities."

"Save me some hot water," Damien called after her.

Thirty minutes later, they were both freshly showered and dressed in the change of clothes they'd had the foresight to pack in preparation for the stakeout. They popped the champagne, ripped open the gift basket, and feasted on the contents while they pored over the map the innkeeper had provided. While Althea was in the shower, Damien had gone downstairs and asked their host about vacant commercial properties in the area.

"He came up with several off the top of his head," Damien explained to Althea, "but only a few sounded remote enough for hiding someone."

"Did he ask why you were interested?"

Damien nodded. "I told him we were thinking about relocating to the area, maybe opening a business."

Althea nodded approvingly. "Good thinking."

Wicked humor glinted in Damien's dark eyes as he drawled, "See? My mind isn't *always* in the gutter."

She laughed. "I never said it was!"

He smiled, his gaze roaming across her damp hair, which she'd shampooed, gelled, and slicked back off her face to let it air dry. His eyes hungrily traced her features, lingering on her mouth so long a flutter of heat ignited in her belly.

"I think I spoke too soon," he said huskily.

Althea stared at him, unable to look away, unable to breathe.

The next thing she knew, he had pulled her from her chair at the table and onto his lap. As she straddled his muscled thighs, the thick, rigid length of his erection pressed against her crotch. It was unbearably arousing, and she let out a ragged moan as his warm lips covered hers. He kissed her, a long, deep, provocative kiss that drugged her senses and left her aching for more.

Despite what common sense told her, despite her resolve to resist temptation and maintain professional boundaries between them, she wanted this, wanted *him* with a ferocity she could no longer deny.

He reached for the hem of her shirt. His hands were

so big, so dark and masculine, that watching them raise her shirt turned her on. He swept it over her head, then tossed it aside. She hadn't bothered with a bra after her shower, and as she watched Damien devouring her with his gaze, her breasts swelled with arousal, her nipples puckering under his masculine appraisal. His shadowed face looked hard, the set of his jaw accentuated in the soft lamplight. His nostrils flared, and his chest rose and fell rapidly.

"You are so damn beautiful," he said, the low, husky timbre of his voice reaching between her legs and making her quiver.

Slowly he bent down and drew her right nipple into his mouth. She gasped. Holding her gaze, he stroked her with his tongue, luscious, velvety strokes that made her arch backward and close her eyes on a deep, shuddering moan. She felt the sensuous pull of his mouth everywhere, filling her loins with a delicious ache. She caught his head, holding him to her, anchoring herself as the wondrous sensations swept through her.

As he kissed his way to her other breast, every nerve ending in her body clamored for release. She whimpered something, maybe his name, and he lifted his head and claimed her mouth, plunging his tongue inside and stroking deep. She sucked greedily on his tongue, and as they played tonsil hockey, he cupped her breasts in his hands and thumbed her wet, sensitized nipples in a manner designed to drive her crazy. She writhed in his lap, grinding against his erection, and he inhaled sharply.

He reached down and cupped her buttocks, squeezing and kneading her round cheeks as he urged her closer. They humped each other, hard, the friction of their movements making her clitoris throb.

With a low, savage oath, Damien lifted her off his

lap and set her on her feet, then quickly went to work removing her jeans. When he saw that she wore no panties, he swore again, hoarsely.

No sooner had she kicked her jeans out of the way than he was lifting her again, depositing her on the small table. She shoved the map out of the way and sent it sailing to the floor. Damien grabbed her thighs and spread them wide to accommodate the breadth of his shoulders as he knelt between her legs.

Watching her face, he pressed a featherlight kiss to one knee, then the other. Althea shivered, anticipation already firing her blood. He took her legs and hooked them over his shoulders. And then slowly, sensually, he began kissing his way up her inner thighs, leaving a path of scorched nerve endings. A ball of liquid heat coiled inside her, tighter and tighter, until she thought she would explode. She licked her lips and leaned back on her elbows.

"So pretty," Damien whispered reverently, his gaze fastened on the slick, swollen folds of her sex beneath a thatch of soft dark curls. He lifted his smoldering eyes to hers. "So damn pretty."

It was one of the most erotic things she'd ever experienced, their gazes locked as he slowly worked his way toward the feminine core of her. It was sensory overload. The brush of his soft lips, the whisper of his breath, the gentle scrape of his stubbled jaw. Her pulse pounded. Her senses were electrified.

At the first touch of his mouth on her sex, she cried out brokenly and flung back her head. His tongue circled her labia, teasing and tormenting. She moaned and rocked her hips as he licked, nibbled, and sucked her clitoris. She closed her eyes and tried to control the trembling that racked her body, but the pleasure was too much. She couldn't take much more.

And then he thrust his tongue deep inside her—and her hips bucked off the table as she came with a loud, mewling cry. He gripped her butt tightly, lapping at her like a hungry tomcat devouring a bowl of cream. Amazingly, she felt another orgasm building in her loins.

But before it broke free, Damien pulled back from her and impatiently tugged his shirt off, casting it aside. Althea rose up on her elbows to watch as he unsnapped his jeans and slid his zipper down over his thick, jutting erection. He retrieved a condom from his wallet and quickly sheathed himself.

Althea's belly quivered with arousal at the sight of his dark, powerful body. She was already reaching for him as he came back to her, sweeping her up and carrying her over to the sofa. She wrapped her legs around his hips, so that by the time he sat down on the edge, the head of his penis was already nudging her slick opening.

Their gazes locked as he thrust into her with one long, erotically painful stroke that made her cry out sharply. He made a harsh sound deep in his throat, and his arms banded around her with steely strength. She clutched his big shoulders, her nails digging into the hard pad of muscle. His hands stroked down her back to her buttocks and he lifted her, sliding her back down his engorged length slowly, inch by inch. She shuddered, her thighs tightening around him, her ankles locking behind his broad back. As he began thrusting into her, her heart hammered in her chest. A mind-numbing pleasure coursed through her veins, unlike anything she'd ever known before meeting this man.

She stared into his face, so brutally handsome it took her breath away. His dark eyes glittered, fierce with arousal and possessiveness. In that moment he owned her. Her mind, body, and soul belonged to him, and he knew it.

He leaned forward, capturing her lips in a rough, marauding kiss that left her breathless and gasping. She whimpered as his thrusts intensified, making her breasts bounce as he plunged in and out of her, harder, faster, taking them higher and higher. Soon the room was filled with their guttural moans and the wet, slapping sounds of their bodies.

Her thighs were taut and shaking, and her stomach muscles clenched as an exquisite pressure built inside her, almost frightening in its intensity. A moment later she sobbed Damien's name as her orgasm gripped her, gripped him, and they came together in a hot, violent rush.

They clutched each other tightly, trembling and panting for breath, a slick coat of sweat sealing their bodies together.

After a few minutes, Damien slowly withdrew from her and brushed a tendril of hair off her damp, flushed face. "I love to watch your face when you come," he whispered. "You blush so hard. It's the most incredible thing I've ever seen."

Althea felt another blush steal across her cheeks, and he laughed, low and husky. Her lips curved. She couldn't even vocalize a response. She felt weak, spent. Thoroughly satiated.

Damien leaned back against the sofa and cradled her protectively in his arms. She clung to his neck, feeling his strong, galloping heartbeat against her own as the perspiration cooled on their skin. He kissed her forehead and stroked her hair in a way that filled her heart with tenderness. She sighed softly, content to lie against him, cuddled and protected, surrounded by his male heat.

They sat in silence for a while and listened to the rain outside, lashing against the windows. In that timeless moment, nothing else existed. Not their jobs, the frustrating case, or the world beyond this room. There was nothing but the two of them, cocooned in their own private, sensual haven.

What have you gotten yourself into, Althea?

More than I bargained for.

She had returned home to bury the ghosts of the past and reclaim her life. At no time had she factored romance into the equation. Meeting Damien Wade at the club had changed all that. By sleeping with him that night, she'd set a course in motion that could not be altered. No matter how hard she tried—and God *knows* she'd tried—the chemistry between them, the connection they shared, was too powerful to resist.

She was falling in love with him.

And the more she fought her feelings, the harder she fell.

She'd tried talking herself out of it by constantly reminding herself of her rule against dating colleagues. When that didn't work, she tried focusing on his flaws. He was too damn bossy, too alpha male. They'd butt heads all the time. And his stubborn insistence upon opening doors for her and holding out her chair would drive her crazy, not to mention his reckless driving.

She'd run the gamut of reasons why she shouldn't fall for Damien. But nothing worked. For every perceived flaw, she could come up with a number of different things she adored about him. Like the way he made her feel with one look, one touch, one smile meant just for her. Or the way he was with his daughter, who had him wrapped around her little finger. She adored his sense of humor, which balanced his fierce intensity. And, yes, damn it, she adored him for being so chivalrous, so protective of her, that he'd even taken the time to open the car door for her before getting himself out of the driving rain.

"Hey," Damien murmured suddenly, placing his finger beneath her chin and tilting her face up to meet his lazy, speculative gaze. "You falling asleep?"

Althea shook her head. "I was just thinking."

"About what?"

No way was she pouring out her heart to him!

She smiled, her flesh tingling as he idly ran his finger up and down her arm. "I was just thinking about how cozy this room is, how comfy that bed looks."

"Yeah? That's funny, 'cause I've been thinking about that bed, too. Wanna know what I've been thinking about doing to you in it?"

The low, husky intimacy in his voice made her shiver. She swallowed and nodded, staring at him.

He gave her a smoldering look. "Better yet, why don't I *show* you?"

Althea trembled with anticipation as he stood with her in his arms and strode purposefully across the room. They tumbled across the queen-size bed, accidentally knocking the lamp to the floor and plunging the room into darkness as their hungry mouths and bodies merged.

Hours later, Damien was awakened by a distant rumble of thunder outside the window. The storm had spent itself, much as he and Althea had done.

His mouth curved in a lazy smile at the thought, and he angled his head to gaze down at her in the shadowy darkness. She lay snuggled against him, her soft, deep breaths fanning his throat, her long, silky leg draped across his thighs.

Memories of last night returned to him.

Althea drove him crazy with lust, made him lose control of himself. Every time they came together he was like an animal with her, heeding only his primal instincts to mate, to conquer. After days of being deprived of her, he'd nearly been too ravenous to worry about using protection, something he'd sworn he would never do again after he got Angelique pregnant.

And now as he reflected upon their night of unbridled sex, he found himself imagining Althea with child. *His* child. Maybe a boy who would look just like him, just as his brothers' sons looked like their fathers, courtesy of those dominant Wade genes. Or maybe a little girl with her mother's bewitching eyes and breathtaking beauty. A little sister for India, one she would cuddle and fuss over. He thought about Althea seated at his breakfast table, smiling and giving his daughter her undivided attention as India animatedly bounced from one subject to the next. He'd been struck by how right, how perfect it felt to have Althea there with them.

Just reliving the cozy family scene made his chest swell with longing, and he leaned down and kissed the top of Althea's head.

In a few hours it would be daylight, and they would get up and go about the business of searching for a missing teenager who never should have been taken from her family in the first place. In a few hours, he and Althea would get up and resume their search for an unknown predator, hoping for a clue that would lead them to his door.

But until then, Damien just wanted to lay there, basking in Althea's addictive warmth, her scent. Her essence.

And then she shifted in her sleep, pressing her lush breasts against his chest, burrowing her thigh between his legs.

And just like that he was hard and aching for her.

She mumbled drowsily as he moved, rolling her gently onto her back. Propping himself on one elbow, he leaned down and kissed her gently, lingeringly. She sighed, a soft, dreamy smile curving her lips. Her nipples puckered tight. He lowered his head, closed his mouth around one dark nipple, and suckled. She shivered, a broken moan escaping her parted lips.

He reached between their bodies and touched her. She was already wet and ready for him. His erection throbbed. He cupped her, his fingers spreading her slick wetness over the soft, swollen folds of her sex. She groaned and arched into his hand, opening her thighs wider.

And he lost it.

He grabbed a condom from his wallet on the night stand and covered himself, then moved on top of Althea and settled between her legs. Telling himself to go easy, not to ravage her, he slowly guided his throbbing penis inside her. She gave a low, throaty moan. He had to clench his teeth against the pleasure of her body stretching around him, her wet, silky heat enveloping him, her clenching muscles pulling at him.

Her lashes fluttered, and her dark, sultry eyes opened and fastened on his face.

His heart contracted. Blood thundered through his veins. Pushing forward, he sank into her until they were fully joined, his whole length buried deep inside her. Her breath left her in a slow hiss. Her eyes went smoky with desire.

He levered himself up on his arms, withdrew almost to the tip, and drove hard into her again. She cried out hoarsely, throwing back her head. Her thighs clamped around him, settling higher on his waist as she opened herself wider to him. He hammered into her, his gaze intent on her face, his jaw clenched, his muscles sweating and quivering.

He tried to order himself to slow down, but he couldn't. He felt primitive, possessive. He couldn't get enough of her. In a near frenzy he thrust into her, reaching deeper with every stroke, voracious in his hunger.

Her firm, luscious breasts bounced up and down from his thrusts. The warm, musky scent of her arousal mingled with his was a heady, potent aphrodisiac that went straight to his head. He felt cocooned in eroticism and heat and something more, something he'd never experienced with any other woman.

And he knew, in that moment, that he'd fallen in love with Althea.

Shaken by the revelation, he watched as she stared up at him, her cheeks flushed, her dark eyes slitting in a way that told him she was on the verge of climaxing. He kept his thrusts steady, all his focus now on giving her the best damn orgasm of her life. She wrapped her arms tightly around him, her nails scoring his back, her breath coming in rapid, shallow pants. He felt her body quivering, straining toward release.

"Let go, sweetheart," he whispered huskily. "Let go for me."

Her neck arched, her body stiffened, and her muscles pulsed and contracted around him as she came, sobbing his name over and over again.

Moments later Damien shuddered and shouted hoarsely with the force of his own powerful release. He emptied himself into her, his hips pumping until he was milked dry, until the violent spasms gradually tapered off.

Then, feeling drained and replete, he lowered himself onto the bed, gathering Althea close. She made a soft little sighing noise and burrowed her face against his chest, mumbling sleepily, "Love you."

Damien froze, lifting his head to stare down at her with a look of incredulity. *Did she just say what I thought she said?*

But Althea's eyes had closed, her body had grown

still, and her breathing was deep and even. She had already fallen back asleep!

Chuckling silently, Damien brushed his lips across her forehead and pulled her tightly into his arms, overcome with tenderness and joy.

"I love you, too," he whispered.

And one way or another, I'm going to make you mine.

Chapter 27

Washington, D.C.
Thursday, October 9
Day 7

Courtney Reese couldn't sleep. She had been tossing and turning all night, mentally replaying the stressful events of the day before. First she'd gotten yelled at by an irate constituent who had called Senator Horton's office to complain about a controversial bill the senator had recently voted in favor of. Then she'd found herself in a verbal sparring match with an aide who worked for a rival senator. Although Courtney got the last word, the delay caused her to be late for a committee meeting, something that rarely, if ever, happened. Shortly after she returned from the meeting, she was told that Althea Pritchard—the niece of a man Courtney despised—was on the phone for her. Althea's probing questions about Claire Thorndike's abduction only served as a painful reminder to Courtney that her young friend was gone and may never be found alive.

Was it any wonder she couldn't sleep?

Courtney blew out a ragged breath and punched her

pillow in frustration. The clock on the nightstand taunted her with the lateness of the hour. Two-twenty.

She'd have to get up in a few hours for her morning jog before she got dressed for work. She needed at least four hours of sleep or she couldn't function, and working for a prominent senator meant she had to be in top form at all times.

Courtney turned over and closed her eyes, but after ten more minutes, sleep continued to elude her. She groaned and rolled onto her back, staring up at the darkened ceiling, her mind still racing.

She was just about to get up and do something productive—like draft a constituent letter for Senator Horton or fold her laundry—when she heard the creak of a floorboard.

Her heart lodged in her throat. The saliva dried in her mouth.

She sat up quickly and reached across the nightstand, switching on the lamp. She swept a panicked look around the large, tastefully furnished bedroom. It was empty. She held her breath, straining to listen for footsteps.

She heard nothing. The apartment was quiet and still.

There's no one else here, she told herself. *It's just your overactive imagination. You're paranoid because of what happened to Claire, and because Althea Pritchard tried to scare you.*

But maybe she was right. Maybe whoever took Claire will come after her friends. At the very least, you should consider getting a security alarm. You're a single woman living alone. You can never be too safe.

Courtney hesitated, deliberating whether to stay in bed or get up and do some work. She had a busy day tomorrow. Well, Senator Horton had a busy day, which meant she did as well. Since she was having such a hard time sleeping, she might as well get up and do something useful.

Decision made, Courtney threw back the covers and climbed out of bed. She had just started across the room when a masked figure dressed in black suddenly appeared in the open doorway.

Courtney screamed.

As the intruder slowly advanced on her, panic shot through her body. Stumbling backward, she grabbed the first thing she could put her hands on and hurled it at him. He calmly batted aside the ceramic flat iron and continued stalking her, silent and menacing.

Courtney wondered if this was what Claire had experienced on the night she was abducted. This mind-numbing terror, a horrifying certainty that her life was about to come to an end.

"P-Please," Courtney begged, her voice quavering with fear. "Y-You can take anything you want. I make good money. I-I have nice things."

He shook his head once. His eyes behind the mask were cold, lifeless.

As she soon would be.

She turned to run, thinking she could barricade herself in the bathroom and call the police with her cell phone, which she'd left on the counter after brushing her teeth.

But it was too late. Her assailant tackled her from behind and knocked her to the floor, pressing something hard against the small of her back. A white-hot blast jolted through her body. Pain shot through her system.

Her last thought before she lost consciousness was that Althea Pritchard had tried to warn her, but she hadn't listened.

* * *

Damien received the call as he and Althea were walking back to the car after checking out their third abandoned building of the morning.

Balducci sounded grim. "I just got a call from D.C. police. Seems that our kidnapper has struck again. Courtney Reese was abducted from her apartment early this morning."

Dread tightened in Damien's gut. "No signs of a struggle?"

"None. Nothing was out of place. When she didn't show up at the office at seven this morning to go over some talking points with Senator Horton, he got worried and started blowing up her cell phone. Seems that Courtney Reese is punctual to a fault, so if she doesn't show up on time for work, people worry. When she didn't answer her phone, Horton called the police. When they arrived at the apartment, Courtney was gone. They started knocking on doors, and it turns out that one of the neighbors thought she heard a scream coming from Courtney's apartment around two-thirty A.M. But the woman decided she was only hearing things, so she didn't call the police." A wary note crept into Balducci's voice. "Is Althea there with you?"

"Yeah." Damien glanced over at Althea, who was watching him intently.

Balducci said quietly, "Then you'd both better come in so I can tell you the rest."

Deep foreboding settled over Damien. "Be right there."

He disconnected and turned to Althea. "That was Balducci. Courtney Reese is missing."

"No," Althea whispered, stricken.

Damien nodded shortly. "Balducci wants us back at the office. Apparently it gets worse."

* * *

Althea took one look at Eddie, seated behind the desk in his office, and knew with a sinking sense of dread that she wasn't going to like what she heard. Still, nothing could have prepared her for the shock that swept through her when he waved her and Damien into chairs and proceeded to tell them what the police had discovered at Courtney Reese's apartment.

"They found a journal in her nightstand drawer." Eddie grimaced, looking like he'd rather kayak through a tsunami than deliver the bad news pressing down on him like an anvil.

Althea waited, the dread twisting and coiling in her stomach. Beside her, Damien shifted in his chair, impatience vibrating in the air around him.

Finally Eddie said in a carefully measured voice, "In the last journal entry dated yesterday, Courtney wrote that when she first heard about Claire's kidnapping, she thought someone had been hired to get rid of her. Because of a secret Courtney had recently told Claire."

Althea frowned. "What kind of secret?"

"According to the journal, Courtney told Claire that she'd had an affair last year with a powerful U.S. senator." He paused, looking grim. "Louis Pritchard."

Althea felt like the air had been knocked from her lungs. She must have swayed, because Damien lurched forward as if to catch her from falling, and Eddie half rose out of his chair with a concerned expression.

"Are you all right?" Damien demanded gruffly.

Althea barely heard the question above the blood pounding in her ears. She stared at Eddie. "What else did the entry say?"

He lowered himself back into his chair, eyeing her warily. "Courtney wrote that she was afraid for her life. She said if anything happened to her, people should know that Louis Pritchard may have been involved."

"That's a lie!" Althea burst out.

Eddie frowned at her. "Althea—"

"Don't you see what's happening? He's trying to frame my uncle!"

"Who?"

"Whoever took Claire. This is all part of the game!"

Eddie traded looks with Damien, who was frowning.

"How do the police even know that Courtney wrote those things?" Althea demanded.

"The handwriting matches the other journal entries," Eddie answered. "But of course they're having it analyzed just to make sure."

"It doesn't matter," Althea said. "The handwriting will match, because he dictated to her what she should write. He forced her to write those things."

"That's possible," Damien agreed.

Eddie shot him a look. The meaning was clear: *Don't encourage this line of thinking.*

Damien ignored the subtle warning. "Did they tell you when the previous journal entry was?"

"We didn't get into specifics. Anyway, what difference does it make?"

Damien shrugged. "If it's been a while since Courtney wrote in the journal, then you have to admit it seems suspicious that an entry suddenly appears the day before she's abducted."

Althea could have kissed him. Not that she hadn't done that enough already. "Damien's right. Everything about this journal entry has to be questioned."

"I agree," Eddie said evenly. "And I'm sure the police feel the same way. Which is why they're going to question your uncle today. To get his side of the story."

"My uncle had nothing to do with these abductions!"

Eddie gave her a long, assessing look. "I understand how difficult this must be for you, Althea," he said quietly.

"But you have to admit there's no way for you to be objective here. He's your uncle, the man who raised you from birth. You'd sooner cut off your left arm than suspect him of these crimes. But you have to look at it from the police's perspective. Your uncle is a very powerful man in Washington; he could become president in the next four years. Obviously a man in his position can't afford to have any skeletons surfacing, or he can pretty much kiss the White House good-bye. If he had an affair with Courtney Reese—"

"He didn't," Althea interjected.

"*If* he did, then he stands to lose a lot if the affair is made public. Not only politically, but personally. So he has motive for wanting to silence Courtney, as well as anyone else she may have confided in. You know as well as I do that if we were talking about anyone other than Louis Pritchard, you'd already be knocking on his door demanding answers."

Althea knew he was right. But they *weren't* talking about anyone else. They were talking about her uncle. *Her uncle!*

In a low, controlled voice, she said, "Do you really expect me to believe that my uncle would have these two women kidnapped and make it look like some psycho out there is reenacting a horrifying experience that his very own *niece* lived through?"

Eddie frowned. "I didn't say it doesn't sound farfetched."

"That's putting it mildly!"

"Come on, Althea," he said impatiently. "You've been at this job long enough to know anything is possible when it comes to people's motives for committing crimes. And the hard, cold reality is that your uncle is a powerful politician who stands to lose everything if an alleged extramarital affair is brought to light. Just ask yourself what *you* would do if you walked into a crime scene and found a journal in which the victim basically ID'd the perpetrator. At the very least, what Courtney Reese wrote in that journal warrants investigating."

"Fine," Althea snapped. "Let's investigate it. Let's ask some tough questions. Assuming my uncle *did* have an affair with Courtney Reese—" She forced herself not to shudder at the very idea. "—how would he have found out that she told Claire Thorndike? 'Cause last I checked, my uncle doesn't travel in the same social circles as seventeen-year-old girls. Did Courtney threaten to confide in Claire, and that's why he got rid of her? Or is he tapping Courtney's phones to monitor who she's talking to? And how can he be sure Claire is the only person she told? Is he going to go on a kidnapping spree, getting rid of everyone Courtney may have confided in? And why kidnap Claire first? If he's trying to conceal the affair, conventional wisdom says he'd get rid of the lover, who may or may not be in possession of the proverbial sperm-stained dress?"

"According to your own theory about this case," Eddie countered, "the perpetrator is reenacting your abduction. That means the protégée goes first, then the mentor. Hence Claire disappeared first."

Althea glared at him for a moment. "My uncle didn't do this!"

Eddie looked at her, his lips thinning to a flat, grim line. "It's clear to me, Pritchard, that you're incapable of remaining objective in this investigation. So you leave me no choice but to remove you from the case."

"What?" The words ricocheted through her brain. "You can't remove me!"

"Wrong. I can, and I just did. If you recall, I had reservations about your involvement in the first place. And now, with this latest development, there's no way you can stay on this case. It's a clear conflict of interest." He looked to Damien. "You know I'm right."

Damien clenched his jaw, his eyes glittering with suppressed anger. "Don't put me in the middle of this," he warned in a low, quelling voice.

Althea's heart sank. She knew what Damien's response meant. If he disagreed with Eddie, he would have said so. But he hadn't. And he was the only one who could possibly change their boss's mind about removing her from the case.

"Please don't reassign me, sir," she said, striving to sound calm, rational. "Damien and I are making progress. If you bring on another agent at this point—"

"I don't need to. Wade is fully capable of representing the Bureau on the task force. That's how it was supposed to be in the first place. I let you talk me into putting you on the case because you accused me of allowing your uncle to dictate the type of investigations you handle." His lips twisted cynically. "Guess the joke's on both of us."

Althea stared at him, half a dozen stinging remarks on the tip of her tongue. But she reined in her temper, remembering that this man, friend or not, could advance her career—or end it.

She drew a deep breath. "I'd really like to stay on and help—"

Eddie's expression hardened. "You're off the case, Pritchard. That's all there is to it." His words, and the cold finality in his voice, slammed through her mind like the metal doors of a jail cell clanging shut.

He jabbed a blunt-tipped finger at her. "Go talk to your squad supervisor. He's got plenty of other cases for you to jump into. And shut the door on your way out. Wade and I have some things to discuss."

Summarily dismissed, Althea rose from her chair without looking at Damien and left the room. The door had barely closed behind her when she heard Damien growl, "Damn it, Balducci, you could have gone a little easier on her. Think how you'd feel in her shoes."

Althea didn't wait around to hear Eddie's response. As she made her way through the labyrinth of halls and down to the Criminal Investigative Division, she pretended not to notice the speculative gazes of other agents she passed. Word traveled fast through the grapevine, especially in an organization like the FBI. And she knew it was only a matter of time before the media would be all over this story, which was sensational enough to rival any political scandal in recent history. It had all the necessary ingredients—sex, lies, and possibly murder.

Althea shuddered, the knot of dread tightening in her stomach as she returned to her cubicle. Ignoring the blinking message light on her phone, she lifted the receiver and dialed her uncle's cell phone. He answered after three rings, sounding shaken.

"It's me, Uncle Louie. Can we meet somewhere in an hour?"

Louis Pritchard had aged in a matter of hours, it seemed.

Pronounced lines of strain bracketed his mouth and his dark, tormented eyes. His broad shoulders, normally proud and erect, sagged beneath his expensive wool overcoat. He entered his niece's apartment and walked over to the sofa, lowering himself down as gingerly as an old man with acute arthritis.

Althea's heart squeezed painfully.

Instead of joining him on the sofa, she sat in the adjacent armchair so she could look at him directly, for what would probably be one of the most painful conversations they'd ever had.

"The police came to my office this morning," Louis began, sounding as shocked as he'd probably felt when the detectives arrived. "I couldn't believe it when they told me what they were there for. I *still* can't believe it."

"Neither can I," Althea murmured.

He looked at her imploringly. "I didn't do anything to those girls, Althea. Before we go any further, I need you to hear that from me. I had nothing to do with those abductions. *Nothing.*"

Althea swallowed hard, tears crowding the back of her throat. "I know you didn't, Uncle Louie. I never doubted your innocence."

He nodded, looking relieved. But not unburdened.

And Althea knew why. "You had an affair with Courtney Reese," she whispered.

His mouth tightened. Pain filled his dark eyes. "I almost did."

"What does that mean? *Almost?*"

He scrubbed his hand over his face and let out a deep, shuddering breath. "I met Courtney two years ago when she first started working for Senator Horton. At the time I sensed that she was, uh, attracted to me, but I never gave it too much thought. I'm in my sixties, old enough to be her father. Anyway, I didn't see much of her until last year, when Horton began sending her to the Armed Services Committee meetings in his absence. She began flirting with me, and I'm not proud of it, but I was flattered. She's a lovely, intelligent young woman, and any man would be lucky to have her.

"We wound up working together on a bill, which meant we met more often and had more than a few lunches together. Courtney became bolder in her flirting. And then one day she just came right out and propositioned me." He shook his head, staring down at his clasped hands in his lap. "I won't pretend that I was surprised. I'd seen it coming for months. And I won't pretend that I wasn't tempted. In fact," he said quietly, "after several invitations, I finally agreed to meet her at a hotel."

Althea said nothing. Her stomach had plummeted. She felt light-headed, as if she were having an out-of-body experience.

After a long, tense moment, Louis lifted his shattered gaze to hers. "You're disappointed in me."

"After the way you raked Malik over the coals for cheating on me," Althea said, with as much composure as she could summon, "you can understand why I might find your actions a bit hypocritical."

Louis flinched, guilt and sorrow filling his eyes. "You're right," he said in a low, chastened voice. "You're absolutely right."

But Althea didn't want to be right. Not about this. "So what happened?"

Her uncle shook his head. "I couldn't go through with it. Despite what you may now believe, Althea, I love your aunt. With all my heart. I always have, and I always will. I realized that having an affair with Courtney Reese, or any other woman, wasn't worth losing my marriage over. And that's what I told Courtney."

"How did she take it?"

Louis grimaced. "Not very well. She accused me of leading her on and not knowing what I wanted. I told her what I wanted was to keep my marriage and my family intact. Needless to say, things have been strained between us ever since."

Althea's mind flashed on her conversation with Courtney yesterday. She'd sensed resentment and hostility in the other woman's voice but had attributed it to political tensions between her uncle and Senator Horton.

"No wonder," she murmured.

Louis didn't hear her, lost in painful recriminations. "I deeply regret the way I handled things with Courtney. If I could go back and undo that moment when I agreed to meet her at the hotel, I would. In a heartbeat. But I can't. I made a terrible mistake, but at least I recognized that before it was too late. *Before* I did something irreversible."

Althea got up, unable to sit still any longer, and paced to the window, turning possibilities over in her mind. "Why would Courtney tell Claire Thorndike that she slept with you?" she wondered aloud, remembering the text message Claire had sent to her mentor, in which Courtney reluctantly confided having an affair with an "important married man" who was black. Was she talking about Louis Pritchard, or someone else?

"I don't know why Courtney would have told *anyone* we slept together, because it's not true," Louis said angrily.

Althea closed her eyes, James Odem's denial whispering through her mind like a cruel taunt: *I can't imagine why Claire would have told her best friend something like that, because it wasn't true. We never made any plans to meet.*

She hadn't believed him, not for one moment. And she'd been right not to. He had lied about his relationship with Claire.

Was her uncle lying?

"I know how bad this looks," he said, desperation edging his voice. "The police told me about the journal. I don't know what Courtney could have been thinking when she wrote that. She never struck me as unstable, but she must be, to have written those things in her journal."

Obviously Claire was more delusional than I thought.

Althea gave herself a hard mental shake, trying to

dislodge the awful whisper of doubt gnawing at her conscience. *Your uncle isn't James Odem. He's never lied to you before. He's not lying to you now!*

"The only explanation I can come up with for any of this is that someone is trying to set me up. A political rival, maybe. Someone who knows that this kind of scandal would effectively slam the door on my future bid for the White House."

Althea turned from the window and crossed the living room to join him on the sofa. Her gaze was intent on his face. "I can think of another explanation."

By the time she'd finished sharing her theory about the journal entry with her uncle, his face was ashen, as if all the blood had drained from his head. "My God," he breathed, staring at Althea. "You haven't told me and Barbara anything about this case. You really *do* believe there's a connection to your kidnapping."

Althea nodded reluctantly. "I didn't want you and Aunt Bobbi to worry about me—any more than you already do. But there are too many things about this case that are reminiscent of what happened before. I think whoever took Courtney planted that journal entry to get *my* attention, not yours." Her lips twisted bitterly. "But there's nothing I can do about it. I've been removed from the case, effective immediately."

Louis frowned. "I never wanted you involved in this investigation in the first place. And with good reason, based on what you've just told me. Let the authorities handle it, baby girl."

She gave a brittle laugh. "I *am* the authorities. If I can't do my job, then I might as well go back to medical school. Don't even think about it," she warned, seeing the thoughtful expression on her uncle's face. "The point is, now I have to rely on my partner to keep me in the loop about the investigation, even though he's probably been ordered not to. How can I help clear your name, Uncle Louie, if I don't know what kind of 'evidence' the police have against you?"

His gaze hardened, his eyes flashing with temper. "Don't you worry about trying to clear my name. You worry about keeping yourself safe. My reputation won't mean a damn thing to me if you're dead."

Impulsively Althea leaned over and looped her arms around his neck. Her uncle hugged her back tightly.

"I'm sorry, sweetheart. I know I've let you down today." His voice, thick with emotion, rumbled against her ear. "I've never told you this before, but when your mother began using drugs, I blamed myself for not doing more to help her. She was my baby sister, and I should've been able to protect her. I thought I was being a good role model for her by going to college and law school, but it wasn't enough. I should have been there for her, and I wasn't. I was caught up in my own life, my own big dreams and ambitions." He swallowed convulsively. "When your mother died after giving birth to you, I held your fragile little body in my hands, and I made a vow to you that I would always be there for you, and I would never give you any reason to question my character or integrity. I deeply regret that my behavior with Courtney Reese has caused you to do that today."

"So do I," Althea admitted quietly. "I've always had you on a pedestal, Uncle Louie. But I guess it's good to know that even our heroes can make mistakes and be human."

Louis kissed the top of her head and hugged her closer. "After I leave here, I'm going home to have a heart-to-heart with your aunt. She's been put through a lot today, and this is probably just the beginning. After we talk, I'm meeting with my attorney and reaching out to my contacts in the police department. One way or another, we're going to get to the bottom of this matter."

And just like that, her uncle was back. The fighter Althea knew and loved.

But she knew it wouldn't be enough to stop what had already been set in motion.

"You've been avoiding my calls." Those were the first words out of Damien's mouth when he showed up on Althea's doorstep that evening.

She looked at him for a moment, then reluctantly opened the door wider and gestured him inside the apartment.

"So much for improved security," she grumbled as he followed her to the kitchen, where she was making herself a cup of chamomile tea. "I see you had no problem getting into the building."

"I didn't think you'd let me in if I buzzed you." Damien leaned in the doorway, his shoulder propped against the jamb as he watched her. "I've been trying to reach you all day. You were gone when I came looking for you after the meeting, and then I called you while I was on the road, but you didn't answer your phone. I started worrying, so I called Anival, but he told me you were in your cubicle. Why didn't you take any of my calls?"

"I was busy." But she wouldn't meet his gaze. "I've got my hands full with the new cases Doherty assigned. What did you want? Was it anything important?"

"Yeah," Damien said gently. "I wanted to know if you were okay. I know it's been a rough day for you."

She gave a dismissive shrug, vigorously stirring sugar into her tea. "Not as rough as it's been for Courtney Reese's family and friends. And for my aunt and uncle, whose marriage has been dissected by every talking head on CNN for the last seven hours."

Damien grimaced. "You shouldn't watch the news."

"What do you expect me to do?" she snapped, temper sparking in her eyes. "Bury my head in the sand and pretend none of this is happening?"

Damien said nothing. It was a rhetorical question, hurled out of anger and frustration.

She retreated to a far corner of the kitchen and brooded over her tea.

Seeking to defuse the tension in the air, Damien sauntered over to the refrigerator and helped himself to a bottle of water. As he twisted off the cap, he said casually, "I thought you'd want to know that I finally had a chance to speak to Patrick Farris."

"Oh?" Her tone was neutral, but he knew he'd caught her attention.

"Not surprisingly, he didn't have anything nice to say about his ex-wife. He called her a 'greedy, vicious, back-stabbing whore without a soul.' When I asked him if he could think of anything from her past that someone might use to blackmail her, he laughed and said he'd already tried to dig up dirt on her. During the divorce proceedings he hired a private investigator to look into her past, but the guy came up with zilch. Farris thinks the P.I. was probably sleeping with Suzette, or she promised him a cut of the divorce settlement in exchange for his silence. Anyway, he's been at his son's house in Virginia for the last two weeks, so that's his alibi."

"What about Corbin?"

"Interestingly enough, Farris says he hasn't seen Corbin in more than a month. He seemed genuinely surprised when I told him that his son had been spotted at the post office near his brother Kyle's house in Virginia. Based on what Farris told me about Corbin, he sounds like a drifter. He wanders from place to place, taking odd jobs here and there, never putting down roots anywhere."

Not unlike your own father, Damien thought. Roderick Wade's bout with mental illness had driven him away from his wife and children, forcing him into a nomadic existence of drifting from one city to another, sporadically checking himself into mental health clinics before the voices in his head became too many and the walls started closing in on him. The last Damien heard, his aging father was staying with a distant relative in Oregon, where he'd been for the last two years—the longest he'd ever remained in one location.

Damien didn't realize he'd divulged all that until Althea said very softly, "I'm sorry. That must have been very hard for you and your family."

Damien blinked to erase the memories of growing up in the shadow of his father's demons, which had haunted their lives as surely as if he'd been present. "I was only four when he left. Reggie and Garrison remember him more than I do."

Althea gazed at him, her eyes soft with compassion.

"Anyway," Damien said gruffly, "I believe Farris was telling the truth. About everything. I don't think he's blackmailing Suzette, and I don't think he's lying about not knowing Corbin's whereabouts. But that doesn't mean I'm ruling out Corbin as a suspect. *Someone* pulled into that driveway last night and took off when he made us. The neighbor I spoke to before said he hadn't seen any cars parked at the house while Farris was in Virginia, but that doesn't mean Corbin can't sneak over late at night and leave early in the morning before any of the neighbors are up."

Althea nodded in agreement.

Damien hesitated, then offered, "I went with Mayhew

to meet with the primary detective assigned to Courtney's case."

Althea stared at him, waiting.

"They found a stack of journals in her apartment and
they're still going through them, but so far they've
found no mention of her alleged affair with your uncle."
A flash of triumph lit Althea's eyes before he continued,
"However, they spoke to some of her colleagues, who
said Courtney was a very private person. So private she
might not have documented something so personal
even in her own journal. Not to mention that she's a
huge fan of political thrillers and a self-confessed conspiracy theorist. Her colleagues said if she was having an
affair with someone as powerful as Louis Pritchard, she
would have been too afraid to write it down anywhere—
unless she suddenly believed her life was in danger."

Althea looked skeptical. "Did any of her colleagues
suspect she was having an affair with my uncle?"

Damien shook his head. "However, Senator Horton
said he sensed some tension between them on numerous occasions. He wanted to ask Courtney about it, but
he didn't want her to think he was prying into her personal life. He spoke very highly of her, said she's a consummate professional and respected by all of her peers."

"Of course," Althea said bitterly. "Are they actually
considering any other suspects? Or is it just my uncle
they want?"

Damien shook his head slowly. "Don't do that."

"Don't do what?" she snapped.

"Don't stand there and act like this is some 'vast right-
wing conspiracy' to get your uncle."

"Why not? That's what it's starting to sound like! It
won't be long before his political rivals and detractors
will start making their rounds on the news programs, demanding his resignation from office. They've probably

already convened a secret meeting in some smoke-filled room somewhere to go over their attack strategy."

Damien gave her a long, measured look. "You know Balducci is right, don't you? You've lost your objectivity in this case."

Hurt flared in her eyes. Hurt and betrayal. "So now you're taking Balducci's side?"

His control snapped. "Damn it, Althea, this isn't about *taking sides!* This is about doing our jobs, leaving no stone unturned. This is about trying to find two missing women! Or have you forgotten about the victims in your crusade to turn your uncle into one?"

She set down her cup with a thud, splashing tea onto the counter. She glared furiously at him. "I spoke to my uncle this morning. He didn't have an affair with Courtney Reese, and I believe him. I don't care what kind of so-called evidence they come up with. My uncle is innocent, and if you can't see what this *really* is, I'm not going to waste my breath trying to convince you!"

Damien clenched his jaw, fighting to rein in his temper. After several tense moments, he blew out a deep breath. "Look, Althea, let's not argue about this anymore. I have to go pick up India from my mom's, and then I'm taking her out to dinner to make up for working late yesterday. Why don't you join us?"

"No, thanks."

Her flat refusal stunned him. He scowled. "So that's how it's going to be? You're going to punish me for disagreeing with you? For speaking the truth?"

Her eyes hardened. "I think it's time for you to leave."

Damien just stared at her. He suddenly remembered that they were supposed to be having dinner with Garrison and Imani that night. Garrison had called Damien earlier to let him know that the invitation was still open, but considering the recent developments in the abduction case, he would understand if Althea wasn't up for socializing. Damien had forgotten to mention it to her, and now it was too late.

The silence stretched between them as they stood there, squaring off across the room from each other, fierce combatants who'd just spent an incredible night of passion together and had awakened in each other's arms. Damien felt an acute sense of loss, sorrow for what could have been.

Without another word he turned and left the apartment, slamming the door behind him.

Literally and figuratively.

Chapter 28

After Damien left, Althea forced herself to return to her office and resume the task of rearranging her bookcase, although the hollow ache of regret in her heart made her want to go lie down on her bed, curl into a fetal position, and bawl her eyes out. She'd lost her temper and lashed out at Damien, perhaps unfairly. But, damn it, he'd provoked her. That dig about her turning her uncle into a victim had been cruel and uncalled for. She'd expected him to be a little more understanding. More supportive. And he'd let her down.

It wouldn't have worked anyway, Althea told herself. *Sooner or later you would have had to choose between him and the job. Better sooner rather than later.*

The thought brought her no consolation.

Giving herself a mental shake, she forced herself to concentrate on the task at hand, shelving the books in alphabetical order, by category. She'd already filled one row with nonfiction titles, which included self-help books as well as the medical journals she'd kept purely for sentimental reasons. She had just reached the end of the *G* section when suddenly she realized which book was missing.

Her thirty-ninth edition of *Gray's Anatomy*.

Althea frowned, a whisper of unease sifting through her. Why would anyone break into her apartment and steal a copy of a medical book? What was the significance?

The kidnapper knows all about your past. He knows you were in medical school. Claire Thorndike wants to become a doctor. That's one of the things you have in common.

James Odem is a surgeon, Althea thought. He works at a hospital that receives generous monetary donations from Spencer Thorndike, the father of the missing girl. So Odem already had a connection to Claire. But *she* contacted him first. She was doing research for her music appreciation class and came across Odem's My-Domain page. That was indisputable.

Althea frowned, tapping her finger against the book she held in her hand. She felt that same frustration she always did on a hard case, that teasing niggle at the back of her mind that she was missing something. Something significant enough to break the case wide open.

What was it?

Think, Althea. Have you forgotten that you recognized James Odem when you saw him at the police station? Try to remember where you've seen him before!

Quickly setting aside the book she'd been holding, Althea crossed to her desk and sat down. She pulled up Mercy Harbor's Web site and went to the page for the neurosurgery department, wondering why she hadn't thought of this before. She clicked through the staff photographs until she came to James Odem's. As she stared at his handsome, unsmiling image, she felt that same whisper of recognition.

So she *hadn't* imagined it.

She perused his biography, noting the impressive list of credentials and published research papers. When she'd finished reading, she began sorting through her

memory bank, concentrating on the last eight years.
She'd spent five years at Stanford, first as an undergraduate and then as a med student. After dropping out of
the program, she'd joined the FBI and accepted an
assignment in Seattle for the next three years.

Althea stared at the computer screen, willing Odem's
photo to trigger a memory.

And then suddenly it happened.

Of course! He'd been a guest lecturer at Stanford
during her junior year. He was invited to the university
to discuss groundbreaking advances in neurology. One
of Althea's professors had passed out a flyer at the end
of class one afternoon, encouraging students to attend
the lecture. Althea had barely glanced at the flyer before
stuffing it into her bookbag and rushing off to another
class. She'd wanted to hear the neurosurgeon speak that
evening, but by the time she remembered and made it
across campus, the lecture was over, and the auditorium
was quickly emptying. She'd lingered in the back for a
few minutes, trying to get a glimpse of Odem through
the crowd of students and professors waiting to speak to
him, but after a while she'd given up and left. She never
gave it another thought.

And even now, it seemed like a long shot. Just because James Odem had lectured at the same university
Althea attended didn't mean he was the kidnapper.
What did he do? Look across a crowded auditorium,
see her, and become obsessed for the next six years?

Highly unlikely.

But then again, there was nothing likely about this
case.

A case you've been removed from, a voice reminded her.

Althea scowled.

Before leaving Mercy Harbor's Web site, she clicked
around some more and came across photos of various

events sponsored by the hospital. Black-tie galas, donor drives, community health forums.

When she stumbled upon a group photo taken at a fund-raiser last year, her hand stilled. She stared at the computer, surprised to find her therapist, Zachary Parminter, posing with the hospital's president and CEO, a board member, the chief of psychiatry. And Spencer Thorndike.

Althea frowned, trying to remember if Dr. Parminter had ever mentioned any connection to Mercy Harbor Hospital. If he had, she'd forgotten. But that was odd. He knew she was from Maryland, and not once had he ever mentioned visiting the state. At the very least, wouldn't his association with Mercy Harbor Hospital have come up when she told him she was being transferred to Baltimore?

And when she spoke to him on Monday, wouldn't he have mentioned meeting Spencer Thorndike before?

He hadn't said a word.

Althea's muscles tensed, a chill of foreboding slithering down her spine.

Was it possible?

No. It couldn't be.

Dr. Parminter *couldn't* have kidnapped Claire Thorndike and Courtney Reese. He had treated Althea for three years, helping her work through her demons. She had confided in him, shared some of her deepest, darkest fears with him. She trusted him implicitly. He wouldn't betray her like this.

But even as she tried to convince herself, a memory surfaced from a dark corner of her mind, fragments of an old conversation.

Did I ever tell you I decided to hold on to some of my medical books? Does that symbolize an unwillingness to let go of the past?

Maybe. Or it could be just as simple as you needing a safety net. If the FBI career doesn't pan out, you can always fall back on medical school. A wry chuckle escaped. *Besides, I happen to think everyone should have a copy of* Gray's Anatomy *in their reading collection.*

Is that your medical opinion?

But of course.

Althea surged to her feet. The bottom dropped out of her stomach, and a cold sweat broke out over her skin.

Just then she heard the soft creak of a floorboard out in the hallway.

Her heart slammed against her ribs.

Why didn't the security alarm go off?

Another creak. Closer.

She yanked open the bottom desk drawer and grabbed the .32, swinging the weapon around just as a figure from her worst nightmare filled the doorway. His image flashed on her brain like quick snapshots. Black clothing, black ski mask, cold eyes, and a thin slash of a mouth.

Time stood still as she and the intruder recognized each other as predator and prey.

And then he advanced on her. And Althea realized, with a sickening sense of dread, that the way he moved was familiar.

She aimed the pistol at his chest. "Don't come any closer or I'll shoot!"

He kept coming. Silent and menacing.

Althea pulled the trigger. There was an empty clicking sound. *No bullets!*

Behind the mask, her assailant smiled.

And then he rushed her.

As Althea swung her leg in a roundhouse kick, he caught it in midair and bent it backward. Pain shot through her body, and she cried out. She saw a flash of something in his hand. A Taser.

Before she could twist out of his grasp, he jammed it against her neck.

And the world went black.

Chapter 29

Even before Althea opened her eyes and took in her surroundings, she knew where her captor had taken her. Back to the cabin.

To the place where it all began.

But even knowing that, nothing could have prepared her for the macabre scene she would encounter when she groggily lifted her head and looked around. She was in the cellar, in the room where she'd been held prisoner eight years ago. But it had been transformed into something that was horrifyingly familiar, horrifyingly surreal. Parminter had re-created his office from Seattle, complete with the pastel seascapes, cordless floor lamps, glass center table, the brown leather chair where he'd sat, and the suede camel couch where she had reclined and talked through her issues on the second Thursday of every month.

Today was the second Thursday.

Only *she* wasn't occupying the couch, Althea realized through the fog clouding her brain. She was seated on a chair, her arms and legs bound with cloth restraints that dug painfully into her flesh.

Arranged beside each other on the couch, their

heads slumped limply forward like rag dolls, were Claire Thorndike and Courtney Reese.

Their eyes were closed, and they were unnaturally still.

Althea's heart thudded, relief mingled with fear. What had he done to them?

And what was he planning to do to all of them?

Fear pulsed through her blood. She swept another glance around the room, taking in more details. When her gaze landed on her copy of *Gray's Anatomy* on a small side table, she froze, chilled to the bone.

"Ah, you're awake. At last."

Althea looked up as Zachary Parminter entered the room. His dark hair was neatly combed, and he wore a beige cashmere sweater over gray wool slacks, looking as if he were merely arriving for one of their monthly therapy sessions.

"What do you think?" he asked as he gestured around the room, inordinately pleased with himself. "I think I captured it rather well, don't you? We could be back in Seattle."

Althea stared at him as he came toward her, a soft, intimate smile on his face that curdled her stomach.

He stopped in front of her, and she instinctively tensed as he leaned down, whispering in her ear, "I've missed you."

She swallowed and closed her eyes as he brushed his lips across her neck. Her skin crawled, but she forced herself not to react, even when she felt him shudder with arousal.

"So beautiful," he murmured. "From the moment you walked into my office that day, I knew you were special. And through the years, after all the patients I've counseled and comforted, there's been no one but you, Althea. You have no idea how many times I dreamed of this moment. Having you here, in this Sacred Room, where your innocence was lost. Every time you were lying on my couch, baring your wounded soul to me, I wondered how you would react if you knew the thoughts I was having. Just imagining your reaction thrilled me even more."

Althea kept her eyes closed, not giving him the satisfaction of knowing how sickened she was, how utterly terrified. Could she have seen a sign, a clue, some foreshadowing of this? she wondered. No, it was impossible. No sane person could have imagined the madness, the depravity, that infected Zachary Parminter.

As he drew back from her with a low chuckle, she opened her eyes to watch him sit down in the leather chair facing her.

"What do you want?" she whispered.

He laughed softly, the sound razoring along her nerve endings. "It's not just what *I* want, Althea. It's what we *both* want."

As she watched, tense and wary, he removed a .32-caliber pistol from under his chair and slowly set it on the glass center table. Althea froze, realizing it was *her* pistol.

He smiled, seeing the stunned recognition in her eyes. "You should have seen the look on your face when you pulled the trigger and realized the gun wasn't loaded. It was priceless. Of course, you had no way of knowing that I had already removed the bullets." His smile turned sinister. "I've been watching you, Althea. Watching your every move. When I realized you don't keep your curtains open late at night, I knew I had to find another way to keep a close eye on you. So I planted some strategically hidden video cameras in your apartment. That's how I knew you were ready for me tonight. Like a good little investigator, you had finally solved the puzzle."

Althea stared at him, her insides quaking with fear

and a terrible sense of violation. "H-How did you get inside my apartment?"

He chuckled. "With a key, of course. One night I waited until the front desk attendant stepped away from his station to use the bathroom, which he did every night like clockwork. I had even timed how long he took—just under four minutes. The keys to every unit in the building are kept in a locked compartment beneath the security desk. If a tenant gets locked out of their apartment, all they have to do is show ID and sign a sheet, and a spare key is temporarily provided to them. It happened rather frequently, I noticed. I knew the attendant would eventually get careless and forget to lock the cabinet, or he would leave the key dangling in the lock. And I was right. Less than two days later, I was able to make a copy of your key." Parminter shook his head, his dark eyes glinting with amusement. "You really should move into a more secure building, Althea. Oh, but wait. It doesn't matter anymore."

Althea's heart jammed at the base of her throat. Her worst fear had been confirmed. He was going to kill her.

Her gaze swung to the silent, unmoving figures on the couch. Claire and Courtney had not stirred once. Something was terribly wrong.

"What have you done to them?" Althea demanded, her voice sharp with panic.

Following the direction of her alarmed gaze, Parminter smiled. "Ah, yes. Courtney and Claire. The mentor and her protégée. Of course, Courtney was never as good a mentor to Claire as Professor Maxwell was to you. After all, she did nothing to stop young Claire from inviting a strange man over to her house while her parents were away. And, shame on the doctor, he actually showed up for the date." He clucked his tongue in disapproval, then chuckled sardonically. "It's a good thing I had already taken Claire. God only knows *what* he would have done to her."

Althea was too concerned about the unconscious women on the couch to fully register the fact that James Odem had, indeed, been at the Thorndike estate on the night of Claire's disappearance.

"What did you give to Claire and Courtney?"

Again Parminter smiled softly. "I gave them a little cocktail, so that you and I could have a little time alone first. We have a lot of catching up to do, Althea. We haven't seen each other since your final session with me a month ago. It was so bittersweet, but I knew we would be reunited soon. I even arrived here in town before you did just to get everything prepared."

As he spoke, Althea began tugging at her restraints— carefully, so he wouldn't notice. But it was no use. They were too tight. She could not escape. There was no way for her to get to the .32 lying just out of reach on the table, taunting her.

She was doomed.

And so were Claire and Courtney.

"What are you going to do?" she asked faintly.

"Wrong again, Althea. It's what *you're* going to do."

She stared at him uncomprehendingly.

"You've never been the same since you were kidnapped eight years ago," he calmly explained. "You were haunted by dreams about your ordeal, terrifying nightmares that coalesced into scenes of unspeakable violence. You were afraid that you had become as unbalanced as the monster who once abducted you. You were worried that you might snap one day and hurt someone." He paused. "At least, that's what I'm going to tell the police when they ask me about your mental stability. I'm going to waive my right to doctor–patient confidentiality and tell them that in my professional opinion, you had never quite recovered from the trauma you experienced. I'm going to tell them that I believe your psychosis led you to reenact your own abduction. You chose Courtney Reese because you found out she was having an affair with your beloved uncle. And once you learned about her friendship with Claire Thorndike, you saw it as a sign. They had almost the same relationship as you and Imani Maxwell. It was the perfect setup. And because your uncle had betrayed your trust, you planted the journal entry at Courtney's apartment, just to cause him a little pain and suffering."

Althea stared at him with horror and revulsion. "No one will believe that," she whispered.

His lips curved in a small, feral smile. "Just as no one believes your uncle had an affair with Courtney, right?"

Her stomach plummeted. "You bastard! You can't do this. I *trusted* you!"

"I know," he sighed, with a look of deep satisfaction. "Which is what makes this that much sweeter. Your *trust*. Your blind faith in me. You can't imagine how intoxicating that is, Althea. To be trusted implicitly simply because I hold a degree, a license that qualifies me to probe human minds."

"You won't get away with this," Althea said with more confidence than she felt.

He laughed softly. "Oh, but I will. You see, the day after your final session with me, I left for my cabin at Lake Tahoe, where, for the last month, I have been enjoying a long-overdue sabbatical. I've even phoned the office a few times to describe the beauty of the lake, the tranquility of my surroundings, the breathtaking sunrises. No one has any reason to suspect I'm anywhere other than where I said I would be."

Althea stared at him, chilled by the level of premeditation, the meticulous planning. And then a thought struck her.

"You're forgetting one thing," she said scornfully.

He looked at her, an amused brow lifted.

"I have an alibi for the nights Claire and Courtney were abducted. I was with Damien Wade."

Fury hardened Parminter's eyes. "I know where you were and what you were doing, whore," he spat contemptuously. "That's why you needed an accomplice."

Althea felt a chill of foreboding. "Who?" she asked faintly.

"Joshua Reed. His father knows your uncle. In fact, his father was one of Louis Pritchard's biggest campaign contributors. So that's your connection to Josh. And once the poor boy had served his purpose, you killed him."

As comprehension dawned, the blood drained from Althea's head. "You . . . you killed Josh?"

He smirked. "No, Althea. *You* did."

Grief and rage swept through her. "You son of a bitch! What kind of sick monster are you?"

Chuckling softly, he removed a short needle and syringe from the front pocket of his sweater. "No more small talk, Althea. It's time to wake our guests. It's time for the Final Act."

Terror and panic gripped her. *"No!"* she shouted.

As he rose and walked over to the couch, her mind raced, frantically thinking of ways to free herself and Claire and Courtney. After surviving her harrowing ordeal at the hand of Anthony Yusef, she'd vowed never again to be a victim. She'd be damned if she let this man—this man she'd trusted and confided in—send her back into the abyss.

"I'm going to enjoy watching you kill Claire and Courtney before you turn the gun on yourself," Parminter murmured as he tapped the syringe. "I've dreamed of nothing else for weeks. I know you thought you had more time to solve this case, since *you* went missing for a month. But unfortunately, I'm on a tight schedule. I'm due back at work in two weeks, you see. And who knows? Maybe if I'm lucky, I'll find another Althea."

As he leaned toward Claire, Althea cried out, "Wait!"

He paused and looked at her.

She licked her dry lips. "Part of what you said about me was right. I *have* been having terrible nightmares about the past, which I've told you about. It seems that no matter what I do, I-I just can't shake the memories. So maybe in a way you're actually doing me a favor. Maybe it's time for me to be put out of my misery once and for all."

He stared at her, his dark eyes narrowing suspiciously.

Swallowing her fear and revulsion, Althea gave him a sultry, inviting smile. "But before we do this, there's something else I've been fantasizing about for a long time, something I never told you. I don't know if you could tell, but I've always been attracted to you, Dr. Parminter. Physically and intellectually. And you know me better than anyone. Sometimes during our sessions, I used to think about what it would be like to kiss you, to feel your hands all over me. To make love to you right there in your office." She feigned an embarrassed chuckle. "I know that's wrong. You were my therapist, not my lover. But now, after hearing what you said about me being special, I realize you must have been feeling the same way. You knew the moment we met that fate had brought us together. I wish we hadn't waited this long to express our feelings to each other."

He stared at her, a solitary muscle ticking in his jaw.

"Why don't you let Claire and Courtney rest awhile longer?" she murmured coaxingly. "I mean, surely you didn't go to all this trouble not to have me at least *once*. That makes no sense at all."

He hesitated, temptation flaring in his eyes.

Please take the bait! Please take the bait!

He did.

As he came toward her, Althea nearly sobbed with relief.

She eyed him seductively as he knelt in front of her. "Let's pretend we're back in your office in Seattle," she purred. "We can make love on the couch. Just move Claire and Courtney out of the way."

Slowly he began loosening the restraints around her ankles. Her heart pounded, adrenaline surging through her veins. Once she was free, she'd have only one shot at the weapon on the table. She'd have to make the most of the opportunity.

But Parminter had suddenly paused in his task. Fearing that he'd changed his mind about accepting her offer, Althea murmured silkily, "I want to touch you. Will you let me touch you?"

He lifted his head and looked at her. And she saw the moment that he came back to his senses. His gaze hardened.

He stood, his fists clenching at his sides.

Not wasting a second, Althea raised her legs and kicked at his chest as hard as she could. She connected with a satisfying thud, sending him staggering back with a surprised grunt of pain. Throwing all her force at him, Althea launched herself forward, chair and all. He didn't have a chance to react before she barreled into him, knocking him backward. Glass shattered as they both crashed into the center table.

"Bitch!" Parminter roared, enraged.

He reached up, slamming his fist into Althea's cheek. Pain erupted in her skull. Lights exploded behind her eyes. The taste of blood bloomed in her mouth.

He shoved her aside roughly and lurched to his feet.

Another burst of pain ricocheted through her as she landed hard on her side, shards of glass penetrating her clothes to stab her skin. Gritting her teeth against the agony, she spied the .32 on the floor nearby, but with her arms still restrained behind the chair, there was nothing she could do.

And he knew it, too.

Slowly, deliberately, he bent down and picked up the gun. Calmly wiping a smear of blood from his mouth, he stuffed the .32 into the front waistband of his slacks. "I applaud your effort, Althea," he sneered. "But I'm afraid it won't be that easy to alter the course of your fate. In fact, it's impossible."

Althea stared into his cruelly smiling face and knew that she'd run out of time.

He came toward her and reached down to lift her upright in the chair.

"FBI! Freeze!"

Althea let out a gasp of relief as she looked past her tormenter and saw Damien standing in the doorway, his weapon drawn and aimed at Parminter's back.

Parminter paused, a look of shock and confusion sweeping across his face. His gaze met Althea's, and she shivered at the cold, calculating gleam in his eyes. Suddenly he whipped the .32 from his waistband and pointed it at her temple.

She squeezed her eyes shut, bracing for death.

A shot blasted through the room, reverberating against the walls. Althea cried out. She jumped as Parminter's body pitched forward, sprawling on top of her. She squirmed, kicking out frantically to dislodge him.

In a few brisk, powerful strides Damien was at her side, his expression fierce as he shoved Parminter's dead weight out of the way. His hands trembled violently as he untied Althea from the chair. Before she could draw breath to speak, he crushed her against him with such force he knocked the air from her lungs. She clung to him, trembling with relief, tears spurting from her eyes.

"How did you find me?"

"I went to your apartment to apologize for what happened earlier," Damien said in a ragged voice. "I got worried when I saw you weren't there. I tracked down your car like I did before."

Althea whispered a prayer of thanks for GPS technology.

A moment later she was jumping up frantically, running to the couch where Claire and Courtney were still unconscious, as silent and still as mannequins. She quickly checked their pulses. Thready. Alarmingly so. What had he drugged them with?

"The police and paramedics are on the way," Damien said, kneeling beside Althea to peer worriedly at the two young women.

"He has a syringe in his pocket!" Althea cried, leaping up and racing over to where Parminter lay. There was a bloody, gaping gash in the middle of his back where Damien had shot him. She rolled the body over, then shuddered at the sight of his lifeless eyes staring up at the ceiling. She quickly dug into his pocket and found the syringe.

As she raced back over to the sofa, Damien was checking the two women's pupils. He dubiously eyed the clear fluid in the syringe that Althea held. "Do you know what that is?"

Althea shook her head. "He was going to wake them up with it."

"How do you know it's not going to finish them off?"

"We have to do *something!* They've been unconscious for a long time. I think he gave them some sort of anesthetic, stronger than what he must have given me. This was going to wake them up," she repeated.

Damien looked wary, but after a moment he nodded. He trusted her.

Althea found a good vein in Claire's right arm and injected her with half the contents of the syringe, then did the same for Courtney.

And then she held her breath.

Moments later Claire groaned softly and stirred awake, followed by Courtney. Their eyes blinked open, and in groggy confusion they stared first at Althea and Damien, then at each other. In unison they burst into tears and hugged each other.

Overcome with emotion, Althea sagged weakly against Damien, whose arms went protectively around her. "You're going to be okay," he whispered into her hair.

No sooner had the words left his mouth than they heard heavy footsteps thundering down the stairs, announcing the arrival of the police officers and paramedics who spilled into the room.

Chapter 30

Baltimore, Maryland
Saturday, October 18

"Slow down. What's the rush?"

As Althea hurried across the crowded parking lot of the downtown sports bar where Damien's surprise party was being held that night, he tugged at her hand, gently pulling her to a stop.

As she turned to face him, his dark eyes searched her face. "You've been acting strange all day. I just want to make sure everything is all right."

Althea gazed into his concerned eyes and couldn't help thinking, for the millionth time, that this was the man who had saved her life. If Damien hadn't shown up when he did, Zachary Parminter would have killed her, as well as Claire and Courtney, a chilling thought that still made Althea shudder.

It had been just over a week since that horrifying night at the cabin in Fredericksburg. The specter of Zachary Parminter's crimes and the sensational events surrounding the case had dominated headlines ever since, relegating the upcoming presidential election to almost an afterthought. A search of the woods behind the cabin had revealed an old underground bunker that the psychologist had used as his hideout. The crime scene team had discovered the prescription drugs and syringes Parminter had used to subdue his victims, as well as a stash of wigs, makeup, contact lenses in various colors, clothing, and costumes used to disguise Parminter as he moved about the city without detection. A chameleon, as the note had suggested. They found receipts for furniture he'd purchased for the macabre stage he'd set at the cabin, as well as for the U-Haul truck he'd rented to deliver the furniture to the remote location. Another receipt provided the name of the local motel he'd called home since leaving Seattle nearly a month ago. He'd paid cash up front and had registered under a false name. Also recovered from the underground bunker were the trophies he had collected from each of his victims, among them Claire's purse, cell phone, bookbag, and a negligee she'd been wearing when he abducted her.

Washington State police were already speculating about Parminter's connection to other missing persons cases, a theory bolstered by the fact that one of the victims was a former patient of his.

The most gruesome discovery was made by Suzette Thorndike, who'd found the mutilated body of Josh Reed slumped inside her car when she emerged from having a late dinner with friends at an Inner Harbor restaurant. Overcome with shock and hysteria, she'd started babbling to her friends, revealing the truth about her affair with Josh and the fact that she'd been paying off Corbin Farris to keep him from exposing her secret past as an underage prostitute, one who'd been driven to shoot and kill a client who refused to pay her. To evade arrest, she'd fled to Baltimore and started a new life. During her hysterical tirade, Suzette even admitted that when Claire disappeared, she'd secretly feared—and hoped—that Corbin had taken the girl as a final payment. Corbin had been apprehended at his father's house and charged with extortion. Suzette had also been taken into custody and returned to her hometown, where there was an outstanding warrant for her arrest.

Claire and Courtney's healing would take time, probably years, just as Althea was still healing from her own wounds—the old and new. At their request, she'd accompanied Claire and Courtney to a support group meeting for victims of violent crime, and the three women were slowly developing a friendship.

Louis Pritchard's name had been cleared when it was revealed that Parminter had planted the journal entry at Courtney's apartment. To quash any further speculation, Courtney had issued a strongly worded statement in which she denied having an affair with the senator. Privately she'd apologized to Althea and Louis for lying to Claire about the affair, admitting that she was mad at Louis for rejecting her and had wanted to somehow punish him.

James Odem was still insisting that he was not at the Thorndike estate on the night Claire disappeared, scoffing at the notion that Parminter had seen him there. Not surprisingly, he and Claire had had no further contact.

Other details from the sensational kidnapping case were still slowly emerging, trickling out to fuel the media's voracious appetite. Althea knew the harrowing events of that night would linger in her memory long after the story died down in the press, but out of such an unspeakable tragedy, she'd found a reason to celebrate. A newfound love.

She and Damien had been inseparable since that night. Partly because they couldn't get enough of each other and partly because Damien wouldn't let her out of his sight. They were working on new cases together at work, and Althea had even moved into his townhouse temporarily. Just until they straightened out the security problems at her apartment building, she told herself, knowing better. She loved waking up in Damien's arms every morning and making love to him before falling asleep every night. She loved hanging out with him and India on the weekend, and looked forward to many more.

She loved Damien. Period.

And after the way he'd saved her life, the *least* she could do was get him to his surprise birthday party on time.

She leaned up and gently kissed him, murmuring, "I'm fine, D-Wade, but if it's all the same to you, I'd really like to get inside the building before I completely freeze my ass off out here. And, no," she warned, seeing the suggestive gleam in his eyes, "I don't need you to warm it up for me."

He chuckled. "You know me so well."

"And I love you, anyway," she quipped.

When they stepped inside the crowded sports bar and were greeted with a cascade of balloons and a roomful of people yelling, "Surprise! Happy Birthday!" Damien's shocked expression was priceless.

He looked down at Althea at his side, her face aglow with triumph. "You got me so good," he murmured in her ear. "It's on now."

Althea grinned saucily. "Bring it on."

They were enveloped by family, friends, and colleagues who laughed at Damien's reaction and congratulated Althea for getting him to the bar without spoiling the surprise. Althea was hugged by Imani and Garrison

Wade, to whom she'd be forever indebted for saving her life—the first time around. Imani, still sporting a soft natural and a fashionably retro look, was as gorgeous as her husband was handsome, and when the couple gazed into each other's eyes, it seemed that no one else existed. Althea was introduced to Reggie Wade—a dentist who shared his brothers' dark good looks—and his wife and three teenage children, who offered shy smiles. Rosemary Wade, the petite matriarch of the family, fussed over Althea and promised to stop by the townhouse with more food to compensate for Damien's lack of "culinary know-how"—the latter said with an affectionate pat on her son's cheek. India, still basking in the glow of mastering Rosemary's blueberry pancakes, traded a secret smile with her father over her grandmother's head.

As Althea and Damien moved through the crowd, smiling and greeting more guests, he kept his arm curved possessively around her waist, a feeling she liked very much.

By the time they joined his family at the table reserved for the guest of honor, the party was in full swing. The bartender dispensed drinks with fluid ease while waiters bustled about delivering fragrant meals on huge plates. The festive sounds of laughter, tinkling glasses, and animated conversations competed with the pulsing music that lured people out on to the dance floor. Among the dancers were Damien, Garrison, and Reggie, who drew a hearty round of applause when they regaled the crowd with their "Wade Shuffle," an old dance they'd made up when they were younger. More than a few murmurs of female appreciation could be heard around the room as the handsome brothers, laughing and clapping one another on the back, made their way off the dance floor.

Someone proposed a toast to the birthday boy, and Damien took center stage to thank his family and friends for the wonderful birthday surprise. Althea was smiling, sipping a fruity cocktail as she watched him from their table, when suddenly his dark gaze fastened on her.

"Many of you don't know this," he said to the guests, "but Althea Pritchard and I met for the first time on my actual birthday two weeks ago. And I have to tell you, as incredible as this party has been, nothing compares to the night I took Althea in my arms and we danced together for the first time."

Althea's heart melted as she smiled at him, oblivious to the appreciative sighs that went up all around her.

But Damien wasn't finished. "I was going to do this over a candlelight dinner tomorrow night, but here is just as good a place as any."

Althea froze, staring at him. Suddenly her heart was thumping.

An air of hushed excitement swept through the room.

Holding her gaze, Damien said huskily, "Althea Lynette Pritchard, will you marry me?"

Althea's eyes widened in shock. She heard collective gasps around the room. Someone plucked the drink from her hand, maybe Keren or Kimberly.

And the next thing Althea knew she was walking, then running across the room to reach Damien. They met halfway, his arms banding tightly around her as he lifted her off the floor and swept her in a circle.

"Yes," Althea whispered, choked with emotion. *"Yes, I'll marry you!"*

Damien grinned broadly, and just in case others had missed her answer, he announced to the guests, "She said yes!"

Loud cheers and clapping erupted around the room.

Althea and Damien kissed deeply and hungrily to a chorus of more applause. They laughed as they drew apart. Damien took her hand and led her to the dance floor, where the slow song they'd danced to that night had just started playing.

As they melted into each other's arms, Damien gazed down at her. "I almost lost you last week, and for as long as I live, I'll never forget that feeling when I thought I might never see you again. It felt like my heart was being ripped out of my body."

"Don't think about that," Althea said tenderly. "We were given a second chance. And now it's up to us to make the most of it, for the rest of our lives."

"I like the sound of that," Damien said huskily. He gently touched her face. "I love you so much."

"I love you, too." Althea smiled softly. "I was thinking maybe we could go back to that bed and breakfast sometime and enjoy some of the, ah, amenities that we were unable to before."

He flashed a wolfish grin. "What're you talking about? I enjoyed *plenty* of amenities that night."

Althea laughed. "You know what I meant."

"I know. And, yes, I'd love to go back there with you. Maybe next weekend."

"That sounds good. We can start planning the wedding, the honeymoon . . . our family."

Damien stared at her, tenderness washing over his face. Without a word he pulled her closer. Althea nestled against his chest, feeling the beat of his heart beneath her palm. Fast and strong. Like the way he drove, and the man he was.

She smiled contentedly. "Damien?"

"Hmm?"

"Do you want to get out of here?"

"Thought you'd never ask," he growled softly.

GREAT BOOKS, GREAT SAVINGS!

When You Visit Our Website:
www.kensingtonbooks.com
You Can Save Money Off The Retail Price
Of Any Book You Purchase!

- All Your Favorite Kensington Authors
- New Releases & Timeless Classics
- Overnight Shipping Available
- eBooks Available For Many Titles
- All Major Credit Cards Accepted

Visit Us Today To Start Saving!
www.kensingtonbooks.com

All Orders Are Subject To Availability.
Shipping and Handling Charges Apply.
Offers and Prices Subject To Change Without Notice.

Look For These Other
Dafina Novels

If I Could
0-7582-0131-1

by Donna Hill
$6.99US/**$9.99**CAN

Thunderland
0-7582-0247-4

by Brandon Massey
$6.99US/**$9.99**CAN

June In Winter
0-7582-0375-6

by Pat Phillips
$6.99US/**$9.99**CAN

Yo Yo Love
0-7582-0239-3

by Daaimah S. Poole
$6.99US/**$9.99**CAN

When Twilight Comes
0-7582-0033-1

by Gwynne Forster
$6.99US/**$9.99**CAN

It's A Thin Line
0-7582-0354-3

by Kimberla Lawson Roby
$6.99US/**$9.99**CAN

Perfect Timing
0-7582-0029-3

by Brenda Jackson
$6.99US/**$9.99**CAN

Never Again Once More
0-7582-0021-8

by Mary B. Morrison
$6.99US/**$8.99**CAN

Available Wherever Books Are Sold!

Check out our website at www.kensingtonbooks.com.

Grab These Dafina Thrillers

From

Brandon Massey

More of the Hottest
African-American Fiction from
Dafina Books

Available Wherever Books Are Sold!

Visit our website at **www.kensingtonbooks.com**.